GROWING MORE HORRIFIED BY THE MOMENT . . .

. . . the half-mad soldier struggled to his feet. Around him he noticed tall hills, even mountains, and the first glimmers of sunlight. Yet, none of them looked at all familiar. None of them at all resembled the peak in which he and his friends had discovered the tomb of Bartuc. Norrec took a step forward, trying to get his bearings.

An unsettling creaking accompanied every motion.

Norrec looked down to discover that not only his hands were clad in metal.

Armor. Everywhere he stared, Norrec only saw the same blood-colored metal plates. He had thought that his shock and horror could not possibly grow worse, but simply gazing at the rest of his body nearly threw the formerly steady soldier into complete panic. His arms, his torso, his legs, the same crimson ~~~~~~~~ ~~~~~~~~ ~~~~~~ the mockery, Norrec ~~~~~~~~~~~~~~~~~~~~'s ancient but still se~~~~~

Bartuc . . . Warlo~~~~~~~~~~~~~~~~~~~~~~k magic had apparen~~~~~~~~~~~~~~~~~~~~t the price of Sadun ~~~~~~~~~~~~~ lives.

DIABLO®

LEGACY
OF
BLOOD

RICHARD A. KNAAK

POCKET BOOKS
New York   London   Toronto   Sydney

This book is a work of fiction. Names, characters, places and incidents are products of the author's imagination or are used fictitiously. Any resemblance to actual events or locales or persons, living or dead, is entirely coincidental.

An *Original* Publication of POCKET BOOKS

POCKET BOOKS, a division of Simon & Schuster, Inc.
1230 Avenue of the Americas, New York, NY 10020

ISBN: 0-671-04155-X

First Pocket Books printing May 2001

10   9   8

POCKET and colophon are registered trademarks of Simon & Schuster, Inc.

Printed in the U.S.A.

To my brother, Win—fellow creative spirit

LEGACY
OF
BLOOD

ONE

The skull gave them a lopsided grin, as if cheerfully inviting the trio to join it for all eternity.

"Looks like we're not the first," Sadun Tryst murmured. The scarred, sinewy fighter tapped the skull with one edge of his knife, causing the fleshless watcher to wobble. Behind the macabre sight, they could just make out the spike that had pierced their predecessor's head, leaving him dangling until time had let all but the skull drop to the floor in a confused heap.

"Did you think we would be?" whispered the tall, cowled figure. If Sadun had a lean, almost acrobatic look to his build, Fauztin seemed nearly cadaverous. The Vizjerei sorcerer moved almost like a phantom as he, too, touched the skull, this time with one gloved finger. "No sorcery here, though. Only crude but sufficient mechanics. Nothing to fear."

"Unless it's your head on the next pole."

The Vizjerei tugged at his thin, gray goatee. His slightly slanted eyes closed once as if in acknowledgment to his partner's last statement. Whereas Sadun had a countenance more akin to an untrustworthy weasel—and sometimes the personality to match—Fauztin reminded some of a withered cat. His nub of a nose, constantly twitching, and the whiskers hanging underneath that nose only added to the illusion.

Neither had ever had a reputation for purity, but Norrec Vizharan would have trusted either with his life—and had several times over. As he joined them, the veteran warrior peered ahead, to where a vast darkness hinted of some major chamber. Thus far, they had explored seven different levels in all and found them curiously devoid of all but the most primitive traps.

They had also found them devoid of any treasure whatsoever, a tremendous disappointment to the tiny party.

"Are you sure there's no sorcery about here, Fauztin? None at all?"

The feline features half-hidden by the cowl wrinkled further in mild offense. The wide shoulders of his voluminous cloak gave Fauztin a foreboding, almost supernatural appearance, especially since he towered over the brawnier Norrec, no small man himself. "You have to ask that, my friend?"

"It's just that it makes no sense! Other than a few minor and pretty pathetic traps, we've encountered nothing to prevent us from reaching the main chamber! Why go through all the trouble of digging this out, then leave it so sparsely defended!"

"I don't call a spider as big as my head *nothing*," Sadun interjected sourly, absently scratching his lengthy but thinning black hair. "Especially as it was *on* my head at the time . . ."

Norrec ignored him. "Is it what I think? Are we too late? Is this Tristram all over again?"

Once before, between serving causes as mercenaries, they had hunted for treasure in a small, troubled village called Tristram. Legend had had it that, in a lair guarded by fiends, there could be found a treasure so very extraordinary in value, it would make kings of those fortunate enough to live to find it. Norrec and his friends had journeyed there, entering the labyrinth in the dead of night without the knowledge of the local populace . . .

And after all their efforts, after battling strange beasts

and narrowly avoiding deadly traps . . . they had found that someone else had stripped the underground maze of nearly anything of value. Only upon returning to the village had they learned the sorry truth, that a great champion had descended into the labyrinth but a few weeks before and supposedly slain the terrible demon, Diablo. He had taken no gold or jewels, but other adventurers who had arrived shortly thereafter had made good use of his handiwork, dealing with the lesser dangers and carrying off all they could find. But a few days' difference had left the trio with nothing to show for their efforts . . .

Norrec himself had also taken no consolation in the words of one villager of dubious sanity who had, as they had prepared to depart, warned that the champion, so-called the Wanderer, had not defeated Diablo but, rather, had accidently freed the foul evil. A questioning glance by Norrec toward Fauztin had been answered at first with an indifferent shrug by the Vizjerei sorcerer.

"There are always stories of escaping demons and terrible curses," Fauztin had added at the time, complete dismissal of the wild warning in his tone. "Diablo is generally in most of the favorites whispered among common folk."

"You don't think there's anything to it?" As a child, Norrec had grown up being scared by his elders with tales of Diablo, Baal, and other monsters of the night, all stories designed to make him be good.

Sadun Tryst had snorted. "You ever seen a demon yourself? Know anyone that had?"

Norrec had not. "Have you, Fauztin? They say Vizjerei can summon demons to do their bidding."

"If I could do that, do you think I would be scrounging in empty labyrinths and tombs?"

And that comment, more than anything else, had convinced Norrec then to chalk the villager's words down as yet another tall tale. In truth, it had not been hard to do.

After all, the only thing that had mattered then to the three had been what mattered now—wealth.

Unfortunately, it seemed more and more likely that once again those riches had eluded them.

As he peered down the passage, Fauztin's other gloved hand tightened around the spell staff he wielded. The jeweled top—the source of their light—flared briefly. "I had hoped I was wrong, but now I fear it is so. We are far from the first to delve this deep into this place."

The slightly graying fighter swore under his breath. He had served under many a commander in his life, most of them during the crusades from Westmarch, and from surviving those various campaigns—often by the skin of his teeth—he had come to one conclusion. No one could hope to rise in the world without money. He had made it as far as captain, been broken in rank thrice, then finally retired in disgust after the last debacle.

War had been Norrec's life since he had been old enough to raise a sword. Once, he had also had something of a family, but they were now as dead as his ideals. He still considered himself a decent man, but decency did not fill one's stomach. There had to be another way, Norrec had decided . . .

And so, with his two comrades, he had gone in search of treasure.

Like Sadun, he had his share of scars, but Norrec's visage otherwise resembled more that of a simple farmer. Wide brown eyes, with a broad, open face and a strong jaw, he would have looked at home behind a hoe. Yet, while that vision occasionally appealed to the sturdy veteran, he knew that he needed the gold to pay for that land. This quest should have led them to riches far beyond his needs, far beyond his dreams . . .

Now, it seemed as if it had all been a waste of time and effort . . . again.

Beside him, Sadun Tryst tossed his knife into the air,

then expertly caught it at the hilt as it fell. He did this twice more, clearly thinking. Norrec could just imagine what he thought about. They had spent months on this particular quest, journeying across the sea to northern Kehjistan, sleeping in the cold and rain, following false trails and empty caves, eating whatever vermin they could find when other hunting proved scarce—and all because of Norrec, the one who had instigated this entire fiasco.

Worse, *this* quest had actually come about because of a dream, a dream concerning a wicked mountain peak bearing some crude resemblance to a dragon's head. Had he dreamt of it only once, perhaps twice, Norrec might have forgotten the image, but over the years, it had repeated itself far too many times. Wherever he had fought, Norrec had watched for the peak, but to no avail. Then, a comrade—later dead—from these chill northern lands had made mention of such a place in passing. Ghosts were said to haunt it and men who traveled near the mountain often disappeared or were discovered years later, all flesh stripped from the shattered bones . . .

There and then, Norrec Vizharan had been certain that destiny had tried to call him here.

But if so—why to a tomb already vandalized?

The entrance had been well hidden in the rock face, but definitely open to the outside. That should have been his first clue to the truth, yet Norrec had refused to even see the discrepancy. All his hopes, all his promises to his companions . . .

"Damn!" He kicked at the nearest wall, only his sturdy boot saving him from a few broken toes. Norrec threw his sword to the ground, continuing to curse his naïveté.

"There's some new general from Westmarch hiring on mercenaries," Sadun helpfully suggested. "They say he's got big ambitions . . ."

"No more war," muttered Norrec, trying not to show

the pain coursing through his foot. "No more trying to die for other people's glory."

"I just thought—"

The lanky sorcerer tapped the ground once with his staff, seeking the attention of both his earthier partners. "At this point, it would be foolish not to go on to the central chamber. Perhaps those who were here before us left a few baubles or coins. We did find a few gold coins in Tristram. Certainly it would not hurt to search a little longer, would it, Norrec?"

He knew that the Vizjerei only sought to assuage his friend's bitter emotions, but still the idea managed to take root in the veteran's mind. All he needed were a few gold coins! He was still young enough to take a bride, begin a new life, maybe even raise a family . . .

Norrec picked up his sword, hefting the weapon that had served him so well over the years. He had kept it cleaned and honed, taking pride in one of the few items truly his own. A look of determination spread across his visage. "Let's go."

"You've a way with words for one using so few," Sadun jested to the sorcerer as they started off.

"And you use so many words for one with so few things worth saying."

The friendly argument between his companions helped settle Norrec's troubled mind. It reminded him of other times, when, between the three of them, they had persevered through worse difficulties.

Yet, the talk died as they approached what surely had to be the last and most significant chamber. Fauztin called a halt, staring briefly at the jewel atop the staff.

"Before we proceed inside, the two of you had better light torches."

They had saved the torches for emergencies, the sorcerer's staff serving well until now. Fauztin said no more, but as Norrec used tinder to light his, he wondered if the

Vizjerei had finally noted sorcery of some significance. If so, then perhaps there still remained some sort of treasure . . .

With his own torch lit, Norrec used it to set Sadun's ablaze. Now surrounded with more secure illumination, the trio set off again.

"I swear," grumbled the wiry Sadun, a few moments later. "I swear that the hair on the back of my head's standing on end!"

Norrec felt the same. Neither fighter argued when the Vizjerei took the lead. The clans of the Far East had long studied the magical arts and Fauztin's people had studied them longer than most. If a situation arose where sorcery had to take a hand, certainly it made sense to leave it to the thin spellcaster. Norrec and Sadun would be there to guard him from other assaults.

The arrangement had worked *so* far.

Unlike the heavy boots of the warriors, the sandaled feet of Fauztin made no sound as he walked. The mage stretched forth his staff and Norrec noticed that, despite its power, the jewel failed to illuminate much. Only the torches seemed to act as they should.

"This is old and powerful. Our predecessors may not have been so fortunate as we first believed. We may find some treasure yet."

And possibly more. Norrec's grip on the sword tightened to the point that his knuckles whitened. He wanted gold, but he also wanted to live to spend it.

With the staff proving unreliable, the two fighters took to the front. That did not mean that Fauztin would no longer be of any aid to the band. Even now, the veteran knew, his magical companion thought out the quickest, surest spells for whatever they might encounter.

"It looks as dark as the grave in there," Sadun mumbled.

Norrec said nothing. Now a few steps ahead of both his comrades, he became the first to actually reach the chamber itself. Despite the dangers that might lurk within, he almost felt drawn to it, as if something inside called to him . . .

A blinding brilliance overwhelmed the trio.

"Gods!" snapped Sadun. "I can't see!"

"Give it a moment," cautioned the sorcerer. "It will pass."

And so it did, but as his eyes adjusted, Norrec Vizharan at last beheld a sight so remarkable that he had to blink twice to make certain it was not a figment of his desires.

The walls were covered in intricate, jeweled patterns in which even he could sense the magic. Precious stones of every type and hue abounded in each pattern, blanketing the chamber in an astonishing display of refracted and reflected colors. In addition, below those magical symbols and no less eye-catching were the very treasures for which the trio had come. Mounds of gold, mounds of silver, mounds of jewels. They added to the overall glitter, making the chamber brighter than day. Each time either fighter shifted his torch, the lighting further altered the appearance of the room, adding new dimensions equally as startling as the last.

Yet, as breathtaking as all this looked, one shocking sight dampened Norrec's enthusiasm greatly.

Strewn across the floor as far as he could see were the many mangled and decaying forms of those who had preceded him and his friends to this foreboding place.

Sadun held his torch toward the nearest one, an almost fleshless corpse still clad in rotting leather armor. "Must've been some battle here."

"These men did not all die at the same time."

Norrec and the smaller soldier looked to Fauztin, who had a troubled expression on his generally emotionless countenance.

"What's that you mean?"

"I mean, Sadun, that some of them have clearly been

dead for far longer, even centuries. This one near your feet is one of the newest. Some of those over there are but bones."

The slight warrior shrugged. "Either way, from the looks of it, they all died pretty nasty."

"There is that."

"So . . . what killed them?"

Here Norrec answered. "Look there. I think they slew each other."

The two corpses he pointed at each had blades thrust into one another's midsections. One, with his mouth still open in what seemed a last, horrified cry, wore garments akin to the other mummified body by Sadun's feet. The other wore only scraps of clothing and only a few strands of hair covered an otherwise clean skeleton.

"You must be mistaken," the Vizjerei replied with a slight shake of his head. "The one warrior is clearly much older than the other."

So Norrec would have supposed if not for the blade thrust into the other corpse's torso. Still, the deaths of two men long, long ago had little bearing on present circumstances. "Fauztin, do you sense anything? Is there some sort of trap here?"

The gaunt figure held his staff before the chamber for a moment, then lowered it again, his disgust quite evident. "There are too many conflicting forces in here, Norrec. I can get no accurate sense of what to seek. I sense nothing directly dangerous—yet."

To the side, Sadun fairly hopped about in impatience. "So do we leave all of this, leave all our dreams, or do we take a little risk and gather ourselves a few empires' worth of coin?"

Norrec and the sorcerer exchanged glances. Neither could see any reason not to continue, especially with so many enticements before them. The veteran warrior finally settled the matter by taking a few steps further into the master chamber. When no great bolt of lightning nor demonic creature struck him down, Sadun and the Vizjerei quickly followed suit.

"There must be a couple dozen at least." Sadun leapt over two skeletal corpses still trapped in struggle. "And that's not counting the ones in little pieces . . ."

"Sadun, shut your mouth or I'll do it for you . . ." Now that he actually walked among them, Norrec wanted no more discussion concerning the dead treasure hunters. It still bothered him that so many had clearly died violently. Surely *someone* had survived. But, if so, why did the coins and other treasure look virtually untouched?

And then something else tore his thoughts from those questions, the sudden realization that beyond the treasure, at the very far end of the chamber, a dais stood atop a naturally formed set of steps. More important, atop that dais lay mortal remains still clad in armor.

"Fauztin . . ." Once the mage had come to his side, Norrec pointed to the dais and muttered, "What do you make of that?"

Fauztin's only reply was to purse his thin lips and carefully make his way toward the platform. Norrec followed close behind.

"It would explain so much . . ." he heard the Vizjerei whisper. "It would explain so many conflicting magical signatures and so many signs of power . . ."

"What're you talking about?"

The sorcerer finally looked back at him. "Come closer and see for yourself."

Norrec did just that. The sense of unease that had earlier filled him now amplified as the veteran peered at the macabre display atop the platform.

He had been a man of military aspirations, that much Norrec could at least tell, even if of the garments only a few tattered remains existed. The fine leather boots lay tipped to each side, pieces of the pants sticking out of them. What likely had once been a silk shirt could barely be seen under the majestic breastplate lying askew on the rib cage. Underneath that, blackened bits of a formerly regal robe covered much of the upper half of the platform. Well-crafted gauntlets and gutter-shaped plates, vambraces, gave the illusion of arms still sinewy and fleshbound; whereas other plates, these overlapping, did the same for the shoulders. Less successful was the armor on the legs, which, along with the bones there, lay askew, as if something had disturbed them at some point.

"Do you see it?" Fauztin asked.

Not certain what exactly he meant, Norrec squinted. Other than the fact that the armor itself seemed colored an unsettling yet familiar shade of red, he could see nothing that would have—

No head. The body on the dais had no head. Norrec glanced past the dais, saw no trace on the floor. He made mention of that to the sorcerer.

"Yes, it is exactly as described," the lanky figure swept toward the platform, almost too eager in the veteran's mind. Fauztin stretched out a hand but held back at the very last moment from touching what lay upon it. "The body placed with the top to the north. The head and helm, separated already in battle, now separated in time and distance in order to ensure an absolute end to the matter. The marks of power set into the walls, there to counter and contain the darkness still within the corpse . . . but . . ." Fauztin's voice trailed off as he continued to stare.

"But what?"

The mage shook his head. "Nothing, I suppose. Perhaps just being so near to him unsettles my nerves more than I like to admit."

By now somewhat exasperated with Fauztin's murky words, Norrec gritted his teeth. "So . . . who is he? Some prince?"

"By Heaven, no! Do you not see?" One gloved finger pointed at the red breast plate. "This is the lost tomb of Bartuc, lord of demons, master of darkest sorcery—"

"*The Warlord of Blood.*" The words escaped Norrec as little more than a gasp. He knew very well the tales of Bartuc, who had risen among the ranks of sorcerers, only to later turn to the darkness, to the demons. Now the redness of the armor made perfect and horrible sense; it was the color of *human blood*.

In his madness, Bartuc, who even the demons who had first seduced him had eventually come to fear, had bathed himself before each battle in the blood of previously fallen foes. His armor, once brilliant gold, had become forever stained by his sinful acts. He had razed cities to the ground, committed atrocities unbounded, and would have continued on forever—so the stories went—if not for the desperate acts of his own brother, Horazon, and other Vizjerei sorcerers who had used what knowledge they retained of the ancient, more natural magics to defeat the fiend. Bartuc and his demon host had been slaughtered just short of victory, the warlord himself decapitated just in the midst of casting a dire counterspell.

Still untrusting of his brother's vast power even in death, Horazon had commanded that Bartuc's body forever be hidden from the sight of men. Why they had not simply burned it, Norrec did not know, but certainly he would have tried. Regardless, rumors had arisen shortly thereafter of places where the Warlord of Blood had been laid to rest. Many had sought out his tomb, especially those of the black arts interested in possible lingering magic, but no one had ever claimed to truly find it.

The Vizjerei likely knew more detail than Norrec, but the veteran fighter understood all too well what they had found. Legend had it that for a time Bartuc had lived among Norrec's own people, that perhaps some of those with whom the soldier had grown up had been, in fact, descendants of the monstrous despot's followers. Yes, Norrec knew very well the legacy of the warlord.

He shuddered and, without thinking, began to back away from the dais. "Fauztin . . . we're leaving this place."

"But surely, my friend—"

"We're *leaving*."

The cowled figure studied Norrec's eyes, then nodded. "Perhaps you are right."

Grateful, Norrec turned to his other companion. "Sadun! Forget everything! We're leaving here! Now—"

Something near the shadowed mouth of the chamber caught his attention, something that moved—and that was *not* Sadun Tryst. The third member of the party presently engaged himself in trying to fill a sack with every manner of jewel he could find.

"Sadun!" snapped the older fighter. "Drop the sack! Quick!"

The thing near the entrance shuffled forward.

"Are you mad?" Sadun called, not even bothering to look over his shoulder. "This is all we've dreamed about!"

A clatter of movement caught Norrec's attention, a clatter of movement from more than one direction. He swallowed as the original figure moved better into view.

The empty sockets of the mummified warrior they had first stepped over greeted his own terrified gaze.

"Sadun! Look to your back!"

Now at last he had his partner's attention. The wiry soldier dropped the sack instantly, whirling about and pulling his blade free. However, when he saw what both Norrec and Fauztin already faced, Sadun Tryst's countenance turned as pale as bone.

One by one they began to rise, from corpse to skeleton,

those who had preceded the trio to this tomb. Now Norrec understood why no one had ever left alive and why he and his friends might soon be added to the grisly ranks.

"*Kosoraq!*"

One of the skeletons nearest to the sorcerer vanished in a burst of orange flame. Fauztin pointed a finger at another, a half-clad ghoul with some traces of his former face still remaining. The Vizjerei repeated the word of power.

Nothing happened.

"My spell—" Stunned, Fauztin failed to notice another skeleton on his left now raising a rusted but still serviceable sword and clearly intending to sever the mage's head from his body.

"Watch it!" Norrec deflected the blow, then thrust. Unfortunately, his attack did nothing, the blade simply passing through the rib cage. In desperation, he kicked at his horrific foe, sending the skeleton crashing into another of the shambling undead.

They were outnumbered several times over by foes who could not be slain by normal means. Norrec saw Sadun, cut off from his two friends, leap to the top of a mound of coins and try to defend himself from two nightmarish warriors, one a cadaverous husk, the other a partial skeleton with one good arm. Several more closed in from behind those two.

"Fauztin! Can you do anything?"

"I am trying a different spell!"

Again the Vizjerei called out a word: this time the two creatures battling with Sadun froze in place. Not one to miss such an opportunity, Tryst swung at the pair with all his might.

Both ghouls shattered into countless pieces, their entire top halves scattered on the stone floor.

"Your powers are back!" Norrec's hopes rose

"They never left me. I fear I have only one chance to use each spell—and most of those still remaining take much time to cast!"

Norrec had no chance to comment on the terrible news, for his own situation had grown even more desperate. He traded quick strikes with first one, then two of the encroaching ranks of undead. The ghouls seemed slow in reaction, for which he gave some thanks, but numbers and perseverance would eventually pay off for these ghastly guardians of the warlord's tomb. Those who had planned this last trap had planned well, for each party that entered added to the ranks that would attack the next. Norrec could imagine where the first undead had come from. He had remarked to his friends early on that although the three had come across sprung traps and dead creatures, no bodies had been found until the skull with the spike in its head. The first party to discover Bartuc's tomb surely had lost some of its numbers on the trek inside, never knowing that those dead comrades would become the survivors' greatest nightmare. And so, with each new group, the ranks of guardians had grown—with Norrec, Sadun, and Fauztin now set to be added.

One of the mummified corpses cut at Norrec's left arm. The veteran used the torch in his other hand to ignite the dry flesh, turning the zombie into a walking inferno. Risking his foot, Norrec kicked the fiery creature into its comrade.

Despite that success, though, the horde of unliving continued to press all three back.

"Norrec!" shouted Sadun from somewhere. "Fauztin! They're coming at me from everywhere!"

Neither could help him, though, both as harried. The mage beat off one skeleton with his staff, but two more quickly filled in the space left. The creatures had begun to move with more fluidity and greater swiftness. Soon, no advantage whatsoever would remain for Norrec and his friends.

Separating him from Fauztin, three ghoulish warriors pressed Norrec Vizharan up the steps and finally against the dais. The bones of the Warlord of Blood rattled in the armor, but, much to the hard pressed veteran's relief, Bartuc did not rise to command this infernal army.

A flash of smoke alerted him to the fact that the sorcerer had managed to deal with yet another of the undead, but Norrec knew that Fauztin could not handle all of them. So far, neither of the fighters had managed much more than a momentary stalemate. Without flesh for their blades to penetrate, without vital organs that could be skewered, knives and swords meant nothing.

The thought of one day rising as one of these and moving to slay the next hapless intruders sent a shiver down Norrec's spine. He moved along the side of the dais as best he could, trying to find some path by which to escape. To his shame, Norrec knew that he would have happily abandoned his comrades if an opening to freedom had abruptly materialized.

His strength flagged. A blade caught him in the thigh. The pain not only made him cry out, but caused Norrec to lose his grip on his sword. The weapon clattered down the steps, disappearing behind the encroaching ghouls.

His leg nearly buckling, Norrec waved the torch at the oncoming attackers with one hand while his other sought some hold on the platform. However, instead of stone his grasping fingers took hold of cold metal that offered no support whatsoever.

His wounded leg finally gave out. Norrec slipped to one knee, pulling the metallic object he had accidentally grabbed with him.

The torch flew away. A sea of grotesque faces filled the warrior's horrified view as Norrec attempted to right himself. The desperate treasure hunter raised the hand with which he had tried to garner some hold, as if by silently beseeching the undead for mercy he could forestall the inevitable.

Only at the last did he realize that the hand he had raised now had somehow become clad in metal—a gauntlet.

The very same gauntlet that he earlier had seen on the skeleton of Bartuc.

Even as this startling discovery registered in his mind, a word that Norrec did not understand ripped forth from his mouth, echoing throughout the chamber. The jeweled patterns in the walls flared bright, brighter, and the unearthly foes of the trio froze in place.

Another word, this one even less intelligible, burst free from the stunned veteran. The patterns of power grew blinding, burning—

—and exploded.

A fearsome wave of pure energy tore through the chamber, coursing over the undead. Shards flew everywhere, forcing Norrec to fold himself into as small a bundle as possible. He prayed that the end would be relatively quick and painless.

The magic consumed the undead where they stood. Bones and dried flesh burned as readily as oil tinder. Their weapons melted, creating piles of slag and ash.

Yet, it did not touch any of the party.

"What's happening? What's happening?" he heard Sadun cry.

The inferno moved with acute precision, sweeping over the tomb's guardians but nothing else. As their numbers dwindled, so too did the intensity of the force, until at last neither remained. The chamber became plunged into near darkness, the only illumination now the two torches and the little bit of light reflected by the many ruined stones.

Norrec gaped at the devastating results, wondering what he had just wrought and whether somehow it heralded an even more terrible situation. He then stared down at the gauntlet, afraid to leave it on, but equally fearful of what might happen if he tried to remove it.

"They . . . they have all been devoured," Fauztin managed, the Vizjerei forcing himself to his feet. His robe had been cut in many places and the thin mage held one arm where blood still flowed from a nasty wound.

Sadun hopped down from where he had been battling. Remarkably, he looked entirely uninjured. "But how?"

How, indeed? Norrec flexed his gloved fingers. The metal felt almost like a second skin, far more comfortable than he could have thought possible. Some of the fear faded as the possibilities of what else he might be able to do became more obvious.

"Norrec," came Fauztin's voice. "When did you put that on?"

He paid no attention, instead thinking that it might be interesting to try the other gauntlet—better yet, the entire suit—and see how it felt. As a young recruit, he had once dreamed of rising to the rank of general and garnering his riches through victory in battle. Now that old, long-faded dream seemed fresh and, for the first time, so very possible . . .

A shadow loomed over his hand. He looked up to see the sorcerer eyeing him in concern.

"Norrec. My friend. Perhaps you should take off that glove."

Take it off? Suddenly, the notion of doing so made absolutely no sense to the soldier. The gauntlet had been the only thing that had saved their lives! Why take it off? Could it . . . could it be that the Vizjerei simply coveted it for himself? In things magic, Fauztin's kind knew no loyalty. If Norrec did not give him the gauntlet, the odds were that Fauztin might simply just take it when his comrade could not stop him.

A part of the veteran's mind tried to dismiss the hateful notions. Fauztin had saved his life more than once. He and Sadun were Norrec's best—and only—friends. The eastern mage would certainly not try something so base . . . would he?

"Norrec, listen to me!" An edge of emotion, perhaps envy, perhaps fear, touched the other's voice. "It is vital right now that you take that gauntlet off. We shall put it back on the platform—"

"What is it?" Sadun called. "What's wrong with him, Fauztin?"

Norrec became convinced that he had been right the *first* time. The sorcerer wanted *his* glove.

"Sadun. Ready your blade. We may have to—"

"My blade? You want me to use it on Norrec?"

Something within the older fighter took control. Norrec watched as if from a distance as the gauntleted hand darted out and caught the Vizjerei by the throat.

"Sa-Sadun! His wrist! Cut at his—"

Out of the corner of his eye, Norrec saw his other companion hesitate, then raise his weapon to attack. A fury such as he had never experienced consumed the veteran. The world grew to a bloody red . . . then turned to utter blackness.

And in that blackness, Norrec Vizharan heard screams.

Two

In the land of Aranoch, at the very northern fringe of the vast, oppressive desert which made up much of that land, the small but resolute army of General Augustus Malevolyn remained encamped. They had set up camp some weeks previous for reasons that still mystified most of the soldiers, but no one dared question the decisions of the general. Most of these men had followed Malevolyn since his early days in Westmarch, and their fanaticism to his cause remained without question. But in silence they wondered why he seemed unwilling to move on.

Many felt certain that it had to do with the more gaudy tent pitched not far from the commander's own, the tent belonging to the witch. Each morning, Malevolyn went to her, evidently seeking portents of the future and making his decisions based upon those. In addition, each evening Galeona made her way to the general's tent—for more personal matters. How much influence she had over his choices, none could truly say, but it had to be substantial.

And as the morning sun began to peek over the horizon, the slim, well-groomed figure of Augustus Malevolyn emerged from his quarters, his pale, clean-shaven features—once described by a now-deceased rival as "the very visage of Lord Death without the kindness inherent"—entirely without expression. Malevolyn stood clad in armor of the darkest ebony save for the crimson border running along every edge, especially around the neck. In addition, the symbol of a red fox over three silver swords decorated the breastplate, the only reminder of the general's far-flung past. Two aides attended the general as he put on ebony and crimson gauntlets that looked as if they had just been forged. In fact, Malevolyn's entire suit looked to be in perfect condition, the result of nightly cleanings by soldiers trained to understand what even a single hint of rust might mean to their lives.

Fully covered save for his head, Malevolyn marched directly toward the sanctum of his sorceress, his mistress. Resembling something of a tentmaker's nightmare, the abode of Galeona looked as if it had been put together like a quilt, with patches of more than two dozen shades of color sewn together over and over. Only those like the general, who saw beyond the facade, might have noticed that the various colors created specific patterns and only those cognizant of the inner workings of sorcery would have known the power inherent in those patterns.

Behind Malevolyn the two aides followed, in the arms of one a covered burden that vaguely resembled something akin in shape to a head. The officer carrying the object moved uneasily, as if what he held filled him with distrust and not a little fear.

The commander did not bother to announce himself, yet just as he reached the closed flap of the witch's tent, a feminine voice, both deep and taunting, bid him enter.

Even though sunlight now toyed with the encampment, the interior of Galeona's tent appeared so dark that, if not for the single oil lamp dangling from the middle of the ceiling, the general and his aides would not have been able to see more than a foot beyond their noses. Had that been so, they would have missed quite a sight, indeed.

Pouches and flasks and items unnamed hung everywhere. Although once offered a case in which to house her wares, the sorceress had declined, finding some purpose in hanging each piece by noose in carefully preselected locations. General Malevolyn did not question this idiosyncrasy; so long as he received his desired answers, Galeona could have hung dry corpses from the ceiling and he would have made no comment.

She nearly did just that. While many of her prizes remained thankfully hidden within containers, those that dangled free included the desiccated forms of several rare creatures and various components of others. In addition, there were a few items that looked to have come from human sources, although full identification would have required too close an inspection.

To further add to the uneasiness her sanctum engendered in all save her commander and lover, the single lamp somehow created shadows that did not move in conjunction with normal reasoning. Ofttimes, Malevolyn's men would see the flame flicker in one direction, but a shadow move in another. The shadows in general also made the tent seem much larger inside than its outer dimensions warranted, as if by stepping in, the newcomers had entered a place not entirely set in the mortal plane.

And as the centerpiece to this unsettling and distracting chamber, the sorceress Galeona presented the most arresting and yet also disturbing vision of all. As she rose from the multicolored pillows covering the patterned carpet below, a fire stirred within each man. Lush, cascading black hair fell back to reveal a round, enticing countenance marked by full red and inviting lips, a generous but pleasing nose, and deep, so very deep, green eyes matched only by the sharp emerald ones of the general himself. Thick lashes half-draped over those eyes as the witch seemed to devour each newcomer in turn simply by looking at him.

"My general . . ." she purred, each word a promise.

Built voluptuously, Galeona displayed her assets as she did every weapon at her command. Her gown had been purposely cut as low as it could without failing its most basic function, and glittering jewels accented the edges near her chest. When she moved, she moved as if the wind gently pushed her along, her thin garments billowing seductively around her.

The visible effect of her charms on Malevolyn proved to be little more than a slight touch of his gloved hand on her deep-brown cheek, which the sorceress accepted as if he caressed her with the softest fur. She smiled, revealing teeth perfect save that they had a slight catlike sharpness to them.

"Galeona . . . my Galeona . . . slept you well?"

"When I actually slept . . . my general."

He chuckled. "Yes, the same myself." His very slight smile faded abruptly, "Until I had the dream."

"Dream?" The momentary intake of breath before she spoke signaled well enough that Galeona took this comment not at all lightly.

"Yes . . ." He moved past her, staring at without actually seeing one of the more macabre pieces of her collection. He toyed with it, moved one of the joints, while he spoke. "The Warlord of Blood arisen . . ."

She swept over to him, a dark angel now at his shoulder, her eyes wide with anticipation. "Tell me all, my general, tell me all . . ."

"I saw the armor without the man struggle from the grave, then bone filled the armor, with muscle and tendon joining afterward. Then flesh covered the body, but it was not Bartuc as his images have shown." The ebony-clad officer seemed disappointed. "A rather mundane face, if anything, but artisans were never known for carvings such as those. Perhaps this was the face of the warlord, although he seemed more a frightened soul in my dream . . ."

"Is that it?"

"No, I saw blood then, on his face, and after it appeared he marched off. I saw mountains give way to hills and hills to sand and then I saw him sink into that sand . . . and there the dream ended."

One of the other officers caught sight of a shadow in one far corner of the tent. It moved, shifting toward the general. Trained by experience not to speak of such things, he swallowed and held his tongue, hoping that the shadow would not, at some later point, turn in his own direction.

Galeona draped herself against General Malevolyn's breastplate, looking up into his eyes. "Have you ever had this dream before, my general?"

"You would have known."

"Yes, I would've. You know how important it is to tell me everything." She separated from him, returning to the pile of plush pillows. A glimmer of sweat covered every revealed portion of her body. "And this most important of all. . . . For this is no ordinary dream, no it is not."

"I suspected as much myself." He waved one negligent hand toward the aide who carried the cloth-covered object. The man stepped forward, at the same time ripping away the material in order to reveal what lay beneath.

A helmet with a ridged crest glistened in the weak light of the single lamp. Old but intact, it would have covered most of the head and visage of its wearer, leaving but two narrowed gaps for the eyes, a slight passage for the nose, and a wider but still narrow horizontal gash for the mouth. The back of the helmet hung low, protecting the neck there, but leaving the throat itself completely open.

Even in the dim illumination one could clearly discern that the helmet had been colored bloodred.

"I thought you might need Bartuc's helm."

"You may be right." Galeona separated herself from Malevolyn, reaching out for the artifact. Her fingers brushed the aide's own and the man shivered. With the general facing away from her and the second officer unable to see from his angle, the sorceress took the opportunity to let one hand briefly caress the aide's wrist. She had tasted him once or twice when her appetite had demanded some change of pace, but knew that he would never dare tell his commander of their encounters. Malevolyn would be more likely to have *him* executed rather than his valued witch.

She took the helmet and placed it on the ground near where she had originally been sitting. The general dismissed his men, then joined Galeona there, placing himself directly across from her.

"Do not fail me, my dear. I am adamant in this."

For the first time, a bit of Galeona's confidence dissipated. Augustus had always been a man of his word, especially when it came to the fates of those who did not live up to his expectations.

Hiding her concern, the dark sorceress placed her hands palm down on the top of the helmet. The general removed his gauntlets and did the same.

The flame in the lamp flickered, seemed to shrink to nearly nothing. The shadows spread, thickened, and yet somehow also seemed more alive, more independent of the frail light. That they had a surreal, unworldly sense to them did not bother General Malevolyn in the least, though. He knew of some of the powers with which Galeona conversed and suspected others. As a military man with imperial ambitions, he saw all as useful tools to his cause.

"Like calls to like, blood to blood . . ." The words slipped readily from Galeona's full lips. She had uttered this litany many times for her patron. "Let that which was his call to that which was his! What the shadow of Bartuc wore must be linked again!"

Malevolyn felt his pulse quicken. The world seemed to pull back from him. Galeona's words echoed, became the only focus.

At first he saw nothing but an eternal gray. Then, before his eyes, an image coalesced in the grayness, an image somewhat familiar to him. He saw again Bartuc's armor and the fact that someone wore it now, but this time the general grew certain that the man before him could not possibly be the legendary warlord.

"Who?" he hissed. "Who?"

Galeona did not answer him, her eyes closed, her head bent back in concentration. A shadow moved behind her, one that Malevolyn vaguely thought resembled some large insect. Then, as the image before him grew, he threw his attention wholly back into identifying and locating this stranger.

"A warrior," the sorceress murmured. "A man of many campaigns."

"Forget that! Where is he? Is he close?" The warlord's armor! After so very long, so many false trails . . .

She twitched from effort. Malevolyn did not care, willing to push her to the very limits and beyond if necessary.

"Mountains . . . cold, chill peaks . . ."

No help there, the world was filled with mountains, especially the north and across the Twin Seas. Even Westmarch had its share.

Galeona shuddered twice. "Blood calls to blood . . ."

He gritted his teeth. Why repeat herself?

"Blood calls to blood!"

She teetered, nearly losing her grip on the helmet. Her link to the spell all but broke. Malevolyn did his best to maintain the vision on his own even though his own magical skills paled in comparison to Galeona's. Yet, for a moment, he managed to fix better on that face. Simple. Nothing at all like a leader. In some ways, panic stricken. Not cowardly, but clearly far out of his element. . . .

The image began to falter. The general silently swore. The armor had been found by some damned foot soldier or deserter who likely had no idea of either its value or its power. "Where *is* he?"

The vision faded away with such abruptness that it

startled even him. At the same time, the dark witch let out a gasp and fell back onto the many pillows, completely shattering the spell.

A tremendous force threw Malevolyn's hands from the helmet. A string of harsh epithets burst from the general's mouth.

With a moan, Galeona slowly rose to a sitting position. She held her head with one hand as she looked at Malevolyn.

He, in turn, considered whether or not to have her whipped. To entice him with the fact that the armor had been found and then to leave him without the knowledge of where it was.

She read his dark look and what it likely meant for her. "I haven't failed you, my general! After all this time, Bartuc's legacy is yours to fulfill!"

"Fulfill?" Malevolyn rose, barely able to keep his frustration and fury in check. "Fulfill? Bartuc commanded demons! He spread his power over much of the world!" The pale commander gestured at the helmet. "I bought that from the peddler as a memento, a symbol of the might I sought to gain! A false artifact, I thought, but well done! The Helmet of Bartuc!" The general let out a harsh laugh. "Only when I put it on did I realize the truth—that it *was* the helmet!"

"Yes, my general!" Galeona quickly rose and put her hands on his chest, her fingers caressing the metal as if it were his own flesh. "And you began to have the dreams, the visions of—"

"*Bartuc* . . . I've seen his victories, seen his glories, seen his strength! I've lived them all . . ."—Malevolyn's tone grew increasingly bitter—"but only in my *dreams*."

"It was fate that brought the helmet to you! Fate and the spirit of Bartuc, don't you see? He means for you to be his successor, trust me," the witch cooed. "There can be no reason, for you're the only one to see these visions without my aid!"

"True." After the first two incidents, each during a period in which Malevolyn had worn the helmet, the general had commanded a few of his most trusted officers to try the artifact on for themselves. Even those who had worn it for several hours had admitted to no subsequent dreams of their own. That, to Augustus Malevolyn, had been proof enough that he had been chosen by the spirit of the warlord to take on his glorious mantle.

Malevolyn knew all that any mortal man could know of Bartuc. He studied every document, researched every legend. While many in the past have shrunken away from the warlord's dark and demonic history—fearing some taint spreading to themselves—the general had devoured each scrap of information.

He could match Bartuc in strategy and physical strength, but Malevolyn himself wielded only the least bit of magic. Barely enough to light a candle. Galeona had provided him with more sorcery—not to mention other pleasures—but to truly be able to emulate the warlord's glory, Malevolyn needed some manner by which to summon and command not one demon, but *many*.

The armor would open that path for him, of that he had become obsessively certain. Malevolyn's extensive research had indicated that Bartuc had imbued the suit with formidable enchantments. The general's own meager powers had already been augmented by the helmet; surely the complete, ensorcelled suit would give him what he desired. Surely the shade of Bartuc wanted that. The visions had to be a sign.

"There is one thing I can tell you, my general," the sorceress whispered. "One thing to encourage you in your quest . . ."

He seized her by her arms. "What? What is it?"

She grimaced momentarily from the pain of his grip. "He—the fool who wears the armor now—he comes nearer!"

"To us?"

"Perhaps, if the helmet and the rest are meant to be with one another, but even if not so, the closer he comes, the better I'll be able to specifically locate him!" Galeona pulled one arm free, then touched Malevolyn's chin. "You can wait just a little longer, my love. Just a little longer. . . ."

Releasing her, the general considered. "You will check each morning and each evening! You will spare no effort! The moment you can identify where this cretin is located, I must know! We shall march immediately after! Nothing must stand between me and my destiny!"

He seized the helmet and, without another word, departed from her tent, his aides quickly falling into line behind him. Malevolyn's mind raced as he pictured himself in the ensorcelled armor. Demonic legions would rise to his command. Cities would fall. An empire spanning . . . spanning the *world* . . . would spring up.

Augustus Malevolyn hugged the helmet almost protectively as he returned to his own quarters. Galeona had the right of it. He only had to be a little more patient. The armor would come to him.

"I will do as you once dreamed of doing," he whispered to the absent shade of Bartuc. "Your legacy *will* be my destiny!" The general's eyes gleamed. "And soon . . ."

The witch shuddered as Malevolyn vanished through the tent's flap. He had grown more unstable of late, especially the longer he wore the ancient helm. On one occasion she had even caught him speaking as if he were the Warlord of Blood himself. Galeona knew that the helmet—and likely all the armor—contained some mysterious magical force, but as of yet she had been able to neither identify nor control it.

If she could control it . . . she would not need her lover

any longer. A pity in some ways, but there were always other males. Other more *malleable* males.

A voice broke the silence, a scratchy, deep voice that even to the witch sounded something akin to the buzzing of a thousand dying flies. "Patience is virtue . . . this one should know! One hundred twenty-three years on this mortal plane in search of the warlord! So long . . . and now it comes together . . ."

Galeona looked around at the shadows, searching for one in particular. She finally noticed it in a far corner of the tent, a wavering, insectlike figure only visible to one who truly looked close. "Be silent! Someone may hear!"

"No one hears when this one chooses," the voice rasped. "Know you that well, human—"

"Then quiet your voice for my sanity, Xazax." The dark-skinned sorceress stared at the shadow but did not approach it. Even after all this time, she did not entirely trust her constant companion.

"So tender the ears of a human." The shadow took more form, now resembling a specific insect, a *praying mantis*. Yet, such a mantis would have been more than seven feet tall, if not more. "So soft and failing their bodies—"

"You'd do well not to talk of failures."

A low, chittering noise spread throughout the tent. Galeona steeled herself, knowing that her companion did not like to be corrected.

Xazax moved, shifting closer. "Tell this one of the vision shared."

"You saw it."

"But this one would hear it from you. . . . Please . . . indulge this one."

"Very well." Taking a deep breath, she described in as good detail as she could the man and the armor. Xazax surely had seen everything, but for some reason the fool always made her go over the visions. Galeona tried to hurry matters by ignoring the man for the most part, going more into the armor itself and the landscape vaguely seen in the background.

Xazax suddenly cut her off. "This one knows that the armor is true! This one knows that it wanders this mortal plane! The human! What about the human?"

"Perfectly ordinary. Nothing special about him."

"Nothing is ordinary! Describe!"

"A soldier. Plain of face. A simple fighter, probably the son of farmers, from the looks of him. Nothing extraordinary. Some poor fool who stumbled onto the armor and, as the general clearly thinks, has no idea what it is."

Again the chittering. The shadow withdrew slightly. When Xazax spoke, he sounded extremely disappointed. "Certain that this mortal journeys nearer?"

"So it seems."

The murky form grew still. Xazax clearly had something in mind. Galeona waited . . . and waited some more. Xazax had no concept of time where others were concerned, only when it came to his own needs and desires.

Two flashes of deep yellow momentarily appeared where the head of the shadow seemed to be. What might have been the outline of an appendage ending in three-clawed digits shifted momentarily into sight, then quickly vanished again.

"Let him come, then. This one will have decided by then whether one puppet is better than another . . ." Xazax's form grew indistinct. All semblance of a mantis, of any creature, faded away. "Let him come . . ."

The shadow melted into the darkened corners.

Galeona swore to herself. She had learned much from the foul creature, increased her power in so many ways because of his past guidance. Yet, much more than Augustus she would have preferred disposing of Xazax, being rid of his horrid self. The general could be manipulated to a point, but not so her secret companion. With Xazax, the sorceress played a continual game of cat and mouse and too often she felt like the latter of the two creatures. However, one did not simply break a pact with Xazax's kind; if done without precautions, Galeona might find herself minus her limbs and her head—all before he finally let her die.

And that made her consider at last something new.

He who wore Bartuc's armor certainly looked to be a warrior, a fighter, and, as she had also described him, a simple man, too. In other words, a fool. Galeona knew well how to manipulate such. As a man, he would be defenseless against her charms; as a fool, he would never realize that fact.

She would have to see how matters went with both the general and Xazax. If it seemed one or the other still worked to her advantage, Galeona would do what she could to tip the balance that way. Malevolyn with the armor his to command could certainly deal with her shadowy partner. However, if Xazax gained the ensorcelled artifacts first, truly he would be the one to follow.

Still, the stranger remained a possibility. Certainly he could be led around by the nose, told what to do. He presented potential where the other two presented risk.

Yes, Galeona intended to keep an eye on this fool for her own good. He would be far more susceptible to her desires than an ambitious and slightly mad military commander—and certainly far less dangerous than a *demon*.

THREE

Blood.

"By all that's holy, Norrec? What've you done?"

"Norrec. My friend. Perhaps you should take off that glove."

Blood.

"Damn you! Damn you!"

"Sa-Sadun! His wrist! Cut—"

Blood everywhere.

"Norrec! For god's sake! My arm!"

"Norrec!"

"Norrec!"

The blood of those closest to him. . . .

"Nooo!"

Norrec raised his head, screaming before he even knew he had awakened. A chill wind snapped him to full consciousness and for the first time he noticed the intense pain in his right cheek. Without thinking much, he put a hand to that cheek.

Cold metal brushed his skin. With a start, Norrec looked at the hand—a hand clothed in a crimson gauntlet, a reddish liquid now staining the fingertips.

Blood.

With great trepidation, he returned his hand to his cheek, touching the flesh with one finger now. By that means, Norrec discovered that he bled in three places. Three valleys had been gouged in his cheek, as if some animal had clawed him.

"Norrec!"

A flash of memory sent shivers through the veteran. Sadun's face, contorted in fear not witnessed by Norrec outside of the most horrible field of battle. Sadun's eyes pleading, his mouth open but no more words escaping.

Sadun's hand . . . tearing desperately at his friend's face.

"No . . ." It could not be as Norrec remembered it.

Another image.

Fauztin on the floor of the tomb, blood pooling on the stones nearby, its source the gaping hole where the Vizjerei's throat had once been.

The sorcerer, at least, had died relatively quickly.

"No . . . no . . . no . . ." Growing more horrified by the moment, the half-mad soldier struggled to his feet. Around him he noticed tall hills, even mountains, and the first glimmers of sunlight. Yet, none of them looked at all familiar. None of them at all resembled the peak in which he and his friends had discovered the tomb of Bartuc. Norrec took a step forward, trying to get his bearings.

An unsettling creaking accompanied every motion.

Norrec looked down to discover that not only his hands were clad in metal.

Armor. Everywhere he stared, Norrec only saw the same blood-colored metal plates. He had thought that his shock and horror could not possibly grow worse, but simply gazing at the rest of his body nearly threw the formerly steady soldier into complete panic. His arms, his torso, his legs, the same crimson armor now hid all. To add to the mockery, Norrec saw that he even wore Bartuc's ancient but still serviceable leather boots.

Bartuc . . . Warlord of Blood. Bartuc, whose dark magic had apparently saved the helpless soldier at the price of Sadun and the sorcerer's lives.

"Damn you!" Gazing down at his hands again, Norrec tore at the gauntlets. He tugged as hard as he could on first the left, then the right. Yet, regardless of which Norrec sought to remove, the metal gloves slid no more than an inch before seeming to catch.

He peered within and, after seeing no impediment, tried once more—but still the gauntlets would not come off. Worse, as the sun rose, for the first time Norrec could see that the blood from his injured cheek had not been the only stains upon the metal. Each finger, even most of each palm, looked as if it had been bathed in a rich, red dye.

But it was not dye that covered them.

"Fauztin," he murmured. "Sadun . . ."

With a roar of outrage, Norrec swung one fist at the nearest rocks, perfectly willing to break every bone in his hand if only it would mean the release of his hand. Instead, though, the rock itself gave way in part, the only damage to Norrec being a violent throbbing throughout his entire arm.

He dropped to his knees. "Nooo . . ."

The wind howled, seeming to mock him. Norrec remained where he was, head cast down, arms dangling. Fragments of what had happened in the tomb flashed through his mind, each painting a scene most diabolic. Sadun and Fauztin, both dead . . . both dead by his hands.

Norrec's head jerked up again. Not exactly by his hands. The damned gauntlets, one of which had saved him from the ghoulish sentinels, had done this. Norrec still blamed himself much for those deaths, for perhaps he might have altered matters if he had removed the first gauntlet immediately, but by himself he would have never slaughtered his friends.

There had to be a way to remove the gloves, even if he had to peel them off piece by piece, taking some of his skin off with the metal.

Determined to do something for himself, the veteran fighter rose again, trying to better identify his surroundings. Unfortunately, he saw little more now than he had on first glance. Mountains and hills. Forest stretching to the north. No sign of habitation, not even a distant plume of smoke.

And, again, nothing resembling the peak in which Bartuc's tomb lay.

"Where in Hell—" He broke off quickly, uneasy at even mentioning that dark and supposedly mythic realm. Even as a child and certainly as a soldier, Norrec had never believed much in either demons or angels, but the horror to which he had been a part had changed some of his opinions. Whether or not demons and angels truly existed, the Warlord of Blood had certainly left a monstrous legacy—a legacy of which Norrec hoped to rid himself quickly.

Hoping that perhaps he had simply been too upset the first time he had tried to remove the gauntlets, Norrec decided to inspect them in yet greater detail. However, as he looked down, he made yet another horrific discovery.

Not only did blood soil the gloves, but it did so the breastplate, too. Worse, on closer study, Norrec saw that the blood had not accidentally splattered the armor but had been purposively and methodically spread across it.

Again he shuddered. Quickly returning to the gauntlets, he sought some latch, some catch, even some dent that might have caused the gloves to stick. Nothing. Nothing held the gauntlets fast. By rights, they should have slid off his hands with a simple shake toward the ground.

The armor. If he could not remove the gauntlets, surely he could unfasten the other pieces. Some had catches readily seen and even with the gauntlets he surely would not have that much trouble undoing them. Other pieces would not have any catches, having been simply designed to slide on and off . . .

Bending down, Norrec tried one leg. He fumbled at the catches at first, then saw how best to secure his hold. With great care, the soldier forced the catch open.

And immediately it snapped shut.

He forced it open again, only to have the same result. Norrec cursed, attempting the catch a third time.

This time, it would not even open.

Attempting several others resulted in the same frustrating results. Worse, when he tried to at least remove the boots—that despite the cold—they, like the gauntlets, slid only so far before refusing to give way.

"This can't be possible . . ." Norrec tugged harder, but again with no visible success.

Madness! These were only garments, pieces of metal and a pair of old if sturdy boots! They had to come off!

Norrec's desperation rose. He was a common man, a man who believed that the sun rose in the morning and the moon at night. Birds flew and fish swam. People wore clothes—but clothes never wore people!

He glared at the bloody palms. "What do you *want* of me? What do you *want*?"

No sepulchral voice arose from around him, telling him of his dark fate. The gauntlets did not suddenly draw words or symbols in the earth. The armor simply would not let go of its new wearer.

Scattered images of his companions' gruesome ends once more tumbled about in his thoughts, making it hard for Norrec to focus. Norrec prayed—pleaded—for them to go away, but suspected that they would forever torment him.

Yet, if he could never be rid of the nightmares, there still might be something he could do about the cursed suit he wore. Fauztin had been a sorcerer of some reputation, but even the Vizjerei had admitted that there were many practitioners more skilled, more knowledgeable, than he.

Norrec would just have to find one of them.

He looked east, then west. To the east he saw nothing but tall and menacing mountains, whereas the west seemed a bit more gentle in scope. True, Norrec knew he might be working under false assumptions, but his best hope, he decided, had to be the latter direction.

The cold wind and moisture already chilling him to the bone, the weary veteran started off on his tremendous trek. It might be that he would die of exposure before he even made it out of the mountains, but some part of him suspected that such would not be so. Bartuc's armor had not seized him simply to let him die in the middle of the wilderness. No, it likely had some other notion in mind, one that would make itself known with time.

Norrec did not look forward to that revelation at all.

The sun vanished into an overcast sky, turning the weather even colder. A wetness also hung in the air. Breathing heavily, Norrec pushed on despite everything. As of yet he had not so much as seen a glimpse to hint that he traveled the right direction. For all the weary veteran knew, he had headed in the exact opposite of where he should have gone. Some mountain kingdom could have been just past the next peak to the east.

Thoughts like that, however frustrating, managed to keep Norrec from completely going mad. Each time he let his thoughts wander, they ever returned to the tomb and the horror of which he had been a part. Fauztin's and Sadun's faces haunted him and every now and then Norrec imagined he saw the pair condemning him from this shadow or that.

But they were dead and, unlike the bloody warlord,

they would stay so. Only Norrec's guilt continued to condemn him.

Around midday, he began to stumble. It finally occurred to him that he had neither eaten nor drunk since waking and the day before he had last supped early. Unless he planned to fall over soon and die, Norrec had to find sustenance of some sort.

But how? He had no weapon, no trap. Water he could find simply by scooping up some of the snow topping the nearby rocks, but actual food looked to be hard to come by.

Deciding he could at least assuage his thirst, Norrec walked over to a small outcropping where the coolness of the shadows had kept a small bit of snow and ice still unmelted. He scooped up what he could and greedily sucked on it, not caring at all about the bits of dust and grass that came with it.

In moments, his head seemed to clear a bit. Spitting out a few fragments of dirt, Norrec pondered what to do next. Not once had he seen any wild animal other than a bird. Without a bow or slingshot, he had no chance to bring down one of the creatures. Yet, he needed food—

His left hand suddenly moved without any regard as to his wishes. The fingers separated and bent inward, almost as if now Norrec clutched an invisible sphere. The gauntleted hand then turned until the palm faced the landscape just before the stunned fighter.

From his lips burst a single word, *"Jezrat!"*

The ground a few feet ahead buckled. Norrec at first thought that a tremor had struck the area, but only a small crevice, perhaps six feet by three, actually formed. The rest of his surroundings did not so much as shiver in the slightest.

His nose wrinkled as noxious fumes arose from the minute but apparently deep fissure. The air burned where yellow tendrils of smoke spread.

"Iskari! Woyut!" The new words came out of his own mouth with great ferocity.

From within the fissure came a horrid, chattering sound. Norrec sought to back up, but his feet would not move. The chattering increased, now a babble of high-pitched, animalistic sounds.

Norrec barely stifled a gasp as a grotesque tusked face thrust itself somewhat unwillingly into the overcast day. A pair of jagged, curved horns rose from the top of the scaly head. Round, yellow orbs with blazing red pupils shied away from the sky, finally focusing with clear bitterness on the human. The creature's squat, porcine nose twitched as if smelling something terrible—something that the fighter realized likely was him.

Twin sets of three-digited talons seized hold of the sides of the fissure as the horrific beast pushed itself up to the surface. Squat, oversized feet with curved nails planted themselves on the ground. Norrec stared down at a thing surely out of the underworld, a vaguely humanoid, hunchbacked denizen of the depths who, while barely reaching his waist, revealed surprising muscle under skin both scaled and furred.

And then a second of the creatures joined the first . . . he immediately followed by a third, a fourth, a fifth . . .

The frightful pack ceased growing in numbers after the sixth, a half a dozen more than Norrec certainly desired. The demonic imps chattered in their incomprehensible language, obviously upset with being here and very clear upon whom they blamed this entire situation. A few opened toothy maws and hissed at Norrec, while others simply scowled.

"Gester! Iskari!" The strange words once more startled him, but their effect on the monstrous pack proved even more astonishing. All signs of defiance faded abruptly as the imps groveled before him, some fairly burying themselves in the ground to prove how lowly they were.

"Dovru Sesti! Dovru Sesti!"

Whatever the phrase meant, it sent the horned brutes scurrying in outright panic. Squealing and chattering, they headed off in different directions as if their very lives depended upon it.

Norrec exhaled. Each time unknown words sprang from his lips, it felt as if his heart stopped. The language sounded akin to that used by Fauztin and other Vizjerei with whom the veteran had made acquaintance over the years, but it also sounded harsher, darker, than anything Norrec's murdered friend had ever spouted, even in the worst of battles.

He had no time to think any more on the subject, for suddenly chattering arose in the distance. Norrec peered to the south, saw two of the monstrosities loping back— the bloody, torn remains of a goat dragging behind them.

He had been hungry and now the suit provided him with its idea of sustenance.

Norrec blanched at the sight of the carcass. He had, of course, often slaughtered animals for food, but the imps had taken some delight in capturing and slaying the unfortunate goat. The head had nearly been ripped from the body and the legs dangled as if all broken. A portion of the goat's flank had been torn away, the blood flowing from that massive wound leaving a stream of crimson behind.

The grotesque creatures dropped the animal in front of Norrec, then backed away. Even as they did so, a third member of their pack returned, this one carrying a small, bloody carcass with vague similarities to a rabbit.

Eyeing the grisly offerings, the wary veteran looked for anything he himself might still consider edible. Exceptional hunters the tusked beasts might be, but their handling left much to be desired.

The other three imps returned within moments, each bearing their own prizes. One, a tattered-looking lizard,

Norrec immediately dismissed. The others, a pair of rabbits, he finally chose in preference to what had been first given to him.

As he reached for them, his left hand again rebelled. The gauntlet passed over the rabbits and as it did, incredible heat threatened to sear Norrec's fingers.

"Damn you!" He managed to stumble back a step. The heat faded quickly again, but his hand still throbbed from the near burning. From where they gathered, the imps chattered, this time sounding quite amused at his discomfort. However, a quick and furious glance silenced them.

His hand nearly normal again, Norrec returned his attention to the rabbits—and found them completely cooked. The scent that arose from them even smelled of certain spices, all enticing.

"So . . . don't think I'm going to thank you for this," he muttered to no one in particular.

Hunger overtaking his good sense, the graying warrior tore into the surprisingly well-prepared meat. He devoured not only one, but both rabbits with great ease. Large, they eventually silenced the cry in his stomach, leaving him to ponder what to do with the rest. Norrec waited, expecting the suit to make the decision for him, but nothing happened.

The pack still watched him, but their gazes often slipped to the meat, finally giving Norrec his own answer. He raised his hand, indicated the goat and the other slaughtered creatures, and waved toward the imps.

They needed no further invitation. With a manic glee that made the seasoned veteran push away, the tiny horde fell upon the meat. They tore into the flesh, sending gobbets and blood flying everywhere. Norrec's own meal grew queasy in his stomach as he watched the demons strip the bones of anything they could devour. He imagined those same claws and teeth on him . . .

"Verash!" So disturbed by the sight before him, Norrec barely reacted to the harsh word bursting from his mouth.

The imps recoiled as if struck. Cowed, they seized what remained of the goat's carcass and dragged it toward the fissure. With some effort, the grotesque creatures deposited the remains in the crevice, then, one by one, followed after it.

The last gave the human a quick and highly curious glance, then vanished into the bowels of the earth.

Before Norrec's wondering eyes, the crevice sealed itself, leaving no trace of its existence.

Walking dead. Haunted armor. Demons from the underworld. Norrec had witnessed magic in the past, even heard tales of dark creatures, but nothing could have ever prepared him for all that had happened since he had first entered that cave. He wished that he could go back and change events, make the decision to leave the tomb before the guardians had risen to slay his band, but Norrec knew he could no more do that than peel the cursed suit from his body.

He needed rest. The trek had been an arduous one and with food in his stomach the desire to go on had faded, at least for the time being. Better to sleep, then continue on refreshed. Perhaps his thoughts would also clear, enable him to better think how to extricate himself from this terrifying situation.

Norrec leaned back, stretching out. After so many years on the battlefield, any spot served as good as another when it came to finding a bed. The armor would make matters uncomfortable, but the tired soldier had suffered worse in that respect.

"What in—?"

His arms and legs pushed him back up to a standing position. Norrec tried to sit down, but no part of his body beneath his neck obeyed.

His arms dropped, swinging from the shoulders as if every muscle had been cut. Norrec's left foot stepped forward; his right followed after.

"I can't go on, damn you! I need some rest!"

The suit cared not a whit, picking up the pace. Left. Right. Left. Right.

"An hour! Two at the most! That's all I need!"

His words echoed uselessly through the mountains and hills. Left. Right. Whether the hapless veteran liked it or not, he would continue his arduous journey.

But to where?

This should never have happened, Kara nervously thought. *By the will of Rathma, this should never have happened!*

The emerald sphere that she had conjured earlier in order to see gave the entire tableau an even more unsettling appearance. Her face, already pale in color, paled further. Kara pulled her lengthy black cloak about her, taking some comfort from its warmth. Under thick lashes, silver, almond-shaped eyes surveyed a scene that her masters surely could never have envisioned. *The tomb is forever safe,* they had always insisted. *Where Vizjerei elemental sorcery falters, our own trusted skills will make the difference.*

But now both the more materialistic Vizjerei and the pragmatic followers of Rathma had apparently failed in their trust. That which they had sought to forever bury from the sight of men had not only been discovered, but had actually been stolen.

Or was there more to it? How powerful could the intruders have been to not only eliminate the undead guardians, but also shatter the unbreakable wards?

Not so powerful that two of them had not died in very violent fashion. Moving with such grace that she seemed almost to glide, the black-clad woman went to the nearest of the corpses. Kara leaned down and, after pushing back several tresses of lengthy, raven-colored hair, inspected the remains.

A wiry man, a battle-scarred war veteran. From one of the distant western lands. Not a pleasant-looking man, even before someone had completely twisted his head around and nearly torn off his arm. The dagger in his chest, surely an exercise in excess, looked to be his own. Which had killed him, even the necromancer could not say—not yet. The gaping wound had bled well, but not as much as it normally should have. Yet, why cut the victim open after snapping his neck?

As silent as death, the slim but curvaceous young woman made her way to the other body. This one she immediately recognized as a Vizjerei, which did not surprise her in the least. Always meddling, always seeking methods by which to gain advantage over one another, the Vizjerei made untrustworthy allies at best. If not for them, this entire situation would never have occurred. Bartuc and his brother had followed the early teachings of the Vizjerei, especially their reckless use of demons for more powerful spells of sorcery. Bartuc had especially excelled in that respect, but his constant interactions with the dark ones had twisted his own thinking, making him believe that demons were his allies. They, in turn, had fed off his growing evil, kindred spirits from both the mortal and infernal planes.

And although Horazon and his fellow mages had slain Bartuc and defeated his demon host, they had found it impossible to destroy the warlord's very corpse. The armor, known to bear several sinister enchantments, had continued to try to serve its function, protecting its master even in death. Only the fact that Bartuc had failed to cover his throat properly had even allowed his foes to decapitate the villain in the first place.

Left with a head and torso that they could not readily

burn, the Vizjerei had come to Kara's own people, search-ing the dense jungles for the reclusive practitioners of a sorcery that balanced life and death, a sorcery that caused their wielders to be branded *necromancer*. Together the two diverse orders worked hard to make certain that Bartuc's remains forever vanished from the face of the world, hopefully even the warlord's enchantments fad-ing to nothing with time.

Kara touched the crimson-soaked throat of the dead sorcerer, noting how most of it had been ripped away with a savageness beyond that of most animals. Unlike the fighter, the mage had died very quickly if still bru-tally. His eyes stared up at her, the horror of what had happened to him still evident. His expression remained a mix of shock and disbelief, almost . . . almost as if he could not believe who his murderer had been.

Yet, how could some force slay a Vizjerei and still fail to stop the other thieves? Had they just been fortunate, barely escaping? Kara frowned; with the undead guardians gone and the wards shattered, *what* had remained that could have hunted the intruders? What?

She wished the others had come with her, but that had not been possible. They had been needed elsewhere—*everywhere,* it seemed. A general ground swelling of forces so very dark had been sensed not only throughout Kehjistan, but also Scosglen. The faithful of Rathma had been spread thinner than in any other period of their existence.

And that left only her, one of the youngest and less-tested of her faith. True, like most of those who followed the path of Rathma, she had been trained to be indepen-dent almost from birth, but now Kara felt she entered ter-ritory for which no amount of teaching or experience could have prepared her.

Perhaps . . . perhaps though, this Vizjerei could still teach her something about what she now faced.

From her belt, Kara removed a delicate-looking but highly resilient dagger, the blade of which had been fashioned in a back-and-forth serpentine manner. Both the blade and the handle had been carved from purest ivory, but there again appearances deceived. Kara would have willingly pitted her own knife against any other, knowing full well that the enchantments placed on it made it stronger and more accurate than most normal weapons.

With neither distaste nor eagerness, the necromancer touched the point to one of the bloodiest areas on the dead Vizjerei's ravaged throat. She turned the blade over and over until the tip had been completely covered. Then, holding the dagger hilt down, Kara muttered her spell.

The deep red splotches on the tip flared bright. She muttered a few more words, concentrating.

The splotches began to change, to grow. They moved as if alive—or remembering life.

Kara, called Nightshadow by her teachers, flipped the dagger over, then thrust the point into the floor.

The blade sank in halfway, not at all impeded by the hard rock surface. Stepping back quickly, Kara watched as the ivory dagger became engulfed by the swelling splotches, which then melded together, creating a vaguely *human* form little taller than the weapon.

Drawing patterns in the air, the necromancer uttered the second and final part of her incantation.

In a blaze of red light, a full-sized figure materialized where the ivory dagger had stood. Completely crimson from head to toe, skin to garments, he stared at her with vacant eyes. He wore the clothes of a Vizjerei sorcerer, the same clothes, in fact, that the corpse on the floor behind him wore.

Kara eagerly beheld the phantasm bearing the likeness of the dead mage. She had done this only once before and under conditions much more favorable. What stood before her most mortals would have called a ghost, a spirit—but in doing so they would have been only partially correct. Drawn forth from the life's blood of the victim, it indeed bore some traces of the dead's spirit, but to fully summon a true specter would have taken more time and trouble and Kara had to act in haste now. This phantasm would surely serve to answer her questions.

"Name yourself!" she demanded.

The mouth moved but no sound came from it. Nonetheless, an answer formed in her mind.

Fauztin . . .

"What happened here?"

The phantasm stared, but did not answer. Kara cursed herself for a fool, realizing that it could only answer questions in a simple way. Taking a breath, she asked, "Did you destroy the undead?"

Some . . .

"Who destroyed the rest?"

Hesitation, then . . . *Norrec.*

Norrec? The name meant nothing to her. "A Vizjerei? A sorcerer?"

To her surprise, the spectral form shook his crimson head ever so slightly. *Norrec . . . Vizharan . . .*

The name again. The last part, *Vizharan*, meant *servant of the Vizjerei* in the old tongue, but that information helped Kara little. This path led her nowhere. She turned to a different and far more important subject. "Did this Norrec take the armor from the dais?"

And again the phantasm shook his head ever so slightly. Kara frowned, recalling nothing in her teachings mentioning this. Perhaps Vizjerei made for more unusual summonings. She pondered her next question with care. With the limitations of the phantasm, the necromancer realized that she could spend all day and night asking and yet still receive no knowledge of value to her mission. Kara would have to—

A sound came from the passage behind her.

The young enchantress whirled about. For just the briefest of moments, she thought she saw a slight bluish light deep within, but it vanished so quickly that Kara had to wonder if she had imagined it. It could have simply been a glow bug or some other insect, but . . .

Cautiously approaching the tunnel, Kara warily peered into the darkness. Had she been too hasty in heading directly to the main chamber? Could this Norrec have been hiding outside, waiting for someone to come?

Absurd, but Kara *had* heard a noise. Of that she felt certain.

And at that moment, she heard it again, this time much farther into the passage.

Muttering a spell, Kara formed a second emerald sphere, which she immediately sent fluttering down the rocky corridor. As it darted along, the dark-haired woman followed after for a few steps, trying to make out what she could.

Still no sign of another intruder, but Kara could not take a chance. Anyone who could so readily slay a Vizjerei certainly offered deadly threat. She could not simply ignore the possibility. Taking a deep breath, the necromancer started down the rocky passage—

—and froze a moment later, swearing at herself for her carelessness. Kara had left her prized dagger behind, and she dared not face a possible foe without it. Not only did it provide her with protection both in the mundane and magical senses, but by leaving it behind, the dark mage even risked possibly losing it to whomever might be stalking the tomb.

She quickly stepped back into the chamber, already preparing in her mind the spell to dismiss the phantasm, only to find that the crimson figure had *already* vanished.

Kara managed but one more step before a further realization struck her just as hard. With the phantasm had vanished her precious *dagger,* yet that alone did not leave her now wide-eyed and unable to even speak.

Both the body of the sorcerer Fauztin and his slighter companion had also disappeared.

FOUR

The sand snake wound swiftly along the shifting desert, its constant undulations keeping the heat of the ground from burning it underneath. Hunting had been poor today but with the sun rising higher, the time had come, like it or not, for the snake to temporarily seek shelter. When the sun had descended some it could come out again, this time hopefully to snag a mouse or beetle. One could not go long in the desert without food, where hunting had always been a difficult business.

Pushing itself hard, the snake traveled up the latest dune, aware that only minutes separated it from shade. Once over this one impediment, it would be home free.

The sand beneath the snake suddenly erupted.

Mandibles more than a foot in length snapped tight around the midsection of the serpent. The snake flailed desperately, trying to slither out. A monstrous head burst through the sand, followed by the first pair of needlelike legs.

Still struggling, the snake struck at its attacker, hissing and trying to use its venom. The fangs, however, could not penetrate the chitinous exoskeleton of the huge arthropod.

One leg pinned down the rear half of the snake. The beetlelike head of the massive predator twisted sharply, at the same time the mandibles squeezing tight.

Flailing, the bloody front half of the serpent dropped to the ground, the head still hissing

The black and red arthropod emerged completely from its hiding place, turning now to the process of dragging its meal to where it could eat in leisure. With its front appendages, the nearly seven-foot long predator began prodding the back half of the serpent.

A shadow suddenly loomed over the hideous creature. Immediately it turned its bulky head and spat at the new intruder.

The corrosive poison splattered against the somewhat ragged silk robe of a bearded and rather wild-eyed elderly man. From above a long, almost beaklike nose, he gazed down briefly at the sizzling mess, then waved one gnarled hand over it. As he did this, the acidic poison and the damage it had already caused completely vanished.

Watery blue eyes focused on the savage insect.

Plumes of smoke arose from the exoskeleton. The beetlelike creature let out a high-pitched squeal, its spindly legs teetering. It tried to flee, but its body seemed no longer to work. The legs buckled and the body crumpled. Parts of the monstrous insect began to drip away, as if the creature was no longer made of shell and flesh, but rather runny wax now melting in the hot sun.

The squealing arthropod collapsed in a molten heap. The mandibles, so deadly to the snake, dissolved into a pool of black liquid that readily sank into the sand. The cries of the dying creature finally cut off and, as the ragged figure watched, what remained of the once-savage predator utterly vanished, draining away like the few drops of rain that annually sought to soothe this parched land.

"Sand maggot. Too many of them about now. So much evil about everywhere," the white-haired patriarch muttered to himself. "So much evil even out here. I must be careful, must be very careful."

He walked past the savaged snake and its just as unfortunate pursuer, heading to another dune just a short distance away. As the bearded hermit neared, the dune suddenly swelled, growing higher and higher, finally forming a doorway within that seemed to lead directly into the underworld itself.

Watery blue eyes turned to survey the oppressive landscape. A momentary shiver ran through the elderly man.

"So much evil . . . I must definitely be careful."

He descended into the dune. The sand immediately began to pull inward the moment he passed through the entrance, filling the passage behind in rapid fashion until no sign remained at all of any opening.

And as the dune settled to normal again, the desert winds continued their shifting of the rest of the landscape, the snake and the sand maggot already joining countless other hapless denizens in a dusty, forgotten burial.

The mountains lay far behind him, although how he had journeyed so far Norrec only half-recalled. At some point he had passed out from exhaustion, but evidently the suit had gone on and on. Despite the fact that none of the effort had actually been his own, every muscle in the veteran's body screamed and every bone felt as if it had broken. His lips were parched from the wind while sweat covered much of his body. Norrec yearned to peel off the armor and run free, but knew the hopelessness of that dream. The armor would do with him as it chose.

And now he stood atop a ridge, staring at the first sign of civilization he had seen in many a day. An unsavory inn, a place that more befitted brigands and highwaymen rather than honest warriors such as himself. However, with darkness about to befall and Norrec nearly done in, the suit seemed to finally register that it had to once more deal with the frailties of its human host.

He marched without desiring to toward the building. Three glum horses stood tethered nearby and at least one more sounded its displeasure from a wretched stable just beyond. Norrec found himself wishing that he had his sword; the armor had not bothered to take that when it had walked out of the tomb with him.

Just before he reached the doorway, the veteran's legs suddenly buckled under him. Norrec quickly caught himself, realizing that Bartuc's damnable armor had granted him the dubious gift of entering on his own, likely in order to avoid notice of anything strange.

Hunger and rest more important to Norrec at the moment than his own pride, the soldier pushed the door wide open. Grimy, suspicious faces looked up, the onlookers a mixture not only of the eastern races, but those on the other side of the Twin Seas as well. Mongrels, all four of them, Norrec saw, and although he certainly held no man's background against him, this group did not look at all like men next to whom he desired to sit.

Kind of place where you gotta watch your back even around the serving wench! Sadun Tryst would have jested. Tryst, of course, would have sat with anyone who would have offered him a drink.

But Sadun was dead.

"Shut the door or go back out!" snarled the one seated nearest.

Norrec obeyed, desiring no confrontations. Forcing himself to act as if he had just ridden in, the weary fighter kept his head high as he walked smartly through the room. His body screamed as he moved, but no one there would know of it. Give these men even the slightest hint of weakness and Norrec suspected that they would make dire use of that fact.

He approached what he assumed to be the innkeeper, a towering heavy-set figure more frightful than his patrons, who stood behind a worn and scratched counter. A bush of dirty brown hair fought its way from under an old travel cap. Beady eyes stared from a round, canine face. Norrec had noted a peculiar odor in the room when he had first entered and now he knew it to originate from the man before him.

Had he thought that the armor would let him leave, Norrec would have walked right out regardless of his needs.

"What?" the innkeeper finally muttered, scratching his extravagant belly. His shirt had been decorated in a variety of stains and even a rip under the arm.

"I need food." That, more than anything else, Norrec had to have quickly.

"I need good coin."

Coin. The desperate soldier fought back growing frustration. Another item that had been left behind with the bloodied corpses of his companions.

His left hand suddenly shot forward, the gauntlet slapping down so hard on the counter that the innkeeper jumped. The men seated at the tables leapt to their feet, some reaching for weapons.

The gauntlet pulled away . . . leaving behind an old but clearly *gold* coin.

Recovering before the rest, Norrec said, "And a room for that, too."

He could feel every pair of eyes avidly staring at the coin. Once more Norrec silently cursed the damnable armor. If it could produce wealth from thin air, it could have at least produced something less conspicuous than gold. Again he wished that he still carried his sword or at least a good, solid knife.

"Got some stew in the pot back there." With a tip of his head the ursine giant indicated the kitchen. "Got a room up the second floor. First on the right."

"I'll eat in there."

"Suit yourself."

The innkeeper vanished in back for a few moments,

then returned with a stained bowl containing something that smelled even worse than he did. Nevertheless, Norrec gratefully accepted it, his hunger so demanding now that, if offered to him again, he would have even eaten the goat the imps had mutilated.

With the bowl in the crook of his arm, Norrec followed the innkeeper's directions to the room. As he walked up the creaking wooden stairway, he heard low muttering down in the common area. His free hand tightened. The gold coin had burned itself into the minds of the men below.

The room proved as dismal as the veteran had expected, a dark, dusty closet with a window so grimy it gave no view of the outside. The bed looked ready to collapse and what had once been white sheets now were permanently gray. The single oil lamp shed barely enough light to illuminate its immediate surroundings, much less the rest of the room.

With no table or chair in the place, Norrec gingerly sat on the bed and began spooning the contents of the bowl into his mouth. If anything, it tasted more vile than he could have imagined, but seemed at least fresh enough not to kill him.

The need to sleep grew more urgent as food filled his stomach. Norrec had to struggle to remain awake long enough to finish and the moment he had the bowl emptied, he dropped it gently on the floor and settled back. In the back of his mind, Norrec continued to worry about those below him, but exhaustion soon overcame even that significant concern.

And as he drifted off to sleep, Norrec began to dream.

He saw himself shouting commands at an infernal army of grotesque horrors his imagination could have never created on its own. Scaled, fiery, nightmarish abominations thirsting for blood—blood Norrec seemed all too willing to give them. Demons they were, but under his complete control. They would raze cities for him, slaughter the inhabitants in his name. Even Hell respected the power of the Warlord of Blood, he . . . *Bartuc*.

At that thought, the soldier finally fought to escape the dream. He could never be Bartuc! Never demand such horror for the sake of his own desires! Never!

Yet such absolute power had its seductive side.

Norrec's internal battle with himself thankfully came to an abrupt halt as a noise suddenly awoke him. Eyes flashing open, he listened for more. What he had heard, the fighter could not say. A small, somewhat insignificant sound, but one that had registered even in his subconscious.

He heard it again, just barely audible through the closed door. The creak of someone slowly and, it seemed, very cautiously ascending.

There were other rooms, true, but the men below had hardly struck Norrec as so polite that they would tread so carefully in order not to disturb him. Had they tromped up the steps without concern, he would have thought nothing of it. However, such caution indicated to the soldier that perhaps they had something else in mind, something not at all to his liking.

If a weary traveler had *one* gold coin, surely he had more . . .

Norrec's hand slipped to where his sword should have been. No hope there. That left him entirely dependent on the armor itself, not necessarily a path he could trust. Perhaps the suit would find one of the thieves more to its liking, opening the way for the soldier's easy slaughter . . .

The creaking ceased.

Norrec pushed himself up as silently as he could.

Two men with drawn knives broke through the dilapidated door, instantly diving toward the figure before them. From behind the pair came a third villain, this one wielding a curved short sword. Each of the attackers matched the rising fighter in height as well as in muscle, and they had the advantage of trapping him in a room with a window too small for Norrec to try to fit through.

He raised a fist, ready to make them pay—

And the fist suddenly held a long, sable sword with wicked teeth set in the edge. Norrec's hand came down with the blade, moving so swiftly that he and his first adversary could only gape.

The blade ripped into the attacker, tearing flesh and sinew without effort. A gaping wound spread across the robber's entire chest as if by magic, blood spilling so fast from it that it took the victim a moment to realize he had been slain.

The first attacker finally slumped to the floor even as his companions came to grips with this sudden, dismaying turn of events. The one with the dagger sought to back away, but his partner pushed forward, daring to match blades. Norrec might have warned the brigand of the foolishness of that, but by then they were locked in combat.

Once, twice—that proved to be all the effort the suit would allow its opponent. As the intruder brought his sword up for a third strike, Norrec's gauntleted hand twisted sharply. The sable blade turned in a mad, zig-zag fashion.

His life fluids spilling from a horrendous slit running from his throat to his waist, the second villain staggered. He dropped his sword as he desperately tried to prevent the inevitable.

As if impatient to end matters, Norrec's hand came up again.

The head of his foe struck the floor, rolling to a corner and coming to rest—all before the torso even began to tip over.

"Gods!" the soldier managed to gasp. He had been trained to fight, not to slaughter.

Clearly aware of what chance he had, the third intruder had already hurried to the doorway. Norrec wanted to let him go, desiring no more bloodshed, but the suit chose otherwise, leaping over the two bodies and chasing after.

At the bottom of the steps, the last of the trio struggled to get around the innkeeper, who appeared to be demanding to know why his friends had failed in their task. Both men looked up to see the crimson figure above them, the dark blade flaring. The innkeeper drew a prodigious long sword from his waist, a weapon so massive Norrec momentarily feared that the suit had overestimated its invulnerability. The other man tried to continue his flight, but a fifth outlaw who suddenly appeared from behind the innkeeper pushed him back toward the fray.

If they expected to meet him on the stairs, they were sorely mistaken. Norrec found himself leaping feet first toward the trio, their astonished faces no doubt matching his own. Two of them managed to back away just in time, but the lone survivor of the earlier debacle stood too horrified to move quickly.

The sinister weapon made short work of him, the blade pushing through until it came out the back, then immediately retracting.

"His right!" snarled the heavy-set innkeeper. "His right!"

The other swordsman obeyed. Norrec knew exactly what the leader planned. Attack from opposite sides, keep the soldier distracted. One of them would surely land a blow, especially the innkeeper, whose weapon had nearly twice the reach of the black one.

"Now!" Both men struck at once, one aiming for Norrec's throat, the other for his legs, where the armor did not cover everywhere. These two had evidently battled side-by-side before, just as Norrec had with Sadun and Fauztin. Had it been his effort alone, the soldier knew that he would have perished there and then. Bartuc's armor, however, fought with a speed and accuracy that nothing human could match. Not only did it force down the larger adversary's gargantuan blade, but it also managed to come up in time to deflect the second villain's strike. More amazing, it followed through with a savage thrust that sank into the throat of the latter man.

And as his companion fell, the innkeeper's iron reserve suddenly melted. Still wielding his sword before him, he began to back toward the doorway. The suit pushed Norrec forward, but did not harry the last of its foes.

Flinging open the door, the innkeeper turned and fled into the night. Now Norrec expected Bartuc's armor to pursue, but instead the suit turned around and marched him over to where one of the other bodies lay. As Norrec knelt beside the corpse, the sable blade dissolved, leaving both hands free.

To his horror, one gauntleted finger thrust into the mortal wound, pulling back only when blood covered much of the upper portion of the digit. Moving to the wooden floor, the finger drew a pattern.

"*Heyat tokaris!*" his mouth suddenly blurted. "*Heyat grendel!*"

The suit backed away and as it did, a plume of rank, greenish smoke arose from the bloody pattern. It quickly formed arms, legs—and tail and wings. A reptilian visage with too many eyes blinked in disdain, disdain that vanished when the demon saw what stood before him.

"Warrrlorrrd . . ." it rasped. The bulbous eyes looked closer. "Warrrlorrrd?"

"*Heskar, grendel! Heskar!*"

The demon nodded. Without another word, the monstrous being headed toward the open door. In the distance, Norrec heard the frantic beats of several fleeing horses.

"*Heskar!*" his mouth demanded again.

The reptilian horror picked up its pace, departing the inn. As it stepped outside, it spread its wings and took off, disappearing into the night.

Norrec did not have to guess its purpose. On the command of Bartuc, it had gone hunting.

"Don't do it," he whispered, now certain that whatever spirit lurked within the armor could hear him. "Let him go!"

The suit turned back toward the first corpse.

"Damn it! Leave him be! He's not worth it!"

Seemingly ignorant to his pleas, it forced him again to bend down near the body. The hand that had earlier touched the wound with but one finger now planted all of them there, letting the blood stain the entire palm.

Outside, a frantic human scream rose high—then cut off with harsh finality.

In Norrec's other hand, a new weapon appeared, this time a scarlet dagger with a double point at the end.

The flapping of wings warned him of the demon's return, but Norrec could not twist his neck enough to see. He heard the heavy breathing of the creature and even the folding of its leathery wings as it settled down in the common room.

"*Nestu veraki . . .* " The dagger shifted toward the corpse's throat. "*Nestu verakuu . . .* "

The veteran soldier shut his eyes, now praying for himself. Enough of his memories concerning his friends' deaths had come back to him to give him indication of what would happen next. Norrec had no desire to face it, would have fled if he could.

"*Nestu hanti . . .* "

But he could do nothing now except try to preserve both his sanity and his soul.

"Nestu hantiri . . ."
The dagger plunged into the throat of the brigand.

General Augustus Malevolyn arose from the sea of pillows, leaving Galeona to whatever dreams a sorceress of her ilk had. Without making a sound, he donned some clothes and stepped out of his tent.

Two sentries snapped to attention, their eyes straight ahead. Malevolyn gave them the slightest of nods, then moved on.

A city of tents spread out to the west, the only homes for the general's dedicated minions. Despite being a landless noble, he had managed to raise a fighting force virtually unequaled in the Western Kingdoms. For a price, he had served the causes of any ruler, garnered for himself the money he had needed for his future ambitions. Now, however, the point had come when he had sworn never to serve another, that some day he, Augustus Malevolyn, would be master of more than this worthless patch of ground.

The general turned his eyes to the south, where the vast desert of Aranoch lay. For some time now, he had felt drawn in that direction, drawn to more than the fact that a tremendous prize, the rich, lush city of Lut Gholein, lay some distance within. Lut Gholein, despite its proximity to the desert, also bordered the Twin Seas. Because of that and the fertile strip of land on which it stood, the kingdom had prospered well. Several times would-be conquerors had thought to add its riches to their coffers, but each attempt had met with total disaster. Lut Gholein had not only proven to be well defended, but it appeared to have a bit of a charmed existence. In fact, in Malevolyn's mind, that charm bordered on outright sorcery. Something watched over the city.

And that something was what most tantalized the commander now. Somehow it had some link to his desire to seize Bartuc's legacy and make it his own. Malevolyn dreamed about it, found himself constantly turning his thoughts toward it.

"Soon," he whispered to himself. "Soon . . ."

And what will you do with that legacy? came the sudden thought in his head. *Emulate Bartuc? Repeat his mistakes as well as his victories?*

"No . . ." He would not do that. For all the warlord's power, for all his command of demon hosts, Bartuc had had one failing that the general could not overlook. Bartuc had not been a career soldier. The fabled Warlord of Blood had been first and foremost a sorcerer. Mages had their uses, especially Galeona, but they were unstable and too focused on their arts. A true commander had to be able to keep his attention on the field of battle, on the logistics and the sudden shifts. That had been part of the reason Augustus Malevolyn had been unable to achieve any true skill with his own sorcerous abilities; his military career had been his true passion.

But with the armor, with the magic of Bartuc, you could be more than him, the perfect fusion of soldier and sorcerer! You could be more than Bartuc, even eclipsing him . . .

"Yesss . . . yesss . . ." The general pictured his image forever engraved in the hearts and minds of those in the future. General Augustus Malevolyn, emperor of the *world*!

And even demons will bow to you, call you master.

Demons. Yes, with the armor his, the ability to summon demons would surely follow. The dreams he had had since first wearing the helm had all pointed to that. Reunite helm with suit and the enchantments within would give him the power.

The suit. . . . His brow furrowed. He needed the suit!

And some fool had it.

Malevolyn would find him, find the witless wretch and peel off the armor piece by piece. Then, he would reward the cretin with the honor of being the first to die at the hands of the new Warlord of Blood.

Yes, the general would make the fool's death a memorable one.

Augustus Malevolyn walked on, dreaming of his glory, dreaming of what he would do with the dark powers he would soon wield. Yet, while he walked and dreamt, he still paid meticulous attention to the encampment, for a good leader always watched to make certain that slovenliness did not spread among his forces. Empires were won and lost because of overlooking such seemingly minor things.

Yet, while Malevolyn noted the care with which his loyal warriors performed their tasks, he failed to notice a shadow not caused by the flickering torches. He also failed to notice that this selfsame shadow had stood behind him moments prior, whispering what the general had believed had been his own thoughts, his own questions.

His own dreams.

The shadow of the demon Xazax shifted toward Galeona's tent, his work this night more than to his satisfaction. This human presented some interesting possibilities, ones that he would explore. It had occurred to him long ago that the armor of Bartuc would never accept an actual demon as its master, for, while the warlord had come to believe in the ways of Hell, he had also carried a basic distrust of anyone but himself. No, if the spirit of Bartuc remained even in part in the ancient armor, it would demand a more susceptible human host, however fragile and temporary their bodies might be.

The general desired to play warlord. That suited Xazax well. The witch had her uses, but a *successor* to the bloody Bartuc—Xazax's lord, Belial, would reward his humble servant well for such a find. Not only had the civil war in

Hell against Azmodan not gone well of late, but troublesome rumors had reached even there that the Prime Evil Diablo had made good his escape from his mortal prison. If so, he would seek to free his brothers Baal and Mephisto from theirs as well, at which point they would then attempt to regain their thrones from Azmodan and Belial. The three would not deal well with demons who had so loyally served their rebellious lieutenants. If Belial fell, so too would Xazax . . .

"What've you been doing?"

The shadow paused just within the entrance of the sorceress's abode. "This one has many tasks and cannot always be at your beck and call, human Galeona . . ." He made a clacking sound, much like a sand maggot might have done just before crushing its prey in its mandibles. "Besides, you slept . . ."

"Not deep enough to not sense your magic in the air. You promised you wouldn't cast any spells around here! Augustus has some skill; he might notice it and wonder what it means!"

"There is no danger of that, this one promises."

"I ask again, demon! What were you doing?"

"Making a little study of the helmet," Xazax lied, shifting to another part of the tent. "Searching for our fool who knows not what he wears . . ."

Her anger turned to interest. "And did you find out where he is? If I could tell Malevolyn more . . ."

The demon chuckled, a scratchy sound like furious bees trapped in a jug. "Why, when we agreed that the armor will never be his?"

"Because he still has the helmet, you fool, and until we find the armor, we still need Augustus because of his connection to the helmet!"

"True," mused the demon. "His ties to it run deep . . . this one would say *blood* deep."

Her chin went up as she flung her hair back, signs that

Xazax had long ago learned meant that the human had grown angry. "And what does *that* mean?"

The shadow did not waver. "This one only meant a jest with that, sorceress. Only a jest. We speak of things concerning Bartuc, do we not?"

"A demon with a sense of humor." Galeona looked not at all amused. "Very well, I'll leave the jesting to you; you leave Augustus to me."

"This one would not seek to take your place in the general's bed . . ."

The sorceress gave the shadow a withering glance, then left the tent. Xazax knew she would hunt down Malevolyn, begin reinforcing her hold on him. The demon respected her abilities in this matter even if he felt confident that in a struggle between Galeona and himself, the witch woman would surely lose. After all, she was mortal, not one of the foul angels. Had she been such, Xazax might have been more concerned. Angels were conniving, working behind the scenes, playing tricks instead of confronting their foes directly.

The shadow of the demon pulled back, secreting himself in the darkest corner. No angels had interfered so far, but Xazax intended to remain wary. If one showed itself, he would take it in his claws and slowly pluck its limbs from it one at a time, all the while listening to the sweet song of its screams.

"Come to me if you dare, angels," he whispered to the darkness. "This one will greet you with open arms . . . and teeth and claws!"

The dim flame from the single oil lamp suddenly flared, briefly illuminating Galeona's tent far more than normal. In that sudden light, the shadow hissed and cringed. The outline of a massive emerald and crimson insect briefly flashed into sight, then quickly faded again as the flame dimmed.

Xazax chittered furiously, grateful that Galeona had

not witnessed his reaction. Oil lamps often flared; he had only been taken by surprise by a mundane act of nature. Nonetheless, the shadow of the demon pressed deeper into the comforting recesses of the tent. There he could safely plot. There he could safely use his power to seek out the human wearing Bartuc's armor.

There he could better watch for cowardly angels.

FIVE

Rumbling storm clouds turned the day as nearly as black as the night had been, but Norrec hardly noticed. His mind still sought to come to grips with the terror of the previous evening and his own limited part in it. More men had died brutally because of Norrec's damned quest for gold; although unlike Sadun and Fauztin these had likely deserved execution for past crimes, their deaths had been too awful as far as the soldier had been concerned. The innkeeper especially had suffered a horrible demise, the returning demon bringing back far too much proof of its thorough handiwork. Norrec only gave thanks that the hellish beast had returned to the nether realm shortly thereafter with its prize.

That, of course, had not enabled Norrec to escape the suit's own monstrous actions afterward. As the desperate fighter moved on, he tried not to look down at the armor, greatly stained by the night's activities. Worse, each passing second Norrec remained aware that his own face still bore a few smudges despite his best attempts to rub everything off. The armor had been very thorough in its foul work.

And while he fought off the horrors in his thoughts, the suit pushed him unceasingly west. Thunder rumbled again and again and the wind howled, but still the armor moved on. Norrec had no doubt that it would keep on moving even if the storm finally broke.

He had been granted one slight boon at least, the garnering of an old, dusty travel cloak hanging on a peg in the common room. The odds had been that it had belonged to the thieving innkeeper, but again Norrec tried to avoid thinking of such things. The cloak obscured much of the armor and offered him a bit of protection should the rains come pouring down. A very small blessing, but one for which he was truly grateful.

The more he headed west, the more the landscape changed, the mountains giving way to smaller hills and even flatlands. Now much farther down in altitude, it also grew increasingly warm. The plant life turned lush, becoming more and more reminiscent of the dense jungles the fighter knew existed further south.

For the first time, Norrec could also smell the sea. What he recalled of the maps he and his companions had carried indicated to him that the more northerly of the Twin Seas could not be that far away at this point. Norrec's original hope had been to head southwest to find one of the Vizjerei, but he had suspicions that the cursed suit had other plans in mind. A fear briefly erupted within him that it might actually try to walk the breadth of the sea, dragging a helpless Norrec into the inky depths. However, so far Bartuc's armor had kept him alive, if not completely well. It apparently needed him breathing in order to achieve its mysterious goals.

And after that?

The wind continued to pick up, nearly buffeting Norrec about despite the determination of the cursed suit to keep on its course. No rain had yet fallen, but the air grew thick and moist and fog began to develop. It became impossible to see very far ahead and although that did not seem at all a bother to the armor, now and then Norrec still feared that it would walk him right off a cliff without ever realizing it.

At midday—which almost might as well have been midnight for all the sun failed to penetrate the cloud cover—imps again came in summons to the unintelligible words spouted unwillingly by Norrec. Even despite the growing fog, it took them but minutes to bring back prey, this time a deer. Norrec ate his fill, then gladly allowed the small, horned demons to drag the rest of the carcass back to their infernal abode.

On and on he trudged, the smell of the sea growing stronger. Norrec could barely see in front of him, but knew that he could not be that far from it—and whatever destination the infernal armor had in mind.

As if reading his thoughts, a building abruptly materialized in the mist . . . followed almost immediately by another. At the same time, he heard voices in the distance, voices clearly of those hard at work.

His hands his own for the moment, the exhausted traveler pulled his cloak tight about him. The less any of the locals saw what he wore underneath, the better.

As he wandered through the town, Norrec sighted a dim but vast shape in the distance. A ship. He wondered whether or not it had just arrived or now prepared to disembark. If the latter, it likely would be the armor's destination. Why else would he have been brought to this specific place?

A figure in mariner's garb came from the opposite direction, a bundle under one arm. He had eyes and features somewhat akin to Fauztin, but with much more animation in his face.

"Ho, traveler! Not a good day to be making your way from the interior, eh?"

"No." Norrec would have walked past the man without another word, his concern that the mariner might become the next of the suit's victims, but his feet suddenly stopped.

This, in turn, caused the other to also halt. Still grinning, the seaman asked, "Where do you hail from? Look to be a westerner to me, though it's a little hard to tell under all that stubble!"

"West, yes," the soldier returned. "I've been on a . . . a pilgrimage."

"In the mountains? Not much up there but a few goats!"

Norrec tried to move his legs, but they would not budge. The armor expected something of him, but would not indicate what. He thought fast and furiously. He had arrived in a harbor town toward which the armor had purposely headed. Norrec had already assumed that it needed transport to some location, possibly even the ship in the distance—

The ship . . .

Pointing toward the murky shape, Norrec asked, "That vessel. Is it heading out soon?"

The mariner twisted his head back to look. "The *Napolys*? She's just come in. Be another two, maybe five days even. Only ship leaving soon's the *Hawksfire*, just down that way." He pointed toward the south, then leaned close—far too close, in Norrec's anxious opinion—and added, "A word of caution there. The *Hawksfire* is not a good vessel. She'll be at the bottom of the sea one of these days, mark me. Best to wait for the *Napolys* or my own fine girl, the *Odyssey*, though that'll mean a week or more. We've need for a little refitting."

Still his legs would not move. What more did the armor want?

Destination? "Can you tell me where each sails to?"

"My own, we're heading for Lut Gholein, but it'll be awhile before we can leave, as I said. The *Napolys* now, that heads for far Kingsport, a long journey but a part of your Western Kingdoms, eh? Get you home faster, I think! That'd be the one for you, eh?"

Norrec noticed no change. "What about the *Hawksfire*?"

"Leaves tomorrow morn, I think, but I warn you against it. One of these days, she'll not make it all the way back from Lut Gholein—and that's if she makes it there in the first place!"

The soldier's legs suddenly started moving again. The suit had finally found out what it wanted to know. Norrec gave the mariner a quick nod. "Thank you."

"Heed my warning well!" the seaman called. "Best to wait!"

Bartuc's armor marched Norrec through the small town, heading to the southern part of the harbor. Mariners and locals glanced at him as he walked by, his western looks not as common here, but none made any comment. For all its tiny size, the port apparently handled a steady business. Norrec supposed that it would have looked more impressive in the sunshine, but doubted that he would ever have the opportunity to see it so.

A sense of unease touched the veteran as he entered the southernmost part of the port. In contrast to what Norrec had seen so far, the area here looked to be in some disrepair and those few figures he noticed nearby struck Norrec as almost as unsavory as the unfortunate fools who had tried to rob him. Worse, the only vessel in sight looked to be most appropriate for a journey desired by a cursed suit of armor.

If some dark spirit had dredged up a long-lost ship from the black depths of the sea, then failed afterward in a half-hearted attempt to make it pass for something still from the land of the living, it would have looked little more baleful than the *Hawksfire* did at that moment. The three masts stood like tall, skeletal sentinels half-wrapped in the shroudlike sails. The figurehead at the bow, once probably a curvaceous mermaid, had been worn down by the elements until it now resembled more an aquatic banshee in midshriek. As for the hull itself, something had long-ago stained the wood nearly to pitch and scars raked the sides, making Norrec wonder if at some point in its colored past the vessel had either served in war or, more likely, had been used more than once as a freebooter.

He saw no crew, only a single, gaunt figure in a worn coat standing near the bow. Despite the uncertainty of taking a voyage on such a ghastly ship, Norrec had no choice but to do as the armor forced him. Without hesitation, it walked its unwilling host up the gangplank toward the rather haggard figure.

"What you want?" The skeleton coalesced into an older man with parchment skin and absolutely no flesh and sinew beneath the thin veil of life. One eye stared sightlessly to a point just to the left of Norrec, while the other, bloodshot, glared suspiciously at the newcomer.

"Passage to Lut Gholein," replied Norrec, trying to end this matter as quickly as he could. If he cooperated, then perhaps the warlord's garments would give him some freedom of movement for awhile.

"Other ships in port!" the captain snapped, his accent thick. Under a broad-rimmed hat he wore his ivory-white hair in a tail. The faded green coat, clearly once that of a naval officer from one of the Western Kingdoms, had likely gone through several owners before this man had laid claim to it. "No time to serve passengers!"

Ignoring the fetid breath, Norrec leaned closer. "I will pay well to get there."

An immediate change came over the captain's demeanor. "Aye?"

Trusting the armor to do as it had done at the inn, the soldier continued. "All I need is a cabin and food. If I'm left alone for the duration of the journey, so much the better. Just get me to Lut Gholein."

The cadaverous figure inspected him. "Armor?" He rubbed his chin. "Officer?"

"Yes." Let him think Norrec some renegade officer on the run. Likely it would raise the price but make the captain more trusting. Norrec obviously needed to be away from here.

The elder man rubbed his bony chin again. Norrec

noted tattoos running from his thin wrist down into the voluminous sleeve of the coat. The notion that this ship had served as a freebooter gained merit.

"Twelve draclin! Bed alone, eat away from crew, talk with crew little! Leave ship when docked!"

Norrec agreed with everything except the price. How much was a draclin worth compared to the coin of his own land?

He need not have bothered worrying. The left hand stretched out, several coins in the gauntlet's palm. The captain eyed them greedily, scooping each from the proffered hand. He bit one to make certain of its worth, then poured all into a ragged pouch on his belt.

"Come!" He hobbled past Norrec, for the first time revealing that his left leg had splints running down each side all the way to the boot. From the extensive binding he saw and his own experiences with field surgery, the veteran suspected that his host could not even stand on the leg without those large splints. The captain should have had the limb better looked at, but both the bindings and the splints appeared as if they had been put on quite some time ago and then forgotten.

However much twelve draclin might be in Norrec's own land, his first viewing of the cabin led him to believe it far too great a price for this. Even the room at the inn had looked more hospitable than what he now confronted. The cabin barely outspanned a closet; only a rickety bunk whose side had been nailed to the back wall represented anything in the way of amenities. The sheets were stained and looked as if they had been crudely cut from the sails, so dark and coarse were they. A smell like rotting fish pervaded the cabin and marks on the floor hinted of some past violence. In the upper corners, spiderwebs larger than Norrec's head wiggled in the breeze let in by the open door and near the edge of the floor, moss of some sort had taken a foothold.

Knowing he had no choice, Norrec hid his disgust. "Thank you, captain—"

"Casco," the skeletal figure grunted. "Inside! Eat at bell! Understand?"

"Yes."

With a curt nod, Captain Casco left him to his own devices. Heeding the man's advice, Norrec shut the door behind him and sat down on the dubious bed. To his further regret, the cabin did not even have a porthole, which might have offered some relief from the stench.

He flexed his hands, then tested his legs. Movement had been granted to him for his cooperation, but for how long, Norrec could not say. He supposed that aboard the *Hawksfire*, the armor expected little trouble. What could Norrec do except step over the rail and sink to the bottom of the sea? As terrible as his situation had grown, he could not yet bring himself to try to end his life, especially in such horrifying fashion. Besides, Norrec doubted that he would be allowed to do even that, not so long as the suit required his living body.

With no notion as to what else to do with his time, he tried his best to go to sleep. Despite the stench—or perhaps because of it—Norrec managed to doze off. Unfortunately, his dreams proved again to be troubled ones, in great part because they did not even seem his own.

Again he lived as Bartuc, taking relish in the dreadful acts he performed. A settlement that hesitated too long in accepting his domination felt the full force of his righteous wrath, the town elders and several other chosen fools drawn, quartered, then flayed for the good of the rest. A Vizjerei caught spying became the centerpiece for a macabre candelabra that illuminated not only the warlord's quarters, but even caused his demonic servants to shudder. A bell sounded . . .

—stirring a grateful Norrec from his sleep. He blinked, finally registering that he had actually slept until the bell for evening meal. While he doubted the food would be anything to his liking, his hunger had become so great that Norrec could not avoid the matter any longer. Besides, he did not want to risk the suit summoning imps to feed him. There was no telling *what* they might decide could be edible . . .

Pulling his cloak tight around him, the fighter stepped out to see several worn, bitter-looking men heading down into the bowel of the ship. Assuming that they, too, planned to eat, Norrec followed them down to a rather seedy-looking mess. In silence the former soldier stood in line, receiving hard bread and a questionable meat dish that almost made him yearn for the thieving innkeeper's fare.

One glance at the surly group convinced Norrec to retire to his room. Carrying his food up to the deck, he paused at the rail for a moment to inhale some of the relatively fresh sea air before going back into the cabin.

A figure standing in the fog-enshrouded dock caught his eye.

The food slipped from his hands, spilling all over the deck, but Norrec did not even notice.

Fauztin. Even with his robes wrapped around him, it could be no other.

The dead eyes of his former comrade stared back at him. Even from where the fighter stood, he could see the gaping hole where the Vizjerei's throat once had been.

"Fool!" Casco roared from behind Norrec. "What mess! You clean up! No help!"

The startled veteran looked over his shoulder at the angry captain, then down at the spilled food. Some of the meat dripped over the toes of Bartuc's boots.

"Clean up! No help! No more food tonight!" Casco limped off, muttering in his native tongue something no doubt derogatory about foreign devils.

Despite the fury of the captain, Norrec immediately forgot the spilled meal, instead quickly returning his gaze to the dock in search of—

Nothing. No sepulchral figure stood staring back at him. The ghastly shade had vanished—if it had ever even been there in the first place.

Hands trembling, he stumbled back, unmindful of anything but the terrifying sight he thought he had just beheld; Fauztin, so clearly dead, condemning him with those empty eyes . . .

Still ignoring Captain Casco's earlier demand that he clean up the mess, Norrec hurried back to his cabin, slamming the door tight behind him and not daring to breathe until he sat once more on the bunk.

He had lost the struggle. The sorcerer's ghost had been the first obvious sign. Norrec had lost the struggle for his sanity. The horrors the cursed armor had put him through had finally torn away the last barriers protecting the veteran's mind. Surely now, the downward spiral into complete madness would be swift. Surely now, he had no hope of saving himself.

Surely now Bartuc's legacy would claim not only his body—but his soul, too.

An exhausted Kara Nightshadow inspected the miserable little port town with some distaste. Accustomed to the beauty of the jungle and the carefully cultivated ways of her kind, she found the port, Gea Kul, reeking of too many unwashed bodies and far too much devotion to materialistic things. As a necromancer, Kara saw the world in balance between the actions of life and that which occurred after death and believed that both aspects should be dealt with accordingly with as much dignity as a soul could muster. What she had so far witnessed in her few minutes here had revealed very little dignity.

It had taken her great effort to reach this place as quickly as she had, effort that had worn her out physically, spiritually, and very much magically. Kara dearly

wanted to get some sleep, but she had come to this place
for reasons that even she did not completely understand
and so needed to at least survey the area in the hopes of
finding some answers.

After the unsettling loss of not only the warlord's
armor but also both her prized dagger and the two
corpses, the young necromancer had used her training to
try to ferret out the locations of all—and that had unerr-
ingly led her to this most unassuming place. What ties
the port might have to all, she could not say, but it clearly
did not bode well. Kara wished that she could have con-
sulted with her teachers, but time had been of the essence
and she had been trained to rely on herself as much as
possible. Delaying the chase only meant it becoming
more difficult to track everything later on. That, she
could not afford. If the thieves planned on taking the
armor overseas, she had to stop them now.

As for the revenants . . . she had no idea what to do
about that unsettling pair. They acted like nothing spoken of in her studies.

Ignoring the unsavory glances from the sailors she
passed, Kara headed for the first inn she found. On the
one hand, the ebony-tressed enchantress needed food,
while on the other, she hoped to garner useful information. Surely those who carried Bartuc's suit had needed a
meal or a drink after such an arduous trek.

The Captain's Table, as the inn had been titled, proved to
be a bit better in appearance than she expected. Although
the building looked old and worn, the gray-haired,
imposing man in charge kept it clean and orderly. Kara
immediately knew that he had once been an officer in
some naval force, from his features likely one of the
wealthier Western Kingdoms. Cheerful for the most part,
the gigantic figure with muttonchop sideburns brooked
no argument from one patron who believed he could
depart without paying. Despite his advanced age, the

innkeeper handled the much younger seaman with ease, not only retrieving the money owed him but also depositing the culprit out in the fog and mud.

Rubbing his hands on his apron, the owner noticed his newest guest. "Good evening, milady!" He bowed graciously despite his growing girth, his entire expression lighting up at the sight of her. "Captain Hanos Jeronnan, your humble servant! May I say you grace my little place!"

Unaccustomed to such open displays toward her, Kara did not answer at first. However, Captain Jeronnan, clearly realizing that he had overwhelmed her, patiently waited for her to recover.

"Thank you, captain," she finally responded. "I seek some food and, if you have the time, the answers to a few questions."

"For you, my lovely little one, I'll make the time!"

He walked off, humming to himself. Kara felt her face reddening. Captain Jeronnan obviously meant nothing forward in his comments, but none of the dark mage's intense training had taught her how to take compliments on her appearance. She knew that some of her brethren found her attractive, but among the followers of Rathma such matters were treated with the formality with which they treated everything.

Seating herself in a side booth, Kara glanced around at the other patrons. Most went about the business of drinking and eating, but a few had other matters in mind. She saw a woman in scandalous garments leaning over a sailor, her offer to him needing little actual conversation. To her right, a pair of men dickered over some deal, babbling in a language of which the necromancer had no knowledge. There were also a few males among the clientele who eyed her with more open interest than Captain Jeronnan had and without his tact. One who showed far too much interest for her own tastes received a stony glare from her silver eyes, a sight so unsettling to him that he quickly turned away, burying his head in drink and visibly shivering for several seconds.

The innkeeper returned with a plate bearing broiled fish and some sea vegetable. He placed that and a mug in front of the necromancer. "Cider in the mug. 'Tis the simplest drink I've got here, milady."

Kara considered telling him something about the strong herbal concoctions developed by the Rathma faithful, but chose to graciously accept the mild drink. She looked at the fish, the spices giving it a very enticing scent. Of course, at this point Kara almost would have been willing to eat it right out of the sea. Still, it pleased her to find such civilized fare here. "What do I owe?"

"Your company alone's worth the price."

She bristled, thinking of the woman plying her wares on one of the customers. "I am no—"

He looked chagrined. "No, no! 'Tis just that I don't get such fair visitors much, lass! I only meant sitting here and answering your questions! No harm meant—" Jeronnan leaned closer, whispering, "and I know better than to try forcing myself on one who follows the ways of Rathma!"

"You know what I am and still you desire to sit with me?"

"Milady, I sailed every sea and all over the Great Ocean. I've seen many a magic, but the most trustworthy of mages were always the faithful of Rathma . . ."

She rewarded him with a slight smile that proved enough to redden his already ruddy cheeks. "Then perhaps you are the man with whom I can trust my questions."

The captain leaned back. "Only when you've first tasted my specialty and given me your fine opinion."

Kara cut into the fish, tasting a small bite. Immediately she cut a second, downing it as quickly as the first.

Jeronnan beamed. "'Tis to your liking, then?"

Indeed, it was. The jungles of the east contained a variety of marvelous spices, but the necromancer had never eaten anything like this fish. In less time than she could have imagined, Kara had devoured a good portion of her meal, so much so that she finally felt like herself again.

Captain Jeronnan had excused himself now and then to deal with his other customers, but by the time she had finished, there remained only two others, a pair of dour-looking sailors clearly too weary to do anything but nurse their ales and food. The innkeeper settled in across from her and waited.

"My name is Kara Nightshadow," she began. "You know what I am."

"Aye, but I've never seen one that looked like you, lass."

Kara pushed on, unwilling at this point to be detoured by niceties. "Captain, have you noticed anyone out of the ordinary here?"

He chuckled. "In Gea Kul? It'd be more extraordinary to see someone ordinary!"

"What about . . . what about a man traveling with armor probably strapped to the back of an animal?" The necromancer paused to consider the implications further. "Or a man wearing armor?"

"We get some soldiers here. Not uncommon."

"In crimson plate?"

Jeronnan's brow wrinkled. "I'd recall that—but, no. No one."

It had been a desperate hope. Kara wanted to ask another, very particular question, but feared that if she did, the captain's easy manner would change. He might be familiar with her kind, but some subjects could be too dark even for him to accept. Walking corpses would certainly be one of those subjects.

Kara opened her mouth with the intention of trying a different track, yet what escaped from her lips proved not to be words but rather a long yawn.

Her companion looked her over. "Pardon me for being blunt, milady, but you look even more pale than you likely usually are. I think you need some good rest."

She sought to dissuade him, only to yawn again. "Perhaps you are right."

"I've got a couple of rooms available, lass. For you, no charge—and nothing expected, if you're worried about it."

"I'll pay you." Kara managed to retrieve some coins from the purse on her belt. "Is this enough?"

He shoved most of it back. "That is . . . and don't go showing all that money around. Not everyone's a kind soul like me!"

The necromancer could barely move. Her legs felt like lead. The spellwork she had utilized to quicker get her to her destination had taken too much from the dark mage. "I think I will go to it immediately, if you will forgive my leaving."

"Best give me a few minutes, lass. I fear that with the help I hire here, it might not be ready for you. Just remain here and I'll be back shortly!"

He hurried off before she could protest. Kara straightened, trying to keep awake. Both the spellwork and her own physical efforts naturally had drained her much, but this exhaustion seemed far more oppressive than it should have been, even taking those matters into account. It almost made her believe—

She pushed herself to her feet, turning to the door at the same time. Perhaps Kara had misjudged Captain Hanos Jeronnan. Perhaps his congenial manner hid a darker side.

Aware that her thinking might well be too muddled, the necromancer stumbled her way toward the entrance, not at all caring what the two sailors in the corner might think. If she made it outside, then perhaps she could clear her mind enough to reconsider. Yes, for all the odious smells of the port itself, the sea air would still no doubt help her regain her balance.

Kara nearly fell through the doorway, so weak had her legs become. Immediately she inhaled. Some of the heaviness in her head evaporated, enough at least for her to get some general sense of her surroundings, but the raven-haired enchantress needed more. She could not decide what to do about the innkeeper until she could think clearly again.

Once more she inhaled, but as her head cleared a bit more, a sense of immediate unease struck Kara.

She looked up into the dark fog and saw a figure in a worn travel cloak standing just a few feet from her. His face remained obscured by the hood of his cloak, but lower Kara could make out one pale hand emerging. In that hand, the figure held a dagger that gleamed even in the mist-enshrouded night.

An ivory dagger.

Kara's dagger.

Another pale hand reached up and pulled back the hood slightly, revealing a face the necromancer had seen but once before. The Vizjerei from Bartuc's tomb.

The Vizjerei who had had his throat torn out.

"Your spell . . . should've worked . . . better on her," a voice croaked from behind her.

Kara tried to turn, her body still moving far too slowly. At the same time, it occurred to her that all her training, all her spellwork, had failed to enable her to notice not one attacker, but two.

A second pale face smiled grimly at her, the man's head tipped slightly to one side as if not entirely connected to his body.

The second corpse from the tomb. The wiry man whose neck had been snapped.

"You leave us . . . no choice."

His hand had been raised, in it another dagger held

hilt up. Even as this fact reached her sluggish brain, the hand of the ghoul came down, swinging hard.

The blow caught Kara Nightshadow on the temple. She spun around once and would have surely cracked her head on the stone path save that the undead creature who had hit her now caught her in his arms. With astonishing tenderness, he lowered the stunned woman to the ground.

"You . . . really . . . leave us . . . no choice."

And with that, she blacked out.

Six

Norrec did not leave his cabin again until time came to retrieve his morning meal. No one spoke to him, especially Captain Casco, who had not forgiven his passenger for leaving the mess near the rail. Norrec actually appreciated the lack of conversation, wanting nothing to slow his return to the safety of his room.

He had slept fitfully during the night, not only haunted by dreams of Bartuc's glory, but now also dread images of Fauztin's vengeful spirit come to claim him. Not until the *Hawksfire* finally set sail did the veteran fighter calm at all. Out on the sea, troubled spirits could certainly not pursue him. In fact, as the ship pushed out onto the stormy waters, it finally began to sound reasonable to Norrec that he had imagined the dreadful vision, that what he had taken for Fauztin had either been but another Vizjerei—for certainly the port lay near enough to their eastern lands—or the complete figment of his own troubled mind.

The latter seemed more and more likely. After all, Norrec had been both physically and mentally torn apart by the demands of the cursed armor. The memories of not only the tomb but the slaughter at the inn remained with him. In addition, the warlord's suit had pushed his endurance to the limits and beyond, forcing the soldier to traverse a rough landscape without hardly any rest and at a pace that would have killed many men. If not for the fact that only part of the effort had been his own,

Norrec suspected that he would definitely have died along the way.

The waves grew choppier as the *Hawksfire* entered deep waters. With each groan of the hull, Norrec became more and more convinced that at some point the sea would crush the worn ship like tinder. Yet, somehow, the *Hawksfire* continued on, riding one wave to the next. In addition, for all their motley outer appearance, Captain Casco and his crew proved quite adept at managing the vessel. They scurried up the ropes, raced across the decks, ever keeping their ship ready to meet the elements.

What they could not entirely keep at bay, though, was the storm. It struck but a few hours out, the sky blackening and lightning flashing all about. The winds picked up, bending the masts and trying to rip the sails. Norrec, who had finally stepped out, quickly gripped the rail as the sea tossed the *Hawksfire* to the side.

"Starboard!" called Casco from the deck. "Starboard!"

The man at the wheel worked to obey, but wind and water battled against him. A second crew member came to his aid, the pair managing to fulfill the captain's orders after great effort.

Rain at last fell, a torrent that forced Norrec back into the cabin. Not only did he know nothing about sailing, but, clad in armor, he risked his life every time he neared the rail. It would take only one strong wave to toss him over the side.

A soiled lantern swinging violently from the ceiling tried desperately to keep the cabin illuminated. Norrec planted himself on the inside corner of the bunk and tried to think. He had not yet completely given up hope of escaping the cursed armor, but so far had no idea as to what to do. It would require powerful sorcery and he knew no one with such abilities. If only he could have asked Fauztin—

The memory of what he had thought he had seen on the dock returned full blown, sending renewed chills through Norrec. Best to forget about Fauztin—and Sadun, too. They were dead.

Night came and still the storm did not abate. Norrec forced himself down to the mess, where he noticed for the first time some of the crew eyeing him with more than disinterest and disdain. Now a few gazes seemed almost hostile, hostile and yet frightened. Norrec had no doubt that it had to do with the armor. Who was he, they must be wondering? The armor spoke of power, of command. Why did such a one as he travel on a miserable vessel such as the *Hawksfire*?

Again he took his meal to the cabin, preferring the solitary atmosphere. This time he found the food slightly more palatable or perhaps the previous meals had just burned away his tongue. Norrec devoured it, then fell back and tried to go to sleep. He did not look forward to sleep, both the dreams of Bartuc and the nightmares surrounding the tomb not at all enticements. However, exhaustion quickly set in and, as a veteran campaigner, Norrec Vizharan knew better than to try to fight it. Even the violent rocking of the *Hawksfire* could not keep his eyes from closing . . .

"*It would be . . . nice to rest,*" came a cracking yet still familiar voice. "*But, after all, they say . . . no rest for the wicked, eh?*"

Norrec bolted to his feet, eyes wide. Barely any light shone from the lantern, but even with what little he had the soldier could see that no one else stood in the room.

"Damn!" Another nightmare. Staring at the lantern, Norrec realized that he must have fallen asleep without realizing it. The voice had been in his head, nowhere else. The voice of a comrade now lost . . .

Sadun's voice.

Thunder crashed. The *Hawksfire* shivered. Norrec gripped the side of the cot, then started to ease himsel' back onto it.

"You should've . . . listened to Fauztin . . . Norrec. Now it . . . may be too late."

He froze where he was, gaze shifting to the door.

"Come to us, friend . . . come to Fauztin . . . and me."

Norrec straightened. "Sadun?"

No reply, but some of the planks just outside the cabin creaked as if someone walked upon them and paused now before his door.

"Someone out there?"

The *Hawksfire* dipped, nearly sending him tumbling. Norrec flattened himself against a wall, eyes never leaving the doorway. Had he imagined Tryst's cracking, laboring voice?

The days since the horror of the tomb had tested the veteran's nerve more than any battle in which he had fought, yet still something within urged Norrec toward the door. Most likely when he opened it there would be nothing. Sadun and the Vizjerei could not be out there, awaiting the friend who had so terribly murdered them. Such things did not happen save in tales spoken in whispers around late night campfires.

But such things as the dreadful armor Norrec wore did not happen outside of those tales, either.

Again the planks creaked. Norrec gritted his teeth, reached toward the latch . . .

The gauntleted hand suddenly twitched—and began to glow a sinister red.

Norrec drew the glove back, watching in wonder as the glow now faded. He reached forward once more, but this time, nothing happened. Steeling himself, Norrec undid the latch, then swung open the door—

Rain and wind battered him, but no fearsome shade stood outside the cabin, bony finger outstretched in condemnation.

Seizing his cloak, Norrec hurried outside, his gaze immediately shifting first to the left, then the right.

Toward the bow he saw the dim shapes of men struggling to keep the sails in order, but of the supposed phantoms, he found not a trace.

The hard tramping of feet made him look in the direction of the stern again, where he saw one of Casco's men running toward the bow. The man would have passed Norrec without a glance, but the soldier seized him. Ignoring the sailor's fierce glare, he shouted, "Did you see anyone out here before you? Anyone standing by my cabin?"

The sailor spat something in another tongue, then pulled away from Norrec as if just touched by a leper. Norrec watched the man run off, then shifted his own attention to the rail. A notion filled his head that he found entirely ludicrous, but still it made him risk fate by actually stepping to the edge and peering over the side.

Waves shattered unceasingly against the timeworn hull of the *Hawksfire*, doing their best, it seemed, to pound through the wood and send the vessel and its occupants to their watery dooms. The sea beyond churned wildly, sometimes rising so high that Norrec had trouble seeing the heavens.

But of his supposed visitor, he saw no sign. No vengeful ghoul clung to the side of the hull. The unforgiving shades of Sadun Tryst and Fauztin had not, after all, been standing outside his cabin door. He had imagined them, just as he had first believed.

"You! What you do out? Inside! Inside!" The hobbling form of Captain Casco closed in on Norrec from the bow. Casco seemed completely outraged that his sole passenger had dared the elements. Norrec doubted it had to do with concern for the veteran's well-being. As with the rest of the crew, a hint of fright tinged Casco's angry words.

"What is it? What's wrong?"

"Wrong?" the cadaverous mariner barked back. "Wrong? Nothing wrong! Back to cabin! Storm outside! You fool?"

Half-tempted to respond "yes" to Casco's question, Norrec did not bother to argue with the man. With the crippled mariner watching, he returned to the cabin, closing the door on Casco's scowling visage. After a moment, Norrec heard him stump away.

The thought of trying to fall asleep again did not at all appeal to Norrec, but he nonetheless tried. At first, questions raced through his thoughts, all but one of which the veteran could answer. That lone question concerned the crimson gauntlet and why it had begun to glow just prior to his going outside to search. If no danger had lurked beyond the door, what reason would the armor have for such a protective measure? True, it had not seized control of him, but still its actions had appeared to have purpose . . .

Norrec fell asleep still pondering the suit's reaction. He did not stir again until a crack of thunder that shook the cabin nearly caused him to tumble out of the makeshift bunk. Disoriented, the soldier tried and failed to calculate just how long he had been asleep. The storm still blew strong, which to Norrec meant that it could not have been more than a few scant hours. Rarely had a storm that he had suffered through lasted more than a day, although he supposed that on the high sea it could be different.

Arms and legs stiff, Norrec stretched, then tried to go back to his slumber.

A long, cracking sound far different from thunder again brought him to his feet. He recognized that sound, even if he had not heard it often. It had been the sound of *wood* breaking.

And on a ship in the midst of a wild storm, that could spell doom for everyone.

Norrec burst out of the cabin, heading toward the bow.

Shouts informed him that the crew already struggled to deal with whatever danger threatened, but he knew how difficult their task would be if what he suspected had truly occurred. Bad enough for the ship to suffer damage, but to try to repair it during such chaos . . .

A moment later, his worst fears had been realized. Just ahead, several sailors fought to keep one of the masts from entirely cracking in two. They pulled on ropes, trying to force the upper portion in place while other men attempted to strengthen the ruined area with planks, nails, and more rope. Norrec, however, could already tell that theirs had become a struggle in futility. More and more the mast leaned dangerously, and when it went the others would surely soon follow.

He wanted to do something, but none of the skills he had learned would have been of aid to the more experienced mariners. Norrec stared at the gauntleted hands, the crimson coloring making them look so mighty, so full of strength. Yet all the vaunted power of Bartuc's legacy would avail him nothing now.

The thought faded as an unsettling blue aura formed without warning around each glove.

Norrec suddenly found himself rushing forward, the suit again in command of his actions. For once, though, the veteran fought little against it, certain of its intentions if not its methods. The armor desired to reach its distant destination, and it could not if it and Norrec sank to the bottom of the sea. For Norrec's life alone, it needed to act.

"Away! Away!" shouted Captain Casco, no doubt certain that his clumsy passenger would just make a terrible situation worse. Norrec, though, barged past him, nearly bowling the crippled mariner over.

The mast creaked ominously, a sure sign that only seconds remained before it toppled into the next. Norrec took a deep breath, anxiously waiting for the suit to act.

"Kesra! Qezal irakus!"

Lightning punctuated each word thrust from the soldier's mouth, but Norrec paid it little mind. What he did notice, what all those around him also surely noticed, was that several shimmering green forms suddenly surrounded, even *clung* to, the ruined mast. They had strong, sleek arms that ended in suckered fingers, but where there should have been legs, the monstrosities had bodies reminiscent of gigantic slugs. The creatures hissed and crawled, their half-seen faces akin to some demented artist's idea of a bat made up like a clown, face paint and all.

The sailors fled in panic, releasing their grip on the ropes and wood. The mast started to fall . . .

The shimmering horde pushed it back in place. While some held it there, others started to crawl around and around the ruined area. As they moved, they left trails of slime over the cracks. At first Norrec had no idea what they intended, but then he noticed that the slime almost immediately hardened, strengthening and stabilizing the mast. Over and over the creatures crawled, a madcap race with no finish line. Their brethren, no longer needed to support the mast, watched and waited, hissing in what seemed encouragement to the ones circling around the pole.

"Kesra! Qezal ranakka!"

The demons quickly crawled from the mast, grouping together. Norrec pulled his gaze from the horrific band, looking over their completed handiwork. Despite the storm, the mast now swayed as if only in a gentle breeze. Not only had they repaired it, but they had reinforced it in such a manner that the odds were it would better survive this voyage than the other two.

As if also satisfied, the suit waved a negligent hand at the demons. A burst of light so bright that Norrec had to shield his eyes covered the foul pack. The creatures' hissing grew stronger, harsher, until, with what seemed a sigh, the light faded out—leaving no trace of the sluglike beasts, not even a single trail of slime.

Seemingly unimpressed, the storm battled on, tossing the *Hawksfire* about. Yet, despite the continued threat of it, the crew hesitated to return to their posts, only doing so when the captain finally shouted at them. The sailors who passed Norrec gave the fighter a wide berth, their fear of him quite clear in their expressions. True, their lives had probably been spared because of the demons summoned, but to know that one who could call forth such horrific apparitions journeyed with them surely shook the men to the very core of their souls.

Norrec, however, did not care, so weary his legs threatened to collapse underneath him. Even though it had been the suit that had cast the spell, he suddenly felt as if he had just rebuilt the entire mast singlehandedly. Norrec waited for the armor to guide him back to the cabin, but now that the danger had been dealt with, apparently it had left matters to him.

The metal plate felt like a thousand pounds as he turned and walked from the deck. Around him, Norrec continued to feel the uneasy stares of the crew of the *Hawksfire*. No doubt they would soon even forget that they owed their lives to his presence and begin to consider what it meant to have a master of demons aboard. Fear had a way of turning to violence . . .

Yet, despite that knowledge, Norrec sought only his bed. He very desperately needed sleep. Even the storm would not be able to keep him awake now. Come the morrow, he would do what he could to explain what had happened.

Norrec only hoped that, in the meantime, none of the crew would attempt anything foolish . . . and fatal.

Darkness. Warm, enveloping darkness.
Kara nestled in it, dwelled in it, found it so comforting that for the longest time she had no desire to leave it. Yet, there came

a point when something—an uneasy feeling, a sense of forebod-
ing—made her turn, shift . . . and try to wake.

She also heard a voice.

"Kara! Lass! Where are you?"

The voice had a familiarity to it, one that slowly drew her up
from oblivion. As she tried to awaken, Kara Nightshadow's
own will aided in the task. This darkness, this nothingness,
held her prisoner. The comfort it offered was a smothering one,
an eternal sleep.

"Kara!"

It no longer even comforted. Now it scratched, crushed, felt
more akin to a casket than a soft bed . . .

"Kara!"

The necromancer's eyes flew open.

She stood imprisoned in a tomb of wood, her limbs
seemingly frozen.

Somewhere a hound barked. The necromancer
blinked, trying to focus better. A few cracks of dim light
shone through, just enough to enable her to better understand what had become of her. Wood tightly surrounded
her on all sides, a hollow tree without major openings.
Somehow, she had been placed here, sealed in here—to
die?

A sense of claustrophobia nearly overwhelmed her.
Kara struggled to move her arms, but could not. They
had been pinned to her sides and wrapped by vegetation
growing in the hollow tree. Worse, moss also covered her
mouth, sealing her lips together. She tried to make a
sound, but, muffled by both the moss and the thick trunk,
Kara knew that no one outside would hear her.

More hounds barked, this time nearer. She fixed on a
voice, Captain Jeronnan's voice, calling her name.

"Kara! Lass! Can you hear me?"

Her legs also could not move, likely for the same reasons as her arms. Physically, Kara had been left completely helpless.

The sense of claustrophobia grew. Although the necromancer had lived much of her short life in seclusion, she had always had freedom of movement, freedom of choice. Her ghoulish attackers had left her without either. Why they had not slain her outright, the desperate dark mage could not say, but if she did not soon escape, her demise would be just as certain . . . and in a far slower, grislier fashion.

And that thought, accompanied by her growing feeling that the tree trunk closed in on her from all sides, pushed Kara as none of her teachers had ever. She wanted to escape, to be free, to not suffer the slow tortures of starvation . . .

Bound as she was, with even her mouth sealed, no sophisticated spell could save her. Yet, raw emotion, so generally kept under control by the followers of Rathma, now bubbled up, demanded to overflow. Kara stared at the wood before her, seeing it as her nemesis, her own tomb.

She would not die this way, not through the dark magic of an undead sorcerer . . .

Not die this way . . .

The interior of the trunk grew hot, stifling. Sweat dripped over the necromancer. The vegetation seemed to tighten around her limbs.

Not die . . .

Her silver eyes flashed bright . . . *brighter* . . .

The tree exploded.

Fragments of wood flew in all directions, bombarding the nearby landscape. Somewhere, Kara heard men swear and dogs whine. She could do nothing for them, though, and, in truth, could do no more for herself. The necromancer fell forward, her arms and legs no longer hindered. The instinctive reaction to put her hands out to save herself kept Kara from striking the ground head first, but did not prevent the jolt when her body hit from causing her to momentarily black out.

Vaguely she heard voices that seemed to draw near. A beast sniffed the ground near her head, its cold nose briefly rubbing against her ear. She heard a command, then felt strong but gentle hands touch her shoulders.

"Kara! What in the name of the Sea Witch happened to you, lass?"

"Jeron—" she managed to utter, the effort nearly doing her in again.

"Easy, lass! Here, you fool! Take the dogs' leashes! I'll see to her!"

"Aye, captain!"

Kara barely noticed the journey back to Gea Kul, save for one moment when the innkeeper, who carried her in his arms, swore at one of his companions for nearly letting the dogs trip him. She drifted into and out of consciousness, now and then recalling her short glimpses of the two undead. Something about them had greatly disturbed her, more than she would have imagined possible.

Even in her present state, it went through Kara's mind that they had been invisible to her senses, that they had played her, not the other way around. Necromancers manipulated the forces of life and death, not the other way around. Yet, the Vizjerei and his grinning companion had toyed with Kara as if she had been less than a first-year novice. How? More to the point, why did they walk the world at all?

The answer had to deal with her earlier error in the tomb. Somehow, although her training had never covered such astounding occurrences, when she had left the phantasm alone, it had been able to seize full control of the body. Then, it must have summoned the companion it had known in life, the pair vanishing by magic before she returned.

A simple explanation, and yet not at all satisfactory. Kara missed something; she felt sure of it.

"Enchantress?"

The word echoed in her skull, drowning out her thoughts. She forced her eyelids open—which Kara had not even realized until now had been closed—and stared up at the concerned visage of Captain Hanos Jeronnan. "What . . . ?"

"Easy, lass! You've gone two days without food and water! Not enough to do you any real harm, but still too much for your own good!"

Two days? She had been trapped in the tree for two days?

"When you vanished that night, I started a search right away, but not until morn came did I find this pouch near the side of the inn." He held up a small, leather pouch in which Kara stored some of the herbs necessary for her calling. Necromancer spells required other ingredients besides blood, although most outsiders never knew that.

Odd, though, that she should lose that pouch. It would have almost required her captors to spend precious time to tear it off, so securely had the young spellcaster generally kept it fastened. Of course, that made even less sense, since the only reason that they would bother to do that might be to actually leave a clue to her kidnapping, hardly something either ghoul would have done.

But, then, they *had* left her alive, if buried in the heart of a dead tree.

She felt so confused. Her irritation must have shown, for the innkeeper immediately sought to aid her. "What is it? Need more water? Blankets?"

"I'm . . ." Her words sounded more akin to the croaking of a frog—or too much like her more vocal assailant. Kara gratefully accepted water, then tried again. "I am all right, captain . . . and I thank you for your care. I will, of course, pay you—"

"I don't like foul language in my establishment, milady! There'll be no more talk of that!"

He truly was a curiosity to her. "Captain Jeronnan, most folk, especially westerners, would rather have left one of my kind to rot in that tree, much less put together a search party. Why do this?"

The huge man looked uncomfortable. "Always watch over my guests, lass."

Despite the aches throughout her body, she pushed herself up to a sitting position. Jeronnan had given her a room such as she could not have imagined in Gea Kul. Clean and comfortable, with no odor of fish, either. Truly a marvel. Yet, Kara did not let her pleasant surroundings deter her from her question. "*Why* do it, captain?"

"I had me a daughter once," he began with much reluctance. "And before you think it, she looked not a bit like you save in also being pretty." Jeronnan cleared his throat. "Her mother was higher born than me, but my naval successes let me rise to where we could wed. Terania was born to us, but her mother never lived much beyond carrying her." A daring tear emerged from the gruff man's eye, one the innkeeper quickly brushed out of existence. "For the next decade and more, I couldn't stand my life because it tore me away from the only one left to me. Finally, I resigned my commission when she was just beginning to blossom into a fair maiden and took her across the sea to a place I remembered being so beautiful. Bless her, Terania never complained, even seemed to thrive here."

"Gea Kul?"

"Don't sound so surprised, lass. Was a much nicer, cleaner place a decade ago. Something foul's touched it since, just as it's touched every other place I hear of these days."

Kara carefully kept her expression neutral. As one of the faithful of Rathma, she knew well that dark powers had begun to spread over the world. The ransacking of Bartuc's tomb only exemplified that fact. The necromancers feared that soon the world would slip out of the delicate balance it needed to maintain, that the tide would shift toward the Lords of Hell.

That demons already walked the world again.

Captain Jeronnan had been talking while she had considered all of this and so Kara had missed his past few words. However, something at the end caught her attention, so much so that she had to blurt, "What?"

By now his face had turned grim, so very grim. "Aye, that's what happened, all right! Two years we lived here, happy as could be possible; then one night I hear her scream from her room, a place no man could get without passing me first! Smashed through her door, I did—and found *no* trace of her. Her window remained locked, her closet I searched well, but she'd somehow vanished from a room with no other good exit."

Jeronnan had searched high and low for his daughter, several of the locals more than willing to join the hunt. For three days, he had looked and for three days he had failed . . . until one night, as he tried to sleep, the captain had heard his daughter calling to him.

A cautious man despite his desperate hopes, he had taken with him the ceremonial blade awarded to him by his admiral. With it, the innkeeper had gone out into the wilds, following the call of his child. For more than an hour he had trekked through the woods and hills, seeking, searching . . .

Finally, near a crooked tree, he had caught sight of his beloved Terania. The girl, her skin so oddly pale—even more so than Kara's—had stood waiting for her father with arms outstretched.

She had called out to him again and Jeronnan had, of course, responded. Sword in one hand, he had taken his daughter close—

Her fangs had nearly ripped out his throat.

Captain Jeronnan had sailed the world, had seen many a marvelous and disturbing thing, had fought pirates and villains in the name of his masters, but no experience in his life had meant more to him than raising his only child.

And nothing had ripped at his soul more than running the creature she had become through the heart.

"It hangs downstairs," he muttered, finishing. "A fine piece of craftsmanship and designed to be practical, too." Almost as an afterthought, the captain added, "Plated in silver or else I'd not be here with you today."

"What happened to her?" Kara knew such tales, but the causes varied.

"The damned thing is, I never found out! Finally managed to push it to the back of my mind until you vanished. Feared that it had come back for you!" A daring tear escaped his eyes. "I still hear her cries . . . both the one when she vanished and the one when I *slew* her."

Jeronnan's unknown horror had not stalked Kara, but the two undead tomb robbers had certainly been waiting, which drew her at last back to her own immediate situation. "Forgive me, captain, for sounding so uncaring about your great loss, but can you tell me if any ships departed during the time I was lost?"

Kara's question caught the grieving man off guard for a moment, but he quickly recovered. "Only ship that's sailed off so far has been the *Hawksfire,* a cursed vessel if I've ever seen one! Surprised it hasn't sunk yet."

Only a single ship had departed. It had to be the one she wanted. "Where was it heading?"

"Lut Gholein. It always sails to Lut Gholein."

She knew the name. A prospering kingdom on the western side of the Twin Seas, a place where merchants from all over the world bought and sold.

Lut Gholein. The Vizjerei and his grinning friend had trekked all the way here from the tomb, moving at a pace only those who felt no exhaustion could maintain. They had specifically come to Gea Kul, whose only good purpose served as a point by which to reach other realms. But why?

There could be only one reason. They pursued the remaining members of their party, the ones who also carried with them Bartuc's armor. Kara suspected that might be only one man, but she had to keep in mind the possibility of more in mind.

So this *Hawksfire* carried either the survivors or the revenants. If the latter, the pair would have to have secreted themselves carefully in order to avoid detection, but she had heard tales of the undead doing whatever they needed while pursuing their victims. Crossing the sea would be difficult, but not impossible.

Lut Gholein. It might yet be only another brief stop, but at least Kara had a particular destination.

"Captain, when is the next ship sailing there?"

"Lass, you're barely able to sit up, much less—"

Silver eyes fixed unblinking at him. "When?"

He rubbed his chin. "Not for a time. Maybe a week, maybe more."

Much too late. By then, both the revenants and those they pursued would be long gone, the armor with them. Even more important than her dagger remained the fact that the bloody warlord's suit moved about. The enchantments within would certainly call out to the ambitious, the evil.

Even those not necessarily human.

"I have funds. Can you recommend a ship I could hire?"

Jeronnan eyed her for a moment. "This is that important?"

"More than you can imagine."

With a sigh, the innkeeper replied, "There's a small but sleek vessel, the *King's Shield*, near the northernmost end of the port. She can sail at any time. Just need a day or two to gather the crew and supplies together."

"Do you think you can convince the owner to hear me out?"

This caused Jeronnan to laugh hard. "No need to worry about that, milady! He's a man who used to follow many a cause, so long as it was a good one!"

Her hopes rose. Already she felt nearly well enough to travel. The *Hawksfire* had a few days head start, but with a good ship, Kara might be able to arrive in Lut Gholein in but a short time after. Her unique skills, combined with a few careful questions, should enable her to follow the trail from there.

"I need to talk with him. I must be able to leave by tomorrow morning."

"Tomorrow morn—"

Again she gave him that gaze. Kara regretted pushing, but more than her health and the patience of this other captain were at stake. "It must be so."

"All right." He shook his head. "I'll get everything ready. We'll set sail in the morning."

Kara was touched by his sudden offer. "It is more than enough that you can convince the *King's Shield*'s captain to take this journey, but you need not tear yourself from your beloved inn! This is no longer your concern."

"I don't like when my guests are nearly killed . . . or worse, lass. Besides, I've been too long on dry land! Be good to feel the sea again!" He leaned nearer, giving her a smile. "And as for convincing the captain, I don't think you understand me yet, enchantress! *I'm* owner of that fine vessel and by all that's holy, I'll see that she sets sail in the morning—or I promise you that there'll truly be hell to pay!"

As he hurried off to see to arrangements, Kara slumped down, caught by his last words. *Hell to pay?*

Captain Hanos Jeronnan had no idea just how fateful his oath just might end up being.

SEVEN

"My men grow restive and I can truly understand their positions, Galeona. Greatness beckons and we have sat here on the edge of the desert!"

" 'Twas by your command that we remained yet longer, my dear Augustus."

He towered over her. "Because you said that soon we would better know the location of Bartuc's armor! We would soon know where this fool brings it!" Malevolyn seized her hair, pulling her up until their faces nearly touched. "Find him, my darling. Find him—or I may have to find myself mourning your passing!"

She let him see no fear. Those who showed fear to the general became much reduced in his eyes, nevermore respected, forever expendable. Galeona had worked long and hard to make certain that she remained invaluable and she would not let that change now.

"I will see what I can do, but it must be accomplished without you this time."

He frowned. "You always required my presence in the past. Why the change now?"

"Because what I must do will require me to delve deeper than I ever have before . . . and if for any reason I am disturbed at the wrong point, not only will it kill me, but it may also perhaps slay anyone nearby."

This clearly impressed even the general. Brow raised, he nodded. "Very well. Is there anything you require of it?"

A voice suddenly spoke in Galeona's head. *There must be . . . some sacrifice.*

The sorceress smiled, wrapping one arm around Malevolyn and putting her lips to his. As she pulled away from the kiss, she absently asked, "Who's failed you most of late, my love?"

His mouth set into a straight edge, unyielding and unforgiving. "Captain Tolos has proven something of a disappointment of late. I think his dedication is slipping."

Her hand stroked Malevolyn's cheek. "Then perhaps I can make him more useful to you."

"I understand. I'll send him to you immediately. Just give me *results*."

"I think you'll be pleased."

"We shall see."

General Malevolyn marched out of the tent. Galeona immediately turned to the shadows, one in particular. "You think it'll be enough?"

"This one can only try," replied Xazax. The shadow separated from the others, moving nearer. Part of the shadow crossed over the sorceress's foot, sending a sensation like approaching death through her.

"I must find him this time! You see how impatient the general gets!"

"This one has waited much longer than the mortal," chittered the shade. "This one desires the finding far more than even him."

They both heard footsteps outside her tent. Xazax's silhouette immediately sank back into the rest of the shadows. Galeona brushed back her hair, then adjusted her arresting garments for best viewing.

"You may enter," she cooed.

A young officer, his helm in the crook of his arm, entered. Red-haired, with a slight beard and eyes too innocent, he looked like a lamb coming to the slaughter.

Galeona remembered his face and the interesting notions that had crossed her mind more than once. "Come closer, Captain Tolos."

"The general sent me," the officer returned in a voice that held just a hint of uncertainty. No doubt he knew well of the sorceress's reputation . . . not to mention her appetites. "He said you had a task for me."

She went to the table where she kept wine for the general, pouring Tolos a cup of the finest. Galeona held it up for him to see, beckoning the man to come to her. Like a fish to the lure, he did just that, his expression still confused.

Pressing the cup into his hand, Galeona led it to his mouth. At the same time, her other hand followed the course of his body, which further increased his anxiety.

"Lady Galeona," Tolos stammered. "the general sent me here for a purpose. It would not do for him to discover—"

"Hush . . ." She pushed the drink to his lips, making him sip. The fiery-tressed soldier swallowed once, twice, before the enchantress lowered the cup again. With her free hand, she brought his lips to hers, keeping them there long. He hesitated for the first few seconds, then pressed hard, lost in her charms.

Enough of frail pleasures, came the demon's voice in her head. *We have work to do . . .*

Behind the enamored officer, the shadow grew, solidified. A sound akin to a dying swarm of flies arose, enough of a noise to finally snap Captain Tolos from the enchantment Galeona had woven over him. The light of the oil lamp let part of a new shadow cross his field of vision, a shadow shaped like nothing human.

Tolos pushed her away, then sought his sword as he turned to face his supposed assassin. "You'll not take me so—"

Whatever words he planned failed him. Captain Tolo

gaped, his skin turning completely white. His fingers still fumbled for the sword, but the overwhelming fear enveloping him made his hand shake so much that he could not maintain any grip on the hilt.

And looming before him, the demon Xazax surely represented a sight capable of instilling such horrific fear. More than seven feet in height, Xazax resembled most a praying mantis, but a mantis as only Hell could create. A mad mix of emerald and crimson colored a body upon which pulsated great golden veins. The head of the demon looked as if someone had peeled off the outer shell of the insect, seeking the equivalent of a skull beneath. Oversized, yellow pupilless orbs stared down at the puny mortal and mandibles wider than a soldier's head—with smaller yet equally savage ones nearer the actual mouth—opened and closed with terrible eagerness. A stench like decaying vegetation pervaded the area surrounding the monstrous creature and even began permeating the tent.

The middle appendages, skeletal arms with three-fingered claws, reached out with lightning speed, dragging the petrified officer near. Tolos finally tried to scream, but the demon spat first, covering his victim's face with a soft, sticky substance.

Xazax's main appendages rose high, two jagged scythes ending in needlelike points.

He thrust both lances through the breast plate of the unfortunate officer, skewering Tolos like a fish.

The body quivered violently, something that seemed to amuse Xazax greatly. Tolos's hands feebly clawed at both his chest and his face, succeeding in freeing neither.

Galeona frowned at the sight, trying to cover her own dread of the demon's physical presence with anger and sarcasm. "If you're done playing, we do have *work* to do."

Xazax let the still-quivering body slide free. Tolos dropped to the ground, his blood-soaked carcass splayed out like some stringless marionette. The hellish mantis prodded the officer's corpse toward her. "Of course."

"I'll draw the patterns. You be ready to channel."

"This one will be prepared, make no mistake about it, human Galeona."

Touching Tolos's chest, the witch began to shape the patterns needed. She drew first a series of concentric circles, afterwards placing a pentagram in the midst of the largest. Galeona then traced in crimson both the marks of summoning and the wards that would protect her and even Xazax from being overwhelmed by the forces of the spell.

After a few minutes' work, Galeona had everything prepared. The sorceress glanced up at her demonic companion.

"This one is ready, as promised," came the raspy reply to her unspoken question.

The mantis approached, his scythelike arms reaching out to touch the center of Galeona's main pattern. A sound that grated the sorceress's ears erupted from Xazax, the demon speaking in a tongue with no earthly origins. She gave thanks that her protective spells kept anyone outside from hearing the creature's unholy voice.

The tent began to shake. A wind arose inside, one that lifted Galeona's hair and blew it back. The oil lamp flickered, at last dousing, but another light, a dank, poison-green aura, emerged from the blood-soaked chest of the dead soldier.

Xazax continued muttering in his demonic tongue, at the same time the mantis drawing new variations in the crimson pattern. Galeona felt forces both natural and hellish come forth, then mix in a combination otherwise impossible in the real world.

She reached out, adding to the demon's variations on the patterns. Now the interior of the tent crackled with energies both in flux and in conflict.

"Speak the words, human," commanded Xazax. "Speak before we are *engulfed* by our own creation . . ."

Galeona did, the ancient syllables spilling from her lips. Each word made her own blood burn, made the horrific veins coursing over her partner flare over and over. The dark sorceress spoke more quickly, knowing that if she faltered, Xazax's fear might yet prove true.

A thing the color of mold and fleshed almost like a toad formed above the body of Captain Tolos. It struggled, twisted, tried to cry out with a mouth not completely formed.

Let . . . me . . . resssst! it demanded.

Deformed beyond even the manner of demons, the grotesque creature sought to swipe first at Galeona, then Xazax. However, the wards that she had set into place caused a blue spark whenever the monstrosity reached out, a spark which clearly hurt the thing much. In frustration, it finally pulled within itself, wrapping spindly, taloned limbs about it as if trying to fold itself up enough to utterly disappear.

"You are ours to command," she told the imprisoned creature.

I . . . must . . . rest!

"You cannot rest until you complete the task we've set for you!"

Nightmarish eyes that dangled loose yet also seemed in some ways human peered at her in open malevolence. *Very well . . . for a time, anyway. What would . . . you have . . . of me?*

"No magic binds your eyes, no barriers block your vision. See for us what we seek and tell us where it is."

The horror above Tolos's cooling body quivered, rumbled. Both Xazax and Galeona bent back at first—until both realized that the thing only *laughed* at their demand.

That . . . is all? For this . . . I am tortured . . . forced to wake and even . . . forced to remember?

Recovering, the witch nodded. "Do it and we'll return you to your sleep."

The eyes swung toward the demon. *Show . . . me what . . . you seek.*

The mantis drew a small circle in the midst of the main pattern. A haze of orange filled the area in which the trapped creature floated. The eyes stared into the haze, seeing what even Galeona could not see.

It becomes . . . clearer . . . what you . . . seek. It will . . . be requiring . . . of a price.

"The payment," interjected Xazax. "you have already tasted a portion of."

Their prisoner gazed down at the body. *Accepted.*

And with but that—a force struck Galeona so hard within her mind that the sorceress fell back, collapsing onto her pillows.

She sailed aboard a vessel of dubious means and reputation, a vessel fighting a storm she found not at all natural. The storm had already ripped apart some of the sails, yet still the ship pressed on.

Curiously, Galeona saw no crew aboard, almost as if only ghosts manned this vessel. However, something tugged at her, demanded she look beyond the deck. Without even moving her feet, the sorceress shifted position, the door of a cabin now before her. Galeona raised one transparent hand, trying to push open that door.

Instead, she drifted through it, entering the cabin like one of the specters she had imagined sailing the ship. Yet, the lone occupant of this sad excuse for a room in no manner resembled the dead. In fact, up close he looked like far more than Galeona had first believed. Very much a soldier. Very much a man.

The witch tried to touch his face, but her hand went through his flesh. Nevertheless, he shifted slightly and almost smiled. Galeona glanced down at the rest of his body, noting how Bartuc's armor fit him well.

Then, a shadow in the corner caught her attention, a shadow with a familiar feel to it. Xazax.

Knowing that she had to tread carefully now, Galeona focused on what she and the demon sought. Once more acting as if she caressed the fighter's cheek, the witch murmured. "Who are you?"

He turned slightly, as if unsettled.

"Who are you?" she repeated.

This time, his lips opened and he mumbled, "Norrec."

She smiled at her success. "On what ship do you sail?"

"Hawksfirrre."

"What is its destination?"

Now he began to turn. A frown appeared on his slumbering visage and he seemed unwilling to answer, even in his dreams.

Determined not to fail in this, the most important of the questions, Galeona repeated herself.

Again, he did not answer. The witch looked up, saw that Xazax's shadow grew stronger. She did not trust the demon to take care, though. In fact, his presence even threatened to jeopardize matters.

The sorceress turned her attention back to Norrec, looming over him and speaking to him now in the seductive tone she generally reserved most for Augustus. "Tell me, my brave, handsome warrior . . . tell Galeona to where you sail . . ."

His mouth opened. "Lut—"

At that moment, the demon's shadow crossed his face.

Norrec's eyes flew open. "What in the name of all—"

And Galeona found herself back in the tent, her eyes staring toward the ceiling, her body covered in a chill sweat.

"You imbecile!" she roared, picking herself up. "What were you thinking?"

Xazax's mandibles snapped open and close. "Thinking that this one could find answers much more quickly than a much distracted female human . . ."

"There are much better ways than fear for discovering secrets! I had him answering everything! A few moments' more and we would have had all we needed to know!" She thought quickly on the subject. "Maybe it's not too late! If—"

She hesitated, staring down at where Tolos lay—or rather, *had* lain.

The body, even the blood that had splattered the carpet, had vanished.

"The dream one has taken his prize," Xazax remarked. "This Captain Tolos will suffer a terrible afterdeath . . ."

"Never mind him! We have to get the Dreamer back—"

Here the mantis vehemently twisted his head back and forth, the closest he could come to shaking it. "This one will not defy a Dreamer in his own domain. Their realm is beyond even that of Hell or Heaven. Here we may command them, but, break the link, and they may take what is theirs." The demon leaned forward. "Do you think your general might part with another soul?"

Galeona ignored his suggestion, thinking what she could say to Malevolyn. She had the names of both the man and his vessel, but what good did that do her? The ship might be sailing anywhere! If only he had managed to blurt out his destination before the demon had fouled matters much! If only—

"He said 'Lut—,'" the witch gasped. "It has to be!"

"You have a thought?"

"Lut Gholein, Xazax! Our fool journeys to Lut Gholein!" Her eyes widened in satisfaction. "He comes to us, just as I first said!"

The monstrous yellow eyes flashed once. "You are certain of this?"

"Very much!" Galeona let out a throaty chuckle, one that would have stirred many a man, but did nothing for the demon. "I must go tell Augustus at once! This will keep him in line for the time being!" She considered further. "Perhaps I can finally convince him to dare the desert. He wants Lut Gholein; this gives him even more reason to want to take it!"

Xazax gave her what for the mantis appeared a puzzled look. "But if the human Malevolyn throws his men at Lut Gholein, he will certainly fail—aah! This one understands! How clever!"

"I don't know what you mean . . . and I've no more time to argue with you! I must tell Augustus that the armor sails toward us as if summoned by our very hand."

She swept out of the tent, leaving the demon to his own devices. Xazax glanced at the spot where the unfortunate officer's body had lain but a short time before, then again at the tent flaps through which the dark-skinned sorceress had passed.

"The armor sails toward us, yes," the mantis chittered, his form beginning to fade back into shadow. "Curious what your general would think of you, though . . . if it did not reach Lut Gholein."

Norrec's eyes flew open. "What in the name of all—"

He paused, already half out of his bunk. Even though the lamp had gone out, Norrec could see well enough to know that he remained the only occupant of the cabin. The woman leaning over him—a sight he would certainly not soon forget—had evidently been the product of his dreams. What exactly she had been doing, the veteran could not say, only that she seemed interested in talking with him.

A beautiful woman who only wants to talk is certain to be after your purse, Fauztin had once pointed out to Sadun Tryst after the latter had nearly lost his meager pay to a female thief. Yet, what harm could a woman in a dream do to Norrec, especially considering his already dire situation?

He wished that he had not awakened. Perhaps if the dream had gone on longer, it would have proved more enticing. Certainly it had been an improvement over his recent nightmares.

Thinking of nightmares, Norrec tried to remember what had actually made him call out. Not the woman. Some sense of foreboding? Not quite right, either. More the feeling that something horrific had been encroaching upon him even as the dark-skinned temptress had leaned nearer . . .

A violent shift in the *Hawksfire* suddenly sent Norrec tumbling. He fell against the cabin door, which swung open without warning.

On his own, Norrec would not have reacted swiftly enough, but one gauntleted hand shot out of its own accord, seizing hold of the door frame and preventing the helpless soldier from crashing through the outside rail and plummeting into the stormy sea. Norrec dragged himself to safety, then pulled himself to his feet, his hands once more his own.

Did Captain Casco no longer have any control over his crew? If they were not careful, they would end up letting the waves and wind tear the *Hawksfire* apart!

He seized a handhold and began fighting his way toward the bow. The roar of the waves and the constant rumble of thunder made it impossible to hear the mariners, but certainly Casco had to be berating them for their carelessness. Certainly the captain would see to it that his crew—

Not a soul stood on the deck of the *Hawksfire*.

Still unwilling to believe his eyes, Norrec glanced up at the wheel. Using strong rope, someone had lashed it into one position, giving at least a semblance of control. However, there any concern for the ship ended. Already some of the lines for the sails fluttered loose, whipping about madly in the storm. One sail had tears in it that threatened to widen quickly unless someone did something.

The crew had to be below. No one would have been insane enough to abandon a serviceable ship, even the *Hawksfire*, in the midst of such violence. Casco had likely summoned them to the mess in order to discuss some drastic measure. Surely that had to be—

The lifeboat that should have been hanging near to where he stood had vanished.

Norrec quickly peered over the rail, but saw only loose ropes battering the hull. No accident had occurred here; someone had definitely lowered the boat into the water.

He ran from rail to rail, confirming his greatest fear. The crew *had* abandoned the *Hawksfire*, leaving both it and Norrec at the mercy of the storm . . .

But why?

It was a question to which he already knew the answer. He recalled the expressions of the crew after the suit had summoned the demons to repair the mast. Fear and horror—and both aimed not at the armor, but rather the man who wore it. The crew had been afraid of the power they believed Norrec wielded. Even from the start of the voyage, there had been a wariness whenever he had entered the mess. They had known even then that he had been no ordinary passenger and the incident involving the mast had more than proven them correct.

Ignoring the rain and wind, he returned once more to the rail, trying to make out any sign of the crew. Unfortunately, they had likely left hours before, making good use of his exhaustion after the summoning. Never mind that they had probably condemned themselves to death on the sea; the mariners had feared more for their eternal souls than their mortal bodies.

But where did that leave Norrec? How could he hope to sail the *Hawksfire* to land by himself, much less even steer a course to Lut Gholein?

A creaking noise directly behind him made the desperate soldier quickly turn.

Looking much bedraggled and not at all pleased to see Norrec, Captain Casco emerged from below deck. He had appeared cadaverous before, now he looked almost like a ghost.

"You . . ." he muttered. "Demon man . . ."

Norrec closed in on him, seizing Casco by the shoulders. "What happened? Where's the crew?"

"Left!" the captain snapped, pulling free. "Drown on sea rather than sail with demon master!" He shoved past Norrec. "Too much work to do! Away!"

The dismayed soldier watched as Casco moved to tighten some lines. His entire crew had abandoned ship, but the captain insisted on not only trying to keep the *Hawksfire* seaworthy, but also on route. It seemed like a mad, pointless exercise, but Casco looked determined to try as best he could.

Following after, Norrec called out, "What can I do to help?"

The soaked mariner gave him a contemptuous glance. "Jump over!"

"But . . ."

Casco ignored him, moving on to the next ropes. Norrec took one step, then realized how futile it would be to get the captain to listen. Casco had reason to both fear and hate him, and the veteran could not blame the man. Because of Norrec, Casco would likely lose both his ship and his life.

Lightning flashed, this time so near that Norrec had to turn away in order to keep from being blinded. Frustrated by his inability to do anything, he headed to the doorway leading below deck. Perhaps out of the storm he could better think.

A few lanterns still provided light as he descended into the bowels of the *Hawksfire*, yet their illumination did not help keep Norrec from being unsettled by the emptiness around him. Everyone but Casco had left the ship, daring certain death in order to be rid of the demon master in their midst. Likely if they had thought that they could have slain him, they would have tried that, but the display of power by the suit had clearly convinced them otherwise.

Which left Norrec wondering how long the *Hawksfire* had before the waves and wind tore it apart.

He glared at the gauntlets, the parts of the armor he most associated with his plight. If not for the suit, he would have never been in this predicament.

"Well?" Norrec nearly spat. "What do you plan to do now? Are we to start swimming if the ship sinks?"

At first he regretted even making the suggestion, fearful that the armor would choose to attempt to do just that. Norrec tried not to picture the heavy armor trying to stay afloat. To him, who had rarely taken to the sea save for short voyages, drowning seemed the most horrible of fates. To suffocate, to have his lungs fill with water as the dark sea engulfed him . . . better to run a blade through his gut instead!

The *Hawksfire* shook, this time in so violent a manner that the hull moaned ominously. Norrec gazed toward the ceiling, wondering if Captain Casco had finally lost what little control of the ship he had briefly had.

Again the vessel shook, the planks literally bending. A few more moments of this and the soldier felt certain that all his darkest fears would soon come true. Already he could feel the waters closing in.

Determined not to fall victim to panic, Norrec raced to the stairway, fighting to keep his footing as he rushed back up on deck. Whatever the mariner might think of him, Norrec had to try to somehow help Casco regain mastery of the *Hawksfire*.

He heard Casco shouting something in his native tongue,

an unending litany of curses, from the sound of it. Norrec looked around, trying to find the captain in the storm.

He found Casco—along with a gigantic nightmare rising from the sea.

A gargantuan horror with what seemed a hundred tentacles and one vast red orb had the bow of the *Hawksfire* in its clutches. The aquatic behemoth resembled a giant squid, but only if some great force had first ripped away its skin and put in place wicked barbs everywhere. Worse, many of the smaller tentacles had, not suction cups, but rather tiny, clawlike hands that grasped and pulled at whatever part of the ship they could reach. Sections of the rail came away readily, as did some of the deck itself. Several hands and tentacles sought for the sails.

Captain Casco ran about the deck, ducking one attacking appendage and swatting at others with a long, hooked pole. On the deck near him, one ripped end of a tentacle flopped around, dark ichor pouring from the torn section. Defying the danger all about him, the mariner continued to try to fend off the monstrous sea creature. The sight looked as absurd as it did terrifying, one lone man trying to stop the inevitable . . .

Once more, Norrec looked down at the gloves, shouting, "Do something!"

The suit did not react.

With nothing else left for him, Norrec looked around, seeking a weapon. Seeing another of the hooked poles, he immediately seized it and ran to Casco's side.

His actions proved most timely for at that moment a pair of clawed hands rose behind the battling captain, reaching for his back. One hand managed to dig into Casco's bony shoulder, causing the captain to cry out.

Norrec brought the hooked pole into play, burying the point in the monstrous hand and pulling with all his might.

To his amazement, the hand tore off, dropping to the

deck. At the same time, though, the second appendage, inhuman claws outstretched, turned toward Norrec. In addition, two tentacles with suction cups darted in from the veteran fighter's right.

Bringing the pole around again, Norrec tore into one of the tentacles, sending it retreating. The hand snapped at him, talons as long as the fingers trying to rip into Norrec's face. He swatted at it with the side of the pole, but missed.

What sort of monster had risen up from the depths? Although he would have willingly admitted that he knew little about life in the Twin Seas, Norrec Vizharan had heard no tales of any creature akin to this ungodly abomination. It looked more like a thing out of a tale of horror, a beast more at home with the demonic imps the suit had earlier summoned.

Demons? Could this creature be some sort of demonic force? Could that explain why the armor had not reacted? It still left so much unexplained, yet . . .

More than a dozen new tentacles, some with the bizarre clawed hands and some not, erupted from the sea, assaulting anew both Casco and Norrec from various directions. More adept at using the hooked pole, the lanky captain disproved his sickly appearance by swiftly tearing into two of the tentacles. Norrec proved not so fortunate, managing to push back a few of the horrors but doing damage to none.

More and more tentacles turned from the task of ripping the ship to pieces to now dealing with the only resistance. One managed to seize Casco's pole, pulling it free with such force that the captain fell to the deck, his bad leg giving out on him at last. Several clawed tentacles encircled him, dragging Casco toward the great behemoth.

Norrec would have helped, but his own troubles grew worse than those of the mariner. Tentacles wound around both legs, then his waist. Two more tore the pole from his hands. The soldier found himself hoisted up into the air, his breath slowly being squeezed out of him despite the enchanted armor.

He screamed as a set of claws raked his left cheek. Somewhere beyond his limited field of vision, Norrec heard Casco uttering oaths even as death prepared to welcome both men.

A serpentine shape curled around Norrec's throat. In desperation, he tugged at it, already aware that his strength would not prove sufficient to save him.

The gauntlet flared a fiery red.

The tentacle instantly uncoiled from his throat, but the glove would not release it. Norrec's other hand, also glowing furiously, came up, seizing the tentacle holding him by the upper part of the waist.

The rest of the behemoth's limbs pulled away, leaving the startled veteran dangling by his hands high above the *Hawksfire*. The storm whipped him about, but Bartuc's armor refused to give up its hold on the gargantuan monster, even when the beast sought to separate the captured tentacles. Norrec screamed, his arms feeling as if they would soon be torn from their sockets.

"*Kosori nimth!*" his mouth shouted. "*Lazarai . . . lazarai!*"

A bolt of lightning struck the leviathan.

The creature shuddered, nearly succeeding in freeing itself of Norrec simply due to its throes of pain. Yet, even then the gauntlets fought to retain hold, clearly the warlord's suit was not finished yet.

"*Kosori nimth!*" the soldier's mouth repeated. "*Lazarai dekadas!*"

A second bolt caught the sea monster directly in its terrifying eye. The bolt burned away the orb with little trouble, sending a shower of hot fluids over Norrec and the ship.

"Dekadas!"

The areas of the tentacles under Norrec's fingers turned a pasty gray. Serpentine flesh grew stony, petrified with startling swiftness.

The leviathan stiffened, its many appendages remaining in whatever position they had been just after the last of the magical words had been spoken. The pasty gray coloring spread rapidly down the two tentacles the hapless soldier held, then coursed along in every direction, covering the giant's body and other limbs in mere seconds.

"Kosori nimth!" Norrec shouted for the third and—so he suspected—final time.

A flash of lightning more intense than either of the others struck the graying sea demon directly in the ruined eye.

The horrific behemoth *shattered*.

The gauntlets released their grip on the crumbling tentacles, at the same time returning control of the hands to Norrec. Suddenly bereft of any hold, the startled fighter frantically grabbed at one of the massive limbs, only to have the piece he seized break off.

He plummeted toward the ship, his only hope that he would die crashing into the hard deck rather than sinking beneath the violent waters.

Eight

"Very curious," Captain Jeronnan muttered, peering far ahead. "Seems like a lifeboat in the distance."

Kara squinted, seeing nothing. The captain evidently had miraculous eyesight. "Is there anyone in it?"

"No one visible, but we'll take a closer look. I'll not risk a single sailor's life just to spare a few minutes . . . hope you understand that, lass."

"Of course!" She felt grateful enough that Jeronnan had arranged this voyage in the first place. He had put his ship and his crew at her disposal, something the necromancer would not have expected from any person. In return, he had accepted such payment as would cover her expenses, but no more. Each time she tried to press, a dark expression would cover his countenance, warning the raven-tressed enchantress that she threatened to tread on the memory of the former naval officer's daughter.

It had taken two days at sea, in fact, before Kara had come to realize that he truly needed this voyage as much as she did. If the tall innkeeper had seemed boisterous before, he now seemed at times ready to burst. Even the constant hint of less than fair weather on the western horizon did nothing to dampen his spirits.

"Mister Drayko!" At Jeronnan's cry, a slim hawk-faced man in perfectly kept officer's garments turned and saluted. Drayko had not acted at all bitter when his master had declared that he would be taking command of this voyage. Clearly Jeronnan's second had great respect and devotion for the innkeeper. "Lifeboat ahead!"

"Aye, captain!" Drayko immediately gave commands for the sailors to prepare for survivors. The crew of the *King's Shield* reacted in quick and orderly fashion, something Kara Nightshadow had already come to expect. Those who served Jeronnan served a man who had lived much of his life following the strict dictates of discipline. This did not mean that he ruled with an iron hand. Jeronnan also believed in the humanity of each of his men, a rare quality in any leader in these times.

The *King's Shield* came up to the lone craft, two sailors immediately preparing lines to draw her in. Jeronnan and Kara stepped down to watch them at work, the necromancer beginning to feel uneasy about this discovery. They followed the same general route that the *Hawksfire* would have used; could this be a boat from that vessel? Had Kara's quest ended so soon, her quarries at the bottom of the sea?

"There's one aboard her," Captain Jeronnan muttered.

True enough, one sailor did lie in the boat, but even as the crew worked to secure the life craft, Kara already noted telltale signs that, for this man, they had arrived too late.

Mister Drayko sent a pair of men down to investigate. Sliding down the ropes, they gingerly turned over the body, which had been lying face down.

Eyes that no longer saw stared up into the heavens.

"Been dead a day," called up one of the men. He grimaced. "Permission to send him to his rest, sir."

Kara did not have to ask what he meant. Out here, there were limitations to what they could do for a corpse. A ceremony . . . and then a watery burial.

Jeronnan nodded his permission, but Kara quickly put

a hand on his arm. "I need to see the body . . . it may tell us something."

"You think it's from the *Hawksfire?*"

"Don't you, captain?"

He frowned. "Aye . . . but what do you plan to do?"

She dared not explain in full. "Find out what happened . . . if I can."

"Very well." Jeronnan signaled for the men to bring the body up. "I'll have a cabin set aside for you, milady! I don't want anyone else witnessing what you plan. They wouldn't understand."

It took but a short time to bring the body to the cabin Jeronnan had chosen. Kara had expected to work with the corpse by herself, but the captain refused to leave. Even when she gave him a rather cursory explanation of what she intended, the former innkeeper refused to depart.

"I've watched men torn apart in battle, seen creatures I doubt you've even heard of, viewed death in a thousand forms . . . and after what happened to my daughter, nothing can ever make me flee again. I'll watch and I'll even help, if it comes to that."

"In that case, please bolt the door. We will not want anyone else seeing this."

After he had obeyed, Kara knelt beside the body. The sailor had been a middle-aged man who had not lived a gentle life. Recalling what little she had learned of the *Hawksfire*, the dark mage grew more suspicious that the boat had been indeed from that desperate vessel.

The men who had brought the body had quickly closed the eyes, but Kara now opened them up again.

"What in the Sea Witch's name are you doing, lass?"

"What has to be done. You may still leave if you wish, captain. It is not necessary that you subject yourself to any of this."

He steeled himself. "I'll stay . . . it's just that a dead man's stare is said to be bad luck."

"He certainly had enough of that." She reached into her pouch, searching for components. Without the dagger, she could not readily summon a phantasm as she had done in Bartuc's tomb. Besides, attempting to do so might have even made Jeronnan change his mind about letting her continue. No, what she had in mind would work well enough, provided that in the process it did not turn the captain against her.

From one tiny pouch Kara pulled forth a pinch of white powder.

"What's that?"

"Ground bone and a mix of herbs." She reached toward the dead sailor's face.

"*Human* bone?"

"Yes." Captain Jeronnan made no noise, no protest, which relieved the necromancer. Kara held the powder over the eyes, then sprinkled both sightless orbs with the white substance.

To his credit, Jeronnan kept his tongue still. Only when she next retrieved a tiny black vial, then reached for the corpse's mouth, did he dare interrupt again. "You're not going to pour that down his gullet, are you, lass?"

She peered up at him. "I mean no desecration, captain. What I do, I do to find out why this man perished. He looks dehydrated, starved, almost as if he has had neither food nor water for more than a week. A very curious state for him to be in if, indeed, he is from the ship we pursue. I would assume the captain there would keep his crew fed, would he not?"

"Casco's a mad, foreign devil, but, aye, he'd still see that his men were fed."

"As I thought. And if this poor soul is not from the *Hawksfire*, it behooves us to find out exactly which vessel he *is* from, too. Don't you agree?"

"Your point's made, lass . . . forgive me."

"There is nothing to forgive." With the top of the vial now removed, she used one hand to open the jaws of the sailor. That accomplished, Kara immediately tipped the vial so that half the contents would quickly drain down into the throat. Satisfied with that, she stoppered the bottle again and leaned back.

"Maybe you could at least tell me how you hope to find out anything."

"You'll see." She would have explained, but Jeronnan did not realize how swiftly she now had to work. In conjunction with the powder, the liquid Kara had used would have an effect lasting but a very short time and the necromancer still had the final part of the spell to cast. Any interruption from here on might waste crucial seconds.

With her finger, Kara drew a circle over the sailor's chest, then extended a line from there along the length of the throat, up the jaw, and finally ending at the mouth. At the same time, she whispered the words of the spell. Once that had been done, Kara tapped the corpse on the chest, once, twice, thrice. All the while, the dark mage kept track of each passing second.

The dead mariner let out an audible gasp as his lungs sought to fill with air.

"Gods above!" blurted Jeronnan, taking a step back. "You've brought him back!"

"No," Kara curtly answered. She had known that the captain would mistake this for a resurrection. Outsiders never understood the many facets of a necromancer's work. The faithful of Rathma did not toy with death as some believed; that went against their teachings. "Now, please, Captain Jeronnan, let me proceed."

He grunted, but otherwise remained silent. Kara leaned over the sailor, looking into the dead eyes. A faint hint of gold radiated from them, a good sign.

She leaned back. "Tell me your name."

From the cold lips emerged a single word. *"Kalkos."*

"From what ship do you hail?"

Another gasp of air, then, *"Hawksfirrrre."*

"So, he *is* from the—"

"Please! No speaking!" To the corpse, she asked, "Did the ship sink?"

"Noooo . . ."

Curious. Then why would this man have abandoned it? "Were there pirates?"

Again a negative response. Kara estimated the time she had remaining and realized that she had better push to the point. "Did everyone abandon ship?"

"Noooo . . ."

"Who remained behind?" The necromancer tried to keep the anticipation out of her voice.

Once more, the corpse inhaled. *"Casco . . . captain . . ."* The mouth shut, something not at all normal. The mariner's body almost seemed reluctant to add more, but then it finally gasped, *"Sssorcererrrr . . ."*

A sorcerer? The answer caught Kara off guard for a moment. She had expected to hear him speak of either the thieves who had stolen the armor or, in view of the crew's desperate act, the two revenants who had attacked her. Certainly their presence would have sent hardened sailors fleeing to the dangers of the sea.

"Describe him!"

The mouth opened, but no words came out. Like the phantasm, this spell allowed only for simple answers. Kara cursed quietly, then altered her question. "What did he wear?"

Inhaling . . . then, *"Armorrrr . . ."*

She stiffened. "Armor? Red armor?"

"Yesss . . ."

Something she had not expected. So, apparently one of the survivors of the tomb had been a sorcerer after all.

Could it be this Norrec Vizharan of which the earlier phantasm had spoken? She repeated the name to the mariner, asking him if he knew it. Unfortunately, that did not prove the case.

Still, Kara had found out much of what she wanted to know. The last time this man Kalkos had seen the *Hawksfire*, it had not only been afloat, but the armor she sought remained aboard.

"Without a crew," she commented to a silent Captain Jeronnan. "The ship cannot sail far, can it?"

"More than likely to go in circles, if only its master and this spellcaster remain aboard." Jeronnan hesitated, then asked, "Haven't you more questions?"

She did, but none that the corpse could answer. Kara dearly wished that she still had her dagger. Then she could have taken more time and summoned up a true spirit, something that could have answered with longer, more coherent statements. Older, more skilled necromancers could have performed such a fantastic feat without the use of a tool, but Kara knew it would still be a few years before she reached that point.

"What about him?" insisted the former naval officer. "What *happened* to him . . . and the rest, for that matter, lass? One day on a rough sea's enough to kill many a man, but there's something unsettling about the look of him . . ."

Feeling somewhat ashamed that Jeronnan had found the need to remind her, Kara quickly leaned over the corpse again. "Where are your comrades?"

No answer. She quickly touched the chest, felt it sink under the slight pressure of her fingers. The liquid component of her spell had begun to wear off.

The necromancer had one chance. The eyes of a dead man often retained the last few images he had witnessed. If the powder she had placed on them still had some potency, then Kara might be able to see those images for herself.

Without looking back at the captain, she said, "Under no circumstances must I be interrupted for the next step. Is that understood?"

"Aye . . ." but Jeronnan said it with much reluctance.

Kara positioned her gaze directly over the sightless orbs, then began muttering. The gold tint to his eyes seized her, pulled her in. The necromancer fought back the instinctive desire to flee from the world of the dead, instead throwing herself fully into the spell she now cast.

And suddenly Kara sat in a boat in the midst of a stormy sea, pulling at the oars with all her might as if the three Prime Evils themselves chased the tiny vessel. The necromancer looked down, saw that her hands were thick, rough, seaman's hands—the hands of Kalkos.

"Where's Pietr's boat?" a bearded man called out to her.

"How would I know?" her own mouth snapped back, the voice deep and bitter. "Just row! Got us a chance if we keep headin' east! That hellish storm's got to end somewhere!"

"We shoulda taken the captain with us!"

"He'd never leave her, not even if she sank! He wants to ride with the demon master, let 'im!"

"Watch out for that wave!" someone else shouted.

Her head turned toward that direction, epithets such as Kara had never imagined men using spitting from her lips. In the distance, she saw two other lifeboats, each crammed tight with desperate men.

The bearded man suddenly stood up, not the wisest thing in such conditions. He gaped at something behind her—behind Kalkos—and pointed frantically. "Look out! Look out!"

Kalkos's gaze shifted as best it could. The sailor continued to man the oars.

At the edge of the the mariner's field of vision emerged a vast, serpentine tentacle.

"Turn about! Turn about!" Kalkos called. "Sit down, Bragga!"

The bearded man dropped to his place. Those able to work the oars desperately tried to turn the boat around.

Over the roar of the waves and the crash of thunder, Kara heard the distant screams of men. Kalkos looked that direction, revealing the horrific sight of scores of tentacles overwhelming one of the other boats. Several men were lifted into the air, some by the suction cups of the tentacles, others by macabre, grasping claws—almost hands—that plucked sailors from the boat as if they were flowers.

Kara expected the sailors to be drawn to the cavernous opening that she now witnessed in the center of a massive, monstrous form, a creature much like a gigantic squid, but with only one massive orb and horrid flesh that marked it as no denizen of this mortal plane. Instead, however, the monster simply held them aloft, using its clawed appendages to attach other sailors to various suckers. The victims cried out, pleading to those in the distance to save them.

"Row, damn you!" Kalkos roared. "Row!"

"I told you he wouldn't let us go! I told you!"

"Be quiet, Bragga! Be—"

A vast wave washed over them, throwing one shouting man overboard. Next to the tiny vessel, an array of tentacles rose from the water, surrounding Kalkos's companions on all sides and reaching hungrily for each.

"At 'em with your blades! It's the only—"

Yet although the men managed to parry the assaults of a few of the demonic arms, one by one they were picked off the boat, screaming—until only Kalkos, one oar used as a weapon . . . remained.

Kara felt a chill as wet tentacles seized her legs, grabbed her arms. She felt the suction cups attach to her body . . . No! This had all happened in the past! This had happened to Kalkos, not her!

Despite recalling that, however, she still felt the mariner's own horror as a new and terrible thing happened. Even despite his clothing, Kalkos felt weaker, drawn—as if the very life were being sucked from his body. His flesh wrinkled, dried despite the wetness all around him. He felt like a water sack whose contents were being swiftly drained . . .

And then, just as all life seemed stolen from him, when his body felt like no more than a dry husk, the tentacles suddenly dropped Kalkos back into the boat. Too late for the sailor to survive, Kalkos already knew that, but better to spend his last few moments of life back in the boat rather than in the gullet of such a hellish beast.

Only when talons dug into his arms and dragged him to a standing position did he come back from the brink enough to register that someone else had joined him in the lifeboat.

No—not *someone*—but *some thing*.

It spoke in a voice reminiscent of a thousand buzzing insects in agony; although Kara strained to make its form out clearly, the eyes of Kalkos no longer saw well. The enchantress could only perceive a terrifying, emerald and red shape looming over the dying sailor, a shape that did not conform to any human standard. Oversized eyes of deep yellow that seemed to have no pupils fixed on the unfortunate Kalkos.

"Death is not your pleasure yet," it chittered. "This one has things it must know! Where is the fool? Where is the armor?"

"I . . ." the mariner coughed. His body felt so very dry, even to Kara. "What . . . ?"

His inhuman inquisitor shook him. A pair of needle-tipped spears came from nowhere, pressing against Kalkos's chest. "This one has no time, human. Can offer you much pain before life flees. Speak!"

From somewhere within, Kalkos found the strength to obey. "The s-stranger . . . armored . . . blood . . . still on . . . Hawksfire!"

"Which way?"

The mariner managed to point.

The demon, for Kara knew it to be one, chittered to itself, then demanded, "Why flee? Why run?"

"He—demons on ship."

The murky creature made a sound unlike any Kara would have expected from one of his kind, a sound that she recognized instantly as a sign of consternation. "Impossible! You lie!"

The sailor did not answer. Kara felt him slipping away. His last attempt to respond to the monstrous figure had drained him of what little he had left of life.

The half-seen creature dropped Kalkos, a jolt of pain coursing through the necromancer as the body struck. She heard the demon chitter again, then spout one comprehendible word.

"Impossible!"

Kara had a lone brief glimpse of the inner side of the lifeboat and the sailor's fingers twitching—and with that, the vision faded.

Inhaling, Kara clutched herself tight, eyes still fixed on the corpse's own.

She felt the nearby presence of Captain Jeronnan. The former naval officer put comforting hands on her shoulders. "Are you all right?"

"How long?" the necromancer murmured. "How long?"

"Since you started whatever you've been doing? A minute, two maybe."

So short a time in the real world, but so long and violent in the memories of the dead. The necromancer had performed this spell before, but she had never faced a death time so horrible as what this Kalkos had suffered.

The *Hawksfire* sailed a day or two ahead of them, no crew left to man the ship save the captain and this sorcerer, Norrec Vizharan. The last name should have warned her: "Servant of the Vizjerei"? More like one of the untrustworthy mages themselves! He had the armor, even had the audacity to wear it! Did he not understand the danger?

Without a crew, even he would have trouble keeping

the ship on course. Kara had a chance to catch him after all, provided that neither the revenants nor the demonic forces she had witnessed in Kalkos's death time had not caught up with the murderer already.

"So," continued Jeronnan, helping her to her feet. "Did you find out anything?"

"Little more," she lied, hoping her eyes would not give her away. "About his death, nothing. However, the *Hawksfire* is definitely still afloat, both the captain and my quarry aboard."

"Then we should catch up to them soon enough. Two men can't do much to keep a ship like that going."

"I believe it is only two days ahead at most."

He nodded, then glanced down at the corpse. "Are you done with him now, lass?"

She forced herself not to shiver at the memories she had shared with the late Kalkos. "Yes. Give him a proper burial."

"He'll get that . . . and then we'll be on our way after the *Hawksfire*."

As he departed the cabin to summon a pair of hands, Kara Nightshadow pulled her cloak about her, her gaze still on the body, but her mind on to what she had just committed herself—herself and every man aboard the *King's Shield*.

"It must be done," the necromancer muttered. "He must be caught and the armor returned to hiding. No matter what the cost . . . and no matter how many *demons*."

"Xazax!"

Galeona waited, but the demon did not respond. She looked around, searching for the telltale shadow. Sometimes Xazax played games, games with dark intentions. The sorceress had no time for games, especially ones that occasionally proved fatal for others than her partner.

"Xazax!"

Still no reply. She snapped her fingers and the lamp blazed brighter—yet still the shadow of the demon did not reveal itself.

Galeona did not care for that. Xazax in the tent, she understood. Xazax elsewhere generally spelled trouble. The mantis sometimes forgot who aided him in secretly walking the mortal plane.

No matter. She had far too much to do. The dark-skinned sorceress turned her fiery gaze on a massive chest positioned in one corner of the garish tent. Taken as it appeared, the chest, made of iron and good strong oak and standing on four stylized leonine paws, would have required two sturdy soldiers to drag it to her and that with much effort on their part. However, as with the demon, Galeona had no time to go searching for strong arms, especially when the enchantress knew that they were all busy packing up the rest of the camp. No, she could handle her own needs at this juncture.

"Come!"

The lower corners of the great chest shone. The metallic paws twitched, the leonine toes spreading, stretching.

The chest began walking.

The massive box wended its way toward Galeona, looking almost like a hound summoned by its mistress. It finally paused within a few inches of the witch, awaiting her next command.

"Open!"

With a long, creaking noise, the lid swung up.

Satisfied, Galeona turned and put her hand under one of the many pieces of her hanging collection. The piece unlatched itself, dropping gently into her waiting palm. The sorceress placed it in the chest, then went on with the next.

One after another, she dropped the items inside. An

onlooker who had observed the entire time would have
begun to notice that, no matter how many things Galeona
put in the chest, it never seemed to completely fill.
Always the witch found room for the next and the
next . . .

But as she neared completion of her task, a slight chill
went up and down her spine. Galeona turned and, after
some searching, found a shadow that had not been present before.

"So! You finally come back! Where've you been?"

The demon did not answer at first, his shadow sinking
deeper into the folds of the tent.

"Augustus has commanded that the entire camp be
struck down. He desires we leave immediately after,
whether preparations are completed in daylight or
night."

Still Xazax did not answer. Galeona paused, not liking
the silence. The mantis tended to babble, not hold his
tongue. "What is it? What's gotten into you?"

"Where does the general seek to go?" the shadow
abruptly asked.

"You have to ask? Lut Gholein, of course."

The demon seemed to consider this. "Yes, this one
would go to Lut Gholein. Yes . . . that might be
best . . ."

She took a step toward the shadow. "What's the matter with you? Where've you been?" When he did not
answer, the witch walked up to the corner of the tent,
growing more furious by the moment. "Either answer
me or—"

"Away!"

The demon burst forth from the shadow, his full monstrous form looming over the human. Galeona let out a
gasp and stumbled backward, at last falling over the pillows still covering much of the floor.

Death in the form of a hellish insect with burning yellow orbs and rapidly snapping mandibles hovered. Claws and sicklelike appendages came within an inch— no more—of Galeona's face and form.

"Cease your chattering and keep from this one! Lut Gholein is our agreed destination! We will talk no more until I choose!"

With that . . . Xazax pulled back into the dark corner, his physical form fading, his shadow growing dimmer. In but a few seconds, the only sign of his continued presence remained just the hint of a monstrous shape among the folds of fabric.

Galeona, however, did not move from where she had fallen until absolutely positive that the mantis would not leap out again. When the sorceress did finally rise, Galeona did so making certain that she rolled away from where the shadow lurked. She had come very close to death, very close to a lingering, *agonizing* death.

Xazax made no more sound, no more movement. Galeona could not recall when she had ever seen the horrific demon act as he had just done. Despite the pact between them, he had been more than willing to slay her if she had not obeyed instantly—something she swore not to forget. The pact should have been impossible for either to break, the only reason they could tolerate one another on such a long-term basis. If Xazax had been willing to risk the consequences of doing away with both that pact and her, then it behooved Galeona more than ever to find a way to rid herself of him . . . which very well meant either the general or the fool. At least with men, she always knew she had some control.

The sorceress turned back to the task of loading the contents of her tent into the chest, but her mind never left the demon's actions. Besides the danger she now perceived in his willingness to risk the consequences of breaking their covenant, his near attack of her had left a question behind to which she dearly desired an answer. It alone would give reason not only for Xazax's unnerving reaction, but also the revelation of an emotion she had never witnessed in him before.

What, Galeona wondered, could possibly have *frightened* the demon so?

Πіпε

The agonizing pain coursing through Norrec Vizharan proved to be the first sign that he had not, after all, perished. That he could breathe also indicated immediately to him that he had not dropped into the sea and that, therefore, he had struck the deck. Why he had not snapped his neck nor broken several other bones, Norrec could only suspect had to be the fault of Bartuc's cursed armor. It had already saved him from the demonic behemoth; a simple, short fall likely had been child's play to it.

Yet, in his heart, the veteran soldier half-wished that it had failed. At least then he would have been rid of the nightmares, the horrors.

Norrec opened his eyes to see that he lay in his cabin. Outside, the storm raged unceasingly. Only two forces could have dragged him back in here, one being the suit. Yet, after what it had done to the tentacled monstrosity, it had seemed weaker, unable to perform any feat. Norrec himself felt so drained, he marveled that he could even move. The weakness felt so odd that the weary soldier wondered if either the armor or the beast had somehow sucked part of his life from him.

At that moment, the door swung open, Captain Casco hobbling into the tiny cabin with a covered bowl in his hand. A scent that Norrec found both enticing and repulsive drifted from the bowl.

"Awake? Good! No waste of food!" Without waiting

for the soldier to rise, the cadaverous mariner handed him the bowl.

Norrec managed to right himself enough to eat. "Thank you."

In return, the captain merely grunted.

"How long have I been out?"

Casco considered the question for a time, possibly wanting to make certain that he understood it. "Day. Little more."

"How's the ship? Did the creature damage it much?"

Again a pause. "Ship always damaged . . . but can still sail, yes."

"How can we possibly sail in a storm with no crew at all?"

The captain scowled. Norrec suspected that he had finally asked the question for which Casco had no good answer. Of course, they could not sail without a crew. Likely the *Hawksfire* went around and around, tossed in random directions by the winds and waves. They might have survived the attack by the monster, but that did not mean that they would reach Lut Gholein.

The monster . . . Norrec's memory of what happened seemed so outrageous that he finally had to ask Casco if what he had seen had been truth.

The captain shrugged. "Saw you fall . . . saw the Sea Witch fall."

The foreign mariner had evidently decided that what he had confronted had been the legendary behemoth mentioned by so many sailors. Norrec believed different, certain after his encounters with the imps and the winged creature at the inn that this had been yet another demonic force—but not one, this time, summoned by the enchanted armor.

Legend spoke of Bartuc's rise to dark glory, first as a pawn of hellish powers, then as a sorcerer both respected and feared by them, and how he had led a legion of demons in his quest to overwhelm all else. No one, though, ever spoke of how the greater demons might have felt about that usurping of their power. Had they now noted the armor's escape from the tomb and so feared that the ghost of Bartuc sought to reestablish his hold over their kind?

His head pounded at such outlandish thoughts. Best he concern himself with his own situation. If the *Hawksfire* remained unmanned, it would continue to meander over the Twin Seas, either sailing on long past the deaths of the only two aboard or finally sinking due to some aspect of the endless storm.

"I'm no seaman," he commented to Casco between bites of food. "But show me what I can do and I'll help. We've got to get the ship back on course."

Now Casco snorted. "Done enough! What more? What more?"

His attitude not only struck Norrec as peculiar, but it also stirred the fighter's own ire. He knew that much of this situation could be blamed on him—or rather, the armor—but his offer to help the captain had been an honest one. Norrec doubted that the suit would prevent him from helping; after all, it had been the one that had truly wanted to reach Lut Gholein, not him.

"Listen! We'll die if we don't get the *Hawksfire* under control! If the storm doesn't take us, then we'll either eventually starve when the supplies go bad or, more likely, strike some rocks and sink like a stone! Is that what you want for your ship?"

The gaunt figure shook his head. "Fool! Fall crack skull?" He had the audacity to seize Norrec by the arm. "Come! Come!"

Putting aside the nearly empty bowl, he followed Casco out into the storm. His legs took a few steps to again get used to the rocking of the ship, but the captain waited for him to catch up. Casco seemed caught between hatred, respect, and fear when it came to his passenger. He did not offer any assistance, but neither did he try to force Norrec along faster than the weakened man could go.

Reaching the open deck, the mariner let Norrec move past him. The veteran fighter held tight to what handrail remained, peering through the heavy rain and trying to see what it had been that Casco sought to show him. All Norrec could make out was the same empty scene he had confronted earlier. No sailors manned the ropes, no helmsman stood at the wheel.

And yet . . . the wheel *turned*. Ropes no longer held it in place. Norrec squinted, certain that the wheel should have been spinning wildly, yet it barely moved, sometimes turning one direction, then adjusting to the other, as if some invisible sailor kept it under control.

A movement to the side caught his attention. Focusing, Norrec at first had the horrible fear that one of the main lines had suddenly untied, only to have it *reloop* itself before his very eyes, then tighten the new knot.

And all around him he began to notice subtle shifts, subtle changes. Ropes adjusted according to the needs of the sails. The sails themselves adjusted as necessary. The wheel continued to counter the churning waves, fixing the *Hawksfire* on a particular route—one that Norrec expected would turn out to be almost directly west.

No crew manned the vessel, but it seemed to the *Hawksfire* not to matter in the least.

"What's going on?" he shouted at the captain.

Casco only gave him a knowing glance.

The armor! Again its power astounded him. It had dealt with the gargantuan demon and now it ensured that its own journey would continue regardless of the mutiny of the crew. The *Hawksfire* would reach port one way or another.

Norrec stumbled away, heading not for his cabin but down into the mess. Casco trailed behind, a captain with no purpose on this voyage. Both men shook off the rain. Casco dug into a chest, pulled out a dusty bottle whose contents he did not offer to his companion. Norrec thought of asking for a drink—he certainly needed one— but thought better of it. His head pounded enough at the moment and he preferred to try to let it clear.

"How long until we reach port?" he finally asked.

Casco put down the bottle just long enough to answer him. "Three. Four days, maybe."

Norrec grimaced. He had hoped for less than that. Three or four more days aboard a vessel where wheels and ropes moved by themselves and his only companion remained a wild-looking captain who thought him a devil in human form.

He rose. "I'll be in my cabin until it's time to eat."

Casco made no move to stop him, the lanky mariner quite content to be alone with his bottle.

Stepping out into the storm, Norrec battled his way back to the tiny cabin. He would have preferred to stay in the much more spacious—not to mention drier—area below deck, but in Casco's presence, the guilt over the troubles Norrec's being here had caused the man ate at the soldier. It amazed him that Casco had not just slit his throat when he had come across the unconscious figure. Of course, after seeing what Norrec had supposedly done, then discovering that even the fall had not killed his unsettling passenger, the captain likely had suspected that any attempt to slay the stranger would end up with Casco the dead party.

He would have probably not been far from wrong.

The rain continued to not only soak Norrec but tried to beat him to the deck. In all his years fighting for one master or another, the veteran had faced harsh weather of all sorts, including blizzards. However, to him this storm had no equal and he could only pray that it would at last end when the *Hawksfire* reached Lut Gholein's port.

That assumed, of course, that the ship *would* reach the port.

The intense rain kept visibility limited, not that there had ever been much to see either aboard ship or among the waves beyond. Nevertheless, Norrec had to continually blink away moisture just to see a few yards ahead of him. Never had the cabin seemed so far away as it did this moment. The heaviness of the armor did not help, either, the metal plate seeming twice its normal weight. Still, at least Norrec did not have to worry about rust settling in; the enchantments cast by Bartuc had clearly kept the suit as new as the day the demon master had first donned it.

Not for the first time, Norrec stumbled. Cursing the weather, he straightened, then wiped his eyes clear again so that he could see just how far away the door to his quarters remained.

A murky figure stared back at him from the aft section of the walkway.

"Casco?" he called out, realizing only afterward that the captain could not have possibly rushed all the way to the stern, not with his bad leg. More to the point, this figure stood taller than the mariner and wore a broad-shouldered cloak reminiscent of a Vizjerei sorcerer—

Reminiscent of *Fauztin's* cloak.

He took a step forward, trying to see better. The figure seemed half mist and Norrec wondered if what stood before him could be only the result of his own tortured, weary mind.

"Fauztin? Fauztin?"

The shadow did not answer.

Norrec pushed another step forward—and the hair on the back of his neck suddenly stiffened.

He whirled around.

A second, somewhat shorter figure near the bow drifted in and out of sight, his wiry form hinting of an acrobat or, more likely, a thief. What looked to be a travel cloak fluttered in the wind, enshrouding and obscuring most of the second figure's detail, but Norrec imagined a dead, still-grinning face, the head cocked slightly to the side because the neck had been broken.

"*Sadun* . . ." he blurted.

His hands suddenly tingled. Norrec glanced down, barely catching a slight red aura about them.

A bolt of lightning struck so near that it lit up the entire ship—so near, in fact, that the stunned fighter almost swore that it touched the *Hawksfire* yet did not damage it in any way. For a moment, the blinding brilliance surrounded Norrec, making him even briefly forget the two specters.

His eyesight finally returned to normal. Blinking, Norrec glanced toward both the bow and stern and saw no sign whatsoever of either of the dire shades.

"Sadun! Tryst!" the frantic fighter shouted. Turning back to the stern, he yelled, "Fauztin!"

Only the storm answered him, rumbling with renewed fury. Unwilling to give up yet, Norrec headed back toward the bow, shouting Sadun's name over and over. He made his way across the open deck, scanning every direction. Why he desired to confront either of his two dead comrades, even Norrec Vizharan could not actually say. To try to apologize? To explain? How could he do that when, even knowing that it had been the armor that had claimed their lives, the former mercenary still blamed himself for not having heeded Fauztin a few precious seconds earlier. Had he done so, he would not be where he was now.

Had he done so, neither of his friends would be dead.

"Tryst! Damn you! If you're real—if you're there—come to me! I'm sorry! I'm sorry!"

A hand fell upon his shoulder.

"Who you call?" demanded Casco. "What you call now?"

Even in the darkness and the rain, Norrec could see the fear rising in the captain's watery eyes. To Casco, either his passenger had gone completely mad or, more likely, Norrec planned to summon yet new demons. Neither choice obviously thrilled the mariner.

"No one . . . nothing!"

"No more demons?"

"No more. None." He pushed past Captain Casco, wanting nothing more than rest, but no longer interested in his cabin. Looking back at the perplexed and frustrated sailor, Norrec asked, "Are there bunks for the crew below?"

Casco nodded glumly. Likely he slept in a cabin near those bunks and did not like the direction of the question. Bad enough he had to share the ship with a summoner of hellish creatures, but now that same demon master planned to sleep nearby. No doubt Casco expected various monsters to go wandering around below deck if that happened . . .

"I'll sleep in one of them." Not caring how the captain surely felt, Norrec headed below deck. Perhaps the battle against the demonic behemoth had taken too much out of him, resurrecting his guilt over the deaths of his comrades. Perhaps he had imagined both of them. That seemed so very likely, just as it seemed likely that he had imagined Fauztin on the dock in Gea Kul. The mutilated bodies of his two friends still lay in the tomb, there to be found by the next eager treasure hunters.

Yet, as he shook off the rain and headed in search of the bunks, a stray thought disturbed him. Norrec stared at his gloved hands, flexed the fingers that, for the moment, obeyed his will. If he had imagined it all, if the shades of Fauztin and Sadun Tryst had not confronted him out on deck, why had the gauntlets glowed, even if only for a moment?

*   *   *

In the dead of night, the army of General Augustus Malevolyn went on the move, entering the vast, terrible desert of Aranoch. Many of the men did not look forward to this march, but they had been given an order and knew no other course of action but to obey. That some of them would surely perish before they reached their destination—assumed to be the lush prize of Lut Gholein—did not deter them in the least. Each hoped that he would be one of the fortunate survivors, one of those who would lay claim to some portion of the wealth of the port kingdom.

At the head of the army rode the general himself, the helmet of Bartuc worn proudly. A faint sphere of light conjured by Galeona floated just ahead of him, marking the path for his steed. That it might also identify him as the most desired target by ambushers did not bother Malevolyn in the least. Clad in the ancient helmet and his own spell-enshrouded armor, the general sought to show the ranks that he feared nothing and that nothing could defeat him.

Galeona traveled beside her lover, outwardly indifferent to everything, but all the while quietly utilizing her sorcery in order to detect any possible threat to the column. Behind the witch came a covered wagon loaded with Malevolyn's folded tent, the various personal items from within it, and—seeming almost as an afterthought—Galeona's wooden chest.

"At last . . . the armor will soon be within my grasp," the general murmured, staring ahead into the darkness. "I can already sense its nearness! With it, I shall be complete! With it, I shall command a host of demons!"

Galeona considered, then dared ask, "Can you be certain that it'll do all this for you, my general? True, the helmet has enchantments and the armor is said to be even more bespelled, but so far the helmet has left us all baffled! What if the armor acts much the same? I pray not, but the secrets of Bartuc may demand more of us than we're able to—"

"No!" He snapped at her with such vehemence that his guards, situated just behind him, immediately drew their swords, perhaps thinking that the sorceress had sought to betray their leader. Augustus Malevolyn signaled them to resheathe their weapons, then glared at Galeona. "It will not be so, my dear! I have seen the glorious visions brought forth by the helmet, the shade of Bartuc surely calling to me to add to his victories! I have seen in each of those visions the power of the armor and helm combined! The spirit of the bloody warlord lives on in the suit, and it is his desire that I become the mortal bearer of his standard!" He waved a hand at the desert. "Why else does the fool who wears it now come to me? He does so because it is destined! I will be Bartuc's successor, I tell you!"

The witch cringed, taken aback by his outburst. "As you say, my general."

Malevolyn abruptly calmed, once more a self-satisfied smile across his face. "As I say. And after that, yes, Lut Gholein will be mine to take. *This* time, I shall not fail."

Galeona had ridden with the commander from Westmarch for some time, likely knew him better than any under his command. Yet, in all that time, the only mention of Lut Gholein had been as an eventual target, one that Malevolyn had dreamed of conquering. She had never heard him speak of it as a past defeat. "You've been there . . . before?"

With something akin to devotion, he gently adjusted the helmet, turning away from her and preventing the sphere from illuminating what of his expression the armor did not already hide. "Yes . . . and if not for my brother . . . it would have been mine for the taking . . . but this time . . . this time, *Viz-jun will fall!*"

"*Viz-jun?*" she blurted, her tone incredulous.

Fortunately, General Malevolyn paid her no mind, attention concentrated on the darkened, shifting sands. Galeona did not repeat the name again, preferring to immediately drop, if not forget, the subject. Perhaps it had been a slip of the tongue, just as something else he had just said had to have been an innocent mistake. After all, the general had much on his mind, so very much . . .

She knew that he had never been to the fabled Kehjistani temple-city, had never yet been across the sea to that land. In addition, Augustus Malevolyn had been an *only* child—and an unwanted bastard at that.

Yet . . . someone else Galeona knew of had not only been to fabled Viz-jun, but had sought to conquer it, to destroy it, only to be thwarted in the end by his own brother.

Bartuc.

With a surreptitious glance, the witch studied the helmet, trying to divine its intentions. The visions that the western commander had experienced had clearly been for his benefit alone; even when she had secretly tried the artifact on, no such images had been shown her. Yet, it appeared that the more Augustus wore it, the more he had trouble differentiating between his own life and that of the monstrous warlord.

Did the helmet perform some sort of enchantment each time these incidents happened? Galeona casually touched a black-jeweled ring on one of the fingers of her left hand, turning the gem in the direction of her lover's head. She mouthed two forbidden words, afterward cautiously glancing to see if the general had noticed her lips moving.

He had not, nor did he now notice the invisible tendrils extending from that ring, tendrils that reached out to touch the helmet in various places. Only Galeona knew that they were there, seeking, probing, trying to detect whatever forces permeated the ancient armor.

Perhaps if she finally discovered how they affected the general, the witch could take the first step toward using those powerful enchantments for her own goals. Even some slight bit of new knowledge would go far toward extending her own abilities—

A flash of crimson light flared from the helmet, illuminating for a stunned Galeona each of the magical tendrils rising from her ring. A surge of power coursed toward her with lightning speed, eating away at the tendrils and converging on her finger. Fearing for herself, the sorceress reached to pull the ring free.

Only mortal, she moved too slow. The streams of crimson light devoured the last of the tendrils, then came together at the black jewel itself.

The gemstone sizzled, turned molten in less than the blink of an eye. The liquefied stone dripped over her finger, burning at her skin, searing her flesh . . .

Galeona managed to bite back a scream, transforming her reaction to the intense pain into a barely audible gasp.

"Did you say something, my dear?" General Malevolyn casually asked, his eyes never leaving the landscape.

She managed to keep her voice calm and assured despite her suffering. "No, Augustus. Just a slight cough . . . a bit of desert sand in my throat."

"Yes, that's a risk here. Perhaps you should cover it with a veil." He said no more, either focused on his duties as commander or lost once more in Bartuc's past.

Galeona carefully looked around. No one had noticed the astounding display of powerful energies in conflict. Only she, with her magical senses, had been witness to both her failure and her punishment.

Giving silent thanks for that bit of fortune at least, she cautiously investigated the damage. The ring had turned to slag, the rare and resilient gem a black, burning stain on her finger. The band she finally managed to remove, but the melted jewel left a permanent and painful ebony blot on her otherwise unmarred hand.

The injury meant little to her overall. She had endured much worse for her craft. No, what bothered Galeona more concerned the helmet's violent reaction to her probing. None of her spells in the past had caused it to respond with such vehemence. It almost seemed as if something within the armor had awakened, something with distinct intentions of its own.

It had always been her assumption that the ancient warlord had cast numerous enchantments of tremendous power on his armor, the better to aid him in battle. Such precautions would have made perfect sense. Yet, what if she had only guessed a part of it? What if even those who had slain Bartuc had not realized the full extent of his mastery of magicks demonic?

Did enchantments alone possess the helm and plate—or had Galeona discovered more?

Did Bartuc himself seek to return from the dead?

✝EП

The *King's Shield* entered the storm late into its fifth day out of Gea Kul. Kara had hoped that the foul weather would break up before they confronted it, but, in truth, those who manned the ship had only themselves to blame for this new situation. Captain Jeronnan commanded an excellent crew, one that understood well the idiosyncrasies of the turbulent sea. The necromancer doubted that any other vessel could have plied the waters as efficiently and with such remarkable speed as this one, which, unfortunately, had virtually guaranteed that the *King's Shield* would outrace even this swiftly moving tempest.

The unfortunate Kalkos had been given a formal burial at sea, Kara adding to the ceremony with a few words of respect based on the funeral traditions of her people. In her eyes, Kalkos had only transcended to another plane, where, in his new existence he and those before him would work to maintain the balance of all things. However, she still felt some guilt, some misgivings, about the prayer she had said, for the pale enchantress had not forgotten her own deep desire to live when she had found herself entombed in the tree. Kara's only way so far to reconcile that with her general beliefs had been to decide that, if she had perished, it would not only have upset the balance, but it would also have left no one who could have tracked down the missing armor. That could not be allowed to happen.

Almost immediately upon entering the storm-tossed waters, Kara Nightshadow took it upon herself to spend much of her time watching the wild seas from the bow. Jeronnan questioned the sanity of this, but she refused all suggestions that she return to the safety of her cabin. He thought that she watched for the *Hawksfire*—in part the truth—but what actually concerned her more had been the possibility that the demons of Kalkos's memories might possibly return, especially the aquatic leviathan that had slain the majority of the other vessel's crew in such a horrible manner. Having still not mentioned its existence to the captain, Kara felt honor-bound to at least keep watch. She also believed that, of all of them, she had the best chance of doing something to either scare it off or possibly distract it while the *King's Shield* attempted to escape.

Even though caught between the harsh rain and the mad sea, Jeronnan's crew remained determined and—to her—quite polite. For a time, Kara had feared that the stories she had always heard about sailors would mean her having to deflect unwanted attention. However, although several of the men clearly admired her—and that despite now knowing her true calling—they did not press. In fact, only Mister Drayko had attempted anything resembling an advance, and he had done so in so formal and cautious a manner that it had almost been as if one of her own had made entreaties. She had kindly and quietly rejected his advance, but had found his attention flattering.

Captain Jeronnan himself had long ago erased any lingering question as to whether he had designs on his passenger. When he did not treat Kara like an aristocratic client, he acted as if at some point she had been adopted into his house. Now and then the former naval officer fussed over her just as Kara suspected he had fussed over Terania. She allowed him to do that, not only because it kept him in good spirits, but because the necromancer also found it made her feel some comfort as well. Growing up, she had not been without parental love, but once her adult training had begun, the faithful of Rathma were expected to put such emotions aside for the better good of learning how best to protect the balance of the world. The balance had to come before all else, even family.

The *King's Shield* leapt up a particularly high wave, crashing down into the water a second or two later. Kara held the rail tight, trying to see past the rain and mist. Although day had begun to give way to night, her eyes, more accustomed to seeing in the dark, let her better view what might lay ahead than any of the more experienced mariners. By now they had surely reached—even *passed*—the waters in which Kalkos and his comrades had perished and that meant that at any moment the entire vessel might be under attack by forces unnatural.

"Lady Kara!" Drayko called from behind her. "It's getting worse! You should really get below!"

"I am fine." Although certainly no highborn lady, the dark mage could not get the men to simply call her by her name. That had been the fault of Jeronnan, who had, on first introducing her to the crew, emphasized the title and, most important, his respect for her. What served their captain well served the crew.

"But the storm—!"

"Thank you for your concern, Mister Drayko."

He already knew better than to argue with her. "Just be careful, my lady!"

As he battled his way back, Kara decided that the consideration she had received from Jeronnan and his men would certainly spoil her for Lut Gholein. There, she knew, she would face the prejudices far more common toward her kind. Necromancers dealt with death and most folk did not like to be reminded of their mortality nor the fact that their spirits could perhaps be affected by those like her afterward.

Despite her refusal to Drayko, the necromancer soon decided that she could not stay at the bow much longer. The coming night, combined with the horrific weather, reduced visibility with each passing second. It was quickly coming to the point where even she would be of no use. Yet, she remained determined to stand her post as long as humanly possible.

Up and down the waves flowed, their continual rise and fall in some ways a monotonous sight despite the spectacle of such raw power at work. Once or twice, she had spotted what she believed some sea creature and much earlier a piece of rotting wood had momentarily broken the cycle, but, other than that, Kara had little to show for her efforts. Of course, that also meant that there had been no sign of the demons, something for which the enchantress could feel grateful.

She wiped the spray and rain from her eyes, turning her gaze one last time to the port side of the *King's Shield*. More waves, more froth, more—

An arm?

Shifting her position, Kara peered into the dark waters, every sense alert.

There! The arm and part of the upper body of a man. She could make out no detail—but swore she saw the waterlogged limb rise of its own accord.

Kara had no quick spell for such a situation and so turned instead back to the deck . . . and the dwindling figure of Jeronnan's second. "Mister Drayko! A man in the sea!"

Fortunately, he heard her immediately. Calling to three other men, Drayko rushed up to where the necromancer stood. "Show me where!"

"Look! Can you see him?"

He studied the mad waters, then nodded grimly. "A head and an arm, and I think it might be moving!" Drayko shouted to the helmsman to bring the ship about, then, in a much more subdued voice, told her, "It's unlikely that we'll be able to save him at this point, but we'll try."

She did not bother to reply, more aware of the odds than even he could be. If the nature of the balance dictated the man's survival, he would be rescued. If not, then, like Kalkos, his soul would go on to the next plane of existence, there to fulfill another role for the balance, as taught in the teachings of Rathma.

Of course, that same balance also dictated that where there remained hope of life, those that could had to struggle to save it. Rathma taught pragmatism, not coldheartedness.

The storm made for rough going, but despite that the *King's Shield* still managed to close in on the feebly struggling form. Unfortunately, the coming of night made the task more and more difficult as the vague figure vanished and reappeared with every new wave.

By this time, Captain Jeronnan had joined his crew, taking over control of the situation. To Kara's surprise, he commanded two sailors to bring bows, sailors Drayko informed her were exceptionally skilled with the weapons.

"Does he mean them to end the man's suffering?" she asked, startled by this side of the former officer. Kara had at least expected him to try to save the unfortunate mariner.

"Just watch, my lady."

Her eyes narrowed in belated understanding as the archers quickly tied rope to their shafts. Rather than trying to simply toss a line to the man in the water, they hoped to use the shafts to better get the ropes within reach. Even with the storm, they could get more precision from using the bows than relying on hands only. A risky venture still, but one with more chance of success.

"Hurry, blast you!" Jeronnan roared.

The two men fired. One arrow soared far past its target, but the second came within a short distance of the rolling form.

"Grab hold!" Drayko shouted. "Grab hold!"

The figure made no move toward the line. Taking a terrible risk, the necromancer leaned over the rail, trying to will the floating rope closer. Perhaps if it actually touched him, he would react. Kara knew elders who could move objects simply by thinking of them, but, as with so much else, her studies in that respect had not yet reached such a point. She could only hope that her desperation combined with what abilities she had already learned might prove enough at this dire moment.

Whether due to her desperate thoughts or merely the whims of the sea, the line came within inches of the man's arm.

"Grab it!" the captain encouraged.

Suddenly, the body jerked. A wave washed over it and, for a few nerve-wracking seconds, the hapless figure vanished. Kara sighted it first, now several yards from either line.

"Damn!" Drayko pounded his fist on the rail. "Either he's dead or—"

The floating form jerked again, almost going under.

The first officer swore. "That's not the waves doing that!"

In growing dread Kara and the crew watched as the body bobbed twice more, then went under again.

This time, it did not reappear.

"The sharks've gotten 'im," one of the sailors finally muttered.

Captain Jeronnan agreed. "Draw in the lines, lads. You did what you could. Odds were he was already dead, anyway, and we've got ourselves to worry about more, eh?"

The mood dampened by the futility of their efforts, the

crew slowly returned to their tasks. Mister Drayko stayed behind for a moment with Kara, who still sought some last glimpse of the lost mariner.

"The sea claims its own," he whispered. "We try to learn to live with it."

"We see it as part of an overall balance," she returned. "but the loss of a life that might have been saved is still to be mourned."

"You'd best come away from there, my lady."

Touching the back of his hand very briefly, Kara replied, "Thank you for your concern, but I wish to remain for a moment. I will be all right."

With reluctance, he left her once again. Alone, the necromancer reached into her cloak and removed from around her throat a small, red icon shaped in the likeness of a fearsome dragon with blazing eyes and savage teeth. The followers of Rathma believed that the world sat upon the back of the great dragon Trag'Oul, who acted as a fulcrum and, as such, helped maintain the celestial balance. All necromancers gave their full respect to the fiery leviathan.

Under her breath, Kara prayed that Trag'Oul would see the unknown man to the next plane of existence. She had prayed the same for the sailor Kalkos, although none of the *King's Shield*'s crew had noticed. Outsiders did not readily comprehend the place of Trag'Oul in the world.

Satisfied that she could do no more, the slim, silver-eyed woman returned to her cabin below deck. Despite her dedication to her task, Kara entered the room with much relief. Standing lookout for demons, then watching the rescue attempt fail, had drained her of much of her strength. During the enchantress's self-imposed task, she had taken only minimal breaks for her meals and had, in truth, been longer on her feet than any of the men. Now all Kara wanted to do was sleep and sleep and sleep some more.

The cabin offered to her by Hanos Jeronnan had been originally set aside for his daughter and so the more austere Kara had to deal with ladylike frills and too-soft pillows. Unlike the crew, she also had a true bed, one secured very well to the floor in order to prevent it from sliding across the room. To further ensure her safety while she slept, the bed also had short, padded rails on each side to keep the occupant from rolling off onto the hard, wooden floor during the worst storms. Kara had already found herself grateful more than once for those rails and especially appreciated them now, so exhausted did she feel. The necromancer doubted that tonight she would have had the strength to hold on by herself.

Throwing off the wet cloak, Kara sat on the bottom edge of the bed, trying to collect her thoughts. Despite the cloak, her garments, too, had been thoroughly soaked, from her jet-black blouse down to her leather pants and boots. The dampness of the blouse made it cling tight, chilling her further. Jeronnan had been dismayed that the necromancer had not brought any other garments with her and had insisted before the voyage on locating at least one more set of clothes. Kara had only relented when he had agreed that they would resemble her own black garments as much as possible. The teachings of Rathma did not include interest in the latest fashions; the necromancer sought only functional, durable clothing.

Grateful now that she had given in even that much, Kara changed quickly into the second set, hanging the others to dry. She had performed the exact same ritual each night of the voyage, doing what she could to keep everything clean. Because one dealt with blood and death did not meant that cleanliness no longer became an option.

For once, the young woman found the so soft bed a very welcome thing. The captain would have been dismayed had he known she slept fully clothed, but on a journey of this nature, Kara could take no chances. If the demons of Kalkos's memories did materialize, she had to be ready for them immediately. Her only compromise to comfort concerned her boots, which, out of respect for Jeronnan and his daughter, she left by the bottom of the bed.

Lantern doused, Kara Nightshadow sank deep into the bed. The wild waves actually worked to more quickly send her drifting off to sleep, rocking the weary mage back and forth, as if in a cradle. The troubles of the world began to recede . . .

Until a faint blue light seeped through her eyelids, pulling her back from slumber.

At first she thought it a figment of some peripheral dream, but then the gradual realization that Kara still sensed it through closed eyes even while awake set every nerve on edge. The dark mage tensed—then spun about in the bed, rising to a kneeling position with her hands pointed toward the source of the surreal illumination.

Situated in a cabin below the waterline, Kara at first imagined that somehow the sea had finally broken through the hull. However, as the last vestiges of sleep faded from her mind, she saw instead something far more unsettling. The blue light from her dreams not only existed, but it now covered a fair portion of the side of her cabin. It had a hazy look to it, almost as if the wall had turned to mist, and pulsated continually. Kara felt her entire body tingle . . .

Through the magical haze stepped not one but *two* water-soaked figures.

She opened her mouth, whether to cast a spell or call out for help, even Kara could not be completely certain. In either case, her voice—and her body as a whole, in fact—failed her. The necromancer did not understand why until one of the dark figures held up a familiar ivory dagger, a dagger that blazed an unsettling blue each time Kara even thought of attempting anything.

The dripping and quite *dead* figure of the Vizjerei sorcerer Fauztin—the gaping hole where his throat had once been only partially obscured by the collar of his cloak—grimly stared at her, his unblinking eyes silently warning Kara of the foolishness of any defiance.

Next to him, his grinning companion shook off some of the seawater. Behind them the blue light faded away, the revenants' magical portal vanishing with it.

The smaller of the two undead took a step toward her, performing a mocking bow. As he did, Kara realized that it had been *his* body she and the crew had seen; *he* had been the helpless mariner. Fauztin and his friend had tricked her and the crew in order to arrange this monstrous visitation.

The ghoul's smile widened, yellow teeth and rotting gums now adding to the initial image of peeling skin and the wet, putrefying flesh beneath. "So . . . very good . . . to see you . . . again . . . necromancer . . ."

If the storm did not end by the time the *Hawksfire* at last reached the harbor of Lut Gholein, then at least it finally eased to something approaching tolerable. For that, Norrec Vizharan gave thanks, just as he gave thanks that the ship had arrived just prior to sunrise, when most of the kingdom would still be asleep and, therefore, would not so much notice the sinister peculiarities of the dark vessel.

The moment the *Hawksfire* docked, the spell cast by the armor ceased, leaving Captain Casco and Norrec to do the best they could to finish matters. The ship drew the stares of those few about, but, fortunately, it seemed that no one had noticed lines adjusting themselves nor sails lowering without physical aid.

When finally the gangplank had been lowered, Casco

made clear with his expression if not words that the time had come for his passenger to disembark—and, hopefully, never return. Norrec reached out a hand in an attempt to make some sort of peace with the skeletal, foreign mariner, but Casco glanced down at the gauntlet with his good eye, then set that same eye unblinking on the soldier's own gaze. After a few seconds of unease, Norrec lowered the hand and quickly walked down the gangplank.

However, a few yards from the *Hawksfire,* he could not help but look back one last time—and therefore saw the captain still watching him closely. For several seconds, the two stared at one another, then Casco slowly raised one hand Norrec's way.

The veteran fighter nodded in return. Seemingly satisfied by this minor exchange, Casco lowered his hand and turned away, now seeming intent only on inspection of his badly damaged vessel.

Norrec had barely taken a step when someone called down to him from another direction.

"The *Hawksfire* tricks fate again," an elderly looking sea captain with almond-shaped eyes, a white tuft of beard, and weathered features remarked from the deck of his own vessel. Despite the early hour and the foul weather, he greeted Norrec with a cheerful smile. "But looks like barely, this time! Rode along with this storm, did ye?"

The soldier only nodded.

"Word to the wise; ye've been fortunate! Not every man that's sailed her has finished the voyage! She's bad luck, especially to her captain!"

More so than ever, thought Norrec, although he dared not tell the other captain. He nodded again, then tried to move on, but the elderly mariner called out once more.

"Here now! After a trip like that, ye've no doubt the need for a tavern! Best one's *Atma*'s! The good lady her-

self still runs it, even what with her husband gone now!
Tell 'em Captain Meshif said to treat ye well!"

"Thank you," Norrec muttered back, hoping that the
short answer would satisfy the much-too-cheerful man.
He wanted to be away from the docks as quickly as possible, still fearful that someone would not only recognize
something amiss with the arrival of the *Hawksfire* but also
link Norrec to it.

Cloak drawn about him, the weary veteran hurried on,
after several anxious minutes at last leaving ships and
warehouses behind and entering the true, fabled Lut
Gholein. He had heard tales about the kingdom often
over the years, but had never visited it before. Sadun
Tryst had said of it that anything a man could buy he
could find here . . . and in great quantities. Ships came
from all over the world, bringing in goods both legal and
not. Lut Gholein represented the most open of markets,
although those who ruled made certain that order was
still constantly maintained.

At no time did the entire city sleep; according to
Sadun, one only had to look long enough and one would
find a place willing to let those seeking exotic entertainments spend their coin no matter what the hour. Of
course, those who could not keep their entertainments
confined to the facilities provided still risked running
afoul of the watchful eye of the Guard, who served the
cause of the sultan with great fervor. Tryst himself had
told some quite lurid tales of Lut Gholein's dungeons . . .

Despite all that had happened to him since the tomb,
Norrec's interest stirred almost immediately as he
walked through the streets. All around him, gaily-
decorated buildings of mortar and stone rose tall, the
banners of the sultan atop each. Along the astonishingly
clean, cobblestone streets that stretched in every direction, the first wagons of the day began to emerge. As if
sprouting from the very shadows, quick-moving figures

in flowing robes began opening tents and doors in preparation for new business. Some of the wagons paused at these tents, suppliers delivering new goods to the vendors.

The storm had dwindled now to a few dark, rumbling clouds, and with its continued lessening, Norrec's mood lightened yet more. So far, the armor had not demanded anything more of him. Perhaps he could, for a time at least, seek his own path. In a place as vast as Lut Gholein, surely there had to be sorcerers of some repute, sorcerers who could help free him of this curse. Under the pretext of admiring the sights—an easy enough thing to do— Norrec would try to keep his eye out for any sign of possible help.

Within moments of the dawn, the streets filled with people of all shapes, sizes, and races. Travelers from as far away as Ensteig and Khanduras walked among dark-clad visitors from Kehjistan and beyond. In fact, there seemed more outsiders than locals. The varied crowd worked in Norrec's favor, enabling him to fit in without much suspicion. Even the armor did not overly mark him, for other figures clad akin to him appeared everywhere. Some of them had clearly disembarked from ships not all that long ago, while others, especially those with the turbaned helms and elegant silver capes fluttering behind their blue-gray breastplates, obviously served the masters of this fair kingdom.

Overall the architecture remained consistent, with the lower floors of buildings a smooth, rectangular shape while quite often the tops tended toward small towers resembling minarets. A peculiar design, especially to one born and raised among the high, turreted castles of lords and the lowly, thatched domiciles of the peasantry, but one with an exotic quality that caused Norrec to marvel over it again and again. No two buildings were exactly the same, either, some being broader, even squat, while others appeared to be making up for the lack of space on the ground by stretching thinner and higher.

A horn sounded and the street around Norrec suddenly emptied of people. Following suit, he narrowly missed being run over by a mounted patrol clad in the same turbaned helms and breastplates he had seen earlier. A lively, active city Lut Gholein might be, but, as Sadun had said, it also looked to be well policed. That made it all the more curious that no one had stopped Norrec on the docks for at least some questioning. Most major seaports kept security strong day and night, but he had seen no one. Despite Lut Gholein's open reputation, it puzzled him.

Hunger and thirst slowly crept up on him as he wandered along. He had eaten some food aboard the *Hawksfire*, but his interest in reaching the docks had kept him from taking his fill. Besides, it had been Norrec's secret hope to find something in the city rather than stomach yet another portion of Casco's unsettling concoctions.

The armor had provided funds before and so with some confidence the veteran looked around. Several taverns and inns of various demeanor dotted the area, but one in particular instantly caught Norrec's eye.

Best one's Atma's! Tell 'em Captain Meshif said to treat ye well! That same tavern stood but a few yards from the soldier, the wooden sign with its bleary-orbed mascot hanging directly over the entrance. A hardy, weathered place, but one still honest enough in looks for him to risk without worry. With as much determination as he could still muster, Norrec headed toward it, hoping against hope that the armor would not suddenly turn him elsewhere.

He entered in peace and of his own free will, something which, along with his new surroundings, raised Norrec's hopes further. Despite the early hour, *Atma*'s had a good business going, most of its customers seamen.

but a few merchants, tourists, and military figures partaking of its offerings as well. Not wanting to draw too much attention to himself, Norrec chose a booth in one corner and sat down.

A slip of a girl, likely too young to be working in any such establishment, came up to take his order. Norrec's nostrils had already pinpointed something cooking in the back and so he risked ordering whatever it might be, plus a mug of ale to rinse it down. The girl curtsied, then hurried off, giving him the opportunity to look around.

He had spent far too much of his life in taverns and inns, but at least this one did not look as if the cooks would be broiling whatever they could catch in their floor traps. The servers kept the tables and floors relatively clean of refuse and none of the customers had so far choked on either their meals or drinks. Overall, *Atma*'s verified his opinion of Lut Gholein as a kingdom in the midst of tremendous prosperity, where everyone appeared to be benefiting, even the lower castes.

The girl returned with his food, which actually looked as good as it smelled. She smiled at him, asking for what seemed to him reasonable coin. Norrec eyed his gloved hand, waiting.

Nothing happened. The gauntlet did not slam down on the table, leaving the proper amount. Norrec tried not to show his sudden anxiety. Had the armor let him trap himself? If he could not pay, at the very least they would throw him out. He glanced toward the door, where two brawny enforcers who had not bothered to look at him on his way in now seemed more than interested in his discussion with the serving girl.

She repeated the amount, this time a less friendly expression on her face. Norrec glared at the glove, thinking, *Come on, damn you! All I want is a good meal! You can do that, can't you?*

Still nothing.

"Is there something wrong?" the girl asked, her expression indicating that she thought she already knew the answer.

Norrec did not reply, closing and opening his hand in the fading hope that some coins would magically appear.

With one glance toward the two enforcers, the young server began to back away. "Excuse me, sir, I . . . I've other tables . . ."

The soldier looked past her, where the muscular pair had begun to move in his direction. The girl's actions had been a clear signal for them to do their work.

He rose, planting his hands on the table. "Wait! It's not what you—"

Under his palm, he heard the tinkle of coins as they struck the table.

She heard them, too, and the smile suddenly returned. Norrec sat back down, indicating the tiny pile now before him. "I'm sorry for the confusion. I've not been to Lut Gholein before and had to think whether I had the right amount. Is this enough?"

Her expression told him all he needed to really know. "Aye, sir! Enough and much more!"

Over her shoulder, he saw the burly pair hesitate. The larger of the duo tapped his companion on the arm and the two men returned to their posts. "Take what you need for food and drink," he told the girl, feeling much relieved. After she had done that, Norrec added, "And the largest coin left for yourself."

"Thank you, sir, thank you!"

She nearly floated back to the counter, from the looks of things having received the largest tip of her life from him. The sight cheered Norrec briefly. At least some little good had come of the cursed armor.

He stared at the gauntlets, well aware of what had just happened. The suit had let him understand without words that *it* and not he controlled the entire situation.

Norrec lived his life through *its* sufferance. To think otherwise was to play the fool.

Regardless of the reality of his dilemma, Norrec managed to enjoy his meal. Compared to Captain Casco's fare, it tasted of Heaven. Thinking of that mystical realm, the soldier pondered his next move. The armor kept a close rein on him, but surely there had to be a way to get past its guard. In a realm as vibrant as Lut Gholein, not only sorcerers but priests had to be found in abundance. Even if the former could do nothing for Norrec, then perhaps a servant of Heaven might. Surely a priest had links to forces far more powerful than the enchanted suit.

But how to speak with one? Norrec wondered if the armor could withstand being on holy ground. Could it be so simple as walking past a church and then throwing himself onto its steps? Would he be able to do even that much?

For a desperate man, it seemed worth the try. The armor needed him alive and relatively well; that alone might give him just enough of an opportunity. At the very least, Norrec had to try for the sake of not only his life, but his soul, too.

He finished his meal, then quickly downed what remained of the ale. During that time, the serving girl came back more than once to see if he needed anything, a clear sign that he had been very generous in his tipping. Norrec gave her one of the smaller coins remaining to him, which caused her smile to somehow grow even wider than before, then he casually asked her about some of the sights of the city.

"There's the arena, of course," the girl, Miram, replied quickly, no doubt having been asked this question more than once by newcomers. "And the palace, too! You must see the palace!" Her eyes took on a dreaming look. "Jerhyn, the sultan, lives there . . ."

This Jerhyn evidently had to be a handsome and fairly

young man judging from Miram's rapt expression. While the sultan's palace surely had to be an intriguing sight, it had not been what he had been searching for. "And besides that?"

"There's also the Aragos Theater near the square with the Cathedral of Tomas the Repentant across from it, but the Zakarum priests only allow visitors at midday and the theater is being repaired. Oh! There's the races on the far north side of the city, horses and dogs—"

Norrec ceased listening, the information he had needed now his. If holy ground or Heaven had any power over the demonic legacy of Bartuc, then this cathedral offered the best hope. The Zakarum Church represented the most powerful order on either side of the Twin Seas.

"—and some old folk and scholars like the ruins of the Vizjerei temple outside the city walls, though there's not much to see any more after the Great Sandstorm . . ."

"Thank you, Miram. That's good enough." He prepared to leave, already trying to think of some roundabout method by which to approach the vicinity of the Zakarum site.

Four figures in the now familiar garb of Lut Gholein's Guard stepped into *Atma's*, but their interest in the tavern had nothing to do with drink. Instead, they looked directly at Norrec, their countenances darkening. He could almost swear that they knew exactly who he was.

With military precision that Norrec would have at other times admired, the foursome spread out, eliminating any hope of bypassing them on the way to the front entrance. Although they had not yet drawn their long, curved swords, each guard kept a hand near the hilt. One wrong action by Norrec and all four blades would come flying out, ready to cut him down.

Pretending to be not at all concerned, the wary fighter turned back to the serving girl, asking, "There's a friend I need to meet in a place located in the street behind this tavern. Do you have another exit in the back?"

"There's one that way." She started to point, but he gently took her hand, dropping another coin in it.

"Thank you, Miram." Gently pushing past her, Norrec moved as if heading toward the counter for one last drink. The four guards hesitated.

Halfway to the counter, he veered toward the back doorway.

Although he could not see them now, Norrec felt certain that the men knew his intentions. He picked up his pace, hoping to reach the exit as quickly as possible. Once out, he could try to lose himself among the growing throngs.

Norrec pushed the door wide, immediately darting through—

—and came to an abrupt halt as rough, strong hands seized him by both arms, holding him fast.

"Resist and it will go the worse for you, westerner!" snapped a swarthy guard with gold tabs on his cloak. He peered past Norrec, saying, "You have done your work well! This is the one! We will take it from here!"

The four who had pursued Norrec from inside stepped past the prisoner, pausing only to salute the officer in charge before wandering off. Norrec grimaced, realizing that he had walked into the most basic of traps.

He had no idea as to the intentions of his captors, but at the moment, they interested him far less than the question as to why Bartuc's armor had not reacted. Surely this situation called for something from it, but so far it seemed unwilling to try to free its host. Why?

"Pay attention, westerner!" the officer came close to slapping Norrec, but finally lowered his hand. "Come peacefully and you will not be mistreated! Resist . . ." The man's hand now slipped to the hilt of his curved sword, his meaning quite clear.

Norrec nodded his understanding. If the armor chose not to resist, he certainly had no intention of trying to fight himself free of this armed patrol.

His captors formed a square of sorts, with their leader in front and Norrec, of course, in the middle. The party headed down the street, away from the larger crowds. Several curious folk watched the procession, but no one seemed at all sympathetic to the foreigner's troubles. Likely they figured that there were always more outsiders, so what difference the loss of one?

No one had as of yet explained exactly for what reason Norrec had been arrested, but he had to assume it had something to do with the *Hawksfire's* arrival. Perhaps he had been wrong when he had thought that no watch had been set at the port. Perhaps Lut Gholein kept a more wary eye on those who arrived by ship than appearances had suggested. It also remained possible that Captain Casco had, after all, reported the goings-on aboard his vessel and the one responsible for the loss of his crew.

The lead guard suddenly veered toward a narrow side street, the rest of the group following close behind. Norrec frowned, no longer thinking of Casco and the *Hawksfire*. His captors now journeyed through less-frequented, more disreputable-looking avenues into which even the brightest day would have had trouble shedding light. The soldier tensed, sensing something suddenly awry with the situation.

They journeyed a little farther, then turned into an alley nearly as dark as night. The band proceeded a few yards into it, then the guards came to an abrupt halt.

His captors stood at attention, seeming to barely even breathe. In fact, the four guards stood at attention with such stillness that Norrec could not help but think that they resembled nothing more than puppets whose master had ceased pulling their strings.

And as if to verify that notion, a portion of the shadows

separated from the rest, shaping itself into an elderly, wrinkled man with long, silver hair and beard and clad in an elegant, broad-shouldered robe clearly fashioned in the style worn by someone Norrec had known so very well . . . Fauztin. However, this figure, this Vizjerei, had not only lived for far longer than Norrec's unfortunate friend, but by being here evidenced quite well the fact that his abilities far outstripped those of the dead mage.

"Leave us . . ." he ordered the guards, his voice strong, commanding, despite his advanced years.

The officer and his men obediently turned, marching back the way they had come.

"They will recall nothing," the Vizjerei commented. "As the others who aided them will recall nothing . . just as I desire . . ." When Norrec attempted to speak, the silver-haired figure cut him off with but a singular glance. "And if you hope to live, westerner . . . you, *too*, will do as I desire . . . *exactly* as I desire."

ELEVEN

"Are you not feeling well, then, lass?" Captain Jeronnan asked. "You've come out of your cabin only to gather your meals, then returned there for the rest of the time."

Kara looked him directly in the eye. "I am well, captain. With the *King's Shield* nearing Lut Gholein, I must prepare for my journey from that point on. There is much for me to consider. I apologize if I appear unfriendly to you and your crew."

"Not unfriendly . . . just more distant." He sighed. "Well, if you need anything, just let me know."

She needed quite a lot, but nothing with which the good captain could help her. "Thank you . . . for everything."

The necromancer felt his eyes on her as she headed for her cabin. Jeronnan would likely have done anything he could for Kara regardless of the situation and she much appreciated that fact. Unfortunately, any aid he might have offered would not have at all helped the enchantress in her present predicament.

As she entered the cabin, Kara saw the two undead standing in the far corner, waiting with the proverbial patience of their kind. Fauztin held the gleaming dagger ready, the Vizjerei's spell upon it ensuring that the necromancer could do nothing against the pair. The yellowed eyes of the mage stared unblinking at her. Kara could never be certain what Fauztin thought, for his expression varied little.

Not so with Sadun Tryst. The other revenant continually smiled, as if he had some jest he wished to share. Kara also found herself constantly desiring to straighten his head, which ever leaned a little too far to one side or another.

The stench of death surrounded them, but so far as she could tell it had not pervaded any part of the ship beyond her cabin. As a necromancer, the foul smell bothered Kara less than most, but she still would have preferred to do without it. Her studies and her faith had ensured that Kara had dealt almost daily with the realm of the dead, but those encounters had ever been on her own terms. Never before had the tables been turned, that the *dead* made her come at their beck and call.

"The good captain . . . leaves you to . . . your self still . . . I hope," Tryst gasped.

"He is concerned for me; that is all."

The wiry ghoul chuckled, a sound like an animal choking on a bone. Perhaps when the man's neck had been broken, a part of the bone there had lodged in his wind pipe. It would explain the way he talked. Even though Sadun Tryst did not need to breathe, he needed air in order to speak.

Of course, with a gaping hole in his throat, Tryst's companion, the Vizjerei, would forever be silent.

"Let us hope . . . that his concern . . . remains distant . . . from this room."

Fauztin pointed to the edge of the bed, a wordless order the dark mage readily understood. Her food held tight in one hand, she perched there, awaiting whatever new command they had of her. So long as the Vizjerei held the dagger, his magic kept Kara Nightshadow in thrall.

Tryst's eyes blinked once, a conscious effort on the part of the corpse. Unlike Fauztin, he worked to pretend that some life remained within his decaying husk. As a mage, the gaunt Vizjerei no doubt saw the situation in more practical, realistic terms. The fighter, on the other hand, appeared to have been a man much in love with all the aspects of life. Behind the smile Kara suspected that this ungodly predicament enraged him more than it did his companion.

"Eat . . ."

Under their unwavering gazes she did. All the while, though, the necromancer rummaged through her memory, trying to recall some bit of knowledge she might use to free herself from all this. That they had not so far touched Kara, much less harmed her in any manner, did not assuage her concerns in the least. The revenants had one goal in mind—to reach their friend, this Norrec Vizharan. If, at some point, it seemed necessary to sacrifice her for the culmination of that goal, Kara felt certain that they would do so without regret.

Vizharan had been their partner, their comrade, and yet he had evidently brutally slain both, then taken off with the armor. Sadun Tryst had not exactly told her all this, but she had come to that conclusion from the fragments of information garnered from conversations with the talkative ghoul. Tryst had never actually even accused Norrec, instead only saying that they needed to find their partner, to end what had begun in the tomb—and that because Kara had not stayed behind as they had wished, *she* would now be a part of their macabre quest.

Kara ate in silence, purposely keeping her gaze from the ungodly pair as much as possible. The less she drew their attention, especially that of Tryst, the better. Unfortunately, just as she reached the bottom of the bowl, the more vocal revenant suddenly rasped, "Is it . . . does it taste . . . good?"

The peculiar question so caught her by surprise that she had to look at him. "What?"

One pale, peeling finger pointed at the bowl. "The food. Does it . . . taste . . . good?"

Some bit remained, more than Kara truly desired at the moment. She considered what she knew of undead, never recalling any with an appetite for fish stew. *Human flesh*, yes, in some cases, but never fish stew. Still, on the off chance that it might ease tensions a little, the necromancer held out the bowl and, in a steady voice, asked, "Would you like to try it?"

Tryst looked at Fauztin, who remained the immovable rock. The slimmer ghoul finally stepped forward, seized the food, then immediately returned to his favored spot. Kara had never known that a walking corpse could move with such speed.

With decaying fingers he took some of the remnants and stuck them in his mouth. Sadun tried to chew, fragments of fish dropping to the floor. Despite the fact that both he and the mage acted as if living, the dead man's body did not completely function as it had previous to his murder.

He suddenly spat out what remained, at the same time a monstrous expression crossing his rotting countenance. "Filth! It tastes . . . it tastes of . . . *death*." Sadun eyed her. "It's too long dead . . . they should have . . . cooked it . . . less . . . a lot less." He considered this crucial matter more, eyes never leaving Kara. "I think . . . maybe they should have . . . not cooked it . . . at all . . . the fresher . . . the better . . . eh?"

The raven-haired woman did not reply at first, having no desire whatsoever to prolong a conversation that might turn to exactly what types of meat the ghoul would think tasted best uncooked. Instead, Kara tried to turn back to the subject of most concern to her—the hunt for Norrec Vizharan.

"You were aboard the *Hawksfire*, weren't you? You were aboard until whatever happened that caused the crew to abandon her."

"Not aboard . . . underneath . . . for the most part . . ."

"Underneath?" She pictured the two clutching the hull, using their inhuman strength to hold on even through the most turbulent of waves. Only a revenant could have accomplished such a harrowing effort. "What do you mean . . . for the most part?"

Sadun shrugged, sending his head wobbling for a moment. "We came aboard . . . for a short . . . time . . . after the fools jumped . . . ship."

"What made them leave?"

"They saw . . . what they didn't like to see . . ."

Not a very helpful answer, but the longer Kara could keep the conversation going, the less time the pair had to think about what else they might need of her—and what it might cost the necromancer.

Once more Kara thought about their unholy perseverance. The revenants had managed to nearly catch up with their prey, even latch themselves onto the hull of his vessel like a pair of lampreys onto a shark. The vision of the two undead clinging to the underside of the *Hawksfire* throughout the violent storm they had earlier mentioned would forever be seared into the necromancer's imagination. Truly Norrec Vizharan would not escape their brutal justice.

And yet . . . he so far had, even with them within yards of his throat.

"If you and he were alone aboard the ship, then why is the hunt not yet over?"

A decidedly grim change came over Tryst's smile, managing to make his general appearance even more ghastly than previous. "It should . . . have been."

He would say no more and when Kara looked to Fauztin, his dark visage revealed nothing. She pondered their responses as rapidly as she could, finally deciding to try to play on their failure aboard the *Hawksfire*. "I can be of more help to you, you know. Next time, nothing will go awry."

This time, Fauztin blinked once. What that meant, the necromancer could not say, but the Vizjerei's action had been for some specific reason.

Sadun Tryst's eyes narrowed slightly. "You'll be . . . of all the . . . help . . . we need. Trust on . . . that . . ."

"But I could be more than your unwilling puppet. I understand what drives you. I understand why you walk the earth. As an ally rather than a prisoner, the possibilities of what you can accomplish grow tenfold and more!"

Silent, the wiry corpse tossed and caught his own dagger a few times, something he had done often since his arrival. Apparently even death could not break some habits. Kara thought he did it whenever he had to concentrate especially hard. "You understand . . . less than you think."

"All I am trying to say is that we need not be adversaries. My spell stirred up your murdered spirits, set you on this quest, and so I feel some responsibility. You seek this Norrec Vizharan, so do I. Why can we not work as allies?"

Again the mage blinked, almost as if he might have wanted to say something—an impossibility, of course. In lieu of that, he glanced down at his companion. The two undead shared a long gaze, which made the enchantress wonder if they communicated in some manner beyond her ken.

The grating sound of Sadun Tryst's unearthly chuckle filled the tiny cabin, but Kara knew better than to hope that Captain Jeronnan or one of the crew would hear. The Vizjerei had cast a spell deadening all sounds within. As far as the men of the *King's Shield* might be concerned, the necromancer made no more noise than if she now slept peacefully.

"My friend . . . he brings up an . . . amusing point. You . . . as our good ally . . . would surely . . . expect your dagger back . . . eh?" When she had no good reply, Tryst added, "Not a bargain . . . we could very much . . . *live* with . . . if you know what I mean."

Kara understood very well. Not only did the dagger give them power over her, but it likely served as a focus for that which let them function on the mortal plane. The ritual blade had been what had first summoned the phantasm of Fauztin and the probable result of taking it from them would be that both bodies would simply collapse, the vengeful shades sent back to the afterlife forever.

This pair would have none of that.

"You'll aid us . . . as we need. You'll serve . . . as the cloak covering . . . the truth from . . . those we meet. You'll do . . . what we can't do . . . in the light of day . . . where all can see . . ."

Fauztin blinked for a third time, a very distressing sign. He had never before taken such a visible interest in their conversations, preferring everything to come from his more vocal companion.

Tryst rose, ever smiling. The more Kara Nightshadow thought of it, the more she realized that the smile never truly left the slimmer ghoul's face save when its owner forcefully chose to make it go, as when the food had so disgusted him. What she had taken for humor looked, in part, to simply be what death had frozen on his countenance. Tryst would likely be smiling even when he ripped out the heart of his treacherous comrade, Norrec.

"And as we must . . . have your cooperation . . . my good friend's suggested a way . . . to make you even more . . . amenable . . . to the situation."

Both he and the Vizjerei approached her.

Kara leapt from the bed. "You have the dagger. You need no other hold over me."

"Fauztin believes . . . we do. I am so . . . sorry."

Despite the unlikely chance of anyone hearing her, she opened her mouth to shout.

The mage blinked for a fourth time—and no sound escaped the necromancer's lips. Her seeming helplessness both horrified and infuriated the pale woman. Kara knew that there were far more experienced practitioners of her arts that could have turned both undead into silent, obedient servants. A few more years and perhaps even she would have been able to do so. Instead, the ghouls had turned her into the puppet—and now they sought to further add to her invisible chains.

Tryst's macabre grin and cold, white eyes filled her view. The breath of decay drifted to her nostrils each time the rotting figure spoke. "Give me . . . your left hand . . . and it'll be . . . less painful."

With no choice left to her, Kara reluctantly obeyed. Sadun Tryst took the hand in his own moldering fingers, caressing it almost as if he and the young enchantress had become lovers. Kara felt a chill run up and down her spine at the thought. She had heard such tales before . . .

"I miss many things . . . about life . . . woman . . . many things . . ."

A heavy hand dropped on his shoulder. Tryst nodded as best his crooked neck allowed, then backed away a step. His grip on her hand remained painfully tight, the ghoul now turning it so that the palm showed.

Fauztin plunged the gleaming dagger into it.

Kara gasped—then realized that while she felt discomfort, she did not feel actual pain. She stared in astonishment, noting and yet not quite believing the sight before her. More than two inches of the curved blade stuck out of the other side of her hand, yet nowhere did she see any trace of blood.

A brilliant yellow glow arose from the area where the dagger had penetrated, a glow that completely bathed her palm.

The Vizjerei at last tried to say something, but only a

thin gasp escaped. Even rewrapping his ruined throat did not work.

"Let me . . ." snarled Tryst. Eyeing the captive necromancer again, he intoned, *"Our lives are . . . your life. Our deaths . . . are your death. Our fate is . . . your fate . . . bounded by this . . . dagger and your . . . soul . . ."*

With that, Fauztin tugged the dagger free. The Vizjerei thrust the blade toward her face, showing Kara that no blood stained it. He then indicated her hand.

She studied her palm, could not even make out the slightest scar. The murdered mage had summoned powerful sorcery for his terrible spell.

Tryst pushed her toward the bed, indicating the young woman sit. "We are . . . one now. If we fail . . . you fail. If we should perish . . . or be betrayed . . . you . . . too . . . will suffer . . . remember that always . . ."

Kara could not help but shiver slightly. They had bound her to them in a manner far more absolute than that which their possession of the dagger had previously done. If anything at all happened to the pair before they could accomplish their dreadful task, Kara's soul would even be dragged back to the underworld with them, forever doomed to wander without rest.

"You did not have to do that!" She looked for some glimmer of sympathy, but found none. Nothing mattered more than avenging what had been done to them. "I would've helped you!"

"Now . . . we can be certain you will." Tryst and Fauztin retreated to the far corner again. The ritual dagger gleamed golden. "Now . . . there'll be . . . no fear . . . of tricks . . . when you meet with . . . the sorcerer."

Despite what they had just done to her, Kara stiffened at the last words. "Sorcerer? In Lut Gholein?"

Fauztin nodded. Sadun Tryst cocked his head more to the side—or perhaps the weight on what remained of his neck simply had proven too much for the moment.

"Yesss . . . a Vizjerei like . . . my friend here . . . an old man . . . with much knowledge . . . and known by . . . the name . . . Drognan."

"My name is Drognan," the cloaked mage remarked as he swept into the chamber. "Please be seated, Norrec Vizharan."

As he gazed around the Vizjerei's sanctum, the sense of unease that had crept over Norrec earlier returned a thousand times stronger. Not only had this elderly but certainly formidable figure drawn the veteran to him with ease, but Drognan understood well exactly what had happened to Norrec—including the quest by the cursed armor.

"I always knew that the curse of Bartuc could not be contained forever," he informed Norrec as the soldier seated himself in an old, weathered chair. "Always knew that."

They had come to this dim chamber after a short trek into even less savory areas of the otherwise rich, energetic kingdom. The doorway through which the pair had entered had seemed to have led into an abandoned, rat-infested building, but once through, the interior had shifted . . . transforming into an ancient but still stately edifice which Drognan informed him had once been rumored to be the home of Horazon, the bloody warlord's brother.

It had been abandoned at some point long after the disappearance of Bartuc's brother, but the spells protecting it from curious eyes had continued to serve their designated purpose—until Drognan had outwitted them while searching for the tomb of the very one who had cast them. Deciding that no one had a more appropriate right to lay claim to the magical abode than himself, the Vizjerei had moved in, then continued his research.

Through an empty hall whose floor had been covered

in a rich tapestry of mosaic patterns that included animals, warriors, and even legendary structures, they had finally reached this particular room, the one that the old mage most called his home. Shelf upon shelf bordered the walls and on each of those shelves had been arranged more books and scrolls than a simple soldier such as Norrec could have ever dreamed existed in all the world. He could read, but few of the titles had been written in the common tongue.

Other than the books, though, only a few other items decorated the shelves, among the most interesting being a single polished skull and a few jars of a dark colored liquid. As for the room itself, its decor consisted chiefly of a well-crafted wooden table and two old but stately chairs. It had all the look of a chamberlain's office such as might have been found in the sultan's palace. Hardly what Norrec would have expected from a Vizjerei or any other sorcerer for that matter. Like most common folk, he had expected to see all sorts of horrifying and grisly objects, the so-called tools of Drognan's trade.

"I am a . . . researcher," the wrinkled figure added suddenly, as if he needed to explain his surroundings.

A researcher who had been the reason why no guards had stopped Norrec on the dock. A researcher who, with but a simple use of his power, had seized the minds of a half dozen soldiers and directed them to bring the foreigner to him.

A researcher who dabbled in dark arts, knew of the deadly enchantments contained in Bartuc's armor—and who had apparently overcome most of them with ease.

And that, more than anything else, had been why Norrec had willingly followed him here. For the first time since the tomb, hope had arisen that someone could at last free him of the parasitic suit.

"It came to me in a vision little more than a week or

two ago." The sorcerer ran wizened fingers along a row of books, obviously searching for one in particular. "The legacy of Bartuc rising anew! I could not believe it at first, naturally, but when it repeated itself, I knew the vision to be a true one."

Since then, Drognan continued, he had performed spell after spell to discover the meaning—and in the process had uncovered Norrec's secret and the journey the armor had forced upon him. Although he had not been able to observe the veteran during the long trek from the tomb, the elderly mage had at least been able to keep track of where that trail seemed to lead. Soon it became apparent that both man and armor would soon be in the Vizjerei's very midst, a fortuitous event as far as Drognan had been concerned.

The sorcerer pulled free one vast tome from the shelf, then placed it gently on a table in the center of the chamber. He began thumbing through it, still talking. "It surprised me not at all, young man, to find out that the armor sought out Lut Gholein. If some lingering, spectral aspect of Bartuc hoped to fulfill his last wishes, then certainly traveling to this fair kingdom makes perfect sense, especially for two particular reasons."

Norrec cared little for what those reasons might be, more concerned with that which the Vizjerei had hinted might be possible to obtain—the fighter's freedom from the suit. "Is the spell in that book?"

The aged sorcerer looked up. "What spell?"

"The one to separate me from this, of course!" Norrec banged the breastplate with one hand. "This damned armor! You said you had some way you could peel it off of me!"

"I believe my earlier words to you were closer to 'if you hope to live, you will do *exactly* as I desire.' "

"But the armor! Damn you, wizard! That's all I care about! Cast a spell! Get it off of me while it's still subdued!"

Looking down on him as a father might a whining child, the silver-haired mage responded, "Of the armor, while I cannot as yet remove it, I assure you that you need not worry about its other enchantments while I have it under my power." Reaching into one of the deep pockets of his robe, Drognan removed what at first seemed a short stick but quickly revealed itself to be much, much, *much* longer. In truth, by the time the sorcerer had it freed from the pocket, the "stick" had swollen in size and length—the latter a good four feet and more—and revealed itself as a spell staff covered in elaborate and glittering runes. "Observe."

Drognan pointed the staff at his guest.

Norrec, who had traveled with Fauztin long enough to know what it meant to be on this end of the magical staff, leapt to his feet. "Wait—"

"*Furiosic!*" shouted the mage.

Flames shot toward the soldier, flames that spread as they moved. A blanket of fire sought to envelop Norrec.

Just a few scant inches from his nose, the fire abruptly died out.

At first Norrec believed that the suit had saved him again, but then he heard the wrinkled figure chuckle. "Not to worry, young man, not even a hair singed! You see now what I mean? My control over the armor is complete! Had I so desired, I could have left you a roasted skeleton and even the suit could not have saved you! Only my canceling of the spell protected you now! Now do sit back down . . ."

The searing heat still burning his nostrils, Norrec slumped back into the old chair. Drognan's unnerving display had proven two things. The first had been that what the elderly sorcerer had claimed had been true; with his magic, he had subdued the enchantments of the armor.

The second had been that Norrec had evidently placed

himself into the hands of a somewhat ruthless and likely *half-mad* wizard.

Yet . . . what else could he have done?

"There is a bottle of wine next to you. Pour yourself some. Calm your nerves."

The offer itself did little to calm Norrec down, for both the bottle mentioned and the table upon which it now sat had not been next to the veteran a second earlier. Still, he kept himself from showing any uncertainty as he first filled a goblet, then sipped some of the contents.

"That should be better." One hand spread over a page in the massive book, Drognan peered at his guest. The staff rested loosely in his other hand. "Do you know anything of the history of Lut Gholein?"

"Not much."

The wizard stepped away from the book. "One fact I will impart upon you immediately, a fact I think central to your situation. Before the rise of Lut Gholein, this region served briefly as a colony of the Empire of Kehjistan. There existed Vizjerei temples and a military presence. However, even by the time of the brothers Bartuc and Horazon, the empire had begun to pull back from this side of the sea. Vizjerei influence remained strong, but a physical presence proved too costly for the most part." An almost childlike smile spread across the dark, narrow features. "It is all quite fascinating, really!"

Norrec, who, under the circumstances cared little about history lessons, frowned.

Seeming not to notice, Drognan continued. "After the war, after Bartuc's defeat and death, the empire never regained its glory. Worse yet, its greatest sorcerer, its shining light, had suffered too much in body and, most pointedly, *mind*. I speak, of course, of Horazon."

"Who came to Lut Gholein," Norrec helpfully added, hoping by doing so that it would assist the rambling elder to reach whatever point he sought to make. Then—perhaps then—Drognan would finally get around to helping the fighter.

"Yes, exactly, Lut Gholein. Not named that yet, of course. Yes, Horazon, who had suffered so terribly even in victory, came to this land, tried to settle into a life of studious pursuit—and then, as I informed you earlier, just disappeared."

The veteran soldier waited for his host to continue, but Drognan only stared back, as if what he had just said explained all.

"You do not understand, I see," the robed sorcerer finally commented.

"I understand that Horazon came to this land and now the cursed armor of his hated brother has come here, too! I also understand that I've had to watch men slaughtered, demons rise from the earth, and know that my life's no longer my own, but that of a dead demon lord!" Norrec rose again, having had enough. Drognan could have easily raised the staff and slain him on the spot, but his own patience had come to an end. "Either help me or slay me, Vizjerei! I've no time for history lessons! I want release from this hell!"

"Sit."

Norrec sat, but this time not of his own accord. A darkness crossed Drognan's features, a darkness that reminded the hapless soldier that this man had readily taken control of not only half a dozen guards, but the damnable suit, too.

"I will save you despite yourself, Norrec Vizharan—although certainly no servant of the Vizjerei are you despite that ancient name! I will save you while at the same time you will lead me to that for which I have searched for more than half my life!"

Whatever spell Drognan used pressed the fighter so tight into the chair that Norrec could barely speak. "What . . . what do you mean? Lead you to what?"

Drognan gave him a nearly incredulous look. "Why, what must surely be buried somewhere under the city itself and what the armor must also be seeking—the tomb of Bartuc's brother, Horazon . . . the legendary *Arcane Sanctuary!*"

TWELVE

As he did each night, General Augustus Malevolyn marched the perimeter of the encampment. Also as he did each night, he studiously observed each detail concerning his men's readiness. Ineptitude meant severe punishment no matter what the soldier's rank.

Yet, one thing the general did different this particular night, a single change that went little noticed by most of his weary men. This night, Malevolyn made his rounds still wearing the crimson helm of Bartuc.

That it did not quite match with the rest of his armor did not concern him in the least. In fact, more and more he considered the possibility of finding some manner by which to dye his present armor a color more akin to that of the helmet. Thus far, though, Malevolyn had come up with but one method by which to possibly match the unique color, a method that surely would have caused a full-scale insurrection.

His hand touched the helm almost lovingly as he adjusted its fit. Malevolyn had noticed some discomfort on Galeona's part when he had earlier refused to remove it, but had simply chalked it up to her fear of his growing might. In truth, when both the helmet and the suit became his, the general would no longer need the witch's magical skills—and while her more earthly talents were most expert, Malevolyn knew that he could always find a more willing, more submissive female to satisfy his other needs.

Of course, such matters of flesh could wait. Lut Gholein called to him. He would not be cheated out of it, as he had been cheated out of Viz-jun.

But are you worthy of it? Are you worthy of the glory, the legacy of Bartuc?

Malevolyn froze. The voice in his head, the one that asked on a previous eve the questions that he himself feared to ask out loud, that proclaimed what he dared not yet proclaim.

Are you worthy? Will you prove yourself? Will you seize your destiny?

A faint glint of light from beyond the encampment caught his attention. He opened his mouth to summon the sentries, then made out the murky figure of one of his own men, a dying torch in one hand, coming toward him from that direction. The dim light of the flames kept the soldier's visage almost a complete shadow even when the man came within a couple of yards of the commander.

"General Malevolyn," whispered the sentry, saluting. "You must come and see this."

"What is it? Have you found something?"

The sentry, though, had already turned back to the darkness. "Better come see, general . . ."

Frowning, Malevolyn followed behind the warrior, one hand gripped on the pommel of his sword. The guard no doubt understood that whatever he had to show his leader had better be of some import or there would be hell to pay. Malevolyn did not like his routine disturbed.

The two wended their way some distance through the uneven landscape. With the sentry in the lead, they crossed over a dune, cautiously making their way down to the other side. Ahead, the dark outline of a rocky ridge loomed over the otherwise sandy region. The general assumed that whatever the guard had noticed had to be out there. If not . . .

The sentry paused. Malevolyn did not even know why the man bothered to carry the torch any longer. The pale, sickly flame did nothing to illuminate the area and if some foe lay ahead, it would only alert them to the presence of the approaching pair. He cursed himself for not having ordered it doused before, but then assumed that, if the soldier had not thought to do so, whatever he had brought the general out to see could not be an enemy.

Spitting granules from his mouth, Augustus Malevolyn muttered, "Well? What did you see? Is it near the rocks?"

"It is difficult to explain, general. You must see it." The shadowed soldier pointed at the ground to the right, "The footing is better there, general. If you'll come . . ."

Perhaps the man had discovered some ruins. Those Malevolyn would have found of interest. The Vizjerei had a long history in and around Aranoch. If this turned out to be the remains of one of their temples, then perhaps it contained some lost secrets of which he could make use.

The ground beneath his foot, the ground on which the sentry had told him to step, gave completely away.

Malevolyn first stumbled, then fell forward. Fearful of losing the helmet, he sacrificed one hand in order to keep it in place, thus losing any chance of halting his fall. The general dropped to both knees, his face but inches from the sand. His right arm, the one that had been forced to support his weight, throbbed with pain. He tried to right himself, but the loose ground at first made it difficult.

He looked up, searching for the fool who had led him into this. "Don't just stand there, you wretch! Help me—"

The sentry had vanished, even his torch nowhere to be seen.

Steadying himself, Malevolyn managed at last to rise. With great caution, he reached for his sword—and found *that* also missing.

Are you worthy? repeated the damnable voice in his head.

From the sand erupted four hideous and only vaguely humanoid forms.

Even in the darkness, the general could make out the hard carapaces, the distorted, beetlelike heads. A pair of arms ending in oversized, sharp pincers completed the look of an insect out of some nightmare, yet these manlike horrors were no product of Malevolyn's imagination. He knew already of the sand maggots, the massive arthropods that hunted for prey in the wilderness of Aranoch and also knew of one of the few hellish creatures that hunted them in turn . . . when human prey could not be found.

Yet, while scarab demons in great numbers had been rumored to be the cause of caravans lost over the years, never had the commander heard of such creatures lurking in the vicinity of as great a force as his own. While not the largest of armies—not *yet*—Malevolyn's disciplined warriors certainly represented a target not at all of temptation to creatures such as these. They preferred smaller, weaker victims.

Such as a lone warrior tricked into walking into their very midst?

Which of his officers had betrayed him he would find out when he located the traitorous sentry. For now, though, Malevolyn had more important matters to consider, such as keeping himself from becoming the scarab demons' next meal.

Are you worthy? the voice repeated again.

As if suddenly prodded to action, one of the grotesque beetles reached for him, its pincers and mandibles clacking wildly in anticipation of a bloody prize. Although not true beasts of Hell despite their name, the scarab demons were certainly monstrous enough foes for any ordinary man to face.

Yet Augustus Malevolyn considered himself no *ordinary* man.

As the savage claws came at him, the general reacted instinctively, his hand swinging forward to deflect as well it could the attack. However, to his surprise—and certainly that of the creature before him—in that empty hand materialized a blade of purest ebony surrounded by a blazing crimson aura that lit up the surrounding area more than any torch. The blade grew even as it cut an arc through the air, yet its weight and its balance remained perfect at all times.

The edge dug into the hard carapace without hesitation, completely severing the pincered appendage, which went flying to the side. The scarab demon let out a high-pitched squeal and backed away, dark fluids dripping from its ruined arm.

General Malevolyn did not pause, caught up in the miraculous turn of events. With expert ease he drove the wondrous blade through the second of his attackers. Even before that monster had fallen, the general turned to the next, forcing it back with his relentless onslaught.

The two remaining creatures joined with the third, seeking to catch the commander from opposing directions. Malevolyn took a step back, repositioned himself, and immediately dispatched the one whose limb he had but moments before cut off. As the other pair fell upon him, the veteran officer twisted, bringing the sword around and beheading one.

A foul-smelling liquid sprayed him as he did it, momentarily blinding the general. The final of his opponents took advantage, first dragging him to the ground, then attempted to remove Malevolyn's head by biting through his throat. Snarling like an animal, Malevolyn blocked the mandibles with his armored forearm, hoping that the plate there would protect the flesh and bone beneath long enough for him to recover.

With one knee, he managed to push his monstrous attacker up a bit, forcing the mandibles away. That gave Malevolyn the angle he needed. Twisting the sword around in his other hand, the general turned the point toward the head of the scarab demon and drove it through the thick, natural armor of the beast with all the force he could muster.

The horrific beetle let out a brief, shrill squeal and dropped dead on top of General Malevolyn.

With only a slight sense of disgust, the commander pushed the carcass away, then rose. His immaculate armor dripped with the life fluids of the scarab demons, but, other than that, they had done him little real harm. He stared at the dark, still forms, both angered at the earlier betrayal yet also feeling a rush of intense satisfaction for having singlehandedly slain the four hellish creatures.

Augustus Malevolyn touched his breastplate, which had become covered with the fluids of the scarab demons. For nearly a minute, he stared at the stench-ridden muck now covering his gauntleted hand. On impulse, Malevolyn touched the breastplate again, but instead of trying to wipe his armor clean, he began to spread the fluids further—just as Bartuc had done with the blood of his human foes.

"So . . . perhaps you *are* worthy . . ."

He spun about, at last sighting the night-enshrouded form of the traitorous sentry. However, common sense now told Malevolyn that what he had taken for one of his own men surely had to be something far more powerful, not to mention *sinister* . . .

"I know you now . . ." he muttered. Then his eyes widened slightly as truth dawned. "Or should I say . . . I know *what* you are . . . *demon* . . ."

The other figure laughed quietly, laughed as no man could. Before the astounded eyes of General Malevolyn, the sentry's shape twisted, grew, changed into that not born of the mortal plane. It towered over the human and where there had been four limbs now six materialized. The foremost appeared as great scythes with needle points, the middle as skeletal hands with deadly claws, and the last, serving as legs, bent back in a manner much like the hind limbs of the insect the demon most resembled.

A mantis. A mantis from Hell.

"Hail to you, General Augustus Malevolyn of Westmarch, warrior, conqueror, emperor—and true heir to the Warlord of Blood." The hideous insect performed a bizarre bow, the sharp points of the scythes digging into the sand. "This one congratulates you on your worthiness . . ."

Malevolyn glanced at his hand, now empty of any weapon. The magical blade had vanished the moment it had no longer been needed—and yet the general felt certain that, in the future, he could summon that blade whenever necessary.

"You're the voice in my head," the commander finally replied. "You're the voice that cajoles me . . ."

The demon tilted his own head to the side, glowing bulbous eyes flaring once. "This one did not cajole . . . simply encouraged."

"And if I had not passed this little test?"

"Then this one would have been terribly disappointed."

The creature's words caused General Malevolyn to chuckle despite the implications in the response. "Damned good thing I didn't fail, then." One hand reached up to adjust the helmet while Malevolyn thought. First had come the visions, then the increase in his otherwise limited powers—and now this magical blade and a demon to boot. Truly it had to be as the mantis had proclaimed; Augustus Malevolyn had indeed earned the mantle of Bartuc.

"You are worthy," the demon chittered. "So says this one—Xazax, I am called—but still one thing remains outside your grasp! One thing must you have before Bartuc you become!"

General Malevolyn understood. "The *armor*. The armor that fool of a peasant wears! Well, it comes to me even now from across the sea! Galeona says it approaches Lut Gholein, which is why we march there now." He considered. "Perhaps now would be a good time to see what she can learn. Maybe with your aid . . ."

"Best to not speak of me to your sorceress, great one!" Xazax chittered with what seemed some anxiety. "Her kind . . . cannot always be trusted. They are better not dealt with at all . . ."

Malevolyn briefly mulled over the demon's statement. Xazax almost spoke as if he and Galeona shared a history, which, in retrospect, would hardly have surprised the general. The witch dealt with dark powers almost on a continuous basis. What did interest him, however, was that this creature did not want her to know what was now being discussed. A falling out? A betrayal? Well, if it served Malevolyn, then so much the better.

He nodded. "Very well. Until I decide what must be done, we'll leave her ignorant of our conversation."

"This one appreciates your understanding . . ."

"By all means." The general had no more time to concern himself with the sorceress. Xazax had raised a point of much more interest to him. "But you spoke of the armor? Do you know something of it?"

Again the foul mantis bowed. Even in the starlight, the general could see the horrendous veins coursing all over its body, veins that pulsated without pause. "By now, this fool has brought it to Lut Gholein . . . but there he can hide it within the city's walls, keep it from he to whom it truly belongs . . ."

"I had thought of that." In fact, General Malevolyn had

considered it much during the journey, considered it and grown more and more enraged, although he had revealed no outward sign of that fury to anyone else. A part of him felt certain that he could seize Lut Gholein and, thus, capture the peasant who wore the armor, but a more practical part had also counted up the losses on his own side and found them far too great. Failure still remained well within the realms of possibility. Malevolyn had, in truth, hoped to keep his army beyond the sight and knowledge of the kingdom and wait for the stranger to head out to the desert on his own. Unfortunately, the general could not necessarily trust that the fool would do as he desired.

Xazax leaned closer. "The kingdom, it is a strong one, with many soldiers well versed in the art of war. He who has the armor would feel quite safe in there."

"I know."

"But this one can give you the key with which to make Lut Gholein yours . . . a force most terrible . . . a force which no mortal army can subdue."

Malevolyn could scarcely believe what he had just heard. "Are you suggesting—"

The demon suddenly looked back toward the camp as if he had heard some sound. After a momentary pause, Xazax quickly returned his attention to the human. "When but a day separates you from the city, we shall speak again. There, you must be prepared to do this . . ."

The commander listened as the demon explained. At first even he felt repulsed by what the creature suggested, but then, as Xazax told him why it must be so, Augustus Malevolyn himself saw the need—and felt the growing excitement.

"You will do this?" the mantis asked.

"Yes . . . yes, I will . . . and gladly."

"Then we shall speak soon." Without warning, Xazax's form began to grow indistinct, quickly becoming more shadow than substance. "Until then, hail to you once again, general! This one honors the successor of Bartuc! This one honors the new master of demons! This one honors the new *Warlord of Blood!*"

With that, the last vestiges of Xazax faded into the night.

General Malevolyn immediately started back to camp, his mind already racing, the words of the monstrous mantis still echoing in his head. This night had become a turning point for him, with all his dreams coming together at last. The demon's test and the manner by which Malevolyn had passed it paled in comparison to what Xazax now offered—the armor and the method that would guarantee that it and Lut Gholein fell into the general's hands with little trouble.

Master of demons, the mantis had said.

One more night to get through. One more night and the *King's Shield* would dock in the port of Lut Gholein.

One more night and Kara would be alone in the strange land, alone save for her two grotesque companions.

She had returned with her evening meal just as before and eaten it under the watchful eyes of the two undead. Fauztin had remained standing in the corner, the dour Vizjerei looking like some macabre statue, but of late Sadun Tryst had edged closer, the more talkative of the two ghouls now seated on a bench built into the wall nearest her bed. The wiry ghoul even tried to make conversation with her on occasion, something that the necromancer could have done well without.

Yet, one subject interested her enough to force her to speak with him for a time and that subject concerned the ever elusive Norrec Vizharan. Kara had noticed something odd about the way Tryst spoke of his former comrade. His words seemed to hold no malice at all for his

murderer. Most of the time, he simply regaled her with
tales of their adventures together. Tryst even seemed to
feel some remorse for the veteran soldier despite the horrible acts Norrec had committed.

"He saved . . . my life . . . three times and more . . ." the
ghoul concluded, after being coaxed once more into
speaking of his treacherous friend. "Never a war . . . as
bad as . . . that one."

"You traveled with him from then on?" The war mentioned by Tryst had apparently taken place in the
Western Kingdoms some nine years before. For men such
as these to stick together for so very long showed a powerful bond of some sort.

"Aye . . . save during . . . Norrec's sickness . . . he left
us . . . for three months . . . and caught up after . . ." The
rotting figure looked to the Vizjerei. "Remember . . .
Fauztin?"

The sorcerer nodded his head ever so slightly. Kara
had expected him to somehow forbid Sadun from going
on with such stories, but Fauztin, too, seemed caught up
in them. In life, both men had clearly respected Norrec
highly and, from what she had heard so far, so now did
the necromancer.

Yet this same Norrec Vizharan had brutally murdered
the pair and revenants did not exist if not fueled by a
sense of revenge and justice that went beyond mortal
comprehension. These two should have harbored only
thoughts of retribution, of the rending of Vizharan's flesh
and the sending of his damned soul to the underworld.
That they still felt anything at all other than that struck
her quite strange. Sadun Tryst and Fauztin did not act at
all like the revenants of which legends had spoken.

"What will you do when you find him?" She had
asked this question but once before and received no clear
answer.

"We'll do . . . what must be . . . done."

Again, a response that did not satisfy her. Why shield Kara from the truth? "After what he did, even your past friendship must mean little. How could Norrec commit so terrible a crime?"

"He did . . . what had to be . . . done." With that equally enigmatic reply, Tryst's smile stretched, revealing more of the yellowed teeth and the gums already receding. Each day, despite their all-consuming quest, the revenants grew less and less human in appearance. They would never completely decay, but their link to their former humanity would continue to shrivel. "You're very beautiful . . ."

"What?" Kara Nightshadow blinked, not certain that she had heard correctly.

"Very beautiful . . . and fresh . . . alive." The ghoul suddenly reached forward, caught a lock of her long, raven-colored hair. "Life's beautiful . . . more so than . . . ever . . ."

She hid a shudder. Sadun Tryst had made his intent quite clear. He still recalled too well the pleasures of life. One of those, food, had sorely disappointed him already. Now, hidden in this tiny cabin for the past couple of days in the constant company of a living woman, he seemed ready to try to relive a different pleasure—and Kara did not know how she could prevent him from trying.

Without warning, Sadun Tryst suddenly turned and glared at his friend. Although Kara had noticed nothing, clearly some communication had passed between the two, communication that did not please the wiry ghoul in the least.

"Leave me . . . at least . . . the illusion . . ."

Fauztin said nothing, his only reaction being to blink once. However, that alone seemed to quell his comrade some.

"I wouldn't have . . . touched her . . . much . . ." Tryst looked her over once before meeting her eyes. "I just—"

A heavy knocking on the door sent him hurrying to the far corner. Kara could not believe her eyes each time the ghoul moved so. She had always read that swiftness could not be termed one of the skills of the undead. In its place, they had persistence, an unholy patience.

Ensconced next to the Vizjerei, he muttered, "Answer."

She did, already suspecting that she knew who it would be. Only two men dared come to her door, one Captain Jeronnan, whom she had just spoken with but a short time before, the other—

"Yes, Mister Drayko?" the sorceress asked, keeping the door open only a crack.

He looked uncomfortable. "My Lady Kara, I realize that you've requested absolute privacy, but . . . but I wondered whether you might join me on the deck for a few minutes."

"Thank you, Mister Drayko, but, as I have said before to the captain, I have much to do before we make landfall." She started to close the door. "Thank you for asking—"

"Not even for a little *fresh* air?"

Something in his tone puzzled her, but the necromancer had no time to think about it. Tryst had made it very clear that she should spend no more time outside than needed to retrieve her food from the mess. The revenants wanted their living puppet where they could see her. "I am sorry, no."

"I thought as much." He turned to leave—then *threw* his shoulder to the door with such force that the door knocked Kara back onto the bed. The blow did not stun her, but she lay there for a moment, completely bewildered by his actions.

Drayko fell to a kneeling position just inside. He looked up, saw the ghouls, and blanched. "By the King of the Depths!"

A dagger suddenly materialized in Tryst's hand.

The mariner reached for his own knife, which Kara saw lay by his side. Drayko had clearly been holding it all along, concealing its presence while he had spoken inanities with the dark mage. All along he had acted with the knowledge that something seemed amiss in the cabin—although likely even Drayko had never imagined the sight before him.

As Sadun Tryst raised his arm, a second figure charged into the tiny room. Ceremonial blade held ready, Captain Hanos Jeronnan shielded his officer from harm. Unlike Drayko, he seemed only mildly surprised at the horrendous figures but a short distance from him. In fact, Jeronnan almost looked pleased to see the two ghouls.

"I won't let it happen again . . ." he murmured. "You'll not take this one . . ."

Kara immediately understood the captain's words. In his mind, the undead represented that invisible monster that had not only taken his daughter from him, but had turned her into a vile creature he had been forced to destroy. Now he thought to wreak his vengeance on them.

And with the silver-plated sword, he had the potential to do just that.

Tryst threw his dagger, again moving with a speed his decrepit form belied. The smaller blade sank into Jeronnan's sword arm, sending the captain staggering. However, the former naval commander did not retreat. Blood dripping down, the ghoul's weapon still half-buried in his flesh, Captain Jeronnan attacked, slicing at his unliving adversary.

His macabre smile seeming to mock, Sadun Tryst reached for the blade, clearly intending to grab it in his hand. As one beyond death, no normal blade could touch him.

The edge of the captain's weapon severed off the lower two fingers.

Pure agony abruptly coursed through Kara, the pain so great that she doubled over, nearly collapsing.

With a hiss, Tryst pulled his maimed hand back. Glaring at Jeronnan, he gasped to his partner, "Do something . . . while I still have . . . a head on my . . . shoulders . . ."

Her eyes blurry from tears, the necromancer nonetheless saw Fauztin blink once.

"Look out!" she managed to cry.

A wall of force erupted from her ceremonial dagger, sending both Jeronnan and Drayko flying against the opposite wall. At the same time, the Vizjerei put his other hand on the wall behind him.

A blue haze spread behind the ghouls, a blue haze that grew rapidly in both height and width.

The two mariners struggled to their feet. Mister Drayko started forward, but Jeronnan pushed him back. "Nay! The only weapon that's good for them is this one! I swear I'll slice them both into fish bait—that is, if even the fish'll take something so rotten! You see to the girl!"

The officer obeyed instantly, hurrying to the Kara's side. "Can you stand?"

With help, Kara found that she could. Although the pain did not leave her, at least it subsided enough for the enchantress to think—and realize what had happened.

Through the dagger, Fauztin had tied her life to the revenants' continued existence. The blow that Jeronnan had landed had not been felt by Sadun Tryst, who had been long past such mortal weaknesses. However, each successful strike against them would, so it appeared, be suffered by *her*.

And so, with a sword gilded in silver, Captain Jeronnan had the capability of not only slicing the undead into the bait he had mentioned, but also in the process slaying the very one he sought to save.

She had to warn him. "Drayko! Jeronnan must stop!"

"It's all right, my lady! The captain knows what he does! His silver blade's just right for dealing with the likes of those! In such close quarters, he'll make quick work of them before the one can cast another spell!" Drayko wrinkled his nose. "Gods, what a stench in here! After you started acting so strangely, Captain Jeronnan finally recalled what had happened to you back in Gea Kul and felt certain that something was up! He summoned me to his cabin after dinner, related his suspicions, then told me to come with him and be prepared for Hell itself—although how close to the truth he meant that even I didn't know!"

The necromancer tried again. "Listen! They've cast an enchantment on me—"

"Which is why you couldn't say anything, aye!" He started to pull her toward the open doorway, where several of Jeronnan's men had gathered. Some had their weapons drawn, but none had yet dared enter, far more fearful of facing the undead than either the captain or his second. "Come on! Let's get you away from them!"

"But that's not the—" Kara stopped as her body suddenly twisted free of its own accord from the officer.

He reached for her arm. "Not that way! You'd better—"

To her dismay, the necromancer's hand folded into a fist—then *struck* her protector hard in the stomach.

While not that harsh a blow, it nevertheless caught Drayko completely by surprise. Jeronnan's second fell back, more startled than injured.

Kara turned toward the undead . . . and saw the grim Vizjerei beckoning her to join them.

Her limbs obeyed despite her best attempts to counter his summons. Behind the ghouls the blue haze had spread to encompass most of the wall. Discovered by the living, the undead now sought to retreat—but with them, they hoped to take their prize.

Kara tried to resist, knowing not only that she had no

desire to go with the duo, but that the only thing beyond that wall lay the dark sea. Tryst and his companion did not need to breathe, but Kara surely did.

Come to me, necromancer . . . she suddenly heard in her head. The eyes of Fauztin stared unblinking into her own, drowning out her own thoughts.

Unable to control herself any longer, Kara ran toward the undead.

"Lass, no!" Captain Jeronnan seized her arm, but his wound kept his grip from tightening much. She tore herself free, then reached forth to take Sadun Tryst's mutilated hand.

"I . . . have her!" the smiling ghoul gasped.

Fauztin grabbed his companion by the shoulder, then purposely fell backwards—vanishing through the blue haze and pulling Tryst with him.

And with Tryst went Kara.

"Grab hold of her!" the captain shouted. Drayko called out something, possibly her name, but by then they were both too late to do anything.

The dark mage fell through the haze—and into the suffocating embrace of the sea.

Thirteen

The tomb of Horazon . . . the Arcane Sanctuary . . .

Norrec Vizharan struggled through a thick, gray webbing, forcing his way down a winding, confusing arrangement of corridors.

Horazon . . .

Ancient statues lined the wall, each the face of someone familiar to him. He recognized Attis Zuun, his fool of an instructor. Korbia, the far too innocent acolyte he had later sacrificed for his goals. Merendi, the council leader who had fallen prey to his well-crafted words of admiration. Jeslyn Kataro, the friend who he had betrayed. Buried behind the webs he found everyone he had ever known—except one.

Everyone except his brother, Horazon.

"Where are you?" Norrec shouted. "Where are you?"

Suddenly, he stood in a darkened chamber, a vast crypt before him. Skeletons in the garb of Vizjerei sorcerers stood at attention in a series of alcoves lining the right and left walls of the room. The symbol of the clan, a dragon bent over a crescent moon, had been carved in the center of the great sarcophagus directly before the armored intruder.

"Horazon!" Norrec cried. "Horazon!"

The name echoed throughout the crypt, seeming to mock him. Angered, he marched up to the stone coffin and reached for the heavy lid.

As he touched it, a moaning arose from the skeletons on each side of him. Norrec almost shrank back, but fury and determination won out over all other emotions. Ignoring the warnings

*of the dead, the soldier wrenched the lid from the sarcophagus
and let it drop to the floor, where it shattered in a thousand
pieces.*

*Within the coffin, Norrec beheld a shrouded form. Sensing
victory, he reached to tear the cloth from the face, to see the
withered and failing countenance of his cursed brother.*

*A hand covered with rotting flesh and burrowing maggots
seized his own at the wrist.*

*He struggled, but the monstrous fingers would not release
him. Worse, to Norrec's horror, the corpse began to sink deeper
and deeper into the coffin, as if the bottom had suddenly given
way to an endless abyss. Try as he might, Norrec could not keep
from being pulled into the sarcophagus, into the pit of darkness
below.*

He screamed as the world of the dead closed in around him—

"Awaken."

Norrec shook, his gauntleted hands reaching to fend
off nightmares. He blinked, gradually realizing that he
still sat in the old chair in Drognan's sanctum. The dream
about his brother's crypt—no, *Bartuc's* brother—had
seemed so real, so horribly real.

"You slept. You dreamed," the elderly Vizjerei commented.

"Yes . . ." Unlike most dreams, however, the veteran
recalled this one quite vividly. In fact, he doubted that he
would ever be able to forget it. "I'm sorry about falling
asleep . . ."

"No need to apologize. After all, I am the one who,
with the aid of some wine, made you sleep . . . and dream
as well."

Sudden anger made Norrec try to leap up from the
chair—only to have Drognan stop him in his tracks with
but a warning hand. "You will sit back down."

"What did you do? How long have I been out?"

"I placed you under shortly after you sat down. As for
how long you slept . . . nearly a day. The night has come

and gone." The sorcerer came closer, the spell staff now used as a cane. Norrec, however, did not read Drognan's use of it as any sign of weakness. "As for why I did it, let us just say that I have taken the first step toward both our goals, my friend." He smiled expectantly. "Now, tell me, what did you see in the dream?"

"Shouldn't you know?"

"I made you dream; I did not decide *what* you dreamed of."

"Are you saying I made up that nightmare myself?"

The ancient mage stroked his silver beard. "Perhaps I had some influence on the choice of subjects . . . but the results were yours alone. Now tell me what you dreamed."

"What's the point of it?"

All friendliness faded from Drognan's tone. "The point is your life."

Aware that he had no true choice in the matter, Norrec finally gave in and told the sorcerer what he wanted to know. In nearly perfect detail, the soldier described the scene, the events, and even the faces and names of the statues. Drognan nodded, quite interested in all of it. He asked questions, dredging up minor details that Norrec had initially forgotten to mention. Nothing seemed too insignificant to the listening mage.

And when it came time to relate the horrifying events taking place in the crypt, the Vizjerei paid very close attention. Drognan seemed to take special delight in having Norrec describe the skeletal mages and the opening of the sarcophagus. Even when Norrec began to shake in recollection of his descent into the abyss, the sorcerer pushed him to continue, to not leave out the most minute bit of information.

"So fascinating!" Drognan burst out when Norrec had finished, completely oblivious to the agony he had just forced the veteran to relive. "So vivid! It must be truth!"

"What . . . must be?"

"You actually saw the tomb! The *true* Arcane Sanctuary! I'm certain of it!"

If he expected Norrec to share in his delight, the wrinkled mage had to have been disappointed. Not only did the soldier not believe that what he had seen could be real . . . but if such a place could exist, Norrec wanted no part of it. After Bartuc's lair, the notion of entering the crypt of his hated brother chilled the otherwise steadfast fighter. He had suffered nothing but misery and terror since this had all begun; Norrec only desired to be free of the enchanted armor.

He said as much to Drognan, who replied, "You will have that chance, Vizharan . . . if you are willing to face the nightmare one more time."

Somehow, Norrec found himself not at all surprised that this would be the sorcerer's response. Both Bartuc and Drognan shared the history of a culture focused much on ambition regardless of the consequences. The Empire of Kehjistan had been founded on that principle and the Vizjerei, its backbone, had delved into demon summoning as a method by which to garner power over all others. Only when those demons had turned upon them had they willingly given up that course—and even these days there existed stories of corrupt Vizjerei who had turned again to the forces of Hell for their might.

Even Fauztin had, at times, hinted of a willingness to take steps beyond what his craft would have deemed safe. However, Norrec liked to believe that his friend would have been less inclined than Drognan to force another to suffer such horrific nightmares not once, but twice—and all for simple gain.

Yet, what choice did the soldier have now? Only Drognan kept the cursed suit from running off with Norrec to who knew what new monstrous destiny . . .

He gazed around at the multitude of books and scrolls

gathered over the years by the elderly Vizjerei. Norrec suspected that they represented only a part of Drognan's storehouse of knowledge. The sorcerer had kept him to this one chamber, but surely hid some of his other secrets from the fighter. Truly, if anyone could free him, the Vizjerei could—but only if Norrec proved willing to pay the price.

Again, what other choice did he have?

"All right! Do what you must . . . and do it soon! I want an end to this!" Yet, even as he said it, Norrec knew that there would never be an end to the horrible guilt he felt.

"Of course." Drognan turned from him, reaching for another massive tome. He perused the pages for a few moments, nodded to himself, then shut the book. "Yes, that should do it."

"Do what?"

Replacing the book, the mage answered, "Despite the enmities between them, Bartuc and Horazon are forever bound together, even in death. That the suit has brought you here to Lut Gholein shows that bond remains strong even after all this time." He frowned. "And your bond with the armor is nearly as great. An unexpected plus, I might add, but one I find myself curious about. Perhaps after this is over, I shall make a study of it."

"You still haven't told me what you want to do," reminded the veteran, not wanting Drognan to become distracted again. He vaguely understood what the sorcerer had said about the bond between the brothers and how the suit had a link to that, but the rest made no sense to him and Norrec did not wish to pursue it any farther. His own connection with the armor had begun with entering Bartuc's tomb and would end when Drognan helped him strip the metal from his body. After that, the Vizjerei could do what he wanted with the suit—preferably *melting* it down to make farm tools or some other such harmless items.

"This time I will cast a spell that should enable us to find the actual physical location of the tomb, which I have always believed might very well be under the *city!*" Drognan's eyes lit up at the possibility. "It will require you to go back into the dream . . . but this time you will do so in a waking state."

"How can I dream if I'm awake?"

The mage rolled his eyes. "Preserve me from the uninitiated! Norrec Vizharan, you shall dream while awake because of my *spell*. Rest assured that you need to know nothing more."

With great reluctance, the weary fighter nodded. "All right, then! Let's get it done!"

"The preparations will take but a few moments . . ."

Coming closer, the elderly Vizjerei used the tip of his staff to draw a circle around the chair. At first Norrec saw nothing of interest in this, but the moment Drognan completed the circle, it suddenly flared to life, glowing a furious yellow and pulsating over and over. Again, the fighter would have jumped out of the chair if not for the warning glance his host gave him. In an attempt to calm down, Norrec reminded himself of the ultimate goal of all of this—freedom. Surely he could face whatever Drognan might put him through for that.

The sorcerer muttered something, then reached out with his left hand to touch Norrec's forehead. The soldier felt a slight jolt, but nothing more.

With his finger, Drognan began drawing symbols in the air, symbols that flashed into and out of existence each time he finished one. Norrec caught only glances of each, although at least one reminded him of one of the wards he had seen in Bartuc's tomb. That made him more wary again, but the time for retreat had already passed and he knew that he had to face whatever resulted from the spellcasting.

"*Shazari . . . Shazari Tomei . . .*"

Norrec's entire body stiffened, almost as if the armor had once more taken control. However, the veteran soldier knew that it could not be that, for Drognan had long ago proven his mastery over the enchanted suit. No, it had to be just another part of the spell.

"Tomei!" the silver-haired mage cried, raising his spell staff high above his head. Despite his advanced years, he looked more terrible, more powerful, than any man Norrec had ever met, even on the battlefield. A white, crackling aura surrounded the Vizjerei, causing Drognan's beard and hair to fluttered about almost as if with a life of their own. *"Shazari Saruphi!"*

Norrec gasped as his body shook violently. A force pushed him hard against the chair. The mage's sanctum suddenly receded from him with such speed it made the fighter dizzy. Norrec felt as if he floated, although neither his arms nor his legs could move at all.

An emerald haze formed before him, a haze with a vaguely circular shape to it. Far, far away, Norrec heard Drognan shout something else, but it seemed drawn out and unintelligible, as if for the Vizjerei time had slowed to a crawl and even sound could move no swifter than a snail.

The haze refined itself, forming a perfect circle now. The emerald mist within that circle then dissipated—and as it did, an image, a place, formed within.

The crypt.

But something about its appearance immediately troubled Norrec. Details seemed altered, incorrect in many ways. The Vizjerei skeletons now wore elaborate armor instead of robes and appeared not to be true dead, but rather cleverly carved from stone. The massive cobwebs gave way instead to tattered tapestries depicting magical creatures such as dragons, rocs, and more. Even the symbol of the brothers' clan had transformed, now a vast bird clutching in its talons the sun.

Norrec tried to say something, but his voice did not work. Once more, though, he heard the painfully belabored words of Drognan. The mage sounded farther away than before.

Suddenly, the image of the crypt receded. Faster and faster it rushed away from Norrec. Although he still sat in the chair, it felt to the fighter as if he ran backwards through the musty corridors leading to Horazon's tomb. Row upon row of statue darted in front of Norrec, vanishing as quickly as the crypt had. Although most faces appeared as little more than blurs, some few he recognized, but not as those from the warlord's dark past. Instead, they were faces from Norrec's own life—Sadun Tryst, Fauztin, Norrec's first commander, some of the women he had loved, and even Captain Casco. A few he did not recognize at all, including a pale but attractive young woman with hair the color of night and eyes so arresting not only for their exotic curve, but for the simple fact that they gleamed silver.

But even the statues finally receded from sight. Now he saw but earth and rock, all tumbling about him as if he burrowed in reverse. Drognan called out something, but he might as well have been silent for all Norrec understood him.

At last, the earth and rock gave way to a more powdery substance . . . *sand*, he belatedly realized. A glimmer of light, perhaps the light of day, spread around the edges of the images.

Norrec!

The veteran shook his head, certain that he had imagined someone calling his name.

Norrec! Vizharan!

It sounded like Drognan, but Drognan as he had never heard the sorcerer. The Vizjerei sounded almost anxious, possibly even fearful.

Vizharan! Fight it!

Something within Norrec stirred, a fear for his very soul . . .

His left hand rose of its own accord.

"No!" he shouted, his own voice seeming distant, disconnected from him.

His other hand rose, his entire body following suit.

He had barely left the chair when a physical force suddenly attempted to halt his unwilling progress. Norrec saw the distorted form of Drognan, staff in both hands, trying to drive the soldier back, away from the vision of the Arcane Sanctuary. He also saw his own gauntleted hands meet those of the Vizjerei, Norrec gripping the staff as if he sought to rip it free.

The staff crackled with energy where the two men held it tight, brilliant yellow bursts where Drognan touched, bloody crimson flashes where Norrec's fingers sought a hold. Norrec could feel powerful sorceries flowing through his very being—

Fight it, Vizharan! called Drognan from somewhere. His mouth never seemed to move, but his expression matched the stress in the words in Norrec's head. *The armor is stronger than I believed! We have been tricked all along!*

No more need have been said. He understood exactly what the mage meant. The enchanted armor had obviously never been under the Vizjerei's control; the suit had simply bided its time, waiting for Drognan to discover that for it which it had so very long sought.

The location of Horazon's tomb.

In some things, then, Drognan had been correct. He had said that Bartuc and his hated brother remained linked forever. So now did Norrec see why the armor had dragged him from one side of the world to the other. Something pulled it toward the final resting place of Horazon, something so powerful that even death had been unable to stop the quest.

The armor had a mind of sorts; certainly it had shown far more cleverness than either Norrec or anyone else he had so far met. Likely when the *Hawksfire* had approached Lut Gholein it had even sensed Drognan's spellwork . . . and somehow knew that it could make use of the Vizjerei in order to further its own sinister goals.

Incredible, unbelievable, improbable—but more than likely the absolute truth.

Energy sizzled between Norrec's gauntlets. Drognan let out a cry and fell back, not dead but obviously stunned. The gloves released their hold on the spell staff, then the right reached for the image before Norrec.

However, as it did, the vision began to shift, to pull away, as if some other force now sought to defeat the suit's evil purpose. The image faded, twisted—

Undeterred, the armor placed the right gauntlet into the very center. A crimson aura appeared around the hand.

"Shazari Giovox!"

As the undesired words fell from his lips, Norrec's body lost all substance. He cried out, but nothing would stop the process. As if a creature of smoke, his form stretched, contorted—and finally *poured* into the dwindling vision.

Not until both Norrec and the magical circle had both vanished did his screaming stop.

This day they had lost one man to sand maggots and another to the heat of the desert itself, yet Galeona noticed that, if anything, Augustus Malevolyn acted more and more cheerful, almost as if he already had not only the armor of Bartuc but the power and glory he dreamed it would give him. That bothered the witch, bothered her more than she would have thought it could. Such a display was hardly like the general. If his disposition had lightened so much, he surely had good reason for it.

Galeona suspected that reason had something to do with Xazax. She had not seen much of the demon of late and that never meant anything good. In fact, since the other night, when Malevolyn had evidently lost his common sense and taken a walk alone in the dark desert, the mantis had acted distant. Twice when the sorceress had found excuses to separate herself from the party and talk with him about their plans, Xazax had remained suspiciously remote in his comments. It almost seemed as if everything for which they had worked together no longer mattered.

Xazax wants the armor, she considered. *But he can't make use of its enchantments himself.*

Yet, if he could not, surely a human dupe could . . . and Augustus presented a quite a distinct possibility there. Already the witch had suspected Xazax of trying to manipulate her lover. Now she felt certain that she had underestimated the mantis.

Galeona had to regain her influence over the general. If not, she risked losing more than her station—the sorceress risked losing her head.

Malevolyn had called for a rest. They had made surprisingly good time and had overall suffered scant losses to their harsh surroundings. A pack of leapers—monstrous, hopping terrors somewhat reptilian in appearance and with spikes along their spines—had harried them for a time, but never had the troops allowed the creatures to come near enough to make use of their long claws and savage teeth. Slaying one had left the others fighting over the carcass. Like most desert creatures, the easy meal, even if it happened to be one of their own, ever won out over battling with something that battled back.

If anything, the sand and heat continued to be their greatest nemesis, which had been why the general had finally relented. Had the choice been solely his, he would have kept going, even if it meant riding his mount to death and then walking on from there.

"I can almost see it," he remarked as she rode up next to him. Malevolyn had taken his horse and moved on a short distance ahead of the column. Now he sat in the saddle, surveying the emptiness ahead. "I can almost taste it. . . ."

She edged her own mount nearer, then extended one hand in order to touch his. General Malevolyn, Bartuc's bloody helm still in place, did not so much as look at her, not a good sign at all.

"And well deserved," she cooed, trying to garner his interest. "Imagine how you'll look when you bear down on Lut Gholein clad in the crimson helm of the warlord! They'll think you to be him come back to life!"

She regretted the words almost at once, recalling how his memories and those of the helmet had earlier melded together. He had not suffered another bout since that last, sinister event, but Galeona still wore the burning reminder of that time on her finger.

Fortunately, Augustus appeared to have his own mind for the moment. He finally looked Galeona's way, sounding pleased with what the sorceress had said. "Yes, that *will* be a wondrous sight—the last one they will ever behold! I can almost picture it now . . . the cries of fear, the looks of horror as they realize their doom and who it is who delivers it."

Perhaps now she had the opportunity for which she had been looking. "You know, my love, while if we still have time, I can cast another search spell for you. With the helmet, it wouldn't be—"

"No." As simple as that. His gaze leaving her, Malevolyn added, "No. That will not be necessary."

He did not see the shiver that coursed through her. With those few words, he had verified her deepest fears. The general had even been adamant about taking any opportunity they could to seek out with sorcery the rest of Bartuc's legendary garb. When the helmet had fallen into his hands in an act even she would have called providential, he had spared no effort in letting her use the artifact to aid in hunting for the suit. Even when they had discovered that this Norrec now walked the earth clad in Malevolyn's prize, he had insisted she still use the helmet at regular intervals to keep track of the wanderer's route.

Now he talked as if he hardly cared, as if he had become so certain of the inevitability of retrieving the armor that he no longer even needed to maintain a magical eye on it. This did not at all sound like the Augustus she had known so inside and out, and Galeona felt it did not entirely have to do with the influence of the helmet. Surely the enchanted artifact had already solidified its hold over him enough to survive a few moments' separation.

And that brought her back to Xazax.

"As you wish," Galeona finally replied. "How soon before we move on again, my love?"

He glanced up in the direction of the sun. "A quarter hour. No more. I will be ready to meet my destiny at the proper time."

She did not ask him to elaborate. A quarter hour would suffice for her work. "I shall leave you to your thoughts, then, my general."

That he did not even nod in dismissal did not surprise her in the least. Yes, Xazax had definitely made his move, likely had even contacted the commander directly. By doing so, the demon had taken the first step toward not only severing his pact with the witch, but seeing her *dead*.

"We'll see whose head lies atop a pike," she muttered. With no shadows in which to hide, Xazax had to remain far from the column until the fall of night. That meant that Galeona could cast her spell with little worry that the treacherous mantis would know of it.

The sorceress found an ideal location behind a dune just beyond the column. She herself had no fear of sand maggots and the like, protective measures cast by her before the journey's beginning still strong. It had been within the limits of her power to do the same for the rest of those in the column, but that would have left Galeona without any ability to cast other spells. She had seen no reason to be so magnanimous. A few less soldiers would not make a difference to her . . .

Dismounting, she took her water flask, then knelt on the hot sand. From the flask the witch poured several precious mouthfuls of the cool liquid onto the parched ground. The moment she felt satisfied with the amount, Galeona shut the flask, then quickly went to work.

Her slim, tapering fingers molded the damp sand into a vaguely human figure the size of a doll. As she refined the form, Galeona muttered the first portion of her spell, attuning her creation to what she desired. The sand figure took on a more male aspect, broad of shoulder with indentations along the torso showing it to be wearing armor.

Knowing that the moisture would not last long, Galeona quickly took out a tiny vial. Still whispering, the sorceress poured a few drops of its contents onto the chest of the sand doll. The vial contained a liquid most precious to her; a small bit of blood that she had sacrificed from her body, then preserved for certain, delicate spellwork.

A representation involving Bartuc's armor needed blood to mark it and, more important, to link Galeona to the figurine she had created. That, in turn, she hoped would enable her to reach out to this Norrec, touch him as she had on the ship. As distant as he had earlier been when she and Xazax had summoned the Dreamer, such a spell cast then would have required far too much of her life's fluids for her to survive the effort. The soldier sacrificed in the tent had served in her place the last time. Now, though, Galeona felt certain that what she attempted here *would* succeed—and with minimal effect on her.

She drew a circle around the effigy, then placed her hands—palms down and fingers splayed—on the left and right sides of her creation. Leaning low, she stared at where the face would have been, whispering the final segment of her spell while intermittently muttering the soldier's name.

"Norrec . . . Norrec . . ."

The world around her receded. Galeona's view shifted, flew along the desert as if she had been transformed into an eagle who soared the skies with the swiftness of the wind. Faster and faster it raced, until she could no longer even see what landscape lay beneath her.

Her spell had worked. Through her own memories of her brief encounter with the fool, she further strengthened the magic by concentrating on his face, his form.

"Norrec . . . show me . . . show me where you are . . ."

Her view suddenly shifted, turned completely black. The abrupt change so caught Galeona by surprise that she nearly broke the spell. Only quick thinking enabled her to maintain the precious link; she would not have time to try again if she failed now. Even this long away from the column might make Augustus suspicious.

"Norrec . . . show me . . ."

His face appeared before her, eyes closed, mouth slack. For a moment, the witch wondered if he had somehow perished, but then she realized that her incantation could not have worked in the first place if that had been the case. The sand effigy demanded a living target.

If not dead, then what had happened? Galeona probed deeper, entered the frame in which Norrec existed. By doing so, she lost all but the thinnest thread of contact with the true world, but, by doing so, she also stood to gain so much more.

And at last, the sorceress saw where her quarry lay.

The knowledge so stunned her that *this* time she could not help but lose her link to him. His face pulled away, receded with such shocking speed that it gave her vertigo. The darkness reappeared, then Galeona found herself falling backwards across the desert, a complete reversal of her journey.

With a gasp, the exhausted witch fell back onto the burning sand.

She ignored the discomfort, ignored everything. The only thing that mattered to her was what she had just learned.

"So . . ." Galeona whispered. "I have you, my pretty puppet."

Fourteen

A harsh rumbling shook Kara Nightshadow, dragging her from the darkness enveloping her. She inhaled, only to quickly start choking. The necromancer tried to breathe, but her lungs would not work properly.

She coughed, suddenly expelling an ocean of water. Over and over, Kara coughed, each time trying to empty her lungs so that she could then fill them up with life-saving air.

At last it became possible to breathe, albeit somewhat raggedly. The necromancer lay still, inhaling again and again in an attempt to regain some balance. Gradually, matters returned near enough to normal for her to begin to sense other things, such as the chill around her and the moisture saturating all her clothes. A gritty substance in her mouth forced her to spit, and she slowly realized that she lay face down on a sandy beach.

Again the world rumbled around her. Forcing her head up, Kara saw that the heavens above had begun to fill with storm clouds much like those of the tempest through which the *King's Shield* had sailed. In fact, she suspected the clouds above to be the precursor of the same storm, now ready to assail much of the eastern coast.

Memories began to return, memories of Captain Jeronnan in battle with the revenants, then the two undead dragging the necromancer through the portal and into the raging sea. After that, however, she could recall nothing whatsoever. How Kara had survived, she could not say. The enchantress did not even know what fate, if any, might have befallen Jeronnan and his men. It had seemed as if the portal had not had any effect on the hull, so if the *King's Shield* had survived that incident, then the odds were good that the vessel would soon make Lut Gholein—if it had not done so already.

Kara blinked, thinking of the city. The fate of the *King's Shield* aside, where by Rathma had *she* ended up? With great effort, the soaked necromancer pushed herself to a kneeling position and peered around.

Her first glimpse of her surroundings told Kara little. Sand and a few hardy plants typical of a coastal environment. She saw no signs of civilization, no signs of any human touch. Ahead of her lay a high ridge, making observation further inland impossible without a bit of a climb. Kara tried to avoid the inevitable by looking left, then right, but neither of those directions offered her more hope. Her only true option remained the ridge.

Still feeling as if she had just expunged both of the Twin Seas from her system, Kara forced herself to her feet. She knew that she should have removed most of her cold wet clothing, but the notion of being discovered by any locals while without much to wear did not appeal to her. Besides, other than the wind, the day itself seemed fairly warm. If she moved around for a while, surely her garments would dry.

Of either Sadun Tryst or Fauztin she saw no sign, but by no means did Kara think herself rid of the two ghouls. Most likely they had all become separated in the fearsome waters. For all she knew, the duo had washed up farther down the coast. If so, it behooved the necromancer to reach Lut Gholein as quickly as possible, perhaps even look for this Vizjerei they had mentioned, this Drognan. She doubted that he willingly worked with the undead; likely they sought the use of his knowledge in order to find their former friend. Whatever the case,

Drognan also represented her best chance of not only freeing herself from any bond to the revenants, but also locating Norrec Vizharan and the armor.

With some struggling, the enchantress made it to the top of the sandy ridge—and there discovered a well-worn road. Better yet, as she looked to the south, she noticed a dim shape on the horizon, a shape Kara believed resembled a city.

Lut Gholein?

With as much eagerness as her weary mind could muster, she started south. If, as she suspected, Lut Gholein lay ahead, it would likely take her a good day to travel that far, especially in her condition. Worse, hunger already gnawed at her stomach, a condition that only grew worse with each step she took. Nevertheless, Kara did not even think of giving in to her weaknesses. So long as she could walk, she would continue on with her mission.

However, Kara had journeyed only a short distance when a clatter behind her made the weary necromancer pause to look over her shoulder. To her relief, she spied two well-laden wagons making their way from the north, a bushy-bearded old man and heavy-set woman in the first, a younger, wide-eyed youth and a girl most likely his sister guiding the second. A family of merchants no doubt on their way to sell their wares in the thriving metropolis. The exhausted necromancer paused, hoping that they would have pity on a bedraggled wanderer.

The elderly man might have driven his team past Kara, but his wife took one look at her and made him stop. They exchanged words with one another for a few moments, then, in the common tongue, the woman asked her. "Are you all right, young one? What's happened? Are you in need of help?"

Almost too tired to answer, the necromancer pointed toward the east. "My ship, it——"

She need not have said anything more. A sad look

came over the elderly woman's round face and even the man gave her sympathy. Anyone living or traveling this near the sea surely knew of its violence. No doubt this had not been the first time the merchants had learned of some seafaring disaster.

The husband leapt down with an agility that belied his age. As he approached, he asked, "Is there anyone more? You the only one?"

"There is . . . no one else. I was . . . the ship may be all right . . . I was . . . washed overboard."

His wife made a tsking sound. "You're still soaked, too, young one! And your clothes are in tatters! Hesia! Find her a blouse and a warm blanket! Those, at least, she must have at once! Hurry!"

Unwilling to accept any charity, Kara fumbled at her belt. To her tremendous relief, the pouch in which she kept her money had somehow managed to remain intact. "I will pay for everything, I promise."

"Rubbish!" remarked the husband, but when she insisted on thrusting some coins in his hand, he nonetheless took most of them.

Hesia, daughter of the merchants Rhubin and Jamili, brought garments that Kara could only believe had to belong to the girl herself. Clearly with an eye toward respecting the stranger's dour garb, she had chosen a black blouse and even a gray knit blanket with which Kara could cover herself. Out of eyesight of Rhubin and his son, Ranul, she changed, feeling much better to be out of the soaked and ruined clothing.

Kara regretted the loss of her cloak even more once she had put on the blouse. Although in keeping with her taste in color, it fit too tight and had been cut too low. Yet, she said nothing, knowing that it had been the best choice available and, more important, something offered to her out of genuine concern. That she had insisted on paying for it did not take away from that.

To her relief, Jamili had Kara ride in the first wagon. Old enough to appreciate women, Ranul had eyed her with casual interest in the beginning and far more pointed interest once the enchantress had dried herself off and changed clothing. She expected no harm from him, but did not want to encourage anything that might cause dissension between herself and her rescuers.

And so, with the help of the kind merchant family, Kara Nightshadow managed to actually reach Lut Gholein more than an hour before sunset. She thought of immediately going to the port to see if Captain Jeronnan had arrived, but the urgency of her quest finally made her decide against it. The hunt for Norrec Vizharan and Bartuc's armor remained paramount.

In the gaily-colored bazaar, she bid farewell to Jamili and her family. Kara returned the blanket with thanks, then searched the marketplace for someone from whom she could buy an inexpensive but serviceable cloak. Doing so used up another valuable hour, but with the hooded garment the necromancer no longer felt so vulnerable. Kara would have replaced some of her other clothes as well, but her funds, much depleted, needed to be preserved now for food.

Questioning the locals carefully brought the dark mage some information concerning the mysterious Drognan. He seemed to live in an old building some distance into the massive city. Few visited him save to purchase elixirs and such. The only time Drognan left his sanctum looked to be when he made excursions to various scholars, seeking information on some pet passion of his.

Following the directions of a vegetable seller who had, on occasion, supplied the Vizjerei with supplies, Kara wended her way through the mazelike streets. The multitude of noises and bright colors wreaked some havoc on her senses, but she managed to not lose her way more than twice. Every so often the necromancer asked a passerby if he or she had seen a man clad in red armor, but not once did anyone say that they had.

Her kidnapping and near drowning in the sea had left her bereft of nearly all her belongings. Other than the pouch in which she had kept her money, only two others had survived. Unfortunately, the powders and chemicals in both had been ruined, save for a couple of vials of no use to her at present. Amazingly enough, the icon of Trag'Oul remained around her throat, for which she thanked the great dragon. It gave her some comfort in this strange land.

The loss of her belongings did not mean that Kara could no longer cast spells, but it did limit her somewhat. Fortunately, her change in garb had so far kept anyone from realizing her calling, even if it had encouraged one or two vendors to try to offer her more than information. Necromancers were not favored in Lut Gholein. The Church of Zakarum, powerful in the kingdom, frowned on their existence even more than it did that of the Vizjerei, who were evidently tolerated here by the young sultan. One or two acolytes from the Church had crossed her path so far, but, other than brief glances, they had not paid any attention to the slim young woman.

With much of what remained of her funds, Kara had purchased enough to carry along with her so that she could eat while she searched for Drognan. The notion of confronting a skilled, experienced Vizjerei bothered her enough, but to do so nearly ready to collapse would have been foolhardy at best. She could not assume that their encounter would necessarily be a friendly one. Animosity had long existed between the two callings.

A trio of soldiers on mounted patrol rode past, their eyes stern and their swords always near at hand. The foremost, evidently the officer in charge, rode a magnificent white stallion while his two subordinates each had brown, well-muscled beasts of their own. Kara had ridden little in her life, but realized as she watched them that, if the trail led outside of Lut Gholein, she would have to find some means of obtaining a horse. The dark mage could not rely on any travel spell out in the desert of Aranoch. Even in her far-off homeland Kara had heard tales of its deadly nature.

Her surroundings suddenly grew decrepit and dank, a complete contrast to the well-kept areas she had first encountered. Kara cursed herself for not having parted with her remaining coins for a usable dagger. The one that Captain Jeronnan had loaned her while aboard the *King's Shield* had been lost at sea. The enchantress began concentrating on her spells, inwardly hoping that she would still have the strength to cast them should the situation prove dire enough.

The necromancer came at last to the old building the vendor had somewhat vaguely described. Despite its decayed appearance, Kara immediately sensed forces at work in and around it. Some felt extremely ancient, surely even more ancient than the edifice itself. Others seemed more recent, including a few that had to have been summoned not all that long ago.

Climbing the outer steps, Kara looked over the ruined doorway, then stepped inside——

——and found herself standing in a timeworn but still magnificent hall that spoke of the glories of another time, another place. While also projecting a sense of long-ago abandonment, the high-columned hall had nothing else in common with the decrepit exterior, so much so that Kara even felt tempted to step outside again to see if perhaps she had somehow entered the wrong building. Here stood no ruin, but rather an ancient wonder still filled with the memories of greatness, of a splendor that even modern Lut Gholein had not yet approached.

The necromancer walked slowly through the hall, her

mission still in mind but her attention distracted by the awesome marble columns, the imposing stone fireplace that covered nearly all of of one far wall, and the massive mosaic floor upon which she cautiously tread.

The floor, in fact, ensnared her attention more and more as Kara walked. In it, the artisan had captured intricate images both fanciful and real. Dragons curled around trees. Lions gave chase after antelope. Fearsome, stony warriors clad in breastplates and kilts did battle with one another.

Something clattered further down the hall.

Kara froze, her gaze shifting that direction. Yet, despite her excellent night vision, she could only make out a shadowed doorway at the far end. The necromancer waited, hesitant to even breathe too loudly. However, when no new noise came, Kara exhaled, realizing that in this ancient edifice bits of marble and stone would, on occasion, fall free. Even the slightest sound echoed here.

And at that moment, something behind her scraped across the marble floor.

She spun about, suddenly certain that the revenants had followed her here and now had chosen to reveal themselves. Against them, Kara could truly do nothing, but that did not mean that she would not struggle. They had already done too much, taken too much.

However, instead of the ever-grinning Sadun Tryst and his sorcerous companion, what greeted her eyes proved to be even more startling.

The gray figure wielding the sturdy blade moved slowly but surely toward her, his intention quite clear. Kara might have taken him for some brigand who had waited in the shadows for her, if not for the fact that she recognized him from but a few seconds earlier. Of course, even if Kara had not recognized the newcomer, she certainly could still make out the many tiny squares of stone composing not only his entire breastplate and kilt—but also his very skin.

The mosaic warrior stalked her, his savage expression exactly the same as when he had existed only as a decoration set in the floor. He swiped at her with the blade—revealing then that while he had the height and width of a living creature, he had no more depth to his form than the tiny stones from which he had been created.

Not for a moment, though, did Kara think this any weakness. The magic that had created such a guardian would not have made him so fragile. Physically striking the mosaic warrior would likely be just like striking a stone wall. She also suspected that the blade would cut just as well as, if not better than, a real one freshly sharpened.

But what had set him into action? Surely Drognan did not set out such a welcome for everyone who walked through the door. No, more likely Kara had been identified by some hidden spell as a necromancer, a dark mage of unknown loyalties. She knew of such detection spells and knew also that many mages utilized them for their own safety. Had Kara not suffered through so much of late, the enchantress felt certain she would have recalled such information earlier—when it might have prevented this deadly encounter.

Rattling came from the floor just behind her macabre assailant, and to the necromancer's consternation, a second warrior arose to join the first. Kara then turned quickly to her right, where yet more noise marked the awakening of a third.

"I mean no harm," she whispered. "I seek your master." Did they even serve Drognan? Kara only assumed that she had come to the right place. Perhaps someone the enchantress had talked to earlier had recognized her for what she was and had sent her here to *die*. Many, especially those of the Zakarum faith, would have considered the loss of a necromancer no loss at all.

The first of the mosaics had nearly come within the striking range of his sword. Kara saw no other choice but to take the offensive.

The words of the spell tripped off her tongue as the necromancer clutched the icon of Trag'Oul and pointed at her first attacker. At the same time, Kara stepped back as a precaution. If her spell worked, the incredible forces she summoned might not be contained to the destruction of the magical guardian.

A swarm of toothy projectiles formed from thin air, then rained down on the nearest of the mosaic warriors. The *Den'Trag*, or *Teeth of the Dragon Trag'Oul*, ripped through the stone body of the guardian, scattering small squares everywhere. The warrior tried to move, but his legs and arms, now missing so many pieces, crumbled. Still wearing his scowl, he attempted one last thrust at her, then collapsed in a shower of stone.

Kara exhaled, relieved to be rid of at least one adversary but praying she still had the strength to deal with the others. Summoning the Den'Trag had taken much out of the already-weary necromancer. Yet, if Kara could do it twice more and thus completely eliminate her unliving foes, then perhaps she could rest afterward.

Once again the necromancer clutched the icon tight, muttering the spell. A few words more and—

An intense rattling all around her caused Kara to falter. She glanced down, saw the many bits of mosaic stone from the fallen warrior now rolling toward one another, gathering in a swiftly growing pile behind the others. To her horror, first the feet, then the legs reformed. Bit by bit the stone warrior rebuilt himself, none the worse for her destructive spell.

The Teeth of Trag'Oul had failed her. Stepping back, Kara entered the darkened hall leading to the doorway. She had other spells at her command, but, combined with her weakness and the enclosed surroundings, none of them seemed likely to help her quickly enough without risking her own life further.

"Verikos!" a voice called. *"Verikos . . . Dianysi!"*

The ungodly trio paused at the cry . . . then each warrior abruptly collapsed, the individual stones dropping to the ground with a harsh clatter that echoed throughout the ancient structure. The stones, however, did not rest where they lay, but rather began to quickly roll back to where the figures had originally been set in the ground, each bit of mosaic returning to its precise location. One by one, they fell into place. Within seconds, the menacing fighters had not only retreated from their attack but had completely reformed as images on the elegant floor.

Kara turned to thank her rescuer, certain that it had to be the enigmatic Drognan. "I thank you for your aid—"

The figure that stood before her could hardly be the venerable, elegantly clad Vizjerei the vendor and others had described. Advanced age seemed the only thing this wild-eyed beggar with long white hair and beard had in common with the mage in question, although even Drognan could not be as old as this man looked. While still somewhat firm of body, his skin had grown so wrinkled and his watery blue eyes so weary that surely he had to be the oldest human alive in all the world.

He put a gnarled finger to thin lips. "Hush!" the beggar whispered much too loudly. "So much evil about! So much danger! We shouldn't have come here!"

"Are you . . . are you Drognan?"

The elderly man blinked, looked confused, then patted his worn, silk robe as if looking for something. After several seconds of this, he finally looked up and replied, "No . . . no, of course not! Now hush! There's too much evil about! We've got to be careful! We've got to be on guard!"

Kara considered. This man had to be a servant or something similar to the mage. Perhaps Drognan even kept him here out of pity for the beggar's madness. She decided to get to the point. Perhaps enough sanity remained within the man so that he could help her with the Vizjerei. "I have to see your master, Drognan. Tell him it concerns something of interest to him, Bartuc's——"

"*Bartuc?*" A ghastly change came over the beggar as he shouted the dead warlord's name. "*Bartuc!* No! The evil's come! I warned you!"

At that moment, another voice called out from the entrance of the building. "Who is it? Who has invaded my sanctum?"

The necromancer turned to speak, but the ragged man moved with amazing swiftness. He clamped a hand over her mouth, then whispered, "Hush! We mustn't be heard! It might be Bartuc!"

Instead, the newcomer proved to be a Vizjerei—and likely the one for whom Kara had been searching. Curiously, he looked as if he had been in some accident, for he had bruises over much of his face and seemed in discomfort each time he put pressure on his right leg. In the crook of one arm, the elderly mage carried a small package. She had no doubt that here stood Drognan, newly arrived from some errand.

"Norrec?" he called. "Vizharan?"

He knew the man Kara hunted! She tried to speak, but for a rather spindly figure, the beggar had incredible strength.

"Hush!" her unwanted companion whispered. "So much evil about! We must be careful! We mustn't be seen!"

Drognan stepped closer, surely able to see them now—and yet, he peered *past* both intruders as if seeing only air.

"Curious . . ." He sniffed the air, then frowned. "Smells as if a necromancer was about . . . but that's absurd." Drognan glanced at the floor, at the warriors in particular. "Yes . . . absurd."

He continued to stare, as if lost in thought. Not once did the mage so much as notice the struggling woman or her odd captor. At last, the sorcerer shook his head, muttered to himself about another lost trail and the need to keep searching, then—much to Kara's dismay—walked past her and the madman. Drognan continued on, heading into the darkness, heading toward the doorway she had earlier sought.

Heading away from someone in desperate need of his aid.

Only when he vanished behind the door did the tattered figure pull his hand from her lips. Planting his face next to hers, he whispered, "We've stayed too long! We'd better go back! Been out much too long! He might find us!"

She knew that he did not mean Drognan. No, judging by his earlier reaction, her captor could only mean one other—*Bartuc.*

He led her along the sculpted floor, to the very center, where the unknown artisan had built out of mosaic tiles an intricate temple like those that might have existed in legendary Viz-jun. Kara would not have followed him that far, but, as with the revenants, the choice of what her body did no longer remained hers. The necromancer could not even call out.

"Soon we'll be safe!" the madcap figure muttered to her. "Soon we'll be safe!"

He stomped down once with his right foot—and suddenly the doorway of the temple opened, *deepened*, becoming an oval hole in the floor in which the necromancer could see a set of steps leading to—to *where?*

"Come, come!" her captor chided her. "Before Bartuc finds us! Come, come!"

Unable to do otherwise, she followed him down into the earth, down toward a distant, yellowish light. As Kara stepped below the level of the floor, the enchantress sensed the stones shifting, the image of the Vizjerei temple returning to its prior state.

"We'll be safe down here," the mad hermit assured her, seeming somewhat more calm now. "My brother will never find us here . . ."

Brother? Had she heard right?

"*Horazon?*" Kara blurted, surprised not only by her conclusion but that she could now articulate it. Evidently her captor had no concerns about anyone hearing her underneath layers of rock and earth.

He looked right at her, the watery eyes focusing hard for the first time. "Do we know each other? I don't think we know each other . . ." When she did not respond immediately, he shrugged and continued on with the trek, still mumbling. "I'm sure we don't know each other but we might know each other . . ."

Kara Nightshadow still had no choice but to follow, not that she much noticed at the moment. Her thoughts reeled, her world entirely turned upside-down.

She had come in search of the Warlord of Blood's armor and had found instead—even despite the many centuries that had passed since their time—Bartuc's living, breathing, and much hated *brother*.

Incredible heat assailed Norrec as he at last came back to his senses. At first he imagined that a fire must have started in Drognan's sanctum, perhaps through the arcane powers of the sinister armor. However, gradually the veteran became aware that the heat, while harsh, did not burn and, in fact, surely had to be from the sun itself.

Rolling over onto his back, Norrec shielded his eyes and tried to get his bearings, only to find a sea of sand in every direction. He grimaced, wondering where he had landed now. In the distance, Norrec thought he noticed darkness, as if a storm approached from that direction. Could Lut Gholein lay somewhere underneath those clouds? It seemed wherever he went, the storm followed. If that were the case now, then at least he knew that he had materialized somewhere west or northwest of the coastal kingdom.

But why?

Drognan had said something about the armor having tricked them. How true those words had been. It had played both the Vizjerei and him for fools, no doubt seeking the mage's aid in locating its goal. Could that have been Horazon's tomb, as Drognan believed? If so, why had Norrec ended up out here in the middle of nowhere?

With great effort, the battered and worn soldier rose. Judging by the sun, he had a little more than an hour or two before nightfall. The walk back to Lut Gholein would take far longer than that, likely two days—and that providing Norrec actually survived the trek. More important, he could not even be certain that the suit would let him return. If what it sought lay out here, it would do everything it could to remain in the desert.

Norrec took a few steps, testing the armor's resolve. When it did nothing to prevent him from heading toward the city, he increased his pace as best he could. At the very least, Norrec needed to find some shelter for the night and the only hope of that lay in a twisted hill of rock barely visible ahead. It would take him until sunset to reach the hill, if not longer, which meant that, despite the heat, he had to move even quicker.

His legs ached horribly as Norrec pushed on. The loose sand and high dunes made it tough going and often Norrec lost sight of his goal for quite some time. He even found himself turned around at one point, the swirling dunes shifting in size and direction even as he tried to cross them.

Yet, despite all that, the hill soon became an aspiration possible to achieve. Norrec prayed that he would find moisture of some sort there; his short time in the desert had already parched him. If he did not find water soon, it would not matter whether he made it to the hill or—

A large, winged shadow crossed over his own . . . followed immediately by a second.

Norrec looked up, trying to see against the sun. He caught glimpses of two or three airborne forms, but could not make them out. Vultures? Quite possible in Aranoch, but these looked much larger and not quite avian in some ways. Norrec's hand slipped to where his sword would have been and once more he cursed Bartuc's armor for putting him through such horrors without a decent weapon of his own.

Despite his flagging strength, the veteran doubled his pace. If he could reach the rock, it would provide him with some defense against the marauding birds. Vultures tended to be scavengers, but this flock looked more aggressive and, in some way he could still not define, unsettling.

The shadows passed over him again, this time much larger, much more distinct. The creatures had descended for a better look.

He barely sensed in time the feathered form dropping on him from behind. With instincts honed on the battlefield, Norrec threw himself to the ground just as talons as great as his hand scraped across his armored back and managed to briefly snag his hair. The hardened fighter grunted as he rolled over, ready to face the birds. Surely he could scare off a few vultures, especially once he let them see he would not simply lie down and die for them.

But *these* were no vultures . . . although their ancestry had certainly come from those desert scavengers.

Nearly as tall as a man and with the wings and head of the avian they so resembled, the four grotesque creatures fluttered just above him, talons on both their feet and their almost human hands ready to tear his head from his body. Their tails ended in whips that lashed out at Norrec as he desperately tried to back away. The demonic birds let out harsh cries as they tried to surround their would-be victim, cries that made Norrec's pulse pound.

He waited for the suit to do something, but Bartuc's armor remained dormant. Swearing, Norrec braced himself. If he had to die here, he would not die like a lamb because he had come to depend on the armor for so much. Nearly all his life, he had served in one war or another. This battle represented little different.

One of the monstrous vultures came within his grasp. Moving with more speed than he thought himself capable of at this point, Norrec seized it by one of its legs and threw it to the ground. Despite their size, the desert terrors were astoundingly light, no doubt because, like their ancestors, their bones were designed for flight. He took advantage of that, using his own considerable mass to pin the shrieking creature down, then twisting the head as hard as he could.

The three survivors harried him even harder as he rose from the limp form, but a different Norrec faced them now, one who had, for the first time in many days, fought a battle of his own and won. As the second dove at him, he grabbed a handful of sand and threw it in the vulpine horror's eyes. The demonic bird blindly whipped its tail at him, giving the veteran soldier the chance to seize the deadly appendage in both hands.

Squawking, the creature tried to fly free. However, Norrec spun the massive avian around again and again, driving back the other pair at the same time. The talons of his captured foe scraped futilely on his gauntleted hands, Bartuc's armor well protecting its host.

Norrec's blood surged. His attackers had come to represent to him more than simply the dangers of the desert. In many ways, they now became the brunt of all his frustration and fury. He had suffered through too many terrible events, suffered too many horrors, and not once had been able to do anything about them. Powerful enchantments saturated the warlord's armor and yet none of it obeyed him. Had it been his to command, he would have used the sorcery of the suit to roast the demonic beast he now held, turn it and its dire companions into fireballs.

His gloves suddenly glowed bright red.

Eagerly, Norrec eyed them, then stared at the vulture demon. Yes, a blazing inferno . . .

He grabbed the furious avian by the neck. The savage beak tried to tear out his face, only increasing his determination to end this battle as quickly and decisively as possible.

Norrec glared at the monster. *"Burn!"*

With a garbled shriek, the winged terror burst into flames, perishing in an instant.

Wasting not a second, the fighter threw the fiery carcass into the nearest of the two survivors, setting that one aflame, too. The last of the avians quickly turned about, flying away as if the hounds of Hell pursued. Norrec paid its retreat no mind, content to finishing off the third.

Its feathers seared away, it tried to emulate its sole surviving comrade, but it had already suffered too much injury. Unable to do more than rise a foot or two above the ground, it could not escape the vengeful fighter. Norrec seized it by one wing, letting the now-pathetic monster claw at his breast plate while he took it by the head.

With one quick jerk, Norrec snapped its neck.

In truth, the battle had taken only a minute or two, but in that short span the veteran soldier had transformed. As he dropped the feathered corpse to the sand, Norrec felt a thrill such as he had never experienced in any war. Not only had he triumphed against the odds, but for once the cursed armor had *obeyed* him. Norrec flexed the fingers, truly admiring the workmanship of the gloves for the first time. Perhaps the encounter with Drognan had changed everything; perhaps now that which had driven the armor to such lengths had finally given in, had even accepted its host as its master . . .

Perhaps he could test it. Surely after all he had seen it do, the armor could perform one basic task at his command.

"All right," he growled. "Listen to me! I need water! I need it now!"

His left hand tingled, twitched slightly, as if the armor wanted to take control—but sought *permission*.

"Do it. I order you!"

The glove pointed to the ground. Norrec knelt, allowed his index finger to draw a circle in the sand. It then drew a looping pattern around that circle, with small crosses in each loop.

Words of power erupted from his lips, but this time Norrec welcomed them.

The entire pattern suddenly crackled, miniature arcs of lightning playing between one end of the design and the other. A tiny fissure opened in the center . . .

Clear, sparkling water bubbled to the surface.

Norrec eagerly bent down, sipping his fill. The water felt cool, sweet, almost as if instead he drank wine. The thirsty fighter savored each swallow until at last he could sip no more.

Leaning back, he took a handful and spilled it on his face. The soothing moisture trickled down his chin, his neck, and into his hot garments.

"That'll be enough," he finally said.

His hand waved over the tiny spring. Immediately the ground healed itself, sealing the fissure and cutting off the flow of water. What remained on the sand quickly sank out of sight.

A feeling of jubilation washed over Norrec, causing him to laugh loud. Twice now, the armor had served him. Twice now, he had been the *master*, not the slave.

Spirits lifted, he headed again for the hill. Now Norrec

no longer worried about whether he would survive the desert. What could he not survive, if the enchantments obeyed him? For that matter, what could he not accomplish? No one had seen such might as the armor wielded since the days of Bartuc! With it, Norrec could make of himself a commander instead of a foot soldier, a leader instead of a follower . . .

A *king* instead of a peasant?

The image enticed him. *King Norrec*, ruler of all he surveyed. Knights would bow before him; ladies of the court would seek his favor. Lands would come under his control. Riches beyond belief would be his to spend . . .

"King Norrec . . . ," he whispered. A smile once again spread across his face, a smile not at all like any Norrec Vizharan had evinced before in his life. In fact, although he could not know it, Norrec's smile resembled almost exactly the smile of another man, one who had lived long, long before the former mercenary.

A man named Bartuc.

FifTeen

Night enshrouded Aranoch and with its coming also returned the demon Xazax to Augustus Malevolyn. The general had been waiting most anxiously for the past hour, pacing back and forth inside his tent. He had dismissed all his officers and ordered that even his guards depart from the vicinity of his quarters. As an added precaution, he had also not permitted any tents within hearing distance. What transpired between Malevolyn and the mantis would be for their ears alone.

Even Galeona had been forbidden to set up her abode nearby, but she had protested little when he had told her. The general had not given that lack of protest much thought, more concerned with the offer made by his new ally. As far as he was concerned, the witch could now pack her things back up and ride off. If she did not, he would likely have to have her slain. Some sort of animosity existed between Xazax and her and, at the moment, Malevolyn needed the demon far more than he needed a very mortal sorceress, whatever her other charms.

Women could be easily replaced; moments of immortality generally could not be.

By Malevolyn's choice, only a single lamp lit the tent. He did not know if the demon cast shadows, but, if so, the less chance of one of his men noticing, the better for the general. Had they known what he and the mantis wished to discuss, they would have all likely fled into the dark desert heedless of the dangers lurking out there.

A flickering movement caught his attention. Augustus Malevolyn turned, noticing that one shadow moved in defiance of the lamp's flame.

"You are here, aren't you?" he murmured.

"This one has come as promised, oh great one . . ."

The shadow deepened, grew substantial. In moments, the hideous form of the hellish mantis loomed over the human. Yet despite the presence of a creature who looked capable of ripping him apart limb by limb, General Malevolyn felt only anticipation. In Xazax, he saw the first of many such monsters who would eventually serve him in every way.

"Lut Gholein lies little more than a day from you now, warlord. Have you changed your mind?"

Changed his mind about gaining the armor? Changed his mind about his destiny? "You waste my time on useless prattle, Xazax. I am firm in my choice."

The bulbous, yellow orbs flared. The mantis's head twisted slightly, as if the demon tried to peer through the closed tent flap. "We spoke briefly of the witch, great warlord. This one has considered that matter much since then and believes still that she must not be part of this . . . or perhaps anything else."

Augustus Malevolyn pretended to brood over this. "She's been of value to me for some time. I would hate to lose her assets."

"She would not agree with what this one has proposed to you, warlord. You may trust this one on that . . ."

The general had not missed Xazax's continual use of the new title and while it pleased Malevolyn to hear it, the demon in no way succeeded in playing to his ego. Malevolyn still considered each detail by its own worth, even Galeona. "What lies between you and her?"

"An agreement made foolishly—and one this one wishes to break."

Not the most clear of answers, but enough to give the general what he needed. He had a possible bargaining chip. "You will give me all I demand? All we discussed?"

"All—and gladly, warlord."

"Then you may have her now, if you wish. I will wait here while you do what you must."

If the demon could possibly ever looked disconcerted, then he did so now. "This one most graciously declines your kind offer, warlord . . . and suggests that perhaps you take the honor *yourself* at some point soon."

The mantis would not or *could* not touch Galeona, just as Malevolyn had expected. Still, to him the matter seemed moot. It would not change his other decision, not in the least. "I will send a detachment to her tent to see that she remains under control. That will at least prevent her from causing any disturbance during our efforts. Perhaps after, I will decide what to do about her. In the meantime, unless there is something else you need to tell me—I would like to begin."

The eyes of the demon flashed again, this time in what seemed immense satisfaction. In that voice that reminded the general of a dying swarm of flies, Xazax replied, "Then . . . you will need *this*, warlord . . ."

In the two skeletal hands, the hellish mantis held a large, twin-bladed dagger made of a black metal, a dagger with runes etched not only in the handle but along the flat sides of the blades. Also in the handle had been embedded two stones, the larger as red as blood, the other as pale as bone. Both stones had a slight gleam to them that came from no outside source.

"Take it . . ." urged the demon.

Augustus Malevolyn did so with eagerness, hefting the massive knife and noting its fine balance.

"What must I do with it?"

"Prick the skin. Let a few drops of blood flow." The mantis cocked his head. "A simple matter . . ."

Dagger in hand, the general hurried to the flap of the tent. He shouted for one of his officers, then glanced over his shoulder at Xazax. "You'd better fade back into——"

But the demon had already anticipated his request, Xazax melting once more into shadow.

A thin, mustached soldier with silver tabs on his shoulders appeared out of the darkness. He rushed up to the tent, then saluted his commander. "Yes, general?"

"Zako." One of his more competent aides. Malevolyn would miss him, but the potential glories outweighed any concern for a single person. "The witch is to be placed under protective arrest. She is not to be allowed to touch any of her belongings nor is she to even so much as raise a finger until I say so."

A grim smile crossed the other soldier's face. Like most of Malevolyn's officers, Zako had no love for this sorceress who had, up until now, influenced their leader so much. "Aye, general! I'll do that, all right!"

Something occurred to the commander. "But first . . . but first bring the guards chosen for this task here. Be quick about it!"

With a swift salute, Zako vanished into the dark, only to return a short time later with four sturdy-looking warriors. Zako ushered them into Malevolyn's tent, then took up his place at the forefront.

"All present, general!" he called out, snapping to attention.

"Very good." Malevolyn gave the small troop a brief inspection, then faced them. "You have all served me loyally time and time again." His fingers stroked the hilt of the dagger, to which none of the five had so far paid much attention. "You have sworn your lives to me more than once . . . and for that I thank you. However, with a prize such as the one awaiting us, I must ask of you one last show of your willingness to serve me unto *death . . ."*

To one side, General Malevolyn noticed a shadow move. Xazax no doubt grew impatient, not understanding the need for the short speech. These men would be the first; therefore, from them would spread word of why their leader now demanded this new proof from them.

"Tomorrow begins a day of glory, a day of destiny, and each of you shall play an integral part! I ask now, my friends, that you verify my faith in you, my hopes in you, with this one last oath!" He held up the dagger for all of them to see. A couple of the guards blinked, but no one otherwise reacted. "Zako! I give you the honor of being the first! Show me your bravery!"

Without hesitation, the mustached officer stepped up and thrust out his ungloved hand. This had not been the first time he had sworn a blood oath to his commander and, of the five, only he no doubt thought that he understood why Malevolyn desired to reemphasize to the men the loyalty they owed the general.

"Palm up." After Zako had obeyed, Malevolyn held the dagger points-down over the fleshiest part—then jabbed his officer's palm.

Zako stifled a gasp, the man keeping his eyes straight ahead, as had been expected of him. Because of that, he did not notice something strange about both the knife and where it had punctured his skin. The two gems in the hilt briefly flashed the moment the points pierced his hand. More curious, although blood flowed from the tiny wounds, little of it actually spread over the palm, most of it seeming drawn toward the black blade—where it then disappeared.

"Have yourself a sip of wine, Zako," Malevolyn offered, pulling back the dagger. As his aide stepped away, the general signaled to the next man, upon whom he repeated the same process.

After all five had been bled, Augustus Malevolyn saluted them. "You have given me your lives. I promise to treat them as the valuable gifts they are. You are dismissed." As the soldiers departed, he called to Zako, "Before you deal with the witch, have Captain Lyconius bring every man under his command to my tent, will you?"

"Aye, general!"

When the others had gone, the voice of Xazax drifted from the shadows. "This goes too slow, warlord. It will take days at this rate."

"No, now it will go much faster. These five have been given an honor, so they see it. Zako will tell Lyconius and he, in turn, will tell his men and so on. I will order the officers to give a ration of drink to each soldier who shows them he has once more sworn his life to my cause. The pace will quicken incredibly, I promise you."

A few seconds later, Lyconius, a thin, fair-haired man older than the general, asked to be admitted. Outside, every soldier under his command awaited. Malevolyn bled the captain first, then had him line the men up. The mention of a ration of drink afterward made each fighter all the more eager to be there.

However, only a few of Lyconius's men had been dealt with when Zako, looking much perturbed, burst into the tent. He knelt on one knee before the commander, head down in shame.

Somewhat irritated at this costly interruption, General Malevolyn barked, "Speak! What is it?"

"General! The witch—she is nowhere to be found!"

Malevolyn tried to conceal his annoyance. "Her belongings; are they still in the tent?"

"Aye, general, but her horse is missing."

Even Galeona would not ride out into the vast desert at night. Taking a casual glance over his shoulder, Malevolyn noticed the shadow of the demon shift. No doubt Xazax did not find this news pleasant either, but at the moment neither man nor demon could afford to waste time on her. If the sorceress had somehow learned of their intention and had chosen to flee, it truly mattered little in the long run to her former lover. What harm could she do? Perhaps, once he wore the armor, he would hunt her down, but now Malevolyn had more important concerns.

"Never mind her, Zako. Return to your normal duties."

Relief in his voice, the aide thanked him, then hurried from the tent. General Malevolyn turned back to his task, bleeding the next man, then commending him for his bravery.

The pace did indeed quicken, just as he had told the mantis it would. The combination of honor and drink caused a line to spread throughout the entire encampment, each man anxious to prove his worth to his master and his fellows. Tomorrow, they felt, the general would lead them to a glorious victory and riches beyond their wildest dreams. That they might be too few to take a stronghold such as Lut Gholein did not occur to them; General Malevolyn would not have made the sudden decision—so *they* assumed—if he did not already have some battle plan ensuring success.

And deep into the night, the last man proved his loyalty, hand out, the dagger already pricking his palm.

The final soldier and the officer who had guided him in both departed after saluting their trusted leader. From without, Augustus Malevolyn could already hear the sounds of celebration, as each of his men savored their ration of drink and toasted their future good fortunes.

"It is done," rasped Xazax, emerging from the shadowy corners. "Each and every one has tasted the dagger's bite and of each and every one the dagger has sipped . . ."

Turning the ceremonial weapon over and over in his hands, the general commented, "Not a single drop, not the tiniest stain. Where did all the blood go?"

"Each to its own, warlord. Each to the one it must go. This one promised you an army against whom even Lut Gholein could not defend long, remember?"

"I recall . . ." He touched the helmet, which he had not taken off once since camp had been made. It seemed so much a part of him now that he swore it would never leave his side, that he would only remove it for necessity's sake. "And I say again, I *accept* the consequences of our deal."

The mantis's body dipped in what might have been an acknowledging bow. "Then, there is no reason not to proceed immediately . . ."

"Tell me what must be done."

"In the sand at your feet, you must draw this symbol." Using one of the skeletal hands, Xazax traced the mark in the air. The general's eyes widened slightly as the demon's gaunt finger left a fiery, orange trail behind, highlighting the symbol.

"Why don't you just do it?"

"It must be done by he who will command. Would you prefer it to be this humble one, warlord?"

Seeing Xazax's point, Malevolyn bent down and drew the mark as it had appeared in the air. To his surprise, as he completed it, strange words suddenly burst from his lips.

"Do not hesitate!" urged the mantis eagerly. "The words were known to him; they will be known to you!"

His words . . . *Bartuc's* words. Augustus Malevolyn let them flow, savoring the power he felt from their use.

"Hold the dagger over the center." When the general had done that, the demon added, "Now . . . speak the name of my infernal lord! Speak the name of *Belial!*"

Belial? "Who is Belial? I know of Baal and Mephisto and Diablo, but not of this Belial. Do you mean Baa—"

"*Speak not that name again!*" Xazax nervously chittered. The mantis twisted his horrific head left and right as if he feared discovery by someone. Evidently finding nothing upon which to base that fear, the demon finally responded in calmer tones, "There is no master in Hell save *Belial.* It is he who offers you this wondrous gift! Recall this always!"

More familiar with the magic arts than the mantis might think him, Malevolyn knew that Hell had once been described as being ruled by the Three Prime Evils. Yet, he also knew of legends which had told of the three brothers cast up onto the mortal plane, their rule over Hell a thing of the past. In fact . . . one of the more obscure legends mentioned Lut Gholein as the possible location of *Baal's* tomb, although even the general doubted the veracity of such a fantastic tale. Who would build a city on top of a demon lord's tomb?

"As you say, Xazax. Belial, it is. I simply wanted to get the name correct."

"Begin again!" the monstrous insect snapped.

Once more the words spilled from Malevolyn's tongue. Once more he held the vampiric dagger high above the center of the symbol—Belial's symbol, the general now realized. At the end of the incantation, the eager commander called out the demon lord's name . . .

"Plunge the dagger into the center—exactly!"

General Malevolyn drove the twin-tipped blade deep into the sand, catching the center of the image perfectly.

Nothing happened. He looked up at the looming horror.

"Step back," Xazax suggested.

And as the would-be conqueror did, a grim, black haze arose around the dagger. While the two watched, the haze rapidly grew, first expanding above the weapon, then finally spreading toward the tent flap. As it drifted outside with what seemed definite purpose to Malevolyn's trained eye, the foreboding haze took on the shape of what looked to be a huge, clawed hand.

"It will not be long now, warlord."

Unconcerned, Malevolyn sought out a goblet of his finest wine. For this night, he chose a new bottle, one that had been packed carefully for countless journeys over desperate landscapes. The general opened it, sniffed the contents, and, with much approval, poured himself a full cup.

At that point, the first of the screams began.

Augustus Malevolyn's hand shook at the sound, but not because of any fear or regret. It was just that he had never heard such a soul-tearing cry, not even from those he had tortured, and the suddenness of it had simply startled the hardened veteran. When the second, the third, and fourth arose, Malevolyn found them not at all disconcerting. He even raised his goblet toward the half-buried dagger and Xazax's unseen lord.

And as he did, the shrieks outside became a chorus of the damned, scores of men crying out at the same time, pleading for some escape. From all around the camp the agonized screams assaulted the general, but he took each in stride. The men—*his* men—had each sworn more than one oath that they would serve him in all things in all ways. Tonight, he had taken that oath to heart, accepting their sacrifices—quite literally—for the better of his quest.

He turned toward the tent flap again. Mistaking the human's reaction, the mantis warned, "It is too late to save them. The pact has been accepted by this one's infernal lord."

"Save them? I merely wished to toast them for what they have given in order to garner me my destiny!"

"Aaah . . ." responded the demon, clearly seeing the true General Malevolyn for the first time. "This one is mistaken . . ."

And on went the screams. A few sounded quite distant, as if some of the men had tried to flee, but they could not flee from something eating away at them from within their very souls. Some, obviously very loyal, called out to their commander, pleading for help. Malevolyn poured himself another goblet, then sat down to wait for the finish.

Gradually, the last of the screams died down, leaving only the nervous whinnying of the horses, who could not understand what had happened. That, too, though, ceased as the heavy silence of the camp affected them as well.

The sudden clank of metal against metal made him look at the demon again, but Xazax said nothing. Outside, the clanking increased, growing both in intensity and nearness. General Malevolyn finished the last of his wine and stood up.

The noise outside abruptly stopped.

"They await you . . . warlord."

Adjusting his armor, especially his helmet, General Augustus Malevolyn stepped outside.

They did indeed wait for him, their ranks perfect. Several held torches, so he could see their faces, the faces he had come to know so well over their years of service to him. They all stood there, Zako, Lyconius, and the rest of the officers, each with their men behind them.

As he stepped into their sight, a cry of salute rose up among the throng, a cry monstrous, brutal, in its tone. It made Malevolyn smile, just as a somewhat closer glance at the foremost visages further enthused the commander. No matter how dark or light their skins had been before, they now had a pale, pasty look to them. As for their mouths, their battle cry had revealed teeth now fanged and tongues long and forked. The eyes—

The eyes were completely red—blood red—and burned with such evil desire that they could be seen even without the aid of a torch. They were not human eyes, but rather eyes that, at least in malignance, more resembled those of the mantis.

Garbed in the very husks of his loyal soldiers, these horrific warriors would be his new legion, his path to glory.

Xazax joined him outside the tent, the hellish mantis no longer needing to be concerned about secrecy. After all, here he stood among his own.

"All hail Malevolyn of Westmarch!" Xazax called out. "All hail, the *Warlord of Blood!*"

And once again, the demonic horde cheered Augustus Malevolyn.

So far from the encampment, Galeona heard nothing, but the witch did sense the striking of the sinister spell. Long associated with the darker aspects of her art, she knew that such incredible emanations of hellish sorcery could only mean that her fears had come to fruition. She had been right to depart when she had or else the enchantress would have certainly joined the fates of Augustus's unsuspecting warriors.

Xazax had underestimated her for the last time. The mantis would have used others to deal with her in order to break the blood pact that they had made some years back. He had chosen the general for his new ally, the demon having always hinted that a new warlord would be of more interest than simply gaining empty armor. Galeona should have realized months ago that he had never intended to continue with their own alliance any longer than necessary.

Yet, what had made him so suddenly choose Augustus over her? Could it really have been fear? Ever since that night when the monstrous insect had nearly done the unthinkable—slain her outright despite the repercussions of directly breaking their pact—the witch had tried to think of what could so disturb a creature of Hell. What fear had sent him scurrying straight to Malevolyn?

In the end, it did not matter. Both Xazax and Augustus could have one another for all she cared. After what she had discovered during her brief spellwork earlier, Galeona had decided that she, in turn, needed neither of the two treacherous creatures. Why settle for always looking over her shoulder when she could be the one who truly commanded?

The sorceress glanced down at her hand as she rode, not the first time she had done so. In her left palm, Galeona held a small crystal which through spells she had tied to her intended destination. So long as the crystal glowed, the enchantress knew that she remained on the right track.

So long as it glowed, she knew that she could find the fool she intended to make her puppet.

In betraying her, Xazax had made one terrible error in judgment. For some reason that she could not yet fathom, the demon could not by himself detect the ancient warlord's armor. He needed human assistance, which had been one of the foremost reasons the two of them had first joined together. That had been why, when he had believed that he knew where the prize lay, the cursed mantis had abandoned her for General Malevolyn. It should not have been at all surprising to her since Galeona had considered doing much the same, but for Xazax, the error would prove a costly one.

The demon no doubt believed that the armor could be found now in nearby Lut Gholein, the location they had

last determined it would head toward. Even she had
assumed that much until her last spell. Where else could
it be but within the coastal kingdom? A lone traveler
either needed to find a caravan there willing to take him
on or wait instead for a ship heading on from Lut
Gholein to one of the more western lands. Either way,
Norrec should have still been within the city walls.

But he was not. At some point, he had left, choosing to
forego sanity and apparently ride out into the desert at a
pace that surely had killed his mount. When Galeona had
discovered his new location, it had stunned her; the veteran fighter practically stood under Augustus's very
nose. If the general had agreed to letting her cast a search
spell when she had originally offered, the armor might
very well even now be his. He could have already been
approaching Lut Gholein clad in the crimson garb of
Bartuc, his loyal witch at his side.

Instead, Galeona now hoped to convince this other
fool that *he* should use it . . . under her masterful guidance, of course. He looked to be a manageable sort of oaf,
one she should readily be able to wrap around her finger.
He also had a not unreasonable countenance, one in some
ways the witch preferred to her former lover. That would
make the task of maintaining control of her new puppet
not so great a chore.

Of course, if Galeona found some better method by
which to harness the astonishing power of the enchantments, it would also not bother her much if she had to do
away with this Norrec. There were always other men,
other fools.

On and on she rode, her only concern that Xazax might
choose to interrupt his activities with Augustus to pursue
his former partner. Of course, that would go against their
pact, too, which would endanger the demon as well as
her. More likely the hellish mantis would forget her for
now, satisfied that he had his grand prize. Later he would

no doubt find the means by which to sever their ties—not to mention her head and limbs.

He would be too late, though. Once she had her pawn ensnared, Galeona would see to it that Xazax, not she, would soon lay scattered over the landscape. Perhaps she would even have Norrec bring the insect's head to her, a pretty trophy with which to begin to rebuild the collection that the sorceress had been forced to leave abandoned tonight.

She peered around, looking for some sign of her prey. In order to lessen the risk of riding around nearly blind because of the darkness, the witch had cast a spell enhancing both the visions of her horse and herself. It enabled the animal to pick a path that would avoid accidents and predators while giving Galeona the ability to better hunt for the soldier.

There! Reining her mount to a halt, the sorceress stared at the distant, shadowed form of a rocky hill. The crystal indicated that her path continued directly that way. Galeona rose in the saddle for a moment, searching for any other likely spot and finding none. As a seasoned warrior, the fool certainly had enough sense to look for reasonable shelter and the small hill before her looked to be the only such choice for many miles around. He had to be there.

Eager now, Galeona urged the horse on. As they neared, she thought she saw a figure just to the left of the hill. Yes . . . most definitely a man seated under an outcropping, his knees drawn up to his chest, his arms resting atop the knees.

He jumped up as the witch approached, for one clad in heavy armor his agility and speed surprising her. Galeona could see him peering back, trying to make her out in the darkness and so far failing. No, not an unpleasant face at all, the guileful sorceress thought. Better than she had recalled from their encounter on the ship. If he would just prove himself to be reasonable, to listen to her, then they would have no troubles with one another and she would not have to so soon begin the search for his eventual replacement.

"Who is it?" Norrec called. "Who are you?"

She dismounted a short distance from him. "Only a fellow wanderer . . . no one who means you harm." Now Galeona simply used the crystal to illuminate the area, let him see the good fortune that had just stepped into his miserable little life. "Someone looking for some warmth . . ."

The witch manipulated the gleaming stone, letting its light cross both her face and torso. She saw his interest immediately. So much the better. He looked to be one readily led around by the nose in return for a few readily given pleasures. The perfect dupe.

His expression suddenly changed and not for the better. "I know you, don't I?" He approached, towering over her. "I need to see your face again."

"Of course." Galeona held the crystal nearer to her features.

"Not enough light," Norrec muttered. "I need more."

He held up his left hand—and in the palm of the gauntlet there suddenly formed a tiny fireball that outshone the crystal a hundredfold.

Galeona could not stifle a gasp. She had expected an uninitiated fool, a fighter with no grasp of sorcery. Instead, he had summoned flame without so much as an effort, something still beyond many well-schooled apprentices.

"That's better . . . I *do* know you . . . your face, anyway! On the *Hawksfire!*" He nodded in immense satisfaction. "I dreamed of you there!"

Recovering, Galeona quickly replied, "And I dreamed of you, too, that time! Dreamed of a warrior, a champion, who could protect me from the evils pursuing me."

As she hoped, her words and tone had an immediate effect on the man. His look of distrust did not completely fade, but now she saw also sympathy—and pride that she looked at him as her savior. The witch pressed nearer to Norrec, staring adoringly into his eyes with her own, half-lidded ones. She surely had him enticed by this point.

"You're in danger?" A protective look crossed his face. He peered beyond Galeona, as if already expecting to see the villains who chased after her.

"They don't know I escaped them just yet. I . . . I dreamed of you again last night, knew that you had to be near, waiting for me." Putting a hand on his breastplate, Galeona leaned forward, but inches between her full lips and his own.

He did not rise to the tempting bait, instead considering some other matter. "You're a sorceress," Norrec finally responded. "What's your name?"

"Galeona . . . and I know from my dreams that my knight is called Norrec."

"Yes . . ." The fighter smiled at the title she had given him. "Are you a powerful sorceress?"

The witch let her hand trace the seams on the armor. "I have some talent in that . . . and other fields as well."

"I could use a sorceress," he muttered almost to himself. "I wanted one to help me deal with this armor . . . but that's not so important any more. I've had time to think, time to put matters in their proper order. There's things I need to do before I go on any further."

Galeona only half-paid attention, already planning ahead. Norrec definitely did not sound as simple a man as the enchantress had first imagined, but he had at least taken her story to heart and accepted her as a companion, if nothing else. As she learned more about him, Galeona would strengthen that tie. He had already revealed some weakness to her charms; the rest of what she desired the witch would gain soon enough.

Of course, if she could help Norrec with whatever concerned him, show her puppet of what valuable assistance she could be, that would shorten her own task. While Galeona did not understand his statement concerning the armor itself, these other matters he had mentioned—whatever they might be—she could surely aid him in accomplishing.

"Of course, I'll help you in any way I can, my knight! I ask only in return that you protect me from those who would do me harm." She turned her gaze briefly to the desert. "They're powerful and have dark arts at their command."

Galeona had wanted to test his reserve, to see the extent he felt sure of the power he apparently wielded. Yet, even to her surprise, Norrec shrugged, then almost casually answered, "Warriors, magic, demons . . . I've no fear of any of them. Those under my protection will come to no harm."

"You've my gratitude," she whispered, leaning up and kissing him hard.

He pulled her away, not out of any disgust, but because he seemed not to have any interest at the moment in what she had offered him. Instead, Norrec appeared once more lost in his other concerns.

"I've thought about it," the fighter finally told the witch. "Thought about why I ended up here of all places. It has to be somewhere near. It tries to keep hidden and from me it can do it . . ." He looked down at her again, something in his eyes suddenly unnerving Galeona a little. "But *you* might be able to find it! You found me, after all! You can probably succeed where Drognan failed."

"I'll do what I can," the dark-skinned enchantress returned, curious as to what so demanded the man's attention. Something of value to her, too, perhaps? "What are we looking for?"

His expression indicated that he found it surprising that she did not already know. *"Horazon's tomb, of course!"* Something in his face changed as he spoke, something that made Galeona look at him again—and this time see a face that she did not entirely recognize. *"My brother's tomb."*

Sixteen

An entire world existed beneath Lut Gholein.

No, corrected Kara, not a world, but something that seemed at least as large as, if not *larger* than, the regal kingdom far above her. The curious and unsettling figure she had identified as an impossibly old Horazon had led her down one confusing corridor to the next and to the next and so on until the necromancer had actually gotten dizzy trying to keep track of her path. She had climbed up and down stairs, walked through door after door, and passed room after room until at last Horazon had brought her to this single chamber, this well-lit and well-furnished bedroom, and told her to sleep.

Kara did not even remember lying down, but now she found herself atop the soft bed, staring up at the intricately-sewn canopy there. She had imagined her quarters aboard the *King's Shield* to be the finest she would ever use, but these set even those to shame. Curiously, the elegant furnishings, while clearly of another time, another place, looked as if they had been made only yesterday. The great wooden bed appeared perfectly polished, the sheets crisp and clean, and the marble floor beneath spotless. The same went for the nightstand next to the bed and the chair in the far corner. On the walls had been hung richly-woven tapestries of decidedly Vizjerei tastes, fantastic creatures and images of astonishing spellwork, all crafted by an expert artisan. If not for the fact that she was presently a prisoner in the lair of a possibly dangerous madman, the enchantress would have felt quite comfortable indeed.

She dared not stay here. While legend had always spoken of Horazon as the brother considered the lesser of two evils, he nonetheless not only remained an ambitious Vizjerei who had once, too, commanded demons to serve him, but who also clearly had lost his sanity over the centuries. Kara wondered how he had even survived for so long. The only records of such extensive life-extending spells had always included the summoning of unearthly powers to help cast them. If Horazon had turned again to demons for his needs—despite his constant mutterings to the contrary—then that would not only explain his present condition but also gave Kara even more reason to find her way out before he returned.

Still clothed, the anxious dark mage slipped out of the bed, heading immediately to the door. It did no good to try to see if Horazon had cast any spells upon it, for his entire sanctum emanated magic to such a staggering degree that she wondered why every spellcaster for hundreds of miles around could not have sensed its presence. Then again, perhaps that same magic explained why they did not. If even a portion of that might had been directed toward hiding Horazon's domain, then the greatest mages in all the world could have stood at its very doorstep and still not noticed the wonder at their feet.

Deciding to take the risk, the necromancer tugged at the handle, only to find the door unmoving. She tried again, with equally dismal results.

It hardly surprised her that she had been locked in, but the truth nevertheless frustrated Kara immensely. The necromancer had been trapped time and time again since beginning this chase and now she wondered whether or not she would be able to escape this prison. Unwilling to give up, Kara touched the handle and muttered a spell of opening. It was a minor incantation, one that actually had its roots in Vizjerei elemental sorcery, but the followers of Rathma had found it one of the few useful creations of the rival calling. That it almost certainly would fail did not escape her, but Kara could think of no other way out of the room that would not require a spell likely to bring the ceiling down on her as well.

The handle *turned*.

Startled by her unlikely success, the necromancer nearly flung open the door. Instead, taking a deep breath, Kara cautiously opened it a crack, then surveyed the outer hallway. Seeing no sign of danger, the dark mage quietly stepped out. She peered both directions, trying to recall by which she had earlier come. After a brief mental debate, Kara turned to the right and ran.

The corridor ended at a stairway that led up, a hopeful sign. Kara pushed herself up the steps, certain that if she kept going the direction she did, the desperate spellcaster would eventually find her way out.

The stairway stopped two flights later, opening up into a much wider corridor. Making certain that Horazon did not seem about, the necromancer crept down the larger hall. Although the room in which she had slept had been well-decorated, the halls themselves seemed positively austere, with only the occasional door breaking the monotony. The one consistently odd element of her surroundings proved to be the yellow light, whose source never proved evident. It came from everywhere at the same time. There were no torches nor anywhere even to put them.

As she hurried along, Kara occasionally felt tempted to try one of the doors, but knew that it behooved her more to find the way out as soon as she could. Any lingering might give Horazon time to discover that she had gone missing. While the necromancer dearly wanted to know more about the mad mage and his sanctum, she desired to do so on her own terms, not his.

Just ahead, the corridor took a hard right turn. Kara stepped up her pace, hoping that the change in direction meant that she had found a passage to the outside. The frustrated enchantress cut around the corner as quickly as she could, praying that somewhere at the end would be another stairway or, better yet, the true exit.

Instead, she found herself facing a blank *wall*.

The hallway simply ended just a few yards after it had begun. Putting both hands to it, the necromancer checked the wall for illusions, magic, even a false front. Unfortunately, for all practical purposes, the barrier before her seemed as solid as it looked even though she could find no good reason at all for its existence.

Stepping back, Kara studied the only other direction. To return to the stairway made no sense, but that left to her only the doors. Surely they did not represent a path out of Horazon's domain.

She went to the first, cautiously opening it. With her luck as it had been so far, Kara feared that her choice would turn out to be the ancient Vizjerei's very own chambers.

Behind the door stood a long, curving passage.

"Is that the trick, then?" she whispered to herself. Did the true way out depend on opening the doors and not following the regular corridors? Trust her demented host to design his underground lair in such an improbable manner!

Eagerly Kara Nightshadow hurried down the hidden corridor, not even bothering to shut the door behind her. Somewhere at the end, she would find escape. Somewhere she would find the way back to the old building or some other secret entrance into Lut Gholein.

Instead, the necromancer found yet *another* door.

She had no choice but to open it. There had been no other passage, no other entrance. However, at least this time Kara opened the door with some hope of success.

She had journeyed for some distance. Horazon's maze-like sanctum had to come to an end here and now.

Another hallway greeted her.

That it resembled the wide one Kara had long left behind did not bother her. Of course, the design would be similar. After all, the same man had created it all.

Then she saw the open door just a short distance to her left.

With great trepidation, the weary necromancer walked over to it. She peeked inside, hoping her guess to be wrong.

The same curved corridor Kara had just traversed greeted the weary woman.

"Trag'Oul, guide me out of the madness!" What point had there been to a corridor that returned to the same hall? Kara blinked as another realization hit her. This door and the one she had returned by had been located on *opposite* sides of the hall. How could she possibly have looped around like that? The corridor would have had to cut through the hallway, a complete impossibility!

Without hesitation Kara headed for the lone door left to her. If it did not lead somewhere other than this hallway, then Horazon's bizarre realm had finally defeated her.

To the necromancer's relief, though, the doorway opened into a vast chamber in which two sets of wide, bannistered staircases flanked a pair of high bronze doors decorated with intricate dragon motifs. A well-preserved marble floor covered the entire expanse of the room and more tapestries covered the stone walls.

Kara stepped into the massive room, debating whether to choose the doors or one of the staircases. The doors looked most tantalizing, being directly across from her, but the stairs, too, enticed the necromancer, either one possibly leading to an exit above ground.

A slight sound above her head made Kara look up—then gasp at what she saw.

Far, far up, Horazon sat in a chair, the white-haired sorcerer mumbling to himself while he ate at a long dining table. The noise Kara had heard had been the madman laying his knife on what looked to be an elaborate gold plate filled with rich meat. Even though so far below, Kara could still smell its succulent flavor. As she watched, Horazon reached for a goblet of wine, the elderly Vizjerei taking a long sip without spilling so much as a drop. That feat especially amazed her, not because she had not thought the insane mage capable of simple table manners—but because he did so while he sat *upside down* on the ceiling.

In fact, the entire tableau was upside down and yet nothing fell toward Kara. The chair, the table, the plates full of fresh food, even Horazon's lengthy beard—all defied basic nature. Gazing around the ceiling in astonishment, the dark mage even saw doors and other staircases that would have suited the mage well in his present position. If not for Horazon and his elaborate meal, it would have been as if she stared at a mirror image above her.

Still drinking, Horazon cocked his head up—or rather *down*—and at last caught sight of the startled young woman.

"Come! Come!" he called to her. "You're late! I don't like people late!"

Fearful that he might use his considerable power to drag her up to the ceiling, perhaps forever eliminating her hopes for escape, Kara rushed across the great hall, heading to the bronze doors. They had to lead somewhere out of his reach! They had to!

With one last look up at her captor, Kara flung open the nearest of the doors and darted through. If she could just keep ahead of him—

"Aaah! Good! Good! Sit there! Sit there!"

Horazon watched her from the other end of a long, elegant table identical to the one at which she had just seen him sitting, only this time it stood not on the ceiling, but rather in the center of the room she had just now entered. The exact same meal, even down to the wine, lay spread before him. Beyond the mage, doorways and staircases just like the necromancer had seen atop the other chamber now served as backdrop to Horazon and his meal.

Unable to prevent herself from doing so, Kara looked up at the ceiling.

Staircases and doorways, all upside down, greeted her gaze.

One of the latter, a bronze giant, stood open—as if someone had flung it aside in haste.

"Rathma, protect me . . ." Kara murmured.

"Sit, girl, sit!" commanded Horazon, totally oblivious to her dismay. "Time to eat! Time to eat!"

And with nothing more she could do to save herself, the necromancer obeyed.

A storm covered the desert, a vast ocean of black, churning clouds that spread all the way from the east to as far west as Augustus Malevolyn could see. Dawn had risen, but it might as well have been just after sunset, so dark had the day begun. Some might have taken such a threatening sky for a bad omen, but the general saw it instead as a sign that his time had come, that his day of destiny was at hand. Lut Gholein lay just ahead and in it he knew cringed the fool who wore the glorious armor—*his* glorious armor.

Xazax had assured him of the last. Where else would the stranger have gone? The winds blew strong, ensuring that no ship would be heading out to sea this day. He *had* to still be in the city.

The general studied Lut Gholein from atop a massive dune. Behind him and entirely invisible to the eyes of the enemy, Malevolyn's demonic host patiently awaited his word. Because of the particular spell utilized, the sinister creatures still wore the shells of his men, although eventually they would be able to discard those. They had needed them to make the passage from Hell to the mortal plane and would yet require them for some time to come. That need, though, did not bother Malevolyn. For the moment, it served better that the enemy thought this tiny army simply mortal. It would make the commanders in Lut Gholein overconfident, arrogant. They would commit themselves to tactics which would expend their might early for a quick victory—but in doing so they would merely be setting themselves up for a slaughter that Malevolyn already much savored.

Xazax joined the human, the mantis finally creeping into sight after being gone far too long. Something about that struck the general as curious. Of all the demons now with him, Xazax clearly had to be the most dominating, yet the insidious insect moved about as if fearful that, even on such a dark day, someone might see him.

"Why do you lurk about? What are you afraid of?" Malevolyn asked, growing a bit suspicious. "Are you expecting something I should know about?"

"This one is afraid of nothing!" the mantis snapped, his mandibles working furiously. "Nothing!" However, in a slightly lower voice, he added, "This one is merely . . . cautious . . ."

"You act as if you fear something."

"No . . . nothing . . ."

General Malevolyn again recalled both Xazax's reaction to the name *Baal* and the fact that Lut Gholein had been said to house underneath it the demon lord's tomb. Could there then be some fact after all to that outlandish tale?

Deciding he could investigate the demon's anxieties later, General Malevolyn turned his gaze back to Lut

Gholein. The city lay unsuspecting. Even now, a contingent of the sultan's forces rode out of the gate on early morning patrol, the riders' attitudes plain to see even from this distance. They did their rounds with the notion that no one would have the audacity to attack, especially by way of the desert. Lut Gholein more feared attacks by sea and on a day as fierce as this one looked to be, the odds of that appeared infinitesimal.

"We will let the patrol come as near as possible," he informed the mantis. "Then we shall take them. I want to see how your warriors act before we seek the city itself."

"Not this one's warriors," corrected Xazax. "*Yours . . .* "

The riders swept out, crisscrossing the land beyond the walls. Malevolyn watched and waited, knowing that their course would soon enough take the patrol to where he wanted them to be.

"Prepare the archers."

A rank of figures stepped forward, inhuman eyes eager. Although they wore but the husks of Malevolyn's men, the demons somehow retained the knowledge and skills of their victims. The faces Augustus Malevolyn glanced at had been the faces of his best archers. Now the demons would prove whether or not they could do as well—or, preferably, better.

"On my mark," he commanded.

They readied their bows. Xazax spoke a single word— and the tips of the arrows blazed.

The turbaned riders drew nearer. Malevolyn shifted his mount, the better to be seen by them.

One of the defenders noted him and called out to the others. The patrol, an estimated forty and more in strength, turned toward the outsider.

"Be ready." He urged his horse a few steps in the direction of the other riders, as if he intended to meet them. They, in turn, rode at a pace that suggested that they were wary, but not very much so.

And at last, the soldiers from Lut Gholein came near enough for General Malevolyn's tastes.

"Now!"

Even the howling wind could not overwhelm the terrible shrieks of the feathered shafts in flight. A rain of death undaunted by the gale fell upon the enemy.

The first of the arrows landed, some missing, some striking well. Malevolyn saw a bolt hit one of the lead riders dead on, the shaft burning through his breastplate as if the latter did not exist, then burying itself deep in the man's chest. Even more shocking, that rider suddenly burst into *flames*, his terrible wound the point of origin. The corpse fell off the frightened horse, colliding with another mount who then shied, throwing his own rider to the ground.

Another shaft caught a guard in the leg, but what seemed a bad wound at best became a new terror as that, too, erupted in fire. Screaming, the soldier frantically slapped at a limb entirely engulfed by quickly spreading flames. His animal, too, shied, sending the unfortunate man to the ground. Even there, the flames would not cease, already spreading up and around the victim's waist.

Of the forty or so riders in the patrol, at least a third lay either dead or near to it, all the bodies afire. Several horses, also lay stricken. The rest of the soldiers fought for control of their panicked steeds.

A smile on his face, Augustus Malevolyn turned back to his deadly horde. "Second and third ranks . . . advance and attack!"

A war cry that would have chilled most men but only served to thrill the general erupted from the throats of those summoned. The demonic warriors poured over the dune. As with Malevolyn's late soldiers, they kept their ranks tight and orderly, yet still he could see the savagery in their movements, the inhuman lust in their continual shouts. In numbers, they more than surpassed those of the riders, but not enough that, under normal circumstances, the patrol could not readily fight their way to freedom.

One of the officers spotted the marauding band and called out a warning. Immediately the survivors of the patrol turned toward Lut Gholein. However, Malevolyn had no intention of letting them go. Glancing at the archers, he ordered another volley.

This time the shafts flew far over his adversaries, just as intended. Moments later, the sand in front of the retreating patrol exploded with fire as the arrows struck the ground. For a few precious seconds, a wall of flame cut off all hope of escape.

Those few precious seconds were all the demons needed to reach their foes.

They swarmed around the riders, swords and spears up. Several riders and horses fell quickly, pin-cushioned. The defenders fought back, thrusting at their assailants. One managed to strike what should have been a mortal blow, only to have Malevolyn's unholy warrior completely ignore the blade in his side while he pulled the stunned soldier off his mount.

An officer from the patrol attempted to organize better resistance. Two of the demons dragged him down. Abandoning their weapons, they tore his armor from his body, then tore into the flesh underneath.

"They are . . . enthusiastic . . ." Xazax remarked with some amusement.

"Just so long as they recall what I said this morning."

"They will do so."

One of the few remaining defenders made a mad break for Lut Gholein. A demon grabbed at his leg and would have brought him down, but another suddenly tore his comrade's clawing fingers from the hapless rider, enabling the human to make good his escape.

"You see? This one promised you that they would obey your orders, warlord . . ."

"Then, as soon as the rest have been dealt with, we'll move forward. You'll remain behind, I trust?"

"For now, warlord . . ." Xazax had suggested that, without a true human form, he would be too obvious a sight for this first struggle. In daylight, the demon could not apparently create sufficiently the illusion of a man, as he had done that night. In fact, had General Malevolyn inspected the shadowed face better during that encounter, he would have seen that no true features had actually existed—just hints of them.

The mantis's explanation for his hesitation had a few holes in it that the general would discuss with him further, but he knew that such a conversation could wait. The armor called to Malevolyn; all he had to do was take the city to get it.

Below, the slaughter of the patrol took but a few short minutes more, the defenders' ranks dwindling with each passing second. More and more the true nature of Malevolyn's force became evident as the demons fell upon the soldiers, drenching the sand with blood.

By this time, the lone survivor had reached the gates of Lut Gholein. Horns blared behind the walls, warning being given to all that the kingdom had been attacked.

"All right! Let's let them see us!" He raised his hand high in the air—and in it formed the fiery, ebony sword that he had used on the scarab demons. "Advance!"

The clouds rumbled and lightning flashed as General Malevolyn's army came out of hiding. Below, the first and second rank formed up, their lines a little more ragged than before. The feast of bloodletting had stirred up the demons there, making them forget some of the human traits they had stolen. Still, so long as they obeyed his commands to the letter, the general could forgive the slight error.

The howling wind whipped Malevolyn's cloak around. He adjusted his helmet, bent his head slightly down to avoid the sand blown into the air. As of yet, the sky had not given any indication of rain, but even that would not stop him now.

Panic must be spreading among the common folk within. The soldiers, however, would, at this moment, be studying his advancing force and determining that, despite the wholesale slaughter of the patrol, this new foe lacked the numbers to be a true threat to them. They would make one of two choices; either defend the walls only—or send out a much larger force seeking retribution for the horrific deaths of which the one surviving guard would speak.

Understanding human emotions, Augustus Malevolyn predicted that they would choose the latter.

"All ranks into line formation!"

The hellish horde spread out, gradually creating two larger, imposing rows. To the commanders in Lut Gholein, it would be clear that the invaders sought to make their force look more impressive. Yet, those same commanders would also think how foolish the newcomers had to be to try such an apparent trick.

Lut Gholein would also wait to see if a second force followed after the first. They would judge the possibility of that by how near to the walls Malevolyn dared lead his troops. The commanders would then decide whether the risk was worth it to crush the first wave, then retreat back inside before any aid might arrive.

The demons began to lose some of the order in their ranks, but for the most part they held as they should. Their new warlord had promised them much blood, much mayhem, and that alone kept them in control. They had but one order to obey once the walls of the city had been breached; the man clad in the crimson armor had to be brought to Malevolyn immediately.

All others they could deal with as they desired.

As he and his force reached the point midway between the mangled bodies of the unfortunate patrol and the very gates of the fabled realm, a long row of turbaned figures with bows suddenly arose at the battlements. In quick fashion, they loosed a storm of arrows, all arced perfectly to wipe out the first line of attackers—including the general himself.

However, as each shaft neared Malevolyn, a brief flash of light erupted around every single one . . . obliterating them before they could touch even his horse. More than a score of arrows vanished in such a way, the archers evidently determined to slay the enemy's leader quickly if they could.

Yet, around him, his warriors fell one after another, shafts sticking out of throats, in sides, even in heads. One by one, the rain of arrows whittled down the first row and even many in the second, leaving the would-be warlord with visible losses of nearly *half* his followers.

Lightning played above Lut Gholein as if marking the next phase of the defenders' intended vengeance. The gates opened, a vast legion of hardened, bitter fighters on both horseback and foot charging in perfect order toward what remained of the murderous invaders. The turbaned warriors spread out, creating a series of rows not only longer than Malevolyn's but also several times thicker. As he had surmised, defending from the battlements had not been satisfying to his adversaries. They would make him and his pay for the butchered riders at the same time garnering some glory for themselves.

"Fools," he muttered, trying hard to hold back a smile. "Impetuous fools!"

General Malevolyn made no move to retreat. In normal combat conditions that would have proven even more costly than his suicidal advance. At least his men could die knowing that they took more of the enemy with them—or so Lut Gholein's commanders must also be thinking.

And as the opposing sides converged, he signaled to one of the few surviving warriors next to him, the one to which had been given the battle horn.

The hellish soldier raised the horn to his lips and blew, sending out a mournful cry throughout the field of combat.

From the sand arose the supposed dead, General Augustus Malevolyn's demons charging forward regardless of the wounds the arrows had inflicted. Armored figures with shafts sticking out of their throats or their eyes moved to meet the stunned defenders, some of whom let out horrified cries and tried to back away only to collide with those advancing behind them. The turbaned lines slowed, faltered, as the horrific sight registered with each man in front.

In a voice that smothered the thunder, Malevolyn roared, "Slay them! Slay them all!"

The demons roared and fell upon their more numerous but merely mortal foes.

They tore into the humans, with their hellish strength completely severing limbs and even heads from those nearest. The foremost of Lut Gholein's defenders perished horribly, several split open completely by swords, others ripped apart by hand while they screamed. Swords and lances had little effect on the general's troops, although occasionally a demon would indeed fall. Yet, despite these one or two losses, the balance of the battle clearly had begun to turn. The bodies of the defenders began to pile up as those in back, still somewhat ignorant of the terrible truth, forced their comrades into the unyielding maw of death.

A horn within the walls sounded and suddenly a new rain of arrows fell upon the invaders. Unfortunately, the new volley had little hope of success and even contributed to the continual slaughter of the defenders on the ground, many of them now falling victim to their own archers. Almost immediately after the first wave of shafts, the horn sounded again, but by that point scores more had perished.

Out among the demons, Malevolyn fought as possessed as the rest of his infernal legion. The ebony blade cut a bloody swathe through his foes, neither armor nor bone slowing it in any fashion. Soon, even his monstrous horde gave him room, the general's viciousness approaching their limits. Malevolyn's black armor had been stained from head to foot in crimson, but, if anything, it spurred him on to harsher, more brutal acts.

The ground around him abruptly exploded. His horse fell hard, dying instantly. More fortunate, General Malevolyn landed a few yards away. The explosion, which would have killed any normal man, did little more than stun him for a few seconds.

Rising, he looked up at the walls to see a pair of robed figures, Vizjerei no doubt in the service of the young sultan. Malevolyn had expected Lut Gholein to throw sorcery at him, but had become so caught up in the massacre that he had forgotten.

A fury such as he had never experienced took hold of him. He recalled Viz-jun, recalled how Horazon and the others had tricked him, led his hellish horde into a trap . . .

"Not *this* time!" Augustus Malevolyn held up a fist, shouted words he had never known before. Above him, the heavens appeared ready to explode.

A fierce wind struck the battlements, but only where the sorcerers stood. Those who watched saw the pair pulled high into the air, where they helplessly flailed about, no doubt trying to cast counterspells.

The warlord brought his fist down hard.

With wild shrieks the two Vizjerei plummeted to the ground as if shot from great bows.

When the sorcerers hit, even the demons backed away, so startled were they by the terrible force with which the pair hit. Only Malevolyn watched with great satisfaction, his first step toward avenging *his* loss at Viz-jun now taken. That his memories had so mingled with Bartuc's that he could no longer tell them apart did not even occur to him any more. There could be only one Warlord of Blood—and he stood nearly at the gates of this trembling city.

His quick eyes caught sight of one among the failing defenders, an officer of high rank. A demon stood before the bearded warrior, the black-clad creature forcing the enemy commander to his knees.

General Malevolyn acted swiftly, summoning the magical sword and driving it through the back of the stunned demon. The monstrous warrior shrieked and the body within the black armor shriveled until nothing remained but a thin, papery layer of dried flesh over bone. A wisp of green smoke rose from the collapsing corpse, smoke that dissipated in the wind.

Stepping over the pile of bones and metal, Malevolyn headed for the officer he had just saved. The general had known that the demon would not have paused in time and the loss of one of his minions meant little to him. After Lut Gholein, he would be able to summon every beast in Hell.

The weakened officer tried to fight him, but with a gesture of his hand, Malevolyn sent the man's own weapon flying—into the throat of one of the other defenders.

He seized the hapless officer by the throat, dragging him up to a standing position. "Hear me and you may live, fool!"

"You might as well slay me now—"

Tightening his grip, Malevolyn held on until the fighter nearly suffocated. At the last, he loosened his fingers slightly, allowing the man to breathe again. "Your life—the life of everyone in Lut Gholein, is mine! Only one thing will save you for the time being! One thing!"

"W-what?" his prisoner gasped, now much more sensible.

"There is a stranger in the city! A man dressed in armor the color of the blood that covers both of us and that you might yet keep running through your veins! Bring him to me! Bring him out through the gates and send him to me!"

He could see the commander calculating the advantages and disadvantages. "You'll—you'll put an end to this battle?"

"I'll put an end to it when I have what I want . . . and until I see him, Lut Gholein will know no peace! Think well on this, for you can already see that your walls will be of little good against me!"

It did not take the man long. "I—I will do it!"

"Then go!" General Malevolyn contemptuously threw the officer back, waving away a pair of demonic soldiers ready to strike the man down. To the enemy commander, he added, "Call a retreat! Any who pass through the gates will not be slaughtered! Any who fail to follow quick enough will serve as fine food for the carrion crows! This is all I grant you—be grateful you get this much!"

The officer fled from him, stumbling in the direction of Lut Gholein. Malevolyn watched him signal to someone up on the walls. A few moments later, a pitiful wail went up from one of the war horns in the city.

An armored figure with eyes that matched the blood on Augustus Malevolyn's armor came up to him. The face had once belonged to Zako. "Let them go, warlord?"

"Of course not. Beat them to the ground, let none survive who do not make it to the gates. Any who do, though, you do not touch and none of you are to enter the city!" He glanced in the direction of the enemy commander, who had not bothered much to wait for his men. "And make sure that *he* survives! He'll have much to tell them."

"Yes, warlord . . ." The Zako demon bowed once, then hesitated. "Not to enter the city? We leave Lut Gholein alone?"

"I want the armor! We will harass them, even do what we can to damage their defenses, but until I have the armor and the head of the one who dared keep it from me, the city will not be touched!" General Malevolyn— *Warlord* Malevolyn—smiled grimly. "I promised them an end to the battle, that Lut Gholein would not know peace until I had the armor. Once I have it, I will give to them exactly what I promised. A *final* end to the battle . . . and the peace of the *grave*."

Seventeen

"What's that sound?" Norrec asked, looking up from the pattern he had drawn in the sand.

Close to his side, Galeona shook her head. "I hear only thunder, my knight."

He rose, listening again. "Sounds like battle . . . from the direction of the city."

"Perhaps a celebration. Maybe it's the sultan's birthday."

Norrec frowned to himself, suspicious of her continual denial of what he certainly recognized. Although his memories and those of Bartuc had intermingled to the point where it had become hard to tell one from the other, both sets of memories now aided him in determining that he heard correctly. The clatter, the shouts . . . they all spoke of violence, of bloodshed . . .

A part of him felt tempted to join in.

No . . . he had more important things to do. Horazon's tomb, what the beguiling witch evidently called the Arcane Sanctuary, had to lie somewhere near, perhaps even beneath where he presently stood.

He knelt down again, ignoring Galeona's momentary look of relief. Something about the pattern he had drawn—an upside-down triangle with circles around each corner and three crescents beneath—did not look right. That the fighter should not have even known of such spells no longer bothered him. Bartuc had known them; therefore, Norrec Vizharan did.

"What's missing?"

The witch hesitated. "One of two things. To search for a person, you would need a pentagram in the middle of the triangle. To search for a place, you would need a larger pentagram surrounding all the rest."

She made perfect sense to him. Norrec grimaced at having forgotten something so simple. He rewarded her with a smile. "Very good."

Despite the fact that her magical skills augmented his own growing abilities and her physical charms enticed his baser nature, not for a minute did the veteran soldier trust his new companion. She told half-truths and hid much from him. He could sense her ambition. The enchantress saw him as useful to her own ends, just as he saw the same where she was concerned. So long as she aided his efforts, Norrec had no trouble accepting her lies. However, if she tried to betray him later on, he had no compunction about dealing with her as he would have any traitor.

Some part within him still did battle with what he had become. Even now, Norrec sensed that such thoughts as he had just had about Galeona went against what the veteran had believed in most of his life. Yet, it seemed so easy to accept those thoughts now.

His mind shifted back to his task. He had to find Horazon's tomb, although *why* still remained a mystery to him. Perhaps when he did discover its whereabouts, then the reason for the quest would finally become clear.

He drew the larger pentagram, choosing to try to find the sanctuary rather than the man. Horazon would be little more than bones, making it somewhat more difficult to fix upon him. The edifice itself represented a larger, more distinct target for the spell.

"Have you cast anything such as this before?"

Galeona gave him a proud look. "Of course, I have!" Her look faltered slightly. "But I've never seen the Arcane Sanctuary nor do I have anything from it."

"That'll be no problem." Norrec already had a plan in mind. He felt certain that he could have both uttered the necessary incantation and focused on the location, but that would have forced him to spread his thoughts and will too much, likely increasing his chance for failure. The Arcane Sanctuary had already appeared to be a place quite unwilling to reveal itself. Even after the armor had fought off Drognan, some other force had pushed Norrec away from his goal. As with Bartuc's own tomb, Horazon's resting place had probably been built with much security in mind. The creators had obviously not wanted it defiled or ransacked and had cast powerful protective measures such as those the soldier had encountered in Drognan's chamber.

But with Galeona casting the spell, Norrec could focus fully on their destination. Surely that would work. If not . . .

He explained it to the witch, who nodded. "It can be done, I think. We must be of one mind, though, or else our own thoughts might work against us."

She reached out her hands. Norrec placed his own in hers. Galeona smiled at him, but something about that smile repelled the veteran rather than attracted him. Again he saw raw ambition in her eyes. The sorceress thought that by proving her usefulness to her companion, she could eventually control him. That, in turn, brought more dark thoughts of his own, thoughts of what he would do to any who believed that they could do such. There could be only one master—and that had to be Norrec.

"Picture it," she muttered. "Picture where you want us to go . . ."

In his mind, Norrec imagined the tomb as he had seen it the first time. He felt certain that the initial vision had been the true one, that the force trying to keep him from the sanctuary had afterward attempted to confuse his memory. The robed skeletons, the stone coffin with the symbol of the dragon over the crescent moon . . . these surely had to be the true images of the tomb.

Holding tight, Galeona leaned back, her eyes closed and her face toward the sky. She swayed as she muttered the incantation, pulling at her companion's gauntleted hands.

Norrec shut his own eyes, the better not to be distracted by the witch's body while he pictured Horazon's resting place. An eagerness swelled within him. This *would* work. He *would* be transported to the Arcane Sanctuary.

And then what?

Norrec had no time to divine an answer to that question, for suddenly he felt his entire body lighten, as if he had become more spirit than flesh. The only tug of weight he felt at all came from his hands, where the sorceress still gripped him tight.

"*Nezarios Aero!*" cried Galeona. "*Aerona Jy!*"

The fighter's body crackled with pure energy.

"*Aerona Jy!*"

A great sense of displacement shook Norrec—

—and in the next moment, his feet landed on *hard stone.*

Eyes immediately opening wide, Norrec Vizharan looked around. Web-enshrouded walls greeted his gaze and within those walls he saw a line of statues, each distinct in face and form, staring back. Not all of them had names that he could recall, but among them he spotted more than one who had known him well—and known his brother, Horazon, too.

But no—Horazon was *not* his brother! Why did he keep thinking that?

"We've done it!" Galeona cried, having at last registered their surroundings. She flung herself on him, kissed him with a fury that could almost not be denied—yet, Norrec desired nothing more than to push her away.

"Yes, this is it," he replied, once he had managed to peel her tentacles from his body.

"There is nothing we can't accomplish *together*," she cooed. "No one who could stand in our way . . ."

Yes, Galeona definitely sought to seal their alliance. The seductive witch understood full well the power he wielded, the power the suit had at last given to him. If she could have, Norrec had no doubts that she would have tried to wear the armor herself—and thereby cut out any need for a partner. The sooner he rid himself of her, the better.

Turning from the devilish woman, Norrec looked down the ancient, musty corridor. A peculiar, yellowish light illuminated the abandoned edifice, a light seemingly without source. He could not recall it from his first incursion into this dark realm, but since everything else looked as it should, Norrec paid the one difference little attention. His goal was at hand.

"This way." Without waiting to see if the sorceress followed, Norrec stomped down the corridor in the direction he felt certain that the sarcophagus lay. Galeona hurried to catch up, the dark-skinned woman slipping an arm around his own as if the two were lovers in the midst of a moonlit walk. He did not struggle free, aware that this way he could also keep *her* under watch.

Now and then a face familiar to him stared out from the dust-ridden statues. Norrec marked each with satisfaction, remembering their order from the vision. Not only did they prove that he headed in the correct direction but particular faces indicated to him that the final chamber had to be only a short distance further.

And yet . . . and yet something about the statues also caused the veteran some unease, for although outwardly they seemed identical to those he recalled, minute alterations in detail began to haunt him. Certain features on some of the faces looked ever so slightly off—the shape of a nose, the curve of a mouth, the strength of a jaw. Most of all, the eyes tended toward different appearances. Never completely, but enough to make Norrec finally pause at one in order to look.

"What is it?" Galeona whispered, anxious to move on to their ultimate destination.

The face he stared at, the face of one Oskul, a round-headed, officious mage who had briefly been Horazon's sponsor to the Vizjerei council, resembled much the visage as Norrec's memory recalled it . . . but the eyes should have been narrower and the artisan had also given the orbs a sleepy look, not at all in keeping with the ever-active personality of the man. Nothing else about the statue seemed out of place, but the eyes proved to be enough to disturb him yet more.

Still, Norrec had been in the tomb for only a short time and had spent only a fraction of it among the ghostly sculptures. Whatever mistakes he now recalled likely had more to do with the artist's failing rather than anything else.

"Nothing," the soldier finally remarked. "Come on."

They journeyed on for a few minutes more—and at last entered the crypt. Norrec smiled as he studied the ancient site. Here, everything looked as it should. In the niches on the left and right, the skeletal figures of the Vizjerei sorcerers silently greeted the newcomers' arrival. The vast stone coffin atop the dais matched perfectly his vision.

The coffin . . .

"*Horazon* . . . " he whispered.

With growing eagerness, Norrec dragged Galeona toward the sarcophagus. The horror he had suffered during his dream visit to this place had been all but forgotten. All Norrec wanted to do now was open the coffin. He left the witch to the side, then reached up to take hold of the lid.

At that moment, his gaze slipped down to the clan markings again, something about them snaring his attention.

The dragon remained as it had been—but now below it lay a fiery star.

He stepped back, the truth dawning slowly on him. There had been too many errors, too many differences in detail . . .

"What's wrong? Why didn't you open it?"

Glaring at the traitorous markings, the veteran fighter snapped, "Because it's not real!" He waved his hand at the legion of dead mages. "I don't think *any* of this is real!"

"But that's mad!" Galeona touched the coffin. "It's as solid as you or I!"

"Is it?" Norrec extended his hand—and as he had hoped, in it he now held the sinister ebony sword. "Let's see what exactly the truth is!"

As Galeona watched in both astonishment and dismay, the soldier raised the sword high above his head, then brought it down hard on the massive sarcophagus.

The blade cut through without pause and yet no line appeared in the coffin. The two halves of the great stone monument did not separate and collapse . . . and the tattered bones of Horazon did not tumble to the floor.

"Illusion . . . or something akin to it." He turned to the horrific throng lined up against the walls, glaring at the dead as if they were to blame. "Where is he? Where's Horazon?"

"Perhaps down another passage . . ." suggested Galeona, her tone indicating she did not completely trust his sanity at the moment.

"Yes, maybe so." Without waiting for her, he charged out of the crypt. For some distance, Norrec followed the single corridor, looking for a side passage, a doorway. Yet, not once could he recall having seen one. In both versions of his dream, it had always been only this single passageway. The great Arcane Sanctuary had always consisted of only this and the actual burial chamber itself. Hardly the immense edifice one would have expected.

Unless what he had seen had been designed simply for the benefit of curious and greedy intruders—and the rest lay hidden elsewhere.

The frustrated fighter paused to glare at the statue of one of his—no, Bartuc's—former rivals. The bearded man smiled in what Norrec felt a very mocking manner.

That brought him to a decision. He raised the black blade again.

"What do you plan to do this time?" snapped Galeona, her patience with him having finally gotten thin. Great power he might wield, but so far Norrec had evidently not impressed her with his running about in circles.

"If there're no passages, I'll make one of my own!"

He glared at the statue, desiring very much to wipe the condescending smile off its face. Here would be the perfect location to begin cutting his way out. Norrec held the sword ready, determined to bring down the mocking effigy with his first blow.

But as he swung, as the blade came within inches of beheading the smiling statue, Norrec's entire surroundings fragmented. The floor rose and the walls pulled away, the rows of statues seeming to fall back as if fainting. The enshrouding webs folded in on themselves, utterly vanishing. Stairs bloomed like flowers, twisting and turning. Part of the floor ceased rising and instead dropped lower, leaving the two standing near a precipice. The only thing that remained consistent through the growing anarchy was the yellowish illumination.

"What've you done?" Galeona cried. "You fool! It's all falling apart!"

Norrec could not answer her, unable even to keep his footing. He fell back, the heavy armor dragging him down. His weapon flew from his grip and as it did, it faded away. The ground shook, keeping him from rising and, worse, rolling him toward the edge.

"Help me up!" he called to the sorceress, growing desperate. The gauntlets tore at the stone floor but could not get a grip anywhere. Around him, the Arcane Sanctuary continued to transform itself without any noticeable rhyme or reason, almost as if the tomb had gone into convulsion as a human might.

Galeona looked his way, hesitated, then looked to her right, where a stairway had suddenly formed.

"Help me, damn it!"

She sneered at him. "What a waste of my time! You, Augustus, Xazax—all of you! Better I relied only on myself! If you can't even pick yourself up, you might as well stay here and die, fool!"

With one last contemptuous glance at Norrec, Galeona started toward the steps.

"No!" Anger and fear vied for supremacy in him, anger and fear of the likes the fighter could never have imagined. As the witch fought her way to what might be freedom—abandoning Norrec to whatever fate awaited him—the urge to strike out, to punish her for her betrayal grew almost overwhelming.

Norrec pointed at her with his left hand. Words of power gathered on his lips, ready to be spoken. With one quick phrase, he would rid himself of the treacherous woman.

"Damn it! No! I won't!" He turned from her, pulled down his hand. Let her flee without him if she liked. He would not have *another* death on his hands.

Unfortunately, the armor did not agree.

The hand rose again, this time against Norrec's will. He struggled to lower it, but as since almost from the beginning of this terrible quest, the soldier found himself not the master, but simply the means. Bartuc's armor sought retribution for Galeona's failing—and it would have that retribution regardless of what its host wanted.

The gauntlet flared crimson.

Their surroundings still in complete flux, the dark-skinned enchantress had only now made it to the twisting staircase. To her misfortune, however, it shifted to the side, forcing her to readjust her path. As Norrec's hand came up, Galeona managed at last to set a foot on the first and second steps.

"No!" shouted Norrec at the gauntlet. He looked at the fleeing woman, who had not bothered to take even the slightest parting glimpse at her struggling companion. "Run! Hurry! Get out of here!"

Only after he had blurted out the warning did Norrec realize what he had done. Those words more than anything else caused Galeona to pause and look over her shoulder, costing her the precious seconds she had needed.

The dark words that the fighter had struggled not to say burst free.

Galeona saw what he did and reacted, striking back. She pointed at the prone figure, mouthing a single harsh word that some memory not of Norrec Vizharan's past recognized as a spell most foul.

Brilliant blue flames surrounded the witch even as she finished speaking. Galeona raised her head and howled once in utter agony—then burned away to ash in the blink of an eye.

Norrec, though, had no time to acknowledge her terrible demise, for suddenly his entire body became wracked in pain, as if each bone within sought to break apart. Norrec could feel even the tiniest of them slowly but inexorably cracking. Although the armor's magic had destroyed her, Galeona had succeeded in her own spellcasting. He screamed, shaking uncontrollably. Worse, despite his agony, the armor did nothing to help and instead appeared to be trying to rise so that it now could use the very staircase upon which the sorceress had perished.

Yet although the suit made it to the steps, it could go no farther. Each time it tried, an invisible force buffeted it back. Norrec's fist slammed against air, sending new shockwaves through the already-suffering man.

"Please!" he croaked, not caring that only the armor could possibly hear him. "Please . . . help . . ."

"Norrec!"

Through tear-drenched eyes, he tried to focus on the voice, a woman's voice. Did the ghost of Galeona call to him to join her in death?

"Norrec Vizharan!"

No . . . a different voice, young but commanding. He managed to turn his head some, although the action caused more torture within. In the distance, a vaguely familiar woman pale of skin but black of hair futilely reached out to him from what appeared to be a crystalline doorway at the top of yet another flight of stairs. Behind her stood another figure, this one male and with long, wild hair and a beard, both as white as snow. He looked suspicious, curious, and frightened all at the same time. He also looked even more familiar than the woman.

To Norrec he could be only one person.

"Horazon?" the soldier blurted.

One of the gloved hands immediately came up, the gauntlet ablaze with magical fury. Bartuc's armor had reacted to the name—and not with pleasure. Norrec could feel the formation of a spell, one that would make Galeona's death seem a peaceful end.

But as if reacting in turn to the armor, an awful moaning arose, as if the very building itself took offense to what it saw. Horazon and the woman suddenly disappeared as the stairway shifted a different direction and new walls formed. Norrec discovered himself suddenly

standing in a high-columned hall that looked as if a
grand ball had just ended. Yet, even that changed quickly.

No matter what the room, no matter where the woman
and Horazon had gone, the armor did not care. Another
spell erupted from the fighter's mouth and a ball of
molten earth flew from his hand, exploding seconds later
against the nearest wall.

The moaning became a *roar*.

The entire sanctuary shook. A tremendous force buffeted Norrec from every side. Worse, he realized that not
only did the air close in on him—but so did the walls and
the ceiling. Even the floor rose.

Norrec raised his arms, now evidently his own again,
in a last futile effort to staff off the onrushing walls.

The meal had been a sumptuous one, better by far than
any Kara could have imagined, including those which
Captain Jeronnan had served her. If not for the fact that
she was the prisoner of an insane mage, she might have
enjoyed it even more.

During the meal, the necromancer had tried on more
than one occasion to pluck some bit of reason from the
white-haired sorcerer, but from Horazon she had only
received babbled words and inconsistent information. At
one point he had spoken of having discovered by accident
the Arcane Sanctuary—the name by which legend called
Horazon's tomb—then he had told Kara that he had built
it all by himself through masterful sorcery. Another time,
Horazon had told his prisoner that he had come to
Aranoch to study the massive convergence of spiritual
ley-lines centered in and around the city's present location. Even she had heard that mages could tap the mystical energies of this region far better than in any other spot
in all the world. However, afterward he had spoken, with
great trepidation, of fleeing to this side of the seas in fear
that his brother's dark legacy still followed him.

Gradually Kara came to feel as if she spoke to two distinct men, one who truly *was* Horazon and another who simply thought he was. She could only think that the terrible trials through which Bartuc's brother had suffered, especially the horrific war against his own sibling, had combined with his centuries-long seclusion to tear apart his already-fragile mind. The necromancer grew somewhat sympathetic to his plight, but never did she forget that not only did this mad sorcerer still keep her in his underground labyrinth against her will, but also that, in times past, his magic had, on occasion, been as black as Bartuc's had ever been.

One other thing Kara had noted that unnerved her as much as her host's sanity. The Arcane Sanctuary itself acted as if more than simply an extension of Horazon's tremendous power. Many times, she could have sworn that it, too, had a mind, a personality, even. Sometimes she would note the room around her shift subtly, the walls moving and the general design transforming even when the wizard paid it no mind. Kara had even noticed that the table and the food changed. More to the point, when the necromancer had tried to push Horazon on the matter of Bartuc, a peculiar darkness had slowly begun to pervade her surroundings—almost as if the edifice itself wished an end to the troubling topic.

When they had finished, Horazon had immediately bid her to rise. Here in his sanctum, he had not babbled too much about 'the evil,' but still the watery-eyed figure acted with caution in all things.

"We must be careful," Horazon had muttered, standing. "At all times we must be careful . . . come . . . there is much to do . . ."

Her thoughts more on escape than his constant warnings, Kara had also risen—only to see a sight so startling that it had made her knock her chair over.

From the table itself had emerged a hand completely

formed of the wood. The hand had seized her empty plate and had dragged it down *into* the table. At the same time, other hands had materialized, each seizing an object and dragging it, too, into the table. Still stunned, Kara had stepped back, only then discovering that the reason she had not heard her chair strike the floor had been because two more appendages formed from the marble at her feet had caught the piece of furniture before it could hit.

"Come!" Horazon had called, his expression now somewhat peevish. He seemed not at all disturbed by the unsettling appendages. "No time to waste, no time to waste!"

While the dining hall had worked to clear itself, he had led her up a flight of stairs, then through a polished, oak door. Behind the door lay another stairway, this one going back down. Despite having wanted to question the trustfulness of their path, the young dark mage had quietly followed even when that set of steps had ended at yet another doorway which seemed to lead back to the vast hall again. Only when Horazon had opened the door and instead of the great hall she had been confronted with a wizard's laboratory had Kara finally blurted out something.

"This is impossible! This room shouldn't be here!"

He had looked at her as if she had been the mad one. "Of course, it should be! I was looking for it, after all! What a silly thing to say! If you look for a room, it should be where you want it, you know!"

"But . . ." Kara had ceased her protest, unable to argue with the facts before her very eyes. Here should have stood the grand room in which she and Horazon had eaten, but instead this imposing if disorderly chamber had greeted her. Thinking back to the impossible journeys she had already made in the sanctuary, the dark-haired spellcaster had finally come to the conclusion that the ancient mage's home could not possibly completely exist on the mortal plane. Even though no architect could have ever solved the physical problems she had encountered, it had been said of the most powerful Vizjerei that some had learned to actually manipulate the very fabric of reality itself, to create for their use what some called "pocket universes" where the laws of nature were what their masters decided it should be.

Could that have been what Horazon had accomplished with the Arcane Sanctuary? Kara could find no other explanation for everything she had experienced. If so, he had created a marvel such as not ever seen before in all the world!

Despite his ragged robe and otherwise unkempt appearance, in this chamber Horazon had taken on a more formidable look. When he had stepped to the center of the room, raising his arms and beckoning to the ceiling, Kara had expected fire and lightning to play from his fingers. She had expected winds to rise from nowhere and perhaps even the Vizjerei's body to glow bright.

Instead, he had simply turned back to her and said, "I brought you here . . . but I don't know *why*."

After taking a moment to register this odd statement, the necromancer had replied, "Is it because of the armor? Your—brother's—armor?"

He had stared up at the ceiling again. "Is it?"

The ceiling, of course, had not answered.

"Horazon . . . you must remember what they did with your brother's body, your people and mine."

Again, the ceiling. "What was done with it? Ah, yes, no wonder I don't remember."

Feeling as if she might as well have been talking to the ceiling herself, Kara had pressed, "Listen to me, Horazon! Someone managed to steal his enchanted armor from the tomb. I've followed them all the way here! He may even be in Lut Gholein at this moment! We need to find him, to take the armor back! There's no telling what evil still lurks within it!"

"Evil?" His eyes had taken on a wide, animalistic look. "Evil? Here?"

Kara had bitten back a curse. She had stirred him up again.

"So much evil about! I must be careful!" A condemning finger had pointed at her. "You must go!"

"Horazon, I——"

It had been at that moment that something had happened, something that passed between the wizard and his lair. Seconds later, she had felt the entire sanctum shiver, a shiver more that of a living thing, not simply a structure caught in some shockwave.

"No, no, no! I must hide! I must hide!" Horazon had looked completely panic stricken. He might have even fled from the chamber, but the room again transformed. The sorcerer's tables of equipment and chemicals receded from the two and from the floor a gigantic, crystalline sphere arose to eye level, a huge hand formed from the stone below keeping it there.

In the center of the sphere, a vision had coalesced, a vision of a man whom Kara Nightshadow had never truly seen but had still been able to identify immediately—thanks to the crimson armor he wore.

"It's him! Norrec Vizharan! He has the armor!"

"Bartuc!" her mad companion had snapped. "No! Bartuc's come for me!"

She had seized him by the arm, daring death in the hopes of finally bringing a conclusion to this dangerous quest. "Horazon! Where is he? Is that part of the sanctuary, too?"

In the sphere, Norrec Vizharan and a dark-skinned woman had rushed through a web-enshrouded corridor filled with ancient statues carved in the fashion of the Vizjerei. Norrec had carried a monstrous black sword and had looked ready to use it. Kara had wondered then if Sadun Tryst had spoken too well of his former friend. Here had looked a man who had seemed very capable of the outrageous murders.

Regardless of the answer to that, Kara had known she could not come this close and fail. "Answer me! Is that part of the sanctuary? It must be!"

"Yes, it is! Now leave me be!" He had torn free from her, headed to the door—only to be stopped there by hands sprouting from the floor and walls, hands that had kept him from abandoning the necromancer.

"What—?" She had been able to say no more, startled by what seemed the vehemence in the hands' actions. Horazon's very stronghold had seemed in rebellion, forcing him to return to Kara.

"Let me go, let me go!" the mad sorcerer had cried out to the ceiling. "It's the evil! I mustn't let it get me!" As the raven-tressed woman had watched, a sullen expression had finally crossed Horazon's wrinkled face. "All right . . . all right . . ."

And so he had returned to the sphere, pointed at the image. By this time, Norrec had confronted one of the statues, shouted something in anger that the crystal did not relay, then raised the black blade as if prepared to strike.

At the same time, Horazon cried, *"Greikos Dominius est Buar! Greiko Dominius Mortu!"*

Chaos had erupted in the scene with walls, floors, and stairs shifting, materializing, or disappearing. In the midst of the madness, the two figures had struggled to survive. However, Norrec Vizharan had been unable to save himself, falling near an edge and then being unable to rise because of the constant motion all around him. The woman—a witch, in Kara's mind—had completely abandoned the helpless fighter, choosing instead to head toward what seemed a fairly stable set of stairs.

"Greiko Dominius Mortu!" her companion snapped.

Something in his tone had made Kara look at Horazon and in his eyes she had read nothing but death for the pair. So, this had been how it would end. Not by the hands of the revenants nor through her own sorcery, but by the fatal spells of Bartuc's own crazed brother. For the witch she had felt nothing, but because of Tryst's tales of the veteran fighter, a spark of sadness had still touched her. Perhaps there had been a good man there once.

But not at that moment. The scene had revealed Norrec determined to slay his wayward partner. He had pointed one gauntleted hand at her, shouted something—

Only then had Kara noticed the look of horror and regret on his face. No satisfaction, no dark intent, only fear for what he would do to the fleeing woman.

But that had made no sense, unless . . .

"What did he say, Horazon? Do you know what he said? I need to know!"

From the crystalline sphere had suddenly burst a man's fearful voice. *"Damn it! I won't!"* Then, *"No! Run! Hurry! Get out of here!"*

Not the bitter shouts of a vengeful murderer and yet the image had still shown him ready to strike down his fleeing companion. However, his expression had continued to belie that notion. Norrec Vizharan had actually appeared as if he battled for control of himself or—or—

Of course! "Horazon! You must stop this! You must help them!"

"Help them? No, no! Destroy them and I destroy the evil at last! Yes, at last!"

Kara had glanced at the sphere again—just in time to witness not only the witch's awful demise, but the woman's own last attack on the fighter. Norrec's cries had filled Horazon's chamber, the sphere apparently still fulfilling the necromancer's previous request.

"Listen to me! The evil is in the armor, not the man! Don't you see? His death would be a travesty, a tipping of the balance!" Frustrated at Horazon's unyielding expression, she had glared up at the ceiling. The wizard seemed to consult some power up there, some power that did not merely exist in his mind. To it she had cried, "Bartuc was the monster, not the one clad in his armor and only Bartuc would take a life so!" Once more gazing at the mad mage, she concluded, "Or is Horazon just like his brother?"

The reaction to her desperate declarations had startled even Kara. From every wall, from even the ceiling and the floor, *mouths* had formed in the stone. Only one word had issued from each, the same word over and over,

"No ... no ... no ... "

The crystalline sphere had suddenly expanded and, even more startling, *opened* up. Within it had arisen a stairway, which Kara had imagined had to lead somehow—as impossible as it had seemed—directly to the struggling Norrec.

Horazon had refused to aid her, but the Arcane Sanctuary had not.

The necromancer had immediately rushed to the crystal, pausing only when she came to the first step. Despite having offered her this path, the enchanted sanctum had continued to assault Norrec, making rescue difficult. Momentarily uncertain, Kara had initially chosen to call to the fighter, to see if he could perhaps make it to her without her having to enter the chaos.

He had responded to the second call—by shouting Horazon's name. Confused, Kara had withdrawn the hand she had offered, a symbolic gesture intended to let him know she had meant only help. As she had done that, he, in turn, had reacted oddly, moving as if he intended not to come to the necromancer—but to slay her.

"The evil awakens . . ." a voice had muttered behind her.

Horazon. She had not realized that he had stepped into sight. Kara had assumed that the mad mage had stayed far from the danger. She had known then why Norrec— or rather the *armor*—had reacted so. The enchanted armor had yet sought to fulfill its creator's greatest desire, to slay the accursed brother.

But before it had been able to strike, the sanctuary had chosen once more to take command of the situation. Norrec and his surroundings had regressed, pulling farther and farther back, almost vanishing from sight. Kara had seen the walls there begin to converge, as if the astonishing edifice had sought to box its adversary in . . . and worse. It had occurred to her only at the last that, with the armor seeking Horazon's imminent destruction, the best choice for the Arcane Sanctuary had been to end this once and for all, even if it meant, after all, the death of an innocent. Better to destroy both the armor and Norrec Vizharan than give Bartuc's legacy another chance to succeed.

But such a death went against the balance that Kara Nightshadow had been trained to preserve. Now, with Norrec's doom looming, the necromancer *leapt* into the chaos within the crystalline sphere, hoping that Horazon's apparently sentient domain would do for her what it would not for the hapless fighter.

Hoping that it would not decide that Kara, too, was expendable.

Eighteen

Norrec could not move, could not even breathe. It felt as if a giant hand had taken hold of him and sought to crush his entire body to a tiny pulp. In some ways he welcomed it, for with his death would at least end his guilt. No one else would die because he had sought to rob a tomb and instead unearthed a nightmare.

Then, just as he prepared himself to die, a tremendous force threw him upward. Norrec flew hard, almost as if he had been fired off by a catapult. So, instead of a crushing death, he would eventually fall to his doom. Unlike the short drop aboard the *Hawksfire*, Norrec felt certain that this time he would not survive.

But something—no, *someone*—caught him by one arm, slowing his flight. Norrec tried to see who it might be, but turning his head toward his would-be rescuer brought about an overwhelming sensation of vertigo. He lost all sense of direction, no longer even able to tell up from down.

Without warning, Norrec struck the ground, the sand doing very little to prevent the jolt from knocking him nearly senseless.

For some time, the battered veteran lay there, cursing the fact that he seemed to end up in such a position more often than necessary. His body ached to his bones and his vision revealed nothing to him but blurs. Yet, despite all that, he at least felt less pain. Whatever spell Galeona had cast before her death had at some point ceased and with it had also gone the crushing suffocation.

He heard thunder and knew from the general grayness his unfocused eyes could make out that he had returned to the storm-swept desert near Lut Gholein. Norrec also sensed that he had not come here alone, that even now, someone stood over him.

"Can you stand?" a familiar female voice asked gently.

He almost told her that he had no desire to, but instead forced himself as best he could to a sitting position. Doing so made his head spin, but at least Norrec felt some pride at accomplishing the simple task by himself.

His vision finally cleared enough for him to see who had spoken. It proved to be the dark-haired woman he had not only seen just before the walls had closed in, but also now recalled as one of the faces on the statues he had passed during his second sojourn into the dream version of Horazon's tomb.

Horazon. Thinking of Bartuc's brother made him recall who he had seen standing near the pale woman. Horazon—still alive after *centuries.*

She mistook his momentary shaking as a part of a possible injury. "Be careful. You have been through much. We do not know how it may have affected you."

"Who are you?"

"My name is Kara Nightshadow," she replied, kneeling so as to get a better look at his face. One slim hand gently touched his cheek. "Does that hurt you?"

In truth, her hand felt good, but he knew better than to tell her so. "No. Are you a healer?"

"Not exactly. I am a follower of Rathma."

"A necromancer?" Surprisingly, the admission did not shock him as much as it once might have. Everything around Norrec of late had concerned death—or worse. A necromancer certainly fit well into the pattern, although he had to admit he had never seen an attractive one before. The few others of her faith that he had come across had been dour figures little different from the dead with whom they communed.

He realized that although she had told him her name he had not introduced himself. "My name's Norrec—"

"Yes. Norrec Vizharan. I know."

"How?" He recalled that she had used his name earlier, yet the two had never actually met as far as he knew. Certainly he would have remembered.

"I have been hunting for you ever since you left Bartuc's tomb with the armor."

"You? But why?"

She leaned back, apparently satisfied that he had not suffered much from their ouster from Horazon's bizarre domain. "Along with the Vizjerei, my people took the responsibility for hiding the warlord's ensorcelled remains. We could not destroy either the body or the armor at that time, but we could keep them from those who might find a use—either corrupted mages or deadly demons."

Norrec remembered the monstrous creature in the sea. "Why demons?"

"Bartuc started out as a pawn of theirs, but even you must know that by the time of his death, even the lords of Hell looked in awe at his power. Although only a portion of his total might, what remains in the armor itself would be enough to entirely upset the delicate balance of life and death in the world . . . and even, perhaps, beyond."

After all that he had seen, he had little trouble believing her. Norrec struggled to his feet, Kara assisting him. He looked down at her, thinking back to what had just happened. "You saved me."

She looked away, almost seeming embarrassed. "I had some part in it."

"I would've died otherwise, right?"

"Very likely."

"Then you saved me—but *why* did you do it? Why not simply let me die? If I had, the armor would've been left with no *host*. It would've been powerless!"

Kara stared him in the eyes. "You did not choose to wear Bartuc's accursed armor, Norrec Vizharan. It chose you, although I do not know why. Whatever it has done, whatever foul deeds it has performed, I felt you innocent of them—and therefore deserving of a chance of life."

"But more might die because of that!" The bitterness must have shown in his expression, for the necromancer withdrew slightly. "My friends, the men at the inn, the *Hawksfire*'s crew, and just now that witch! How many more must perish—and most before my eyes?"

She put a hand on his own. Norrec feared for her, but the suit did nothing. Perhaps whatever fueled its evil task lay dormant for a time—or perhaps it simply awaited the best moment to strike. "There is a way to end this," Kara replied. "We must remove the armor."

Norrec burst out laughing. He laughed long and hard—and with no hope. "Woman, don't you think I've tried? Don't you think the first chance I had I pulled at both gloves, attempted to peel off every bit of plate? I couldn't even remove the damned *boots*. They're all sealed to my body, as if a very part of my flesh! The only way you'll be able to remove the suit is if you take my skin off with it!"

"I understand the trouble. I understand also that, under most circumstances, no spellcaster would have the power to undo what the armor has done—"

"Then what could you possibly hope to accomplish?" the frustrated soldier snapped. "You should've let me die just now! It would've been better for all!"

Despite his outburst, the raven-haired woman remained calm. She glanced around before answering, as if looking for someone or something. "He did not follow. I should have known."

"Who . . . Horazon?"

Kara nodded. "So you recognized him, too?"

Exhaling, Norrec explained, "My memories . . . my memories are confused. Some of them I know are mine, but others . . ." He hesitated, certain she would find him mad for what he believed. " . . . the others belonged to Bartuc, I think."

"Yes, very likely they did."

"That doesn't surprise you?"

"In legend, the warlord and his crimson suit seemed as one. Over time, he imbued it with one mighty enchantment after another, transforming it into more than simply pieces of metal. By the time of his death, it had been said that the armor acted as if a loyal dog, its own magic protecting and fighting for Bartuc as hard as he himself would. Small wonder that his life has been imprinted upon it . . . and that some of those vile memories have seeped into your *own* mind."

The weary veteran shuddered. "And the longer I wear it, the more I'll succumb. There's been times I actually thought I *was* Bartuc!"

"Which is why we must remove it." She frowned. "We must try to convince Horazon to do it. I feel he is the only one who has the capability."

Norrec did not exactly like that notion. The last time he and the bearded elder had seen one another, the armor had reacted instantly and with clear malice. "That may stir up the suit again. It may even be why it's being so quiet now." Something suddenly struck him. "It *wants* him. It wants Horazon. All this damn distance, all the things it's put me through—it's all been because it wants to slay Bartuc's brother!"

Her expression indicated that she had come to much the same conclusion. "Yes. Blood calls to blood, as they say, even if the blood between two is bad. Horazon helped slay his brother at the battle of Viz-jun and the armor must have preserved that memory within it. Now, after all this time, it has risen and seeks to repay the deed—even though Horazon should have been dead centuries ago."

"But he isn't. Blood calls to blood, you said. It must've known he was still alive." Norrec shook his head. "Which doesn't explain why it waited so long. Gods! It's all insane!"

Kara took him by the arm. "Horazon must have the answer. Somehow we must find our way back to him. I feel that he is the only hope by which we can put an end to the warlord's curse."

"Put an end to it, someone says?" rasped a voice of no human origin. "No . . . no. . . . This one desires otherwise he does . . ."

Kara stared past Norrec, who immediately began to turn

"Look—" was as far as the necromancer got.

What resembled a sharp, needlelike lance darted down toward him. It would have caught Norrec through the head, but at the last, Kara pushed him aside. Unfortunately for both of them, the wicked lance continued its downward thrust unabated—and buried itself in the woman's chest.

The lance quickly withdrew. Kara gasped, collapsing Blood spilled over her blouse. Norrec froze momentarily, then, knowing he could do nothing for her if he, too, perished, the veteran fighter turned to confront their attacker.

Yet, what greeted his horrified eyes proved to be no warrior, but rather a thing born of nightmares. It most resembled a towering insect, but one clearly spawned in more hellish climes. Pulsating veins crosscrossed its grotesque form. What he had taken for a lance had actually been one of the creature's own appendages, a lengthy, sicklelike arm ending in a deadly point. Beneath the sickles, savage skeletal hands with claws opened and closed. Somehow, the massive horror managed to support itself on two lengthy hind limbs bent back in the manner of the mantis it so resembled.

"This one came in search of a treacherous, wandering witch, but such a prize will serve better! Long has this one hunted for you, for the power you wield . . ."

Even dazed, Norrec knew that the demon—for what other creature could this be—meant the armor, not the man.

"You killed her!" he managed to reply.

Blood dripping from one sickle, the mantis dipped his head. "One less mortal makes no difference. Where is the witch? Where is Galeona?"

He knew her? Norrec did not find that at all surprising. Even half under the spell of the armor, he had known that much of her story had been lies. "Dead. The armor killed her."

An intake of breath indicated to him that the demon found this startling. "She is dead? Of course! This one sensed something amiss—but did not suspect that!"

He began to emit a peculiar, rattling noise which the soldier at first thought anger. Only after a time, however, did it become clear that the monstrous insect *laughed*.

"The bond is severed, yet still this one roams the mortal plane! The tie is broken, but the blood spell preserves! This one could have slain her all along! What a fool Xazax has been!"

Norrec took the demon's enjoyment as a chance to look at Kara. Her entire chest had turned crimson and from where he stood he could not tell if she even breathed. It pained him to have her, the one who had tried to save him, die before his very eyes without being able to do anything about it.

Spurred on by anger, Norrec took a step toward the mantis—or at least *tried* to do so. Unfortunately, his legs, his entire body, refused to obey him.

"Damn you!" he roared at the suit. "Not now!"

Xazax ceased laughing. The deep, yellow orbs fixed on

the helpless human. "Fool! Think you to command the greatness of Bartuc? This one thought to peel the armor off your cold corpse, but now Xazax sees this would have proven a terrible blunder! You are needed—at least for the time being!"

The mantis raised one spearlike tip toward the breastplate. Immediately, Norrec's left hand reached out, but not in defense. Instead, to his horror, it touched the demon's own appendage as if in acknowledgment.

"You would be whole, would you not?" Xazax asked of the suit. "You would desire the return of the helm separated from you so long ago? This one can take you to it . . . if you like."

In response, one booted foot stepped forward. Even Norrec knew what the lone movement meant.

"Then go we shall . . . but it must be done quickly." The mantis turned and started off.

Norrec had no choice but to follow, the armor soon marching alongside the demon. Behind the desperate soldier, Kara bled away the last drops of her life, but he could do no more for her than he could for himself. In some ways, Norrec envied the pale woman. The necromancer's suffering had already all but ended; his would only get worse. His last hope had been crushed.

"Heaven help me . . ." he whispered.

The mantis apparently had sharp hearing, for he immediately fell upon the hopeless words. *"Heaven?* No angel will there be to help you, fool of a human! Too afraid, they are! Too cowardly! We walk the world in numbers, the demon master awakes, and the human stronghold of Lut Gholein prepares to suffer a horrific end! *Heaven?* You would do better to pray to Hell!"

And as they continued on toward their destination, Norrec could not help but think that on this the demon might just speak the truth.

* * *

Kara felt her life ebbing away, but she could do nothing about it. The demonic creature she had seen had moved with inhuman swiftness. Perhaps she had saved Norrec, but even that the necromancer doubted.

She drifted along, each drop of blood leaving her body bringing her close to taking her next step in the overall scheme of the balance. Yet despite her deep beliefs, Kara wanted nothing more at the moment than to return to the mortal plane. She had left too much undone, had left Norrec in a position that he could not possibly survive without her aid. Worse, demons walked her world, further evidence that every follower of Rathma was badly needed. She *had* to return.

But such choices were generally not given to the dying.

"What should we do?" a voice in the distance asked, a voice that Kara felt she knew.

"He said that we should give it back when we felt we must. I feel we must."

"But without it—"

"We will still have time, Sadun."

"He may have said so, but I don't trust him!"

A brief, throaty chuckle. *"Trust you to be the only one capable of not trusting one of his grand kind."*

"Save the remarks . . . if it's got to be done, let's do it."

"As you say."

Kara suddenly felt a great weight upon her chest—a weight that felt so good that she eagerly welcomed it, took it into her very being. It had a tremendous familiarity to it that caused her to reminisce about little things, such as her mother feeding her fruit, a butterfly the color of rainbows landing on her knee while she studied in the forest, the smell of Captain Jeronnan's freshly cooked meals . . . even a brief glimpse of Norrec Vizharan's weathered but not unhandsome face.

The necromancer suddenly gasped as *life* enfolded her again.

She blinked, feeling the sand, the wind. Thunder rumbled and somewhere distant she heard what seemed the sounds of battle.

"It did . . . as he said . . . it would. I should've . . . used it . . . on myself."

Kara knew that voice now, although it had changed some from just a few seconds before. Now it sounded more as she would have expected it to sound—the rasping words of a dead man.

"I know . . . I know . . ." Sadun Tryst retorted to some silent response. "Only her . . ."

Opening her eyes, the enchantress stared up at the solemn forms of the grinning revenant and his Vizjerei companion. "What—how did you find me?"

"We never lost . . . you. We let you . . . go . . . and followed." His eyes narrowed. "But here in . . . Aranoch . . . we knew you . . . were around, but . . . could not see . . . you . . . until now."

They did not know exactly where she had gone when Horazon had led her down into his underground sanctum. The spell binding her to them had kept them in the general area, but both the sanctuary's location and its incredible magic had left the revenants baffled. She could have been directly underneath and neither would have noticed.

Her strength returning, the dark mage tried to push herself up a bit. Something slid from her chest. Kara instinctively caught it with one hand and marveled. Her dagger!

Tryst's smile had taken a decidedly bitter turn. "The bond is . . . broken. The life force . . . we took . . . is yours. . . ." He looked frustrated. "We have . . . no more . . . hold . . . over you."

The necromancer looked down at her chest. Blood covered most of the blouse, but the horrible wound inflicted on her by the demon had sealed over, the only sign of its earlier presence a circular mark, as if someone had tattooed Kara there.

"Looks . . . much healed."

She covered the area up again, glaring at the undead, despite the fact that he and Fauztin had just gifted her with a second chance at life. "How did you do that? I've never heard of such a feat!"

The wiry corpse shrugged, his head tipping to the other side. "He—my friend . . . said that the dagger . . . was a part . . . of you. When you were . . . bound to us . . . some part of you . . . came with. We returned it . . . to make you alive." He grimaced as best he could. "Nothing keeps . . . you tied to . . . us any more."

"Except one thing. Norrec." Kara forced herself up. Tryst stood back, but, to her astonishment, Fauztin lent a hand. She hesitated at first, but realized that the revenant only meant to help. "Thank you."

Fauztin blinked . . . then rewarded her with a brief, tight-lipped smile.

"You bring life . . . to the deadest of . . . the dead . . . now . . . we're even . . ." Sadun Tryst jested.

"What about Norrec?"

"We think . . . he nears . . . Lut Gholein."

Even though they had saved her, the necromancer could not let them slay their former friend. "Norrec is not responsible for your deaths. What happened to you he could not prevent."

The two stared back at her. At last, Fauztin blinked again and Tryst replied, "We know."

"But then why—?" Kara stopped. All along she had assumed that they hunted their murderer, who, naturally, could only be Norrec. Only now, looking at the duo, did she understand that her misconceptions had led her astray.

"You do not pursue Norrec in order to exact revenge on him—you pursue Bartuc's *armor*." Although they did not answer her, she knew that she had not been wrong. "You could have told me!"

Tryst did not reply to that, either, instead abruptly announcing to Kara, "The city is under . . . siege."

Under siege? When had that happened? "By who?"

"One who . . . also seeks . . . to raise the dead . . . or at least . . . the bloody specter of . . . Bartuc."

Where did all these madmen come from, Kara wondered—and that made her think of the ragged figure from whom she had most recently escaped. Turning around, she looked for some sign of the Arcane Sanctuary, but to no avail. The desert sands swirled in the wind, the dunes looking as if they had remained untouched for years. Yet, somewhere around here the earth had opened up and deposited her and Norrec on the ground.

Not caring what the revenants might make of her peculiar actions, Kara called out, "Horazon! Listen to me! You can help us—and we can help you! Help us save Norrec—and put an end to Bartuc's legacy!"

She waited, the wind whipping her hair and sand stinging her face. Kara waited for Horazon to materialize or at least send her some sign that he listened.

But nothing happened.

At last, Sadun Tryst broke the silence. "We can't . . . wait here any longer . . . while you call . . . more ghosts . . ."

"I'm not calling—" the necromancer stopped. Of what use trying to explain to the revenants that Horazon had survived the centuries and lived, albeit as a madman, under their very feet? For that matter, why had she even hoped that Bartuc's brother would join with them in this dire venture? He had already shown that, if it had been up to him alone, Norrec would have perished along with the armor. Some legends concerning Horazon had painted him as a hero in comparison to his brother, but this same hero had also summoned demons, bending them to his will. Yes, his war against Bartuc had definitely been about self-preservation as much as anything else. There would be no aid from the ancient Vizjerei.

"We go . . ." Tryst added. "You come . . . or not . . . your choice, necromancer."

What else could Kara do? Even without Horazon, she had to go after Norrec. The demon must have taken him to the one besieging Lut Gholein, but for what reason? Did they hope to destroy what remained of the veteran fighter's own mind, enabling the ghostly memories of the Warlord of Blood to completely take over? A terrifying thought for all people everywhere, not simply poor Norrec. Many scholars had assumed, quite rightly, that, had he defeated his brother, Bartuc would have wreaked his evil upon the rest of the world until it had all fallen under his heel. Now, it seemed, like Kara, he had a second chance to succeed.

As a follower of Rathma, she could not permit that—even if it meant having to kill the armor's host. The thought left her cold, but if the balance after all required Norrec to be slain, then so be it. Even her own life did not matter if only it meant that she put an end to the danger.

"I will come with you," the necromancer finally replied.

Fauztin nodded, then pointed in the direction of Lut Gholein.

"Time is . . . wasting . . . he says."

The revenants flanked Kara as the trio set off, a fact which did not escape her. The wind had already wiped clean much of Norrec's trail, but Tryst and the Vizjerei had no apparent trouble following. The bond to what had murdered them enabled the pair to follow anywhere, any place.

"What about the demon?" Kara asked. He had designs

on the armor, too, and would certainly fight anyone who sought to take it away from him.

Tryst pointed at her dagger, which now hung from the dark mage's belt. "That . . . is our best bet."

"How?"

"Just use it . . . and pray." He looked as if he intended to say more, but Fauztin gave him a glance that silenced the smaller of the ghouls immediately.

What secret did they still hold from her? Had she underestimated them? Did they still plan to use her as a puppet? Now was certainly not the time to hold back anything that might mean the difference between victory and death.

"What do you—"

"We'll deal . . . with the armor . . ." Sadun commented, cutting her off, "and Norrec."

His tone indicated that there would be no further conversation on this or any other subject. Kara considered trying anyway, but decided not to aggravate relations with the duo. The revenants acted in no manner she could readily predict, going against everything she had been taught about their kind. Half the time, they acted as if they still had hearts that pumped, blood that flowed. The rest of the time, they moved on with the silent determination for which such undead had been fabled. Truly, a unique situation. . . but then, everything about this matter had been unique.

Deadly, too.

She pictured Norrec in her mind, wondering what he must be going through at the moment. The image of the demon overshadowed the fighter, causing the necromancer to bite her lip in concern. There also appeared in her mind the shadow of a third figure, the one who now led the assault on the coastal kingdom. What part did he play? What did he gain in all this? He could not simply desire to have Norrec become a second Bartuc—that would be the same as signing his own death warrant. Bartuc had never either willingly served nor allied himself with any other mortal.

She would have the chance to discover the answers to her many questions soon enough. As to whether she would live long enough to appreciate those answers—Kara had severe doubts.

ΠΙΠΕΤΕΕΠ

More than an hour had past and still Lut Gholein had not given up the armor. General Malevolyn barely contained his righteous anger, wondering if they had already found it and thought that somehow they could use its magic against him. If so, they would be sorely mistaken. The armor would never work for their cause and, if tampered with, would likely strike out at those investigating it. No, Bartuc's legacy belonged to him and him alone.

In keeping with his threat, his demon horde continued to assault the walls. The grounds near Lut Gholein had been littered with the mangled remains of not only those who had earlier failed to reach the gates, but also several who had fallen from above. The demon archers had proven in many ways superior shots to even the men whose bodies they now inhabited. In addition, the six catapults that he had brought along now wreaked more havoc in the city itself. Protected by demonic sorceries, the siege machines, in turn, suffered no damage from Lut Gholein's return fire.

He watched as those at the nearest catapult prepared yet another fiery gift for the inhabitants. General Malevolyn had saved the weapons for just this, showing his adversaries that he would permit them no respite. Either they gave him what he desired or even their high walls would not save them—not that he would let such limited barriers save them in the end, anyway.

And the end was very near. Lut Gholein, the general

decided, had just run out of time. He would let the catapults fire their present volley, then give the command for
his full forces to strike. The people within thought that
their gates would hold against the invaders, but even
now they underestimated the might of demons. It would
be a simple matter to remove the one obstacle to the
horde's entrance into the city . . . and from there would
begin a day of death so bloody that Lut Gholein's fall
would be spoken of in terrified whispered by all other
men for years to come.

Once more, the crimson armor of the Warlord of Blood
would cast the shadow of fear across the entire world.

Augustus Malevolyn suddenly stiffened as an unsettling sensation filled him. He quickly turned to look
behind him, certain that he *had* to see who—or what—
approached from the rear.

And over a dune came a familiar sight, Xazax moving
along the sand. That the demon had dared come so near
to Lut Gholein during the day puzzled the general—until
he saw who walked beside the monstrous insect.

"*The armor . . .* " he whispered almost reverently.

Forgetting his demon soldiers, forgetting Lut Gholein,
Malevolyn charged toward the oncoming pair. In all his
life he had never experienced so glorious a moment.
Bartuc's armor came toward him. His greatest desire had
at last come to fruition!

Why the simpleton who had stolen it from the tomb
still lived to wear it, only Xazax could say. It amazed
Malevolyn that the mantis had let the man live this long.
Perhaps Xazax simply had not wanted to bother with carrying the suit back himself and had forced the fool to
bring it along. Well, for that deed, the least the general
could do would be to grant the armor's present wearer a
relatively quick and painless death.

"And what prize is this you bring, my friend?"

The mantis sounded quite pleased with himself. "A

gift surely proving this one's intentions match those of the warlord. This one gives you one Norrec Vizharan— mercenary, tomb robber, and host for the glorious armor of Bartuc!"

"Mercenary and tomb robber . . ." General Malevolyn chuckled. "Perhaps I should hire you on for your expertise. Certainly I should congratulate you for bringing to me at last the final step in my ascension to glory!"

"You—want this suit?" The fool sounded incredulous, as if he, who had worn it so long, could not comprehend its majesty, appreciate its power . . .

"Of course! I want nothing more!" The general tapped his helmet. He saw that Norrec Vizharan instantly recognized the link between them. "I am General Augustus Malevolyn, late of Westmarch, a land, from your looks, I think you know. As you see, I wear the helm, lost when Bartuc's head and body were separated by the fools who by fluke managed to slay him. So fearful—and rightly so!—of his tremendous power, they placed body and head on opposite sides of the world, then secreted both in places from which they thought no one would be able to take them!"

"They were wrong . . ." muttered the mercenary.

"Of course! The spirit of the Warlord of Blood would not be denied! He called to his own, awaited those whose links to him would stir the powers to life, to new horizons!"

"What do you mean?"

Malevolyn sighed. He supposed he should have slain the fool out of hand, but the commander's mood had grown so light that he decided to at least explain what Norrec had obviously never understood. Reaching up, General Malevolyn gently removed the helmet. He felt at some slight loss as it left his head, but assured himself that soon it would be back in place again.

"I did not know its secret then, but I know now . . . for

the artifact itself revealed it to me. Even you, I daresay, do not know the full truth, friend Xazax."

The mantis performed a mock bow. "This one would be delighted to be enlightened, warlord . . ."

"And you shall!" He grinned at Norrec. "I would wager to say that many died in the tomb before you came along, eh?"

Vizharan's expression darkened. "Too many . . . some of them were friends."

"You'll be joining them soon, have no fear . . ." The ebony-clad officer let Norrec get a better view of the helmet. "I daresay it was the same with this. The same fate for every minor tomb robber until one—one with a very special, *inherent* trait that gave him just enough of an advantage." Malevolyn's hands suddenly began to shake slightly. Quickly but still with an air of casualness, he replaced the helm. An instant feeling of relief washed over him, although he made certain not to let either the man or the demon know. "Can you guess what you and he had in common?"

"A cursed life?"

"More a magnificent heritage. In both of you, the blood of greatness flowed, albeit in quite a watered state."

This explanation only made Norrec frown. "He and I— were related?"

"Yes, although in his case that bloodline had become even more diluted. It gave him the right to take the helmet, but he proved too weak to be of use and so it let him be slain. With his death, it grew dormant again, waiting for one more worthy . . ." The general proudly indicated himself. "And it finally found me, as you see."

"You share the same blood, too?"

"Very good. Yes, I do. Far less tainted than that which flowed through that fool and, I have no doubt, far less tainted than you. Yes, Norrec Vizharan, you might say that you and I and he who discovered the head and helm are all *cousins*—several times removed, of course."

"But who—" the soldier's eyes widened, truth at last dawning. "That's not *possible!*"

Xazax said nothing, but clearly he still did not understand. Demons did not always comprehend human mating and the result of it. True, some of their kind knew the process and, indeed, bred rapidly at times through its use, but they bred as animals, without any concern for bloodlines.

"Oh, yes, cousin." Malevolyn smiled broadly. "we are all the progeny of the grand and noble *Bartuc* himself!"

The mantis clacked his mandibles together, rightly impressed. He looked even more pleased with himself, likely because he had chosen rightly in joining forces with Augustus Malevolyn.

As for Norrec, he took no evident pleasure in the revelation, like so many lesser mortals not at all understanding what Bartuc had nearly accomplished. How many men had earned the respect and fear of not only their fellows, but Heaven and Hell, too? It disappointed the general slightly, for, as he had said, the two were indeed cousins of a sort. Of course, since Norrec only had a few moments left to his life, the disappointment was not all that great. A fool removed was still a fool removed, always a plus in the world.

"Blood calls to blood . . ." Norrec muttered, staring down at the sand. "Blood to blood, she said . . ."

"Indeed! And that was why with you, the armor could act as it could not for so many centuries. Great power lay dormant within it, but power without life. In you flowed the life that had given that sorcery a spark. It was as if two halves, separated for so long, came together to create the whole!"

"Bartuc's blood . . ."

Augustus Malevolyn pursed his lips. "Yes, we've

gone over that . . . you mentioned 'she'? My Galeona, perhaps?"

"A necromancer, warlord," Xazax interjected. "Quite dead now." He lifted one sickle limb up, indicating the cause. "But as for the witch—she is also no more."

"A pity, but I suppose it had to be, anyway." Something occurred to the slim commander. "Excuse me a moment, will you?"

He turned back to where his hellish warriors harassed Lut Gholein, picturing the demon who wore the face of Zako.

In the distance, the ghoulish minion suddenly turned from his task at the lead catapult and rushed toward Malevolyn. The moment he reached the general, the demon went down on one knee. "Yes, warlord—" A sharp intake of breath escaped the false Zako as he suddenly noticed Norrec and the armor. "Your—your command?"

"The city has no more value. It is yours to play with."

A savage, toothy grin spread an impossible distance across the dead man's features. "You're very gracious, warlord . . ."

General Malevolyn nodded, then waved him off. "Go! Let no life be spared. Lut Gholein will serve as notice of what hope any other kingdom, any other power, has against me."

The thing with Zako's face rushed off, fairly bouncing up and down with glee as he hurried to tell the others. The horde would ravage the city, leave nothing standing. In many ways, it would assuage the warlord for what had happened at Vin-Jun.

Vin-Jun. Malevolyn's chest swelled with anticipation. Now that he had the armor, even Kehjistan, legendary home of the Vizjerei, would fall to him.

His hand traced the fox and swords crest on his own breastplate. Long ago, after he had slain his birth father and burned down the house that had never acknowledged him, Augustus Malevolyn had decided to bear the symbol of that house on his armor in order to remind himself that what he wanted he would always be able to take. Now, though, the time had come to set aside that symbol for a better one. The bloodred suit of Bartuc.

He turned back to Xazax and the mercenary. "Well, shall we begin?"

Xazax prodded Norrec forward. The man stumbled, then dared to glare at the demon. Malevolyn's opinion of his distant cousin rose a notch. At least the buffoon had some nerve.

But the words spat bitterly from Norrec's mouth did not at all please the new warlord. "I can't give it to you."

"What do you mean by that?"

"It won't come off. I've tried again and again and it won't come off, not even the boots! I've no control over the armor whatsoever! I thought I did, but it was all a trick! What I do, where I go—the armor always decides!"

His tragic situation amused General Malevolyn. "Sounds almost like a comic opera! Is there any truth to this, Xazax?"

"This one would have to say the fool speaks the truth, warlord. He could not even move to save the necromancer . . ."

"How fascinating. Still, a problem not at all difficult to solve." He raised a hand toward Norrec. "Not with the power now at my command."

The spell summoned from memories other than his own should have enabled Malevolyn to desiccate the soldier within the very armor, leaving but a dried husk easily removed. Bartuc had used the spell and used it well during his reign and never once had it failed him.

But now it did. Norrec Vizharan stood wide-eyed but untouched. He looked as if he had truly expected to die, which made the failure of so strong a spell all the more puzzling

Xazax it was who suggested the reason. "Your spell encompasses the entire body, warlord. Perhaps the suit reacts instantly as if attacked itself."

"A good point. Then we shall just have to do something a little more personal." He stretched out his hand—and the demon blade appeared in it. "Beheading him should sever the armor's link. It needs a live host, not a corpse."

As he approached, the general noted the mercenary struggling within the suit, trying desperately to make it move. Malevolyn took the lack of reaction by Bartuc's armor as a sign that he had chosen the right method this time. One swift slash would do it. In some ways, Vizharan should have considered himself honored. Had not the first great warlord perished much the same way? Perhaps Malevolyn would keep the man's head for a trophy, a reminder of this wondrous day.

"I shall remember you always, Norrec, my cousin. Remember you for all you have given me."

General Augustus Malevolyn readied the ebony sword, taking expert aim at his target's throat. Yes . . . one swift slash. Much more elegant than simply hacking away until the head fell off.

Smiling, he performed the killing stroke—

—only to have his blade resound off an *identical* one now held in Norrec's left hand.

"What in the name of *Hell?*"

The mercenary looked as startled as him. Behind Norrec Vizharan, the monstrous demon clacked and chittered in open consternation.

Norrec—or rather the *armor*—shifted into a combat stance, the other black blade ready for any attack by the general.

A peculiar expression spread across the soldier's countenance, an expression both bewildered and bemused. After a moment's hesitation, he even dared speak to

Malevolyn. "I guess it might not think you're the right choice for it, general. I guess we'll be forced to fight over it. I'm sorry, believe me, I am."

Malevolyn fought back his growing rage. He could ill afford to lose his temper now. In a calm tone, he returned, "Then fight we shall, Vizharan—and when I claim the armor, the victory will be that much the sweeter for this battle!"

He swung at Norrec.

Xazax feared that he had made a terrible error. Now before him stood two mortals clad in pieces of Bartuc's armor, two mortals who both seemed capable of wielding to some extent the warlord's ancient sorcery. Yet, the mantis had thrown in his lot with Malevolyn, who had, until now, seemed the destined successor. The suit of armor, however, clearly saw matters differently, choosing to defend its quite unwilling host.

The demon had worked hard to convince his infernal lord, Belial, to sacrifice so many hellish minions to this effort. Belial had only agreed because he, too, had thought that a new Bartuc could give him the edge he needed not only against his rival, but the possible return of any of the three Prime Evils. If Xazax had assumed wrongly, if Norrec Vizharan somehow managed to win, it would look as if Belial's lieutenant had completely mismanaged the entire affair. Belial did not suffer incompetence in his servants.

Now, watching the two prepare for the struggle, he also felt certain that the suit had played him in particular for a fool. It had come with him as if docile, as if it only wished to reunite itself with the helmet, then join the demon's cause. However, now the mantis believed that it sought the helmet only—and after that intended to turn upon *him*.

It must have known that Xazax had been the one who

had brought the aquatic behemoth to the mortal plane and, who, after questioning the dying mariner, had sent that monster to attack the ship. At the time, Xazax had thought he could quicken matters, take the armor before it ever reached dry land. Galeona had guided him to a fair approximation of where Norrec Vizharan could be found. It should have been a simple matter for the hellish beast to rip the puny wooden vessel apart, then strip the armor from the dead man's body . . .

Only . . . only the armor had not only fended off the titanic creature, it had slain the demon with hardly any effort. The result had been so startling that it had sent Xazax fleeing in panic. He had never expected the enchanted armor to unleash such overwhelming power . . .

The mantis fixed his gaze on the back of the mercenary, his decision made. With Malevolyn as the warlord, Xazax had something spectacular to show his master, an ally with whom they could crush Azmodan and, if necessary, the *three*. However, with Norrec Vizharan the unwilling host, Belial would surely not be nearly so pleased.

And when his master was displeased . . . those who failed him suffered much for it.

The demon raised one sickle, biding his time. In the heat of combat, it would take only one strike. The general might complain about his loss of glory, but he would soon come around. Then, they could return to the ravaging of Lut Gholein.

And from there . . . the rest of the mortal realm.

Norrec did not even feel a fraction of the confidence he tried to portray to General Malevolyn. While his words concerning the suit's reluctance to part from him had been true, that did not mean that he trusted in the ability of the enchanted armor to defeat the helmed officer. In truth, Malevolyn looked as if the link between him and the helmet far surpassed the questionable alliance Norrec suffered. Not only did Malevolyn share in the knowledge and skills of the Warlord of Blood, but the general also had his own not inconsiderable abilities. In combination with what the helmet offered, even the armor would likely not be able to stand long against the dedicated commander.

The general came at him, attacking with such fury that the suit had to step back in order to save Norrec. Again and again the fiery blades clashed, each time sending plumes of flame flying. Had they fought in any other domain save the sandy desert, the odds of a fire starting would have been quite likely. Norrec himself worried that some stray spark would land on his hair or blind him in one eye. Bad enough already that he had to participate in the desperate struggle without having any choice as to defense or attack, for, from what he quickly saw, the armor had some gaps in its knowledge of swordplay. True, it countered Malevolyn's strikes, but Norrec watched at least one evident opening go wasted. Had not the bloody warlord learned how to properly handle a blade?

"A bit like fighting one's self, isn't it?" sneered his adversary. Augustus Malevolyn seemed to be enjoying himself, so certain of victory did he no doubt feel.

Norrec said nothing in return, wishing that, even if he had to die, it would be through his own efforts, not the failures of the enchanted armor.

Malevolyn's blade passed within inches of his head. Norrec swore, muttering quietly to the armor, "If you can't do better than that, I should be the one leading!"

"Do you really think so?" retorted the general, expression no longer amused. "You think a simpleton like you worthier to bear the title, carry on the legacy, than I would be?"

The suit suddenly had to defend against a series of lightning-swift attacks by Malevolyn. Norrec silently cursed the general's exceptional hearing; the man believed that the mercenary had mocked him.

He had served under many a skilled officer, battled many a talented foe, but Norrec could not recall any with the adaptability of Augustus Malevolyn. Only the fact that the general fought as much with Bartuc's skills as his own enabled the suit to anticipate most of his moves. Even then, if not for the other protections of the armor, Norrec would have already been dead twice.

"You are fortunate that the enchantments protect you so well." The slim commander said as he momentarily backed away. "Else this matter would have been settled already."

"But if I'd died so quickly, it would've meant that the armor wasn't as special as you hoped."

Malevolyn chuckled. "True! You have some wits about you after all. Shall we see what they look like spilled out on the sand?"

Again he thrust up, over, and around Norrec's guard. Twice Bartuc's plate nearly failed the soldier. Norrec gritted his teeth; the ancient warlord had been a good swordsman, but his methods were those of the Vizjerei. After so many years in the company of Fauztin—who could handle a sword well despite being a mage—the veteran fighter probably knew more about the advantages and disadvantages of their fighting style than even the general here. Malevolyn appeared to have accepted that melding his skills with those of Bartuc only meant the better, yet, if Norrec himself had been combatting the man, he could have possibly threatened Malevolyn's life at least twice.

He suddenly screamed, his right ear feeling as if it had burst into flames. General Malevolyn had finally landed a blow, albeit a glancing one. Unfortunately, with the magical swords even that meant an agonizing injury. Norrec's entire ear throbbed, but fortunately, despite the wound, he could still hear with it. Yet, one more strike like that . . .

If only he could enter the fight himself. If only the suit could understand that he had a better chance. He knew the weaknesses, knew also the western styles the general used. There were some tricks that Norrec doubted that even the helmed commander had learned. As a mercenary, one picked up such tricks to make up for deficiencies in formal training—and more than once they had saved the veteran.

Let me fight . . . or at least let me fight alongside you!

The suit ignored him. It deflected Malevolyn's latest attack, then tried countering with a move recognizable to the veteran from some of Fauztin's own occasional sessions of sword practice. However, Norrec also knew that the Vizjerei people had also developed a countermove to *that* attack—and a moment later Malevolyn proved him right by using it to keep the armor from succeeding.

So far, the battle had been all the general's. It could not go on much longer. Bartuc's plate might desire Norrec as its simple, malleable host, but if matters continued as they presently did, it would soon have to bow to the skill and might of General Malevolyn and his own enchanted helmet.

Caught up in his darkening thoughts, Norrec barely noticed his foe suddenly thrust toward his face. The veteran fighter immediately raised his own sword, barely pushing Malevolyn's blade aside. Had he failed to do so, the general's weapon would have cut right through Norrec's skull, coming out the back.

And then it came to Norrec that *he* and not the armor had just defended against the nearly fatal assault.

He had no time to mull over the sudden shift, for Malevolyn did not slow his advance. The would-be warlord cut again and again at Norrec, forcing him backward in the direction of the watching Xazax.

Yet, despite the precariousness of his situation, Norrec's hopes rose. If he died, he would die his own man.

Augustus Malevolyn tried a move the soldier recognized from one of his first forays as a mercenary. The maneuver took skill and cunning and oft times succeeded, but from a willing commander Norrec had learned how it could be turned to the opponent's advantage . . .

"What?" Malevolyn's gaping expression enthused Norrec Vizharan as he turned what should have been a near-mortal blow by the general into a sudden counterattack that forced the veteran's foe to retreat or lose his own head.

Wasting no time, Norrec sought to push the general back until the soft sand made the man stumble or even fall, but at the last moment, Malevolyn succeeded in turning the duel back into a stalemate.

"Well," the helmed figure gasped. "Seems that the suit can learn like a man. Interesting. I wouldn't have thought it would've known that last move."

Norrec refrained from telling him the truth. Any advantage he had, however small, he would use. Yet, he could not help keep a slight, grim smile from briefly crossing his weary visage.

"You smile? You think it learning a trick or two enough? Then let's see how it and you fare if we change the rules a little . . ."

Malevolyn's free hand suddenly came up—and a brilliant sunburst exploded in Norrec's eyes.

He swung wildly, managing twice to parry the general—then a tremendous force ripped the sword from his grip. Norrec stepped back, lost his footing—and tumbled back onto the sand.

Through vision still suffering the aftereffects of Malevolyn's treacherous spell, the fallen fighter saw the murky form of his triumphant opponent loom over him. In each hand General Malevolyn held a black sword.

"The battle is done. I will say well fought, cousin. It only occurred to me at the last that you seemed a bit more eager than earlier—as if you had joined the duel yourself. So you finally thought that working with the armor would save you? A good notion, but clearly decided upon much too late."

"Waste no time!" snapped Xazax from somewhere behind Norrec. "Strike! Strike!"

Ignoring the demon, Malevolyn hefted the two swords, admiring them. "Perfect balance in each. I can wield both with no fear of crossing myself up. Interesting, too, that yours still exists. I would have thought it would have faded away once out of your hands, but I suppose that since I immediately grabbed it, that made all the difference. Bartuc's enchantments are full of surprises, are they not?"

Still trying to focus better, Norrec suddenly felt his left hand tingle. He knew the sensation, had experienced it before. The suit intended some ploy, but exactly what ploy the fighter did not know—

Yes, he *did* know. The knowledge filled Norrec's head, instantly enabling him not only to understand the enchanted armor's part in this, but the man's as well. For this to succeed, both would have to work together. Neither alone stood a chance of success.

Norrec fought back a grin. Instead, he satisfied himself with answering his adversary. "Yes . . . they are."

The left gauntlet flared.

Norrec's lost sword transformed into an inky shadow swarming over Malevolyn's arm and head.

Swearing, the general released his grip on his own weapon and gestured toward the hungering shadow. From his mouth came ancient words, Vizjerei words. A green luminescence radiated from his fingertips, eating away in turn at the shadow.

Yet, as Malevolyn focused his attention on this new menace, Norrec leapt up at him—just as the armor had desired. As the shadow faded away under the brunt of the general's own spell, Norrec seized Malevolyn by the hands and the two wrestled. This close, neither dared use Bartuc's sorcery unless certain.

"The battle's even again, general!" murmured Norrec, for the first time feeling as if he, not anyone else, had command of the situation. The armor and he had a common goal at last—triumph over this foul foe. Exhilaration filled him as he grappled, exhilaration at the thought of Malevolyn lying dead at his feet.

And the fact that much of that newfound determination and confidence might possibly have come from a source other than himself did not enter his mind. Nor did it occur to Norrec that, if he did slay the one who wore the crimson helm—then he had as good as cursed himself to the fate that Bartuc's armor had long chosen for him.

Xazax watched the sudden turn of events with great dismay. The shifting tide in the battle had caught even him unaware and now the mortal with whom he had chosen to ally himself risked defeat. Xazax could not take that risk; he had to ensure that this duel ended with Malevolyn as the victor.

The giant mantis poised to strike—

Twenty

Kara stepped over the winding dune—and into yet another nightmare.

In the distance, black armored warriors battered at Lut Gholein's gates, shouting with a murderous glee almost inhuman. The defenders above continuously fired down at them, but curiously their many arrows had no visible effect whatsoever as far as she could see, almost as if the invaders had somehow made themselves invulnerable to mortal weapons. Judging by what else she could see, the necromancer felt fairly certain that the straining gates would soon crash inward, gaining this savage force entrance.

However, the terrible struggle there paled in her mind in comparison to the duel taking place not far from her right. She had found Norrec again, yet with him she had also found not only the demon, but a furious figure clad in armor akin to the men attacking Lut Gholein—akin, that is, save for his crimson helmet.

The necromancer immediately recognized Bartuc's helm. Now matters made more sense. The armor of the warlord sought to reunite, but it had *two* hosts with which to contend and only one who could end up with the prize. Unfortunately for Norrec, he stood to lose everything no matter what the outcome of the combat. Slay his foe and he became the armor's puppet; fail in the struggle and he died at the feet of the new Warlord of Blood.

Kara eyed the trio for several moments, trying to consider what best to do. Unable to come up with a satisfying answer, she turned back to her decaying companions. "They're locked together and the demon's only a few yards behind him! What do you—"

She talked to the air. Both Tryst and Fauztin had completely vanished, the sand revealing no trace of their path. It was as if they had simply flown into the air and vanished.

Regrettably, that left the necromancer's decision completely up to her and time looked to be rapidly running out. Norrec had brought the battle to a more even level again, but as Kara watched, the hellish mantis began to move toward the combatants. Kara could think of only one reason why he would do so at such a juncture.

Knowing that she had no other option remaining, the dark mage leapt forward, racing for the back of the imposing demon. If she could get near enough, she had a chance.

The mantis raised one wicked limb high, awaiting the ideal moment to strike . . .

Kara realized that she would not make it—unless, of course, she took a desperate gamble. In her hand the necromancer already held her ceremonial dagger, which Sadun Tryst had suggested she might need. Until now, though, her fear of possibly losing it again had kept Kara from considering such an act. The weapon was a part of her calling, a part of her very *being*.

And the only way she could possibly save Norrec.

Without hesitation, she took aim at the foul creature—

Now! Xazax thought. *Now!*

But just as the mantis chose to attack, fire burst within him, coursing through his entire body with astonishing swiftness. The monstrous insect stumbled, nearly falling on top of the two fighting figures. Xazax swiveled his head so as to see the cause of his agony and found in his back a gleaming dagger made of something other than metal. He recognized quickly the intricate runes in the protruding handle and knew then why such a minuscule weapon could cause him so much pain.

A necromancer's ceremonial dagger . . . but the only such being Xazax had come across he had quickly murdered, so surely it could not be—

But there she came, hurtling toward him despite the fact that she should have been dead. The mantis knew where he had struck her, knew that no human could have rightly survived the blow, not even those who dealt in life and death such as she.

"You cannot be!" he demanded of her, a sense of dread building quickly within. For all their chaotic origins, demons had a very set sense of how things worked. Humans were fragile; rip, stab, cut, or tear them apart in certain ways and they would die. Once dead, they stayed so unless summoned back in the form of some ghoulish servant. This female defied the rules . . . "Dead you were and dead you should stay!"

"The balance dictates the terms of life and death, demon, hardly you." She made her right hand into a fist and pointed at him.

An incredible weakness spread through the demon. Xazax teetered, then caught himself. The necromancer's spell should not have affected him so thoroughly, but with her dagger in him, he became far more susceptible to anything she cast.

That situation could not be allowed to continue long.

Summoning what reserves he had, the mantis used his upper appendages to stir up the sand, then send it flying into the face of the enchantress. As she fought to regain her sight, Xazax's middle limbs bent back in a most impossible manner and sought out the treacherous dagger.

It burned, burned terribly, but he forced himself to seize the hilt and try to pull it free. The demon roared as he tugged at the enchanted blade, so great did the pain grow.

He would rend her into bloody gobbets for this abominable act. He would pinion her, then peel away every layer of skin, every bit of muscle—all while her heart still beat.

But just as the monstrous insect felt the blade begin to loosen, the necromancer uttered her final spell.

And before Xazax's eyes materialized a luminescent being so glorious his very presence burned the eyes of the demonic mantis. He looked manlike, but with all imperfections washed away. His hair flowed golden and the beauty of his countenance affected even the demon. However, even overwhelmed by the robed figure's presence, Xazax did not fail to notice the majestic, gleaming sword that the vision wielded with expert grace . . .

"Angel!!"

Xazax knew that what he saw had to be an hallucination. Necromancers had reputations for being able to cast such terrifying illusions directly into the minds of their enemies—and yet even that knowledge could not keep the primal fear from drowning the demon's senses. In the end, Xazax only knew that one of Heaven's imperious warriors now came for *him*.

With an inhuman cry, the cowardly mantis turned from Kara and fled. As he did, the dagger slipped from his wound, causing the escaping demon to leave a steady stream of thick, black ichor trailing behind him in the sand.

Kara Nightshadow watched as her adversary disappeared into the wastes of Aranoch. She would have preferred a more final conclusion to her encounter with the mantis, but in her present state of exhaustion, that conclusion could have just as well gone against her. The spell would keep him from any foul play for some time, at least long enough, so Kara hoped, to deal with the unholy threat of the armor.

She picked up her dagger and turned to where Norrec and his own foe still battled. The necromancer frowned. If the helmed stranger won, her course would be quick and clear. The dagger would see to a swift end to the second coming of the Warlord of Blood.

And if Norrec won?

Kara had no choice there, even. Without a host, the armor could cause no more harm. Whoever won between them—she would have to make certain that the victor did not live long enough to draw another breath.

Neither Norrec nor his adversary noticed the battle taking place beside them, so desperate had their own struggle become. The gauntleted hands of the two flared again and again as dark sorceries burst into life and immediately died. Although Malevolyn did not wear the armored suit of Bartuc, the helm alone gave him strength and power matching that now wielded by a willing Norrec. Because of that, the fight continued to be a stalemate, although both men knew that eventually the end would come for one.

"I am destined to take his place!" snarled Augustus Malevolyn. "I am more than just his blood! I am his kindred spirit, his will reborn! I am Bartuc come back to the mortal plane to reclaim his rightful place!"

"You're no more his successor than I am," returned Norrec, not at all aware that his own expression matched that of the arrogant commander. "His blood is mine as well! The armor chose me! Maybe you should think about that!"

"I will not be denied!" The general slipped one boot under the soldier's leg, forcing Norrec off balance.

They tumbled to the ground, Malevolyn on top. The

sand softened some of the blow when Norrec's head hit, but still the veteran fighter lay momentarily dazed. Taking advantage of the situation, General Malevolyn forced his hand toward his rival's visage.

"I will remove your face, your entire head," he hissed at Norrec. "Let us see then who the armor thinks more worthy . . ."

The general's red and black gauntlet blazed with wild magic, Malevolyn's fingers only an inch or two from making good his dire promise. One hand pinned by his foe's own and the other trapped between their armored bodies, Norrec had little hope of preventing the sadistic general from accomplishing what he desired . . .

At that moment, though, Norrec sensed movement behind him, as if a third person had joined the fray. Malevolyn looked up at the newcomer—and the triumphant sneer on his countenance switched to an expression of utter bafflement.

"You—" he managed to blurt.

Something within Norrec urged him to take advantage. He slipped the one hand free from the general's, then immediately struck Malevolyn hard in the chin. A brief burst of raw magical energy accompanied Norrec's strike, sending the helmed figure flying back as if pulled by a string attached to his head. Malevolyn dropped to the sand some distance away with a harsh thud, the general too stunned at first to rise.

Focused only on victory now, the veteran fighter rose and charged toward his fallen foe. In his growing certainty that he had been meant all along to triumph, Norrec nearly threw himself on top of the general—an action which would have cost him his life.

In Malevolyn's hand materialized one of the black blades. Norrec barely had time to twist out of its deadly reach, dropping to the sand just beside the other fighter. General Malevolyn rolled away, ending up in a crouched position. He kept the sword between them, his mocking expression quite evident even within the bloodred helmet.

"I have you now!"

Leaping forward, he *thrust*.

The tip of the ebony blade sank deep . . . deep into the chest of *General Augustus Malevolyn*.

The sinister noble's resummoning of his enchanted sword had immediately reminded Norrec that he, too, could call his own weapon back into play. In his haste to at last be done with the mercenary, Malevolyn had evidently not considered that last part. As his sword came at Norrec, Norrec rolled forward, at the same time thinking his own demonic blade into existence.

Augustus Malevolyn's thrust had come within a hair of slicing the veteran's skull in half.

Norrec's had materialized already a third of the way through his adversary's torso.

Malevolyn gaped at his wound, the blade having skewered him so quickly that his body had not quite yet registered that death was upon it. The general dropped his own weapon, which instantly faded away.

In past battles, Norrec Vizharan had taken no pleasure in the deaths of his foes. He had been paid for a task and he had performed that task, but war had never been a pleasure for him. Now, however, he felt a chill run up and down his spine, a chill that stirred him, made him desire more of such bloodshed . . .

He stood up, and walked over to the gaping general, who only now slipped to his knees.

"You don't need this any more, *cousin*."

With great force, Norrec tore the crimson helmet from Augustus Malevolyn's head. Malevolyn screamed when he did, although not from any physical pain. Norrec understood what so troubled the man more than even the lethal thrust, understood because at that moment he would have felt the same if someone had tried to rip the armor from his body. The power inherent in Bartuc's suit seduced both of them, but in Malevolyn's case, he had lost the duel and, therefore, lost all right to that power.

Laying the helmet to the side, Norrec took hold of the hilt of his sword. With easy effort, he pulled it free, then inspected the blade itself. No blood stained it. Truly a marvel. It had served him well here, served him as grandly as it had done at *Viz-jun* . . .

A gauntleted hand grabbed at him. General Malevolyn, a manic look on his face, tried desperately to grapple with Norrec.

Norrec shoved him back and grinned. "The war's over, general." He readied the sword. "Time to retire."

One easy sweep left General Augustus Malevolyn's head rolling in the sand. The headless torso joined it a moment later.

As he reached down to retrieve the fabled helmet, a feminine voice called out to the exhausted but also exhilarated veteran. "Norrec? Are you all right?"

He turned to face Kara, pleased in more than one manner by her unexpected resurrection. In the short time since they had met, she had proven her loyalty to him by sacrificing her lesser existence for his. Had she remained dead, Norrec would have honored her memory, but now that she had somehow cheated Xazax's murderous strike he instead considered her further uses. The necromancer had shown some skill and likely had more sense than the untrustworthy Galeona. Her not unpleasing face and form also made him consider her as possibly worthy of being his consort—and what sane woman would spurn the offer of becoming consort to the *Warlord of Blood*?

"I'm well, Kara Nightshadow . . . very well!" He opened his one hand and let the magical sword fall free. As the weapon vanished, Norrec took the helmet in both hands and raised it over his head. "In fact, I am far *better* than well!"

"Wait!" The raven-tressed woman rushed up to him, concern in her almond-shaped eyes. Pretty eyes, the new warlord decided, eyes reminiscent of another woman he had briefly known during his apprenticeship in Kehjistan. "The helmet . . ."

"Yes . . . it's mine at last . . . I'm now complete."

She pressed against him, placing one hand on the breastplate. Her eyes seemed to implore. "Is this truly what you want, Norrec? After all we spoke of earlier, do you now really desire to wear the helmet, to give yourself up to Bartuc's ghost?"

"Give myself up? Woman, do you know *who* I am? I'm his own blood! Blood calls to blood, remember? In a way, I already *am* Bartuc; I just didn't know it! Who better to carry on? Who better to bear the title, the legacy?"

"Bartuc's shade himself?" she countered. "There will not be any more Norrec Vizharan, not in mind and soul . . . and if the armor has its way, I daresay that even in form you will begin to resemble your predecessor. It will be Bartuc who wears the suit. Bartuc who reclaims his role. *Bartuc* who slaughters more innocents, just as he—not you—slaughtered your *friends* . . ."

Friends. . . . The horrific images of the mangled, blood-soaked bodies of Sadun Tryst and Fauztin blossomed once more in Norrec's beleaguered mind. They had been brutally murdered and he had suffered terrible guilt for those murders for each waking moment since then. He recalled quite succinctly how the armor had slain each—and now Kara spoke of other deaths to come.

He lowered the helmet slightly, battling with himself. "No, I can't let that happen . . . I can't . . ."

His arms suddenly rose again, holding the helmet just above his head.

"*No!*" Norrec roared, his denial aimed now at the enchanted suit. "She's right, damn you! I won't be a part of your bloody campaign—"

But what foolishness . . . a voice so much like his own whispered in his mind. *The power is yours . . . you can do with it what you wish . . . a world of order, where no kingdom wars, where no one is poor . . . that is the true legacy . . . that is all Bartuc sought . . .*

It sounded so very good. Simply place the helmet on his head and Norrec would be able to change the world to what it should be. The demons would even serve him in this monumental task, their wills subservient to the power of the warlord. He would create a perfect realm, one that even Heaven would *envy*.

And all he had to do was put on the helmet, accept his destiny . . .

He suddenly felt Kara shift—

One hand slipped from the helmet, seizing the necromancer's own in an iron grip that made Kara gasp. From her own hand slipped a gleaming blade of what looked like bone or ivory.

She had been about to use it on *him*.

"Stupid female . . . " Norrec snapped, not noticing that his voice did not entirely sound as it should. He shoved her to the sand. *"Stay put! I'll deal with you in a moment!"*

Despite his warning, the dark mage tried to rise, but arms of sand arose from each side, pinning her to the ground. More sand flowed over her mouth, preventing her from casting any verbal spells.

Eyes bright in anticipation, Norrec took hold of the helmet again—and placed it on his head.

A world such as he had never known now lay open to him. He saw the might he wielded, the legions he could command. The destiny thwarted by his fellow Vizjerei could once more be attained.

The Warlord of Blood lived again.

But a warlord needed soldiers. Leaving Kara to struggle, Norrec climbed to the top of the dune and stared at Lut Gholein. With avid interest he watched the demonic warriors tear at the walls and gates. The city could not be more than a few moments from bloody destruction. He would let his horde have their fun, let them race through Lut Gholein slaying every man, woman, and child—then reveal to them his return to the mortal plane.

He imagined the blood flowing everywhere, the blood of all those who feared and hated him. The blood of those who would perish at his command—

The dune exploded around him, a pair of dark forms leaping up out of the sand. Two strong sets of hands seized his arms, twisting him back.

"Hello . . . old friend . . ." a horrifyingly familiar voice whispered on one side of him. "It's been . . . a lifetime . . . since we last . . . saw you . . ."

The hold the armor had over Norrec shattered for the moment as recognition mixed with sudden terror. "S-Sadun?"

He turned in the direction of the voice—and stared close into the peeling, decaying visage of his dead companion.

"You haven't . . . forgotten us . . . how nice . . ." The ghoulish figure smiled, revealing the blackened gums and yellowed teeth.

Unable to flee, Norrec turned his head the other way—only to find Fauztin there. The murdered Vizjerei's collar had slipped, showing the tattered, crusted gap in his throat.

"No . . . no . . . no . . ."

They pulled him back down the dune, back toward where Kara still fought to free herself.

"We tried to . . . see you on . . . the ship . . . Norrec," Tryst went on. "But you certainly . . . didn't seem . . . so willing to see . . . us . . ."

Their eyes never blinked and the stench of death became apparent the longer they held him so near. Their very presence overwhelmed Norrec so much that even the armor could not demand control. "I'm sorry! I'm so sorry! Sadun—Fauztin—I'm so sorry!"

"He's sorry . . . Fauztin," commented the wiry undead. "Did you know . . . that?"

Norrec glanced at the gaunt Vizjerei, who nodded solemnly.

"We accept . . . your apology . . . but . . . I'm afraid . . . we've no choice . . . with what we . . . now do . . . my friend . . ."

With remarkable speed and strength, Sadun Tryst tore the helmet from Norrec's head.

It felt as if the revenant had ripped the veteran's skull off as well, so great did the pain of separation feel. Now Norrec truly understood how Malevolyn had felt. He cried out, pulling at his captors with a fury even they grew hard-pressed to combat.

"Hold . . . him! Hold—"

Both gauntlets flared a furious crimson. Even caught up in the intense agony coursing through him, Norrec noted the gloves and feared . . . feared for his friends who had already died once because of his inability to do anything to stop the armor's damnable actions. That their troubled spirits had followed him, he understood completely. Such an injustice demanded retribution. Unfortunately, the armor had no intention of granting them that opportunity.

The area around Norrec exploded, sending the two undead hurtling away and ripping through the dune from which they had just descended. He stared in horror at the two bodies, fearing that once more they had perished.

"No! Not again! I won't let you do it again!" The veteran fighter seized one hand in the other and although both struggled, this time his determination proved too great even for Bartuc's legacy. Norrec tugged, using his own suffering to augment his strength . . .

The right gauntlet came free.

Without hesitation he threw it as far away as he could. Immediately the suit tried to turn that way, seek after its lost member, but Norrec would no longer be denied. He forced the armor a different direction, that of Lut Gholein, now visible through the collapsing gap in the dune.

How long he controlled the power and not the other way around, the soldier could not say. Norrec only knew that he had to try to make as much right as possible. So long as his outrage, his guilt, fueled his actions, he had the advantage—and Lut Gholein had little enough time.

He raised the free hand toward the distant city. The demons had at last torn their way past one of the gates. Norrec could hesitate no longer.

The words he spoke had never been taught to him. They had been Bartuc's words, Bartuc's magic. But Bartuc's memories—his *ancestor's* memories—had become just as much Norrec's by this point. He knew what they could do, knew what they *had* to do, and so he willingly spoke them even though that part of him still in thrall to the armor struggled to prevent it from happening.

Had he been witness to the wicked spellwork performed by Malevolyn and Xazax in the general's tent, Norrec might have noted that what he said almost sounded like Malevolyn's incantation, but chanted in reverse. As it was, he simply knew that if he did nothing, an entire city would become awash in the blood of its people.

And at the end of that incantation, the descendent of the Warlord of Blood shouted out two last words. *"Mortias Diablum! Mortias Diablum!"*

Within the gates of Lut Gholein, the defenders stood and fought, knowing already that they battled men without souls, men who were not men but something far more monstrous. Yet, the sultan's warriors braced themselves for death even as the citizens prepared to weather the dangerous storm waters and try to escape.

The captains of the ships had little hope, though, already one of their vessels swamped and another shattered against the side of the docks. The waves roared inland, making it dangerous even to stand near the water. Three men had already been washed off as they had tried to prepare the vessels for refugees.

But as all hope faded, a sight both unsettling and miraculous happened. Just within the city walls, the fiery-eyed soldiers in black stopped, turned their heads back in clear dismay—and then let loose with a chorus of unearthly, savage howls.

Then, from out of the backs of each erupted hideous, spectral forms with grotesque, inhuman faces and limbs twisted and clawed. Those who witnessed the event would later say they saw both rage and despair on those demonic faces just before the specters, screaming piteously, were cast out into Aranoch in a thousand different directions.

For a moment, the army of darkness stood at attention, weapons ready, suddenly empty eyes staring straight. Then, as if all within them had been drained away along with the phantoms, each of the monstrous soldiers began to *collapse* in on himself. One by one, then row by row, the invaders dropped—bones, faded flesh, and fragments of plate spilling into piles that left more than one of Lut Gholein's defenders unable to hold onto the contents of their own stomachs.

One of the commanders, the very one whom General Augustus Malevolyn had ordered to find Norrec Vizharan, became the first to mouth what everyone else thought. Stepping toward the nearest of the grisly sets of remains, the officer gingerly prodded it.

"They're dead . . ." he finally muttered, unable to believe he and the rest of his people would live after all. "They're dead . . . but how?"

"Norrec."

He turned to find Kara free, the gleaming ivory dagger ready in her hand. From his left and right came the two revenants, the determination of the dead forever tattooed on their expressions.

"Kara." He glanced at his former comrades. "Fauztin. Sadun."

"Norrec," continued the necromancer. "Please listen to me."

"No!" The mercenary instantly regretted his harsh tone. She only sought to do what even he knew had to be done. "No . . . listen to me instead. I—I've got some control over the armor now, but I can feel that already slipping away. I guess I'm just too exhausted to fight it much longer . . ."

"How could you even manage to fight it at all?"

"He is . . . Bartuc's progeny . . . after all," remarked Sadun. "Something that the . . . armor needed . . . in order to . . . fulfill its destiny . . . but that it . . . did not . . . understand worked . . . both ways. What other . . . answer?"

She lowered her gaze. Norrec could read the pain in them. Although a necromancer, the pale woman felt no pleasure or satisfaction in slaying one who had not chosen to cause such evil. Yet so long as he lived, all humanity lay threatened.

"You'd better do it quick. One swift thrust straight through the throat. It's the only way!"

"Norrec—"

"Hurry—before my mind changes!" He did not simply refer to any sudden reluctance on his part, and they all knew it. The risk remained that at any second the armor might transform him again into the ideal host for its insidious desires.

"Norrec—"

"Do it!"

"This is not . . . how it was . . . supposed to be . . ." rasped Tryst in open bitterness. "Fauztin! He swore . . . to us . . ."

The Vizjerei, of course, said nothing, instead moving toward Norrec. With great reluctance, Sadun slowly followed suit. Norrec swallowed, hoping the madness would end soon.

The hand still gloved suddenly rose.

Fauztin seized it in his own.

"Best do . . . as he says . . . necromancer . . ." a sullen Tryst murmured. "Looks like . . . we don't have . . . long . . ."

Kara came toward him, clearly steeling herself for what she had to do. "I'm sorry, Norrec. This is not how I would wish it, not as it should be . . ."

"Nor is it how it *will* be," a peculiar, almost hollow voice answered.

Horazon stood a short distance behind the necromancer, but Horazon with something different about him. The glimpse Norrec had earlier had of the ancient mage had made him think of Horazon as a cowardly looking hermit most likely bereft of most of his wits. However, this figure, while still clad in rags and with hair like uncut weeds, had a presence that made all else around him seem insignificant. Norrec had a suspicion now what had made Malevolyn look up at that most vital moment in the battle, for surely the ancient mage's appearance would have shocked the half-possessed general as well . . .

A massive, unexpected surge of bitterness and hatred welled up within the fighter, all aimed at his foul brother—

No! Horazon was not his brother! Once again the armor sought to reestablish its control, rekindle the insidious spirit of *Bartuc*. Norrec managed to fight the emotions down, but he knew that next time the suit would likely prevail.

The robed figure moved purposefully toward him and as he did, Norrec noticed a curious shimmer around him. The captive warrior squinted, trying to make out what caused it.

Horazon's entire body had been *encased* in a thin layer of glittering, almost transparent sand grains.

"Blood calls to blood," the Vizjerei murmured. His eyes stared brightly, never blinking. Even the two undead holding onto Norrec seemed taken aback by his presence. "And blood will end this travesty now."

Norrec could feel the will of the suit battering at his mind, struggling physically with his body. Only the combined efforts of he and his comrades kept it from succeeding for the moment.

"Horazon?" Kara whispered. The white-haired sorcerer glanced her way—and the woman stepped back. "No—you are *him*, but you also are *not*."

He gave her—gave all of them—a condescending smile. "This living shell is another's, a too-curious sorcerer who long ago found the Arcane Sanctuary by accident, but in the process lost his senses forever. I have watched over him ever since, feeling some responsibility . . ." Foregoing any further explanation as to what in the underground sanctum might have destroyed a mind so, the glittering figure glanced at his borrowed hands. "So fragile is flesh. More stable and lasting are earth and stone . . ."

"You!" Kara gaped, her eyes nearly as wide open as her mouth. "I know you at last! He talked to you, seemed to even obey you—the great Horazon seemed so *willing* to obey you—which made no sense until now! *You* are the presence I felt—the presence of the very *sanctuary* itself!"

He nodded, his own eyes never blinking once. "Yes . . . over time it just seemed the natural path, the natural way of things . . ."

Still battling the insidious incursions of Bartuc's enchanted armor, it took Norrec a moment longer to understand—and when he did the answer so astounded him that he nearly dropped his defenses.

Horazon and the Arcane Sanctuary were one and the *same*.

"My own mind almost shattered by what I had been through, I came here to escape the memories, escape the horror, and so I built my sanctum and dwelled underneath the sand, away from the events of the world." A smile crossed the false Horazon's face, the sort of smile attempted by someone who had all but forgotten such minor mortal practices. "And as I kept remaking my domain over and over in my own image, it became more me than the faltering shell I wore—until at last, one day, I gave what remained within and took upon a new, stronger, and far more durable form . . . and so I have been ever since—"

Horazon might have gone on further, but at that moment, Norrec's world turned bloodred. He felt an all-consuming rage build. He would not be denied again! Horazon had escaped his wrath at Viz-jun, but even if he had to burn away the entire desert, the *warlord* would have his final vengeance!

Horazon's puppet looked his way again, holding out one hand as if asking something of the armored figure.

A gauntlet—the same one Norrec had earlier torn off and thrown away—materialized on the aged sorcerer's own hand.

"Blood calls to blood . . . and I am calling you, brother. Our war is over. Our time is over. *We* are over. Your power negates mine. Mine negates yours. Join me now where we both belong . . . far from the sight of men . . ."

The other gauntlet tore free from Norrec, flying over to the glittering figure's ungloved hand. Then, in rapid succession, each piece of armor from his legs, torso, and arms flew forth, the crimson suit quickly remaking itself bit by bit on the elder's body. Somewhere along the way, the torn, stained robe of the hermit vanished, replaced by other garments more suitable to the armor. Even the boots Bartuc had worn left Norrec to join the rest of the suit. The false Horazon raised his arms as his astonishing work went on, eyes never blinking, lips set grimly.

With each loss, Norrec's mind edged nearer to what it had more or less been like before the armor had claimed him. The memories and thoughts became wholly his own, not that of a murderous demon master. Yet, he could never be rid of the terrible days since the tomb, never be rid of the horrors and death of which he had played an unwilling but great part.

And when it was done, the white-haired figure stretched out a gauntleted hand again, summoning the helmet. Placing that in the crook of one arm, Horazon's puppet looked over Norrec and the others.

"It is time for the world to forget Bartuc and Horazon. You would do well to do the same, all of you."

"Wait!" Kara dared approach the enigmatic form. "One question. Please tell me—did you send this one," she indicated Horazon's host. "To find me in Lut Gholein?"

"Yes . . . I sensed something amiss and knew that a necromancer so near—a necromancer who should not be in the city above—had to be involved. I needed you closer so that I could discover why. As you slept, as you ate, I learned what I needed to know from you." He stepped back from her, from all of them. "Our conversation is at an end. I leave you on your own now. Remember this, though; the Arcane Sanctuary exists in many places, has many doorways—but I advise you now to *never* seek it again."

His darkening tone left them with no doubt as to what he meant by the last. Horazon had no desire to be a part of the living world again. Those who would disturb him would risk much.

He suddenly seemed to lose form and substance, bits of him crumbling away as if even flesh and metal had become grains of sand. With each second, the armored mage looked less like anything mortal and more a very part of the landscape.

"Norrec Vizharan," Horazon called in that odd, echoing voice. "It is time to create your own legacy . . ."

Clad in the same garments he had worn upon entering Bartuc's tomb—even his own boots having somehow been returned to him by the astounding sorcerer—Norrec pulled free from the revenants and started forward. "Wait! What do you mean by that?"

But Horazon's host, now a man completely of sand, only shook his head. Of all of him, only the eyes remained somewhat human. Even as Norrec neared, the figure shrank, his sandy form melting into the dunes around. By the time the veteran fighter reached the area it was already too late . . . only a small lump of loose grains remained to mark Horazon's past presence.

Seconds later, even that no longer existed.

"It's over," Kara quietly remarked.

"Yes . . . it is," agreed Sadun Tryst.

Something in his tone made Norrec now turn to the two ghouls. Both undead had a peculiar look in their eye, as if they waited for something else to happen.

The necromancer guessed first. "Your quest is over, is it not? Just as with Horazon, your time in this world is at an end."

Fauztin nodded. Sadun gave what seemed a sad grin—or perhaps his failing flesh and muscle simply made it seem so. "He came . . . when he felt . . . the armor stir . . . but too late . . . so he granted us . . . this chase . . .

but with . . . the promise that . . . when it finished . . . so would we."

"*He?*" Norrec asked, joining Kara.

"But it was my spell and my dagger that brought you back!"

"His trickery . . . to throw you . . . off . . ." The smaller of the undead looked around. "Sanctimonious . . . bastard . . . can't even show up . . . now that it's . . . over . . ."

However, as he finished, a brilliant blue light suddenly shone down on the four, turning their small patch of desert as bright as, if not brighter than, a cloudless day at noontime.

Sadun Tryst would have spat in disgust, if such a simple feat had been within his ability any more. Instead, he shook his head—or rather, let it rock back and forth once—then added, "Should've known . . . better . . . damned strutting . . . angel!"

Angel? Norrec looked up in the direction of the light, but found no source for it, much less an angel. Still, what else could explain so much?

The ghoul glared at it. "At least . . . show yourself . . ." When nothing happened, he glanced at Norrec and added, "Typical. Just like . . . his kind . . . hiding in the . . . shadows . . . pretending they're . . . above it all . . . but putting their hands . . . in everything."

"I know this light," Kara muttered. "I caught a glimpse of it in the tomb. It's what drew me away from your bodies."

"He likes . . . his tricks . . . the archangel does." Tryst eyed Fauztin, who nodded again. To the two living members, the wiry revenant continued, "And for his . . . last one—"

"Damn you, Sadun, no!" Norrec scowled at the heavens, scowled at the unseen archangel. "It's not fair! They had no choice in the matter—"

"Please . . . it's . . . time . . . and we . . . want it so . . . Norrec . . ."

"You can't mean it!"

Sadun chuckled, a harsh sound. "I swear it . . . on my . . . life, friend . . ."

The blue light focused suddenly on the revenants, bathing them in such brilliance that Norrec had to shield his eyes. Fauztin and the smaller ghoul became harder and harder to see.

"Time to . . . buy that . . . farm . . . you always wanted . . . Norrec . . ."

The light flared then, becoming so intense that it momentarily blinded the veteran and his companion. Fortunately for both, the burst lasted only a few seconds, but even with that, by the time their eyes recovered, it was to find that not only had the heavenly illumination completely faded away—but with it had gone the two undead.

Norrec stared at the spot, at first unable to speak.

A hand touched his own. Kara Nightshadow gave him a look of sympathy. "They have moved on to the next step in the eternal journey, on to their next role in helping to maintain the balance of the world."

"Maybe . . ." Wherever they had gone, Norrec knew that he could be of no aid to them. The best he could do was keep their memories alive in him—and do something with his own life in honor of the friendship the three had built. He glanced up again, noticed for the first time that the ever-present storm clouds had finally quieted. In fact, they had already begun to dwindle to the point where patches of clear sky could be made out.

"What will you do now?" the necromancer asked him.

"I don't know." He glanced in the direction of Lut Gholein, the only sign of civilization for days. "Go there first, I suppose. See if they need any help cleaning up. After that . . . I just don't know. What about you?"

She, too, looked to the far-off city, giving him a chance to study her profile. "Lut Gholein makes sense also.

Besides, I wish to discover whether Captain Jeronnan and the *King's Shield* are there. I owe him a debt. He treated me well, as if I were his own daughter—and he probably fears I drowned at sea."

Having no desire to part from her company just yet, Norrec responded, "I'll come with you, then, if you don't mind."

That brought an unexpected smile from Kara. Norrec liked it when the dark-haired woman smiled. "Not at all."

Recalling the ways of the many nobles he had served, Norrec offered her his arm, which, after a moment's hesitation, the necromancer took. Then, together, the weary pair made their way through what remained of the ruined dune and headed back toward civilization. Neither looked behind them to where the head and body of General Augustus Malevolyn already lay half-covered by the drifting sand, where Horazon and the armor had faded into the desert itself. The weary, battered soldier especially had no desire to be reminded of what had happened—and what *could* have happened if matters had taken a turn to the dark.

The legacy of Bartuc, the legacy of the Warlord of Blood, had been buried once again from the sight and knowledge of all . . . this time hopefully forever.

EPILOGUE

Night fell upon the desert of Aranoch, a solemn, brood-
ing night. The creatures of the day hurried to the safety of
their lairs while those who hunted in the darkness came
forth in search of careless prey . . .

And from beneath the sand slowly emerged a monstrous form, one that would have sent maggots, scarabs,
and vulture demons fleeing in mindless panic. Mandibles
snapped open and closed several times and bulbous yellow orbs that glowed faintly in the darkness carefully
perused the unyielding landscape, searching . . . searching somewhat fearfully.

Xazax rose unsteadily, a pool of brackish, black fluids
underneath him. The wound caused by the necromancer's dagger refused to be healed by his power and
the mantis knew that he could not yet petition his lord
Belial to help him. By this time, Belial would know of his
failure and, worse, the decimation of the infernal horde
summoned to aid General Malevolyn.

The mantis had sensed the terrible spell being cast
even as he had fled. Who had been responsible for it, he
could only guess, but it had meant the certain end for
most of the lesser demons. Summoning such numbers in
so quick a fashion had required each hellish warrior to be
initially *bound* to the mortal shell they had been given.
With the passing of time, even as little as a month, they
would have grown more adapted to this plane, been able
to fully cast off the husks. This new spell, though, had

torn them from their earthly anchors far too soon. Only the strongest would survive the extraordinary forces unleashed by the abrupt separation. In human terms it would have been akin to removing a baby from the womb more than a month before its proper birth time. Only the strongest would survive . . .

The few survivors would be condemned to wander Aranoch without any guidance, unable to return to Hell without aid. Unlike Xazax, most these demons lacked sense enough to plan beyond the moment; Belial had relied on his lieutenant for their guidance.

In that lay the mantis's only hope for redemption. His dark lord might forgive him if Xazax managed to gather those who remained and sent them back to Hell. For that, the demon would need another human dupe capable of sorcery, but there were always plenty of those. Of more immediate importance, however, was the necessity of finding prey of his own, something to provide the energy he heeded to combat his wound. The mantis would have preferred a nice, ripe merchant camped out for the night, but at this point, anything he could catch would have to do.

Nervously the demon moved about on the sand. The cursed necromancer's spell still lingered, albeit with less influence than before. Illusions of angels and other fearful sights on occasion materialized before Xazax, but with effort each time he managed to fight off the urge to flee.

When he had regained his strength, recovered from his wounds, the mantis would find Norrec Vizharan and the female. He would impale each, making certain that they lived, then slowly work on peeling the flesh from first one, then the other. After that, Xazax would devour them slowly, savoring each bloody morsel—

Xazax . . .

He froze, waves of fear seeking to wash over him. *Damn the human's spell!* Would the last vestiges of it never fade away? How many illusions, how many whispering voices, would the demon have to suffer before it all stopped?

Smelled you from afar . . . knew you immediately . . .

The giant mantis looked around, but saw nothing. So, it was only in his head this time. He could suffer that well enough—

A shadow darker than the night swept across Xazax, completely startling the wounded monster.

Cunning . . . lying . . . traitorous little bug . . .

Xazax froze. None of the creations of the female's spellwork had ever spoken in his mind with such elaborate conviction.

"Who dares?" he rasped, turning in the direction from which he sensed the voice in his head somehow originated. "Who—"

And before the hellish mantis loomed the most terrible of all the nightmares he could have dreamed. The demon's mandibles stretched wide and a single, almost plaintively spoken word tried unsuccessfully to completely escape.

"Diab—"

A scream punctuated the stillness of the nighttime desert, a scream seemingly of no earthly origin. It caused the various creatures of Aranoch to pause in whatever they had been doing and listen in absolute terror. Even long after the cry abruptly cut off, they remained unmoving, fearful that whatever had preyed upon the source of the mournful sound might next be coming for them.

And among those of Belial's demons that yet survived from the debacle at Lut Gholein, that fear took a greater form. They sensed what had happened, sensed the force behind it—and knew that for them and the humans of this mortal plane the *nightmare* might just be beginning . . .

About the Author

RICHARD A. KNAAK is the author of more than twenty fantasy novels and over a dozen short pieces, including the *New York Times* bestseller *The Legend of Huma* for the Dragonlance series. Aside from his extensive work in Dragonlance, he is best known for his popular Dragonrealm series, which is now available again in trade paperback. His other works include several contemporary fantasies, including *Frostwing* and *King of the Grey*, also available again. In addition to *Legacy of Blood*, he has written *Day of the Dragon* for the Warcraft series and will soon return to Diablo for a second tale. He is also at work on a major trilogy for Dragonlance.

Those interested in learning more about his projects should check out his Web site at http://www.sff.net/people/knaak.

TOP **10**
SANTA FE, TAOS
& ALBUQUERQUE

DK
EYEWITNESS TRAVEL

Left **Santuario de Chimayó** Center **A Guadalupe Street scene** Right **Exhibit, Museum Hill**

LONDON, NEW YORK,
MELBOURNE, MUNICH AND DELHI
www.dk.com

Printed and bound in China by South China Printing Co. Ltd.

First American edition 2006

Published in the United States by:
Dorling Kindersley Limited
80 Strand, London WC2R 0RL, UK

12 13 14 15 10 9 8 7 6 5 4 3 2 1

Reprinted with revisions 2009, 2010, 2012

**Copyright © 2006, 2012
Dorling Kindersley Limited, London**

A catalog record for this book is available from the Library of Congress.

ISSN 1479-344X
ISBN: 978-0-7566-8547-8

Within each Top 10 list in this book, no hierarchy of quality or popularity is implied. All 10 are, in the editor's opinion, of roughly equal merit.

MIX
Paper from
responsible sources
FSC™ C018179

Contents

Santa Fe, Taos, & Albuquerque's Top 10

The information in this DK Eyewitness Top 10 Travel Guide is checked regularly.
Every effort has been made to ensure that this book is as up-to-date as possible at the time of going to press. Some details, however, such as telephone numbers, opening hours, prices, gallery hanging arrangements and travel information are liable to change. The publishers cannot accept responsibility for any consequences arising from the use of this book, nor for any material on third party websites, and cannot guarantee that any website address in this book will be a suitable source of travel information. We value the views and suggestions of our readers very highly. Please write to: Publisher, DK Eyewitness Travel Guides, Dorling Kindersley, 80 Strand, London WC2R 0RL, UK, or email: travelguides@dk.com.